THE FRIEND SITUATION

THE BILLIONAIRE SITUATION SERIES

LYRA PARISH

CONTENT WARNING

This book includes "on-page" adult content and language unsuitable for minors.

OFFICIAL PLAYLIST

MILLION DOLLAR BABY - Tommy Richman
Stepping Stone - Brooke Alexx
Sailor Song - Gigi Perez
Damn I Wish I Was Your Lover - Sophie B. Hawkins
Guilty as Sin? - Taylor Swift
When You Say My Name - Chandler Leighton
Casual - Chapell Roan
Like You Mean It - Steven Rodriguez
Maroon - Taylor Swift
Für Elise - Toms Mucenieks
Hey Daddy (Daddy's Home) - USHER
Wildest Dreams (Taylor's Version) - Taylor Swift
Ordinary - Alex Warren

LISTEN TO THIS PLAYLIST:
https://bit.ly/thefriendsituationplaylist

*To the real ones who just want to get
drunk on the vibes of falling in love.*

Weston Calloway is waiting for you, gorgeous.

What if he's written 'mine' on my upper thigh
Only in my mind?

-Taylor Swift, Guilty as Sin?

1

CARLEE

"That's the one," Lexi, my best friend, tells me over FaceTime. It's the fifth dress I've slid on and modeled for her in the past twenty minutes.

The black silk bodice clings to my small frame and hugs my waist; the cool fabric presses against my warm skin. I strut inside my tiny bedroom, glancing at the two paintings on the wall before I spin around to face the screen. The chiffon skirt flows around me.

"Does it give *new year, new me* energy?"

It's the second week of January, and I just have a feeling this year is going to be different.

"Yes, and it's *perfect* for date night as long as you have a coat. It's freezing outside, literally," she says.

"Thanks, *Mom*." I smile. "Now, which shoes?"

I hold up a pair of chunky wedges that add a playful edge, ankle boots that scream confidence, and strappy heels with ribbons that tie up my legs, like I'm a present waiting to be unwrapped.

"The last ones, unless they'll make you taller than him."

"Oh, babe, you know short kings aren't my thing. I need a six-foot-something, or get the hell outta here," I remind her. "I won't give up my heels for anyone."

"That's the energy I like to see," she says.

Lexi always reminds me never to settle on men or clothes.

We've been besties since we were naive eighteen-year-olds, freshmen at New York University. We instantly bonded because we had grown up in small Texas towns. It feels like yesterday, but now we're navigating being thirty together. Getting older is a weird concept.

I sit on the edge of my twin bed, lacing the wide silk ribbons up my calves as anticipation creeps in.

"Are you sure you like this better than the blue minidress?"

It hangs on the edge of my full-length mirror, taunting me. It's an insurance policy for getting some D.

"Don't doubt me. He'll *love* it." Confidence radiates from her.

I stand, studying my ensemble in the mirror. I tilt my head, pushing my dark brown hair over my bare shoulders. The bodice swoops down in the back, showing just enough skin. "Lexi, if I wear this, he might fall *in love* with me," I mutter.

It's almost too elegant, like what one would wear to an engagement party. I trust her judgment, though.

"What's his name again? I'll add him to the long list of wannabe lovers." Her laughter calms my nerves.

"Trever. T-R-E-V-E-R. Like *forever*. And if he says *I love you* tonight, I swear I'll lose my shit. If you jinxed me ..."

"You've got the magic touch with men," she says.

"Feels like a curse," I groan. "I just want to have an easy conversation with the possibility of being split in half without forcing commitment. I want to have fun."

Over the past two years, I've gone on countless dates. At some point in the first thirty days, each has confessed their feelings, and love is always involved. It's ridiculous.

If I'm ever blindsided by an *I love you*, I dump them immediately because we're not on the same page. I'm convinced someone is teaching this unhinged behavior at bro school, and I'm growing exhausted.

In my early twenties, I was into the *let's fall fast and hard, exchanging* I love yous *within two weeks* instalove behavior. Now, it's a gigantic red flag.

At thirty, I crave a man who can match me emotionally. In New York, it's as easy as finding a needle in a haystack. Abigail, my sister, says I'm being too picky for my age and that my options are dwindling, like I'm thirty going on seventy-five. Did I mention she's been divorced twice and she's only four years older than me?

I may be single, but I'm *not* desperate to be loved by anyone or to rush into marriage. My past relationship trauma could partially be to blame for that, but I've learned to embrace my independence and love myself without a man's approval. It took a lot to become this confident. Even if I don't need a man, I'd still like one.

"How long have you known Trever? Where are you meeting him?"

She leans back on the plush couch, running her fingers through her dark hair. Her wedding ring sparkles like a star, reflecting the overhead light of her luxurious penthouse. It has the most incredible view of Central Park.

The sun sets behind her, and the sky is golden, but it's not just the fading light that gives her that glow. My best friend is madly in love with her husband, Easton Calloway, who also happens to be one of the wealthiest men on the planet. She wears her happiness like a badge of honor while trying to hide her pregnancy from the media.

It's *beautiful.* And if I'm honest, I'm just a *tad* jealous.

Weston Calloway, her husband's identical twin brother and my coconspirator, secretly played matchmaker. For months, we worked together and meticulously planned. While Lexi and Easton's first encounter was a disaster, it still worked out. We were given the honor of watching them fall deeply in love.

Weston and I swore never to share what we'd done, and that

secret sits next to our friendship, which we've kept hidden for nearly a year.

Secrets. When it comes to Weston, I have a chamber of them.

Lexi clears her throat, pulling me from my runaway thoughts of *him*.

"Are you gonna give me details about this date, or do I need to call Brody to do surveillance?" she asks.

"I don't need a bodyguard, Lex. Trever would be scared shitless with Brody around. However, he is a fine piece of man candy. Is he still single?"

Lexi nods. "He's a robot. He'll be single forever."

Brody looms larger than life in my mind. He's Easton and Weston's cousin, but also their bodyguard. That man is covered with ink and wears a glare that screams, *Don't fuck with me.* It's a Calloway trait though.

"*Lex*, I don't need a babysitter."

She can make it happen with one phone call.

"It comes from a good place in my heart, I promise. I worry when you meet these strange men from these apps. There are too many pervs out there who only want one thing from you because you're drop-dead gorgeous, and—"

"Thanks for gassing me up, but what if I only want one thing from them? You sound like my brothers." I shake my head, the corners of my mouth twisting into a smirk. "God forbid I use men for the *only* good thing they have to offer me right now."

"No, no, no. I *want* you to have tons of raunchy, mind-blowing sex—but with the *right* person, even if it's only temporary. You deserve to have fun. I've just watched too much true crime lately."

Her expression softens, revealing her genuine concern. I appreciate how much she cares.

"Lex, you know I've taken tons of self-defense classes. Not to mention, I grew up fighting my asshole cousins and brothers. I can put a man two times bigger than me on his back in eight seconds flat."

"I know, but I still worry about you," she explains, resting her hand on her belly.

Lexi is more like a sister to me than my *actual* sister has ever been. She's the family I chose, and she wants the best for me.

"I'll be fine, I promise. Thank you. It means a lot." I grab some pearl earrings and a silver tennis bracelet I bought for my birthday. It's my lucky charm. Something amazing *always* happens when I wear it.

"If this doesn't work out, I have someone you can date. How do you feel about previously married men?" she asks teasingly.

It's a question I've avoided answering because I know why she's asking.

"Stop trying to hook me up with Weston," I say sternly, my heart thumping harder at the mere mention of his name. Anytime he crosses my thoughts, my pulse quickens in a way that both excites and terrifies me.

"*You* brought him up, not me," she singsongs. "But speaking of Weston, you two would be great together. He's kind. Funny. Outgoing. Plus, he's always been your hall pass."

"Lexi!" My eyes widen. Not many people know that. "I've since replaced him with Jensen Ackles. And I don't care if he's close to fifty. He's *fine*."

"He's married. Weston, on the other hand …" She's not even being subtle with what she's doing.

"Technically, he's married too," I say, knowing his divorce hasn't been finalized yet.

"It will be over any day now. You know that."

"We'll see. Now, do you want to hear about my date, or would you like to keep talking about your brother-in-law? My ride will be here in thirty minutes." I abruptly change the subject.

"Tell me," she says, moving to the edge of the couch cushion and leaning in to catch every detail.

"Okay, so Trever works in finance, and I've known him for two and a half weeks. This is our third date, and I'm meeting him at The Marquee for drinks."

"Oh, wow. Extravagant for a third date."

"Right? If I go home with him, I'll send you my location in case I go missing. Anything else?"

"Don't joke like that." She stares me down. Her gaze pierces through my facade like she's sorting through my thoughts. "Trever's getting dumped tonight." Certainty fills her tone.

"What? *No*. I'm hoping he takes me back to his place." I lower my voice. "He's *packing*, and he seems very experienced. Plus, you know a man in a tailored suit is a wet dream of mine. Big O material. I could use someone who can deliver, if you know what I mean. It's been a year, Lex. One. Year. My lady parts are going to seal themselves shut." I shake my head.

"Not happening. It's already over between you two. I can see it on your face," she confirms.

Nothing I say will convince her otherwise. She's giving me her cocky Little Miss Know It All attitude, which drives me crazy. However, she does know me better than anyone else.

"Are you sure you're not delusional from being pregnant? Or maybe it's love that's poisoned your thoughts." I wink at her, trying to lighten the mood. I pin one side of my hair out of my face, then lightly spritz perfume behind my ear.

Last September, Lexi and Easton invited me and Weston over so they could tell us they were pregnant. It's a secret they're hiding from everyone until it becomes too noticeable to hide. The Calloways are strategic and great at keeping things hidden.

"Delusional? Maybe my baby has a sixth sense about these things." She closes her eyes, rubbing her tiny belly like it's a Magic 8 Ball. "I predict it ends within *two* hours and you don't go home with him. Life is too short to spend on crappy dates. Love happens when you least expect it."

"I cannot pass up the *only* opportunity I've *ever* had to enter The Marquee. You know it's been on my wish list for years. Plus, I don't cancel dates at the last minute. Sorry, but no, I can't," I explain.

"Not even for a million bucks?" she asks, eyebrows raised.

"Not even *ten* million. It's karma I don't want. Seven years of bad-luck shit." My tone sharpens as I remember the sting of being ditched. It's a douche move, and she knows my integrity can't be bought.

"Trever has reliable fling potential and is only searching for something short-term. If it doesn't work out, I'll continue down the dating app queue until I find someone who vibes with me," I add as the city ambience drifts through the poorly insulated walls of my apartment. It's affordable, so I can't complain.

"What is it that Carlee Jolly wants?" she asks curiously.

I sigh, searching for the right words.

She clears her throat. "What about a six-two man who's stacked with muscles? Tattoos. Baby blues. Messy hair you can run your fingers through. He comes with a fun personality and maybe a teeny-tiny bit of baggage, but it's nothing you can't handle."

"Give him a chance to heal from his dirty-as-fuck divorce. Jeez, I really hope you don't do to him what you do to me. Relentless," I state, carrying my phone to the bathroom to apply dark red lipstick. I uncap it, looking down at the rich color. It's the cherry on top of this seductive look I'm going for tonight.

"You haven't ever really moved on from—"

"Do not say his name," I warn.

She opens her mouth to speak, and I quickly interrupt her again, "*Seriously. Please.*"

"It's just superstition," Lexi says. "*Samson.*"

"Oh my God! *Lex!* Do you have any idea what you've done? He's like Beetlejuice. His entire family is. You do realize that, right?" I growl out, annoyed.

Samson is the last man I wanted to think about today. Sometimes, I still can't believe we're not in one another's life. We went from friends to lovers to strangers.

"You know the only way to get over someone is to get under someone else," she states as I put lipstick on my bottom and top lip.

"The only way to get over someone you deeply loved is to fall in love harder than you ever have before. That scares the shit out of me, Lex. I don't know if I'd be able to survive another breakup like that. It took years. Maybe I'm the problem." I let out a long sigh.

"I don't think so," Lexi says. "Life is too short to settle on shitty men."

"That's why I think a no-strings-attached arrangement with the *possibility* of falling in love is what I need. No pressure, but just having adult fun."

"Do you want to be exclusive with someone?" Lexi asks.

"I don't care," I say. "I'd be fine with something casual until one of us found someone else."

"A situationship?" She grins. "That would be great for both of you."

"Not with Weston, okay? You know he's completely out of—"

"So, you won't be gracing us with your presence tonight?" I hear a voice ask in a deep, familiar rasp.

My league. I finish my thought, even if my words were interrupted.

I glance at the phone screen. Her hubby is leaning over her shoulder for a closer look at me, and his presence shocks me.

"Oh my God, Lex, I thought we were alone!"

Easton glances at her with a teasing grin. "You were wrong, babe."

"Wrong? Pfft," Lexi says and clenches her teeth. "She'll be here."

"I hope you didn't hear our *entire* conversation," I groan.

"He was on his phone, reading articles. Not paying attention to us at all," she says, then glances at him.

"Speak freely. Your *secrets* are always safe with me. Anyway, I suppose we won't order to-go food from Frankie's for you. I was hoping you'd join us for movie night." His tone is neutral.

Frankie's has the best burgers in the city, and the owner is one of Easton's old college buddies.

"Apologies, but I have a hot date tonight." I smile. "Some of us are still on the market, *Easton*. Not everyone is as lucky as you two."

"Easton? Hmm." He narrows his gaze, the corners of his mouth twitching up, as if he's trying to suppress a grin.

My smile falters.

"Weston?" His name escapes me like a whisper. Knowing *he* overheard our entire conversation. I'm mortified.

Something unknown ticks between us like a time bomb. The connection we share isn't one I've ever experienced with a man, and I'm so fucking afraid of losing it, losing him.

"Am I Easton or Weston?" he asks, blinking incredulously. "Take a guess."

I study him, now completely unsure which Calloway brother stands before me. It's nearly impossible to tell them apart, and they're professionals at mirroring each other's personalities.

Weston is Mr. Popularity, the life of any party. If you give that man a spotlight, he shines like a diamond under it. Beneath the charm, he's a master of disguise, capable of mimicking Easton's mannerisms with uncanny precision.

Only two people on this planet can tell them apart—Lexi and Billie, their sister. They can still fool their parents.

I've asked Lexi several times how she can figure them out, and she said when Easton touches her, she immediately knows it's him, like they're bonded.

"I don't know. I'm not a Calloway expert," I say.

"Well"—Lexi clears her throat—"since you won't ditch, maybe you'll consider leaving early. Otherwise, Weston will be the third wheel," she says, glancing back at him, confirming it for me.

I smack my lips together as adrenaline courses through me. I move the screen closer to my face, and Weston lifts a brow.

He's impeccably dressed in a tailored three-piece suit, the fabric hugs his muscular form. His hair is a wild mess, as if he just ran his fingers through it in frustration or excitement. Was it because of me? Or something I said?

We spark a silent conversation that only the two of us can comprehend.

Scruff lines his chiseled jaw, accentuating those deep blue eyes that pierce right through me. It should be illegal for any man to look this damn good. And he knows it too.

Lexi watches us, allowing our stare down to continue. Her expression is already scheming. I wish she'd believe me when I say it won't work. There are too many boxes on his list, and there are too many reasons why I can't be the woman to check them.

"Nice seeing you again, *Weston*," I mutter, keeping my tone level as warmth floods my cheeks.

"Carlee." He places his hands in his pockets, leaning closer and chewing on the edge of his pouty plump lip.

Weston's a flirty bastard, and even his presence—regardless of the screen between us—gives me palpitations.

I'm not special though.

The man has this effect on everyone. Weston's a professional at holding a gaze and making people feel *seen*. Combine that with his addictive personality, and it's obvious why so many women have fallen madly and obsessively in love with him over the years.

The world revolves around Weston and his chaotic, dazzling life, and I can't help but wonder if I'm just another star caught in his gravitational pull.

I'd be lying if I said I wasn't *always* curious about him, but that comes with being a pop culture reporter. The more I learned about these luxurious lifestyles, the more fascinated I became. It's why I created LuxLeaks and the pseudonym LadyLux.

Weston's lore runs deep, and I consider myself an expert on him. It's both a blessing and a curse.

"Wow. That dress looks *incredible* on you," he says, his gaze sliding up and down the screen, taking in every one of my curves.

The compliment hangs in the air.

I offer him a small smile, aware that politeness is the currency of our interactions when Lexi and Easton are near. "Thanks. It looks incredible *off* of me too."

The words spill out, and I remind myself we're not hanging out in Sluggers alone. Sluggers is the dive bar at the bottom of a basement where we've been secretly meeting for nearly a year.

"Mmm. I don't doubt that."

That is not the response I expected.

For a fleeting moment, I swear his eyes darken with something deeper, something more dangerous. I'm *almost* immune to him, but the walls I've constructed around our friendship are not impenetrable. Drunk me has attempted to bridge that gap with a kiss, but each time, I was met with a firm rejection.

"You two would be so good together," she encourages. "I know you both very well. Trust me on this."

I quickly shift my focus away from Weston and our nuclear chemistry.

"Please tell me he didn't hear our *entire* conversation," I say between clenched teeth.

"I heard *every* word," Weston answers, crossing his arms over his broad chest. The corners of his mouth twitch in amusement.

"Don't you have a date or something tonight? Isn't it time to switch to your new woman of the week?"

"I'm free tonight. And if you must know, I'm on a cycle of a date every three days," he explains, just as Easton makes himself comfortable next to Lexi.

"Hi, darling. Sorry that phone call took so long. My dad had a lot to say," he whispers to her.

She greets him with an eager kiss, pulling her from this conversation.

I glance over at Weston, who's intently watching me. I can't help but smile.

"Hey, Carlee," Easton says as he pulls away.

"Hi," I tell him as he turns back toward his brother.

"That's over one hundred and twenty dates in a year. How do you have a life?" Easton asks.

"I make it work." Weston shrugs, his demeanor lighthearted.

"Your dick must be *raw*." Easton casually chuckles, tucking a loose strand of hair behind Lexi's ear as he admires her. It's obvious how in love he is with her.

"Oh, little Westie is fantastic." Weston grabs his crotch with a teasing grin. "Might amp it up to a date every night though. Put him through his paces like I'm in my twenties again." His laughter fills the space.

Easton rolls his eyes.

"Don't believe me?" Weston questions.

"I'm gonna let y'all go now. I'm running out of time," I say, my Southern accent slipping out.

"Aww," Lexi groans.

I'm not interested in hearing about the women Weston is banging. After all, I see enough about his life online while I scour for juicy tidbits for my blog.

"Good luck getting laid tonight," Weston quips, effortlessly stealing my attention like a thief in the night. His mouth twists into a devilish grin. "Hope Double-E Trever gives you the big O."

"Thanks. I hope he does too," I say confidently, not ashamed of my intentions. "Could use a few."

"So, your hall pass? That true?"

Weston winks at me, and the warmth spreads through me.

"Lexi, you're fired as a best friend," I snap at her.

"I'm sorry," she says.

"Maybe I'll see you soon?" Weston's blues burn into my greens.

"Doubt it," I say.

He gives me a smug-as-fuck smile, then walks away.

A storm brews within me.

"I'm so mad at you right now," I say to Lexi. My voice is barely above a whisper as I avoid glancing in Easton's direction.

He's focused on his phone, his dark hair falling over his forehead.

She scoffs. "Don't be. You two are a *perfect* match. Trust me when I say I *know* these things. It's written all over his face. Someone has to push you both, so I volunteered as tribute."

Lexi grabs Easton at his side, and he squirms away from her, holding back laughter.

"You saw it, didn't you?" she asks him.

"I'm not getting involved," he mutters with a chuckle as she continues to tickle him.

Lexi has tried very hard to push Weston and me together since August when she believes we met.

She's relentless.

"Convinced Easton's the only logical person in the room," I offer, a hint of sarcasm creeping into my voice as I try to regain some control.

He chuckles, and it breaks through my frazzled thoughts. "You're damn right about that. Dealing with both of them is a full-time job." He tilts his head at me, as if he knows about me and Weston.

I won't admit anything.

"Babe"—Lexi laughs, her voice light and teasing—"I'm not teaming up with Weston. Ever. He's the *devil*."

I hear him snicker in the background, an intoxicating sound that sends my mind spiraling into inappropriate territories. The dirty thoughts I've had about that man are enough to banish me straight to hell with no regrets.

"Whatcha want on your burger? Order it like usual?" Lexi asks me.

"No thanks! But I'll check in and give you an update. Hopefully, I *won't* see you tonight!"

"Mayo, tomatoes, and cheese, right?" she asks, unfazed by my attempts to escape her.

"Bye!" I end the call, knowing I need to get my mind right and push thoughts of Weston out of my head.

We're just friends. It's all we can ever be.

2

CARLEE

W hen the rideshare finally arrives outside my apartment, I lock my door and leave. Each step toward the car is filled with excitement. Lexi was right about the heavy coat, and I'm so damn glad I wore gloves because it's in the upper thirties outside. Right now, I'm comfortable.

Once I'm inside the Lexus, I confirm the location with the driver, and we take off.

The Marquee is an exclusive club that the rich and famous frequent in the heart of the Theater District. A reservation is required to enter, and securing one without deep connections is impossible. I'm still not sure how Trever pulled it off, but the pop culture queen inside of me wants to know.

The establishment has kept detailed records of every person who has walked through its doors since it opened in the late 1800s. Being allowed to write my name inside the leather-bound guest book causes excitement to course through me. My signature will join the ranks of the world leaders and celebrities who have graced this space with their presence.

My phone vibrates in my deep coat pocket, and I pull it out. A smile spreads across my face when I see who it is.

Weston.

Since we met, he's *always* texted me first. The last thing I want to do is seem needy, and I try to respect his boundaries, knowing how busy he is running a multibillion-dollar company. Anytime he reaches out, it's a little reminder that I'm on his mind, and I cherish being there.

> **WESTON**
>
> Too bad you won't be joining us tonight.

> **CARLEE**
>
> I'd ignore you per our secret friendship agreement.

> **WESTON**
>
> I doubt you'd succeed, especially with Lexi trying to force us together. You weren't kidding; she sucks at this.

I can't help but chuckle as the plush leather of the car seat surrounds me in comfort. I'm glad I treated myself tonight and chose the luxury upgrade.

> **CARLEE**
>
> Do NOT entertain her. It's not her first attempt at hooking me up with her partner's brother. Warning: it always ends horribly.

> **WESTON**
>
> I'm aware. You were the topic of conversation before you interrupted our very interesting chat. But happy to learn I was your hall pass.

> **CARLEE**
>
> Say a prayer for Lexi because she's DEAD.

> **WESTON**
>
> I actually feel pretty fucking special.

As we zoom down the street, I can't shake the excitement that dances in my stomach.

CARLEE

You were replaced. Sorry, friend. Don't get jealous though. I've only ever done deep dives on you.

WESTON

And you enjoyed every second.

I did.

Just because we're friends doesn't mean he hasn't always been my dirty little secret.

Since I started LuxLeaks over a decade ago, I've had a soft spot for Weston, feeling an overwhelming urge to defend him against misinterpretations. His complexity often goes unnoticed by the masses, but I feel like I have him figured out. There's an understanding between us.

Even after he learned I was behind LuxLeaks, he still allows me to peel back more layers of who he is.

WESTON

Just so you know, I've never encouraged Lexi to talk about you.

CARLEE

I bet you don't encourage her to stop either.

WESTON

Smart girl.

I read his text message and imagine his cute-as-hell smirk.

CARLEE

I'll tell you whatever you want to know. Ask me.

WESTON

Really?

CARLEE

I don't have anything to hide.

WESTON

I might have to test this theory.

CARLEE

Does it go both ways?

WESTON

What you already know about me makes you dangerous.

CARLEE

I prefer the word powerful.

WESTON

And that's why you're dangerous. Because you know it gives you power.

CARLEE

After I told you who I was, you still chose to be my friend. Kinda your fault.

WESTON

And I'd do it again and again and a-fucking-gain. No regrets, Firefly.

CARLEE

You mean that?

WESTON

With everything I am.

Weston said I was a tiny ball of light in the darkness that had swallowed him whole, hence the nickname. When we officially met, I had already known how much he needed a friend and offered what I could—myself and my time. I hadn't sought him out, but I had known exactly who he was when our eyes locked. Becoming Weston Calloway's friend was a case of being at the right place at the right time.

When his divorce was made public over a year ago, ridiculous rumors about him were splashed across the internet. For months, he became a recluse and hid from the media.

Amid the finely crafted smear campaign, I became his only friend and confidant, other than his brother. Our bond is unbreakable.

CARLEE

Aww, thanks!

WESTON

No prob, bestie.

I'm relieved he clarified.

Don't get me wrong; I'm comfortable being friend-zoned, and I have been since we met. It allows me to slip into the role of being one of the boys. It's safer for both of us.

CARLEE

Don't ever let Lexi find out you call me that. She gets super jealous.

WESTON

What if I get jealous?

CARLEE

Do you?

WESTON

You have no fucking idea.

He's not flirting.

It's something I repeat to myself each time I speak to him.

WESTON

LadyLux hasn't posted this week.

CARLEE

She extended her break.

WESTON

Is she still on a three-month cruise, gang-banging those twenty-year-old rich kids?

CARLEE

😄 Yep!

It's one of the absurd rumors bubbling up in gossip circles about my absence. I've posted weekly articles for twelve years— filling pages with intricate details of the exciting lives of Manhattan's elite—but now my silence is deafening. People have noticed I've been MIA.

My blog has recently earned some money, but my main income is from working at the W—a lavish hotel in Manhattan, where I scrub the glittering surfaces for the *filthy* rich. In its luxurious setting, I'm overlooked, playing the role of a quiet housekeeper who doesn't make eye contact. When I slip on that uniform, I become invisible to the guests. I navigate the marbled floors and three-story penthouses with purpose. Being a housekeeper is more than just a paycheck. It's my access to the secrets of the wealthy.

WESTON

Earlier, I wasn't just giving you a compliment, like you thought. I meant what I said.

I hate that he can read my expressions so easily. He shouldn't be able to do that.

CARLEE

I meant what I said too. But thanks. Happy you approve, bestie. When will I see you again?

WESTON

When you leave him and come to me.

I nearly melt into a puddle at the weight of his words.

WESTON

Anyway, good luck tonight. Hope he's the one.

CARLEE

Me too.

I stare out the window, searching for a distraction as I replay how I became friends with Weston Calloway.

For years, he was nothing more than a public persona I analyzed and critiqued in my articles. That man was only a distant star I observed. Now, we secretly text and meet weekly, and our conversations are always lighthearted. Every day, Weston proves he's exactly the man I've *always* believed him to be.

Before we became friends, I championed him from afar, my heart rallying for him. Now, it's my mission to see him happy again. He deserves it after the hell he's endured with his ex over the past year.

The car stops outside The Marquee, its iconic entrance illuminated in an inviting glow. I thank my driver and step out onto the red carpet that leads to the door. My heart gallops as I approach the entrance, the chiffon of my dress flowing behind me.

Once my identity is confirmed, my coat is taken. I sign my name across the next open line in the guest book. It feels surreal. I smooth my hand over the ivory paper, knowing I'm now a part of The Marquee's records.

As the double wooden doors swing open, I pause to take it all in, my breath catching in my throat. I've only ever seen it in photos that were captured in secret. Each shot an act of rebellion, thanks to the strict no-camera policy.

Crimson velvet drapes hang lazily from the ceiling to the floor, and they surround the perimeter. Candles flicker on the polished bar top, crafted from the wood of one of Broadway's first stages. It's a silent testament to its rich history. I can almost imagine the whispered conversations and laughter that have echoed off these walls over the decades. If this building could talk, what stories would it tell?

I scan the room, and the romantic energy surrounds me. Eventually, I spot Trever and approach him, weaving through clusters of elegantly dressed couples mingling and laughing. Once

I'm close, he stands, placing a gentle kiss on my lips. It catches me off guard, but I go with it.

"Wow," he whispers, pulling away, gently grabbing my hand and taking me in as if he's memorizing every detail. "You're ... *gorgeous*, Carlee."

"Thanks." A blush creeps onto my cheeks, warmth flooding my face at his compliment.

Trever is undeniably attractive, with golden-brown eyes and messy dirty-blond hair that falls around his forehead. Based on his dating profile photos, I know his chiseled abs trail down the V that points to his package. It's a hidden treasure beneath his tailored suit.

He pulls the barstool out for me—a charming gesture—and I happily sit. So far, so good. Maybe tonight will go exactly how I want it to. I might not be desperate for love, but great sex is another story.

"Would you like a drink?" he politely asks, leaning in, his voice low.

"Martini, extra dirty," I reply.

Anticipation brews as the bartender approaches.

"Extra dirty?" he questions, his smile widening as he settles into the seat beside me. "My *favorite*."

He places our order and turns his attention back to me. His gaze is steady and full of intrigue.

"How was your week?" he asks, inhaling my sweet skin.

"I met up with a friend for a couple of drinks on Wednesday. Work was fine, and I even deep-cleaned my apartment. Adulting at its finest."

I keep the struggle with my blog to myself, a secret too precious to share. No one can ever find out who's behind LuxLeaks. Right now, only a handful of people know—Lexi, Weston, Easton, and Brody. They'd never snitch.

"Did you tell your friend about me?" he inquires just as our drinks are placed in front of us, their crystal glasses gleaming.

I smile. "Actually, I did."

Weston wasn't happy about it and rolled his eyes when I showed him Trever's photos.

"Yeah? What did *she* say?" he asks, arching a brow.

Presumptuous to think it was a woman. I'm not sure he'd want to know Weston said he looked like a fuckboy. I smile, remembering how I told him he'd know, considering he's the president of the fuckboy team.

"I was given a *good luck*, but I don't think we'll need it," I reply, taking a casual sip of my drink and popping an olive into my mouth. The salty flavor mixes deliciously with the gin.

"You're right," he whispers, his breath warm against my ear.

Then Trever wraps an arm around the back of my barstool. I *want* to feel something—anything. Even a teeny-tiny spark.

Could he be the man to finally give me that elusive big O? He's confident, like he possesses the skills to take me to the edge. But then again, I thought that about many I'd given chances to in the past, and they failed.

"What about you?" I ask, shifting the focus back to him.

He sighs, a deep, weary sound. "Work this week was difficult. So tiring."

"Oh, I'm sorry to hear that," I respond with genuine concern in my voice.

"After I cut our last date short, I've been working nonstop," he continues, his gaze drifting like he's recalling a distant memory. The investment project he's involved in consumes him.

I glance around the room, absorbing the dreamy ambience, distracted from his business jargon. The atmosphere inspires intimate conversation, yet here we are, entangled in corporate chatter. With the right person, this place would be romantic.

"And the outrageous import fees …" he adds, his voice trailing off.

I watch Trever intently, nodding when I think it's appropriate while realizing how deeply he's obsessed with his job. Within five minutes, I confirm he's not boyfriend material, but maybe he can move into the fling category.

The night isn't over yet.

"This deal could redefine how the market views manufacturing," he continues, his passion undeniable. "The payoff could be *huge.*" He emphasizes the last word, then finishes off his drink while signaling for another round.

He throws around phrases like *leverage, assets,* and *return on investment* without taking a single breath, his words flowing like an unending waterfall. I can hardly keep up, mainly because I don't care that much.

After thirty minutes, he finally pauses, and I take the opportunity to excuse myself.

"I think I need to visit the ladies' room."

"Sure," he replies, already distracted by his phone as I tap out.

As soon as I'm out of sight, I let out a yawn. This evening feels more like a business meeting than a date. It's a disappointing twist after a promising start.

Turning down the dark hallway, I pull my phone from the pocket in my dress. The screen lights up my face in the dimness as I quickly type a message to Lexi.

CARLEE
Checking in.

LEXI
How's it going?

CARLEE
Awful!

LEXI
Glad I ordered you a burger! Yay! I mean, aww, that's so sad. See you soon!

CARLEE
UGH!!!

LEXI

I LOVE it when I'm right. Kinda like how I know
you and Weston will fall madly in love, and then
you'll officially be my sister. A DREAM!

That's not happening. He has a specific type of woman he pursues.

My complete opposite.

No lines have ever been crossed between us—not even once. And they never can be.

I ignore her text.

CARLEE

I'll see you soon, but can you be on your best
behavior? Especially now that Weston knows he
was my hall pass! WTF?!

I want to tell her to stop revealing things about me to him, but I can't. It would blow our cover, and the last thing I need is for Lexi to jeopardize the delicate balance we've created.

LEXI

He finds it endearing, I promise.

CARLEE

I bet he does!

Once in the restroom, I comb my fingers through my hair. I reapply lipstick, loving the deep shade of crimson. Standing before the mirror, I can't shake the nagging thought that I'm undatable.

Is it my expectations that ruin everything?

Maybe Trever's nervous, fumbling for conversation, so he's sticking with what he's comfortable with. I take a deep breath, not ready to completely give up, and decide I'll change the subject the first chance I get. Maybe I can salvage this date before it slips away entirely.

My phone vibrates, and I unlock it.

WESTON

How are things?

CARLEE

Amazing!

WESTON

Liar.

CARLEE

Liar?

WESTON

Yep. Because you wouldn't have texted me back if it was.

CARLEE

Did Lexi tell you what I just texted her?

WESTON

Nope! Swear.

CARLEE

Quick question. Am I hard to talk to?

WESTON

Not at all.

With a renewed sense of purpose, I return to the bar. As I step back into the main area, I glance across the faces of couples lost in deep conversation.

My eyes quickly find Trever, only to find him talking on his phone. A fresh martini waits in front of him, glistening with droplets of condensation.

My empty barstool sits between him and a man with broad shoulders, wearing a stark black suit, exuding an air of confidence that's hard to ignore.

As I take a few steps forward, an unsettling familiarity grips me. I recognize the dark, messy hair from behind.

My heart kicks into overdrive, and I stop walking.

I blink hard, trying to convince myself he's not a daydream, that I'm not imagining things.

Sitting right next to my barstool is *Weston fucking Calloway.*

3

WESTON

A s I scroll through my phone, a text suddenly pops up and
pulls me from my thoughts.

LEXI

She's leaving early! Is this when I tell you I TOLD
YOU SO?!

WESTON

You're awful. You should be rooting for your bestie
to have a good time.

LEXI

MARRY HER.

WESTON

For the last time, I can't marry anyone right now.

LEXI

MARRY HER WHEN YOUR DIVORCE IS
FINALIZED!

WESTON

Lex.

LEXI

When is it supposed to be over?

WESTON

Soon. Weeks.

With a sigh, I swipe to my brother's contact, hoping for a distraction.

WESTON

Control your wife.

EASTON

Impossible.

WESTON

You're enjoying this.

EASTON

It's amusing, watching you get your balls busted.

WESTON

And she thinks I'M the evil twin.

EASTON

Aren't you?

WESTON

We both know you are.

EASTON

Maybe Lexi is right about you and Carlee.

WESTON

I thought you weren't getting involved?

EASTON

I'm not.

I reluctantly focus back on the phone conversation Trever is having a couple of barstools down. Carlee's empty seat is between us, and I'm impatiently waiting for her to return after texting her.

"Nah, man. I can't make it tonight. I'm going home with someone. Yeah, the girl I met a few weeks ago," Trever says with a chuckle.

His casual tone irritates me. I can't believe she'd been on more than one date with this douche.

"Yeah. Gorgeous. Tiny thing with a very nice ass. Perky tits. Her nipples have been hard for me all night. I think I could fall in love with this girl, maybe even marry her," he boasts. "She's eating up every word I say. I guess we'll see. Maybe I'll just fuck her raw until I'm bored. Would be a good lay. Seems like a little freak."

My jaw clenches tight.

"I have another date tomorrow night too. I dunno. Carlee feels special. Catch you up with what happens later." He ends the call, smirking, completely oblivious to the anger he's stirring within me.

I take a deep breath, trying to stay calm, but every fiber of my being wants to lash out. This motherfucker needs to be laid out on the floor. He doesn't deserve her time, and he certainly doesn't deserve *her*.

I down the bourbon in one swift motion, the burn calming my nerves. I signal for another, one that I'll try to savor, needing to steady the storm roiling inside me. As I wait for round two, I catch the familiar hint of her perfume.

Carlee Jean Jolly, from Merryville, Texas, smells like vanilla with a hint of cinnamon. It's intoxicating, swirling around me, and it puts me in a choke hold. I'm convinced I could locate her in a crowded room while blindfolded. Her scent is home, familiar, and comforting, and it drives me crazy. *She* drives me crazy.

"Pardon me," Carlee mutters as she slides onto the barstool beside me.

Her fingers gently brush along my back. It's a simple gesture, yet it holds so much behind it.

"No problem." I meet her sparkling greens, losing myself in their depths, feeling like time stands still.

I glance down at her pretty lips, which curl into a shy smile as I sip my bourbon, trying to mask the onslaught of emotions brewing beneath my skin. Our gazes lock as the world around us fades to obscurity. We engage in a silent conversation; unspoken words connect us in this dimly lit bar.

I tilt my head, along with my glass, watching the rich brown liquid swirl at the bottom. She's surprised I'm here, and she's silently wondering why. I've asked myself the same question since I walked through that fucking door.

I *shouldn't* be caught in this limbo of desire and restraint. But I had an unshakable urge to witness her with another man, a form of self-inflicted torture that only reiterates what's truly at stake—*her*.

Carlee returns her attention to tedious Trever.

"Sorry, what were you saying? Something about import fees?" Carlee continues, straining to find interest.

I'll give her an A for effort, but this date is pathetic.

Trever is birth control in human form.

"Ah, right." He dives back into his spiel about foreign taxes and fees, blissfully unaware that he's as exciting as watching paint dry. He wouldn't recognize a hint if it punched him in the face.

His monotonous finance talk is painfully unengaging. He hasn't allowed Carlee to speak for longer than three seconds, and it's infuriating. Even if she wanted to go home with him, which I can sense she doesn't, I'd never fucking allow it.

Call me a cockblock—I don't care.

Lexi was right about one thing: Carlee deserves to be with someone who will treat her right. Trever isn't the one.

"Don't you find that interesting?"

"Wow, yeah," Carlee responds, twirling the straws in her martini glass before downing the rest of it. She unlocks her phone to check the time, perhaps gauging how much longer she'll have to endure this.

I take the opportunity to text her.

WESTON

For fucks sake, how are you surviving this?

CARLEE

I told you I have the worst luck.

WESTON

Sluggers after this?

Carlee glances down at her phone and laughs, a sweet sound that pierces through the monotony of Trever's dialogue. It's the first time I've seen her chuckle since she sat down, and I take pride in knowing I sparked that glimmer of joy.

Visiting Sluggers is one of her bad dating rituals. After *every* failed date, she goes inside and has a shot of tequila before heading home.

It's also where *we* met.

Carlee was a faint glow in the darkness, my Firefly.

My phone buzzes with her reply.

CARLEE

After movie night.

It's confirmation that she'll be at my brother's. It makes me smile.

WESTON

It's a date.

CARLEE

Do you want it to be?

"*Do you?*" I barely whisper, letting the question float between us.

I shift my arm just enough to brush against hers, my fingertip touching her skin. The world around us fades away again.

I pick up my bourbon, shooting the rest back in one swift

motion. Two shots down. Stiffening the nerves feels necessary, but I think I need another.

The vintage light bulbs let out just enough light for me to catch the subtle uptick in her pulse. Something stirs between us, unspoken and undeniable, but I won't admit it. Neither will she. We're too stubborn.

"Are you okay?" Trever interrupts his own monologue, finally directing his attention toward Carlee.

She nervously chuckles. "I'm great."

A lie.

Trever continues his droning, and she glances at her empty glass—a silent plea for an escape.

"Excuse me." I catch the attention of the bartender with a wave. "I'd like to order the lady a drink. It's *desperately* needed."

Trever's rambling stops, and his eyes bore into me, confusion and irritation flaring in his gaze. I ignore him because a lion doesn't care if a dog barks. No one intimidates me.

"Miss?" The bartender turns to Carlee.

A flirty smirk dances on her pretty, kissable lips, hinting at her seductive spirit. She enjoys me being here—I can tell.

"The most expensive bottle of wine you have. With two glasses, please?" she asks, then glances at me.

"Make it three glasses," I say, breaking the tension surrounding us. "She forgot to request a glass for the finance guy."

"What's his fucking problem?" Trever mutters, his voice bitter.

"He's just being polite," Carlee interjects, her tone calm and confident. "You have nothing to worry about."

I don't know which of us she's reassuring, but it feels like that last part was directed toward *me*.

Flecks of gold dance in her irises, capturing the light.

Am I worried? *Absolutely not.*

Trever's disrespect and what he said on the phone gnaw at me.

"Yeah, I think he does have a problem," Trever continues, his agitation obvious as he leans forward, his arms crossed defiantly.

"I don't have a problem. *Yet.*" I turn to him, keeping my tone sharp and cool. "I can ruin your life with one phone call, so don't fuck with me, little boy. Calm down and enjoy your date, if that's what you call this."

Carlee's a player in this game. If this were baseball, she'd be in the major leagues—graceful, strategic, and in absolute control. She's no damsel in distress, and she doesn't need rescuing. But I'd bet my entire inheritance that when she walked through that door, Double-E Trever wasn't a passing thought. There was only one man on her mind.

"Is that a threat?" Trever asks, his eyes narrowing in challenge.

He's too stupid to understand it's a promise.

I glare at him like I'm the Grim Reaper. In less than five minutes, I could unearth everything about him—his background, his ambitions, and his family. That silly little finance job he clings to? I could buy the company right now and fire his ass first thing in the morning without giving it a second thought.

He leans closer to Carlee, his fingers brushing along the exposed skin on her back. Thinking about his grubby little hands on her makes my jaw clench.

"Do you want to get out of here? We can go somewhere more private and finish our conversation," Trever whispers. "I think I'm falling for you."

She immediately stills, and her demeanor changes in a snap.

"No, no," she says, pulling away from his grasp. She's so close we touch.

The brief contact between her body and mine sends an inferno raging through me, igniting desires I've learned to ignore.

Why am I here again?

"I forgot I promised my best friend I'd meet up with her at eight thirty," Carlee explains sweetly, her voice a melody that doesn't defuse his annoyance.

I glance down at my watch, noting the cruel passage of time. It's a waste of precious minutes we'll never get back.

Trever growls with frustration, the sound feral. "I thought you were free *all* night? Isn't that what you told me?"

I don't like his fucking tone with her. It's laced with entitlement and anger, which only amplifies my need to protect her.

"I wanted to see you," she says, her honesty cutting through the fog of the situation.

Her expression is final, and she's done playing cat and mouse with this man. Just as her lips part to say more, a twenty-year-old bottle of merlot is set on the bar top like a trophy.

Carlee studies it.

"How much is this?" I ask.

"Ten thousand," the bartender replies.

"Carry on," I tell him with a dismissive wave.

The bartender carefully removes the cork with a practiced flick of the wrist and pours the dark liquid into three glasses.

The rich, velvety scent of the wine fills the air, making my mouth water. Trever glares at the two-thousand-dollar glass of merlot as if it personally insulted him.

"This is bullshit. When will I see you again?" His words drip with rudeness as he disregards Carlee's demeanor. It's obvious she's growing uncomfortable by his tone.

"Watch your fucking tone when speaking to her," I finally say, my voice straining.

Carlee sits straighter. "I'm sorry, Trever. This isn't going to work out between us." Her Southern accent says *hello*, a melodic reminder of the roots she tries to bury.

"You're breaking up with me?" Trever snaps back, his voice crackling with disbelief.

His reaction catches her off guard.

"Trever," she says sharply as the nice version of her vanishes, replaced by a fierce resolve, "be realistic. We're on our third date. You ditched me after thirty minutes the last time we were together." Her tone is unwavering. "We are *not* dating. Look at how you've treated me tonight. You're self-centered and married to your job."

Ruthless. I've never personally witnessed this side of her before, and it simultaneously captivates and terrifies me.

"You're a bitch," he retorts, pulling a hundred-dollar bill out of his wallet with exaggerated disdain. "I'm not paying for your drinks."

"I've got it," I say, glaring at him, my hand instinctively returning to the back of Carlee's stool. "Goodbye, Trever."

"Fuck you. She won't suck your dick either," he hisses as he storms away.

As he retreats, Carlee picks up her wineglass, taking three large gulps as if seeking solace.

Neither of us speaks for five minutes, but our bodies are as close as they can be without sharing a chair.

"I'm—"

"I'm—"

We stumble over each other in synchronicity.

"Go ahead," I offer, hoping she isn't upset. "You first."

"I'm happy to see you," she admits. "Your turn."

I open my mouth, then close it again because that's not the response I expected. "I was going to offer an apology."

"Save it for when it's needed. It's not in this instance." Her brows rise, and she glances around, a smile breaking across her face as her gaze dances over the candles flickering on the bar top.

A second later, she shifts her barstool, creating space between us. It's a deliberate move, a precaution, in case anyone is watching our casual exchange too closely.

"What's on your mind?" I ask.

"When I arrived, I imagined how nice this would be with the right company. And then *you* appeared." She tilts her head, eyes sparkling.

"Were you thinking about me?" I ask. The weight of the moment shimmers with unspoken chemistry.

"Maybe." She takes another sip of wine, the liquid gliding down her throat, and I can't help but admire the way her lips wrap around the glass's edge.

"Don't make me blush," I tease, trying to keep the mood light.

She chuckles. "Is a Calloway even capable?"

"Hmm," I muse, realizing she has no idea how breathtakingly gorgeous she is under these lights.

I'd get on my knees and worship her if I could, but deep down, I'd grapple with my own fear—wondering if I could ever fully give myself and my heart to someone again. That's why there are unspoken rules to our friendship, deep lines drawn in the sand that neither of us dares to cross. Not to mention, she won't give herself permission to really fall in love.

As I discreetly watched Carlee from across the bar, I knew she wasn't into Trever. If they had genuinely hit it off, I'd have left, ensuring she never knew I was here. But seeing her with him only confirmed that our relationship was lightning in a bottle.

"He said he was falling in love with me," she says, her brows knitting together in confusion. "Why is *that* the go-to?"

I shrug. "Maybe it's true?"

"Doubt it." Annoyance coats her tone, and she avoids eye contact.

I know what she's doing, pretending we're strangers to anyone who might catch a glimpse of us. The muted buzz of conversation and soft clinking of glasses surround us.

"You're the type of woman men *want* to settle down with," I reply, my voice steady, hoping to navigate the delicate topic with care.

"I think you've pegged me wrong, Weston," she counters.

I wish with every fiber of my being that she could see her how I do. She draws me in like a moth to the flame.

"You go on dates with men who you'd never actually date long-term," I say.

My honesty is sharp yet gentle. I don't want to cut too deep, but she deserves the truth, and I know she can handle it.

Carlee nervously chuckles.

"Laugh, but you know it's reality," I assert, leaning closer, my voice dropping to a conspiratorial whisper. "You set yourself up for failure so you can continue being single. The chase is a game to you. One you're not ready to give up yet."

"Maybe you do have me figured out," she finally concedes, her voice thoughtful, tinged with curiosity and a touch of vulnerability.

"I think it's because you're afraid of *actually* falling in love," I say without regret.

I sip the wine, letting the bold dryness wash over my palate while she contemplates my words. Silence swallows us whole as an eternity passes between us.

"Wow, how much do I owe you for my therapy session?" she asks teasingly.

Spilling truths is a familiar routine we've fallen into since we became friends. We don't hold back from one another because there is no time for bullshit.

"Don't worry; I'll add it to your bill," I tell her, the corners of my mouth lifting in a smirk. I lean back in my barstool, enjoying how her laughter lights up the dim room.

"And how will I ever repay you?" she asks, her demeanor flirty.

"I'm sure I'll think of something," I reply.

The promise hovers in the air between us, charged with unspoken possibilities.

More people filter into the bar area, but it's a Friday night, so that's unsurprising. The hum of chatter surrounds us, blending with the occasional clinking of glasses and the rich jazz floating from the stage across the room.

Carlee licks her red lips, and she captivates my thoughts. I can't help but wonder how the merlot tastes on her tongue.

"What's on your mind?" she asks.

Her gaze moves from my mouth to the sleek tie around my neck; that tight knot draws her attention like a magnet. I'm her kryptonite.

"You're eye-fucking me. You should stop that." I don't *ever* let that shit slide. I want—and *need*—her to be acutely aware when she looks at me like I'm utterly irresistible.

"Blame the suit," she replies, an amused smile playing at the corners of her mouth.

A well-dressed man is her thing. It always has been. She's never denied her preferences, and I admire that about her.

We sit in comfortable silence for a few more minutes. There are too many unspoken words and lingering glances.

"Have you heard the recent Weston Calloway rumor?" she asks, breaking the spell.

"Which one?" I lean closer, inviting her to share the latest scandal.

Several have made their rounds this week, each more outrageous than the last.

"There was a blind item dropped about you and your *secret* girlfriend." She studies me intently, her eyes sparkling with curiosity. "Who is she?"

4

WESTON

With fast fingers, Carlee types into her phone, and the bright screen reveals her features. She sets it on the bar, and my eyes scan over the post. The site has been around for decades, and it's one my publicist watches. Everyone from celebrities to the general public knows about it.

Blind Item #13

Mr. Playboy Billionaire may be going through a dirty divorce with the gold-digger demon, but he has a secret girlfriend he's been seeing for months. It doesn't matter how many "dates" he publicly goes on. His heart belongs to the woman he's trying to keep hidden.

"That anonymous website is full of unconfirmed gossip," I say, trying to sound dismissive, but the weight of the accusation lingers in the air.

"There are confirmed truths shared here too," she argues, her tone unwavering. "You won't tell me?"

"If I were seeing someone regularly, you'd know, I promise," I assure.

"I'd love to be the one to reveal her," she says. "What a comeback that would be for LadyLux."

I smirk, my mind reeling. "Sorry to disappoint you."

"Kinda glad though." She swirls the wine in her glass. "I have a feeling whoever you end up with won't appreciate our friendship."

Her words hit harder than I care to admit.

"If anyone had issues with us, I'd dump them. Lena, my ex, isolated me from my friends for years. Somehow, she wedged herself between me and Easton. I won't allow anyone to have that sort of control over me again," I explain, my voice firm. "Our friendship is nonnegotiable."

Silence stretches between us, filled with the unspoken fears that hover like fog in the early morning.

"What about you? What if your boyfriend told you to stop seeing me? Would you?" I ask.

Carlee's expression softens. "You'll have to end our friendship, Wes. It's nonnegotiable for me as well."

I love it when she shortens my name like that, as if she's claiming a piece of me for herself.

"Music to my ears," I admit as I empty the bottle of wine into our glasses.

The mood shifts, and I need to change the subject before I drown in the depths of our connection. "I'm curious. Why Trever?"

"His profile made me laugh."

"Laughter is happiness in its rawest form," I mutter, contemplating the joy that bubbles up when I'm with her.

"Where happiness lives, true love follows," she continues.

I think about my past relationships. Could that be what's been missing?

Her brows lift. "Is something wrong?"

"No." I shake my head. "All is well."

"You have that look on your face. Is it pity? Because if so—"

"No," I say, my tone firm. "It's *admiration*."

"Oh." She pauses, trying to hold back a smile, but ultimately fails. "Carry on then. I kind of like the thought of you being my secret admirer."

If she only knew.

I lick my lips, and warmth spreads through me. This woman has no idea how deep my feelings run. She's completely immune to my charm unless she's had a drink or two, and even then, I wonder if it truly counts. My buried emotions keep me tethered, and yet here she is, blissfully unaware of what she does to me.

Carlee finishes her glass and hiccups with a grin. "Sorry it was so expensive."

She's already tipsy.

"Expensive?" I chuckle, genuinely relaxed when she's close. "If I had known it would end your shitty *date* sooner, I'd have sent two bottles over as soon as you arrived."

"*Wait*, when I arrived? You were already here?" Her mouth falls open in surprise, and it's adorable.

I nod. "I had to witness this monstrosity for myself. You know, for research."

"Ah. And how would you feel if I showed up and watched one of your dates like a stalker?"

I chew on the corner of my lip, the idea enticing. "What are you doing tomorrow night? I'll get you a reservation."

She's full of skepticism. "You're serious?"

"Maybe you can determine my relationship issues?"

"Okay," she says with a hint of mischief in her gaze. "I'll call your bluff. I'm free."

I smirk. "Mmm. This will be fun."

She laughs, a melodic sound that dances between us. My heart pounds just a little harder.

"You realize I could write the Weston Calloway dating manual before sunrise, right? I already know why you suck."

"Oh, really?" I enjoy the banter. "Enlighten me."

"You *rush* things with every woman you've ever been with. I don't know if it's fuckboy behavior or if you're just a hopeless romantic, but it's definitely a dating cycle. You have to give it longer than two months. I'm not sure you've ever been in love. It all seems like lust to me."

"Hilarious." I lean back, the weight of her words sinking in. "It *might* be a cycle, but I know what it's like to fall madly and deeply in love with someone. It's obsessive. Dangerous. Addictive."

"Where's the proof?" Her head tilts as she challenges me.

I glance down at her mouth, and her breath catches. Together, we're electrifying. There's a magnetic pull between us that I can't keep ignoring. I wonder what she'd do if I slid my lips across hers. Would that be enough evidence for her?

"You *choose* not to see what's right in front of you," I say, lowering my voice.

She doesn't get it—not even with the millions of hints I've dropped or the moments we've shared that linger like stardust across the summer sky. Not even with the blind items posted that are *clearly* about us.

Somehow, I'm still hiding in plain sight.

Carlee's approach to finding love is calculated. She knows exactly what she wants in a partner, but runs when she finds it. I've witnessed it a lot this year.

But I'm not perfect either.

I struggle to trust my decision-making skills after the mistake of marrying someone as awful as Lena. The memory of that toxic relationship still looms like a dark cloud over me. That's why I'm so hesitant to seriously date again.

"I've predicted every one of your major breakups since I was eighteen years old," Carlee says with a serious glint in her eyes.

"Maybe you should pick my next girlfriend then," I offer, half joking.

"Me?" Her brows furrow in disbelief. "Why?"

"Why not?" I reply, a smile tugging at my lips. "You're a *Westoncyclopedia*. You would immediately know who'd be compatible with me. Plus, you're a *great* matchmaker, considering you keep taking all the credit for Lexi and Easton."

A grin spreads across her lips. "You're serious?"

"What do I have to lose?" *Other than her.*

I quickly shoot a text to the restaurant I'm visiting tomorrow. The response is immediate.

"Reservation made," I state.

"I look forward to it." A hint of cockiness drips from her tone as if she's already taking pride in this little venture of ours.

"It shouldn't be this easy, should it?" The question has lingered in my mind since we met last on Wednesday.

"What's that?" she asks.

"*Us.* Our friendship," I say.

"But shouldn't it? When it's easy, that means it's right. Sometimes, we meet people who we instantly connect with—friends who will stay in our lives forever. They're the family we choose. Look at me and Lexi. Me and you. It's serendipity. Completely meant to be. Wouldn't have it any other way," she admits.

It's the little things she says that strike a chord within me. I appreciate her sincerity; she doesn't just string words together for the sake of conversation. She wears her heart on her sleeve and isn't afraid to share her inner thoughts and feelings with me. That's trust—something we've built brick by brick.

I'm convinced Carlee sees the world through heart-shaped, rose-colored glasses. I wish I could.

She's right though; relationships should be easy.

That's just never been my experience, *except with her.*

"That was my trauma talking again," I acknowledge, a weight settling in my stomach.

For years, I fought tooth and nail for a woman who *never* truly loved me. Lena was obsessed with what being married to me could bring her—money, fame, and endless connections—all while smothering me in layers of deceitful lies.

"Healing takes time, Weston," Carlee says gently, her fingers briefly wrapping around my hand under the bar, squeezing me with assurance.

When she pulls away, I instantly feel the hollow ache.

Carlee understands to an extent, but she has no idea how deeply my ex-fueled anxiety runs. I'm still navigating the treacherous waters of trust, working to mend the fractures of my heart that Lena left behind. Every day is a struggle. Every day, I find myself questioning who is seeking to exploit my family's name and the connections it brings. It's a place I don't want to be.

Carlee is the only woman I've let into my world since Lena tried to dismantle it. She's sunshine on a cloudy day.

"Were you contemplating going home with Double-E?" I ask curiously.

"No. I knew within the first five minutes that I wouldn't," she replies, leaning closer, her voice dropping to a whisper. "Doubt he could've gotten the job done. Not sure he knows where the little man in the boat is."

I burst into laughter, the sound genuine. "You were serious earlier—about your sex life?"

"You weren't supposed to hear any of that," she groans, her cheeks tinged with a rosy hue.

"Not my fault Lexi had you on speaker. But I'm sorry to hear that. Condolences to your lady parts."

"Appreciate it. I've learned that if I want something done right, I have to do it myself."

She winks at me, and I find myself lost in thought—imagining her alone in her bedroom, shadows flickering around as she explores her body.

Shit.

I swallow hard, adjusting myself, desperate to push the visual away as she locks her gaze on me, sultry and mischievous.

She smirks with a brow popped as if she saw my thoughts. "I've had lots of practice."

"You're tipsy," I mutter, my pulse quickening.

Anytime her inhibitions fall, she throws away our carefully constructed boundaries. She test-drives my willpower, forcing me to reject every advance she makes.

Carlee bats her long lashes. "This is when things get fun."

The scent of her perfume surrounds me as I lean in close. "As much as I don't want to cut this short, I have to go. A car waits for you outside. I'll see you there."

She grabs my hand.

"How did you know I was going to ditch tonight?" Her breath is hot against my skin.

"When you didn't choose the blue dress."

"Seriously?" She creates space between us, the air suddenly charged with something more.

"Yeah. And I caught a glimpse of your expression. Hope to never see that look on your face again," I say truthfully.

"Never," she whispers. Vulnerability flashing in her eyes. "I *always* look forward to us."

"Let's keep it that way." I shoot her a wink. "See you soon."

"Soon," she repeats, and I catch a glint of something.

I pay the bill, careful not to meet her gaze as I move toward the exit. Leaving her is always the hardest part.

I climb into the back of the SUV, sinking into the leather seat as my driver zooms away. Anticipation and excitement coil in my stomach as I text her the details for tomorrow night.

CARLEE
We're going to Ambrosia? Are you serious?

WESTON
Yes.

CARLEE
But the dress code …

WESTON

I'll take care of it. Don't forget I have fuck-you money. Anything else?

CARLEE

I guess not.

WESTON

Great. A car will pick you up at seven sharp tomorrow night. Wardrobe will be delivered an hour prior.

CARLEE

I cannot believe we're going to Ambrosia.

WESTON

You're too easy to please.

CARLEE

We both know that's a lie.

The vehicle rolls to a stop on the curb in front of Frankie's. The sign might be faded, and the windows are covered in grime, but the aroma is irresistible. They serve the best burgers in the city, and my mouth waters at the thought.

As soon as I enter, the bell above the door clanks against the glass, announcing my presence. I check my watch, a wave of guilt washing over me as I move toward the counter, knowing I'm late.

Frankie stands with his arms crossed, an exaggerated glare etched on his face. Not a good sign.

"Apologies," I say, shaking my head with a laugh, hoping to defuse his irritation.

"When Lexi told me she was sending *you*, I knew you'd be an hour and a half late. I didn't start on the order because this food is made to be eaten fresh," he says, his tone a mix of annoyance and amusement.

I let out a relieved breath. "You're a lifesaver."

"You're right," he barks out. "You *owe* me, Calloway."

"I had a drink with a friend and lost track of time," I explain, offering a faint smile as I think about Carlee.

"With your secret girlfriend?" he questions, raising an eyebrow.

"Please," I tell him firmly. "You know that's bullshit."

"Is it?" Frankie watches me closely, his gaze sharp and unwavering, but I don't answer. His smirk tells me he's enjoying this. "You always have an excuse. At least the secret girlfriend one is plausible and forgivable."

"Can I get one of those colas in a bottle?" I ask, glancing at the fridge packed with colorful drinks.

He pops the top with a satisfying crack and hands it to me, the icy bottle cool against my fingers. I sit in one of the mismatched chairs and wobbly tables that threaten to topple over.

I have to sober up.

The last thing I want is to walk into Easton's as drunk as Carlee. My brother is *too* smart and pays attention to details. He'll see right through me, as he always does.

Fifteen minutes pass in a blur as I scroll through my text conversations with her. The flirting is undeniable, and a smile creeps onto my lips, one I try to suppress but can't.

"Why are you cheesing like that?" Frankie asks, his voice cutting through my daydream.

He holds up two large paper bags. The scent of food floats through the air, causing my mouth to water. He hands me the sacks, and they're heavier than I expected.

"Holy shit. What did they order?"

He shakes his head with amusement. "You know, I've seen that same expression on your brother's face."

"Not sure what you're talking about. You're imagining things," I reply.

"Enjoy your *date* tonight," he mumbles, grabbing my empty soda bottle and placing it in the recycling bin with a clattering thud. The sound echoes through the small dining room as he opens the door for me with exaggerated chivalry that makes me roll my eyes.

I walk outside, the bags snug in my grasp. "Date?"

"It's four meals—Lexi's and Easton's orders, plus yours and Carlee's."

"See ya, Frankie," I say, sucking in cool, fresh air.

"Hot damn. Carlee *is* your secret girlfriend."

I roll my eyes again. "God, not you too. Also, keep that shit quiet. That's how rumors get started."

He gives me a wide, mischievous grin and a wave goodbye. "Whatever you say, Calloway."

Am I that transparent? *Fuck.*

5

WESTON

I'm dropped off in front of Park Towers—the high-rise where Easton and I have property. I returned to my penthouse at The Park after my divorce was officially filed, seeking proximity to my brother. My ex was a professional at isolating me from everyone who cared about me—something I will *never* allow to happen again.

The elevator soars upward like a speeding bullet. Soon, the doors are opening to the foyer of his home, nicknamed *the diamond in the sky* for its dazzling blue windows that sparkle at night.

As I enter, I spot Carlee perched on the small couch with a glass of wine, radiating allure in her skintight blue dress. I open my mouth, then close it again, momentarily taken aback.

"Weston. Nice seeing you again," she says, knowing we spent the last hour together.

"The pleasure is *always* mine." A devilish smirk plays on my lips at the thought of her changing clothes for me.

She thinks she's so fucking sly, and I love it.

"Rizzing me up, Weston," she says as I walk past her. "Appreciated."

I glance at Lexi, who's grinning wide. "Sorry it took me so long. Time slipped away, as it always does."

"That's why I sent you. I wanted to give Carlee time to arrive," Lexi replies, glancing between us and nodding.

I find it adorable that she believes I need assistance with Carlee. I don't.

Easton grabs the bags from my hands, raising an eyebrow as we engage in a silent conversation. I wonder if he can detect the alcohol on my breath or catch the lingering scent of The Marquee on my clothes. It's distinct. Maybe that's why Carlee changed clothes.

He opens his mouth to speak, but I shake my head, cutting him off. Has he already guessed that we were together?

"You're confirming *that* for me later," he says, his voice low enough for only me to hear.

"*No*, I'm not," I murmur.

There's no way I'll tell him where I was. It's my business, and while I typically share most things with him, I don't discuss Carlee with anyone. It's also why I'm still puzzled by that blind item. No one knows.

"You will tell me."

"It's not up for discussion," I assert firmly.

I'm not ready to share whatever *this* is. I don't have an explanation.

I pass Carlee as I move toward the kitchen. "How was your date?"

"The end was my favorite part," she replies with a wink.

"I bet it was." A current zips between us. "Too bad it didn't work out."

Easton studies us, and I maintain a neutral expression. Mirroring his calm demeanor always throws him off. I become unreadable.

WWED? (What would Easton do?)

She shrugs. "It's fine. I have another date scheduled after I leave here. It's not a huge loss."

"Moving on so quickly?" Lexi probes, sounding almost concerned that Carlee might find the love of her life after this. "Maybe you should reschedule," Lexi suggests, not realizing she's literally working *against* me right now.

"I don't ditch my dates," she reminds her confidently.

"Well, I hope that one ends with a happy ending," I quip, unable to resist the temptation to tease.

Carlee snorts. "Now, that would be a dream come true."

"A dream, huh?" I chuckle as Easton places everything on the counter.

I wish he weren't zeroed in on me. My brother is piecing together bits of information he's gathered from this conversation, and I try to ignore him.

"Oh, I have a date tomorrow as well," Carlee says excitedly as we move to the bartop.

It's so hard not to smile, but I can't break character with Easton so close. I hate it when he does this to me, but I continue to be a chameleon.

The chandelier glitters above us, and the city lights glow warmly as we dig into our food. Carlee sits beside me, her knee brushing against mine. Our eyes meet, and I flash her a small smile as she picks up her burger. She blushes.

I glance at my brother, and he gives me a shit-eating grin. He knows we were together. It only took him twelve minutes.

I clear my throat. "Lex, did you tell Frankie this was a dinner date?" I take a bite of my cheeseburger.

"I don't think the word *date* came out of my mouth. It could have though. Is that what this is?"

I turn to Carlee. "Speaking of dates, just to be clear, you're going on another date *tonight*, right?"

"Yes," Carlee confirms.

"And people think *I'm* the serial dater," I scoff.

"You are." She snorts. "You go on several dates each week and have a secret girlfriend. I think that's the very definition of being a serial dater, wouldn't you agree?"

"Secret girlfriend?" Easton tilts his head, puzzled.

I haven't had a chance to chat with him yet.

I clear my throat. "There's a rumor circulating that I have a secret girlfriend, and the dates I've been going on are a cover-up to keep her hidden."

"Is it true?" Easton questions.

"No," I explain, "it's not."

His smile fades, replaced by a look of irritation. "Who would spread something like that?"

"A liar who needs to keep their fucking opinions to themselves. And if I ever find out who started this, I swear I will make their life a living hell."

Lexi wears a concerned expression, but Carlee keeps the mood light.

"Just tell us who she is," Carlee insists. "LadyLux would love to know."

"There is no secret girlfriend. Unless you're volunteering for the role," I say.

Carlee's breath hitches, but I catch it.

"Yes!" Lexi nods, wiping her mouth with a napkin. "That's actually a *great* idea. Play into the rumors."

"Pfft. No thanks." Carlee takes a bite of her burger, but I see the fire behind her eyes.

I enjoy the clever comebacks that roll off her tongue.

Lexi and Easton exchange glances as I reach over and dip a fry into Carlee's ketchup.

"Pardon me, sir. You have your own. I don't like sharing what's mine." She points toward the unopened packets.

"You also don't play nicely with others," I quip.

She laughs. "That's why I'm single. It's probably why you are too."

"Oh, I'm *very* kind. Attentive. *Love* to please," I insist.

Carlee nearly chokes but recovers, forcing her food down with a gulp of wine.

"Are you okay?" I ask, ready to perform the Heimlich maneuver if necessary.

She gives me a thumbs-up while coughing. "It went down the wrong way. I'm good."

Lexi glances between us, an amused look on her face. "You two are getting married."

"Really?" I placate her. "How long do I have before the wedding?"

Lexi tilts her head. "You're in phase one right now. I'm guessing it'll be within six months."

Carlee's brows knit together, and her smile fades. "Wait, you're serious."

"Of course I am," Lexi confirms.

Carlee bursts into laughter. "You believe I'll marry Weston within six months? Lex, he's not even divorced yet. Who knows how long that could take?"

"I'm working on it, my sweets," I say, shooting her a wink. "It's almost over. A month at max."

I've fought my ex for everything she's tried to claim, including half of the inheritance I received after marrying her. A smaller settlement might work because she's quickly running out of money after I cut her off.

If I knew I had a real chance with Carlee, I'd pay whatever it took to rid myself of Lena. Until then, I'll keep battling her until she exhausts herself or runs out of funds. I'd bet on the latter happening first.

"Do I need to give you a list of reasons why you'd be really great partners?" Lexi asks.

"No. And do not entertain her, Weston." Carlee scrunches her nose, looking undeniably cute.

"Even Easton agrees with me," Lexi interjects.

"Weston can make decisions on his own. Trust me, he knows how love works," Easton reiterates.

"Thank you," I say with a wide grin, lifting my hand toward my brother. "Appreciate that."

My brother gives me a pointed look. He sees right through me. He knows there's something more lingering between me and Carlee, and the smirk playing on his lips confirms it.

"Hmm," he says, wiping his mouth with a napkin, cockiness still present.

"What is it?" Lexi asks.

"Just figured something out," Easton replies, returning his attention to his wife. "But it's not important."

He can recognize love in me just as easily as I can in him.

"You're *not* shocked by this revelation?" Carlee asks me skeptically.

"Lexi has been harping on this for months like she's hypnotizing me into believing we're meant to be together. It's nothing to panic over."

"Has it worked?" Easton asks with a chuckle.

"Don't start," I warn.

Carlee glares at Lexi. "I honestly thought this horrible matchmaking tactic was a joke just to patronize me."

Her denial is adorable, and I can barely handle it.

"I'm not apologizing." Lexi grins. "You'll thank me later. *Trust* me."

"Do you know how often you've told me to trust you and it's gone horribly wrong? A handful of times, Lex. Well, over ten. You should stop with the matchmaking. At least let us become friends."

Ah, smart girl. Carlee's a mastermind, skillfully laying the groundwork for our friendship to be recognized, so no one will be surprised *if* we're seen together. She's cunning, and while I can see through her carefully executed moves, I appreciate that she's making them.

"You want me to be your *friend*? Hmm. I'll need to think about that before agreeing. Seems like a commitment."

Carlee might actually be offended. "I'm a *great* friend. I give amazing advice. I'm very *easy* ... to be around. Plus, I'm pretty, and I have a sense of humor. I'm the whole package."

She's flirting, almost as if she knows I hang on to every word she says.

"Be careful, Weston. Every other dude she's befriended fell madly in love with her, and it ruined the friendship," Lexi says.

I glance at Carlee. "Is that true?"

She forces a smile. It's not something she's shared with me.

"It's the truth. It's why I'm *always* very hesitant to be friends with men. I quickly become their late-night fantasy. No man has *ever* been able to leave their emotions at the door."

"Thankfully, I don't have emotions." I smirk, understanding that I'm different.

I was Carlee's fantasy before becoming a part of her life.

She knows so much about me like she's hacked into my brain and written things I've never admitted to anyone—not even my brother.

Carlee *could* pen a manual on me. If she did, I wonder how she'd weave together the words of *our* chapter. She doesn't realize this is just the beginning.

Carlee notices I'm lost in thought. I smile at her—a genuine one.

"Yeah, that means I'd have to friend-zone you pretty hard," Carlee says. "Hope you're prepared for that."

"Same. And I'm a professional, completely unbreakable," I assure her with a laugh, but she already knows that to be true.

This statement confuses Easton because he's reading between the lines. He knows me too well to ignore anything I say. Our minds are too similar.

Carlee bats her long lashes. "So, friends?"

"To be determined."

My little Firefly glows in the dark, and I grin as I focus back on my food. I'll be her friend forever if that's the path she chooses.

"Being friends first makes the sex *so* much better," Lexi says.

My brother's cheeks redden. Carlee notices.

"Oh my God. Calloways *can* blush. Good to know."

"You're imagining things," he says, but he's smiling.

Throughout dinner, Carlee and I exchange unspoken words and too many stolen glances to count as our arms brush together. I want to be closer to her.

Afterward, Lexi and Easton take the long couch. I remove my suit jacket and roll up my sleeves before joining Carlee on the other one. There's a cushion's width between us, but I wish there weren't. As the movie rolls on, I'm lost in my thoughts. At the hour and fifteen minute mark, she finishes her wine and moves to the kitchen to put her glass away.

I haven't had any alcohol since I arrived. I'm sober because I need to be. When Carlee returns, she sits beside me, and our bodies mold together.

"Who picked *Titanic*? This movie is long," she whispers as she glances down at my lips.

It would be so easy to kiss her right now as Jack draws Rose like one of his French girls.

I glance over and notice Easton and Lexi are asleep. Heat floods through me as her body presses against mine. I lean in, and my mouth traces the shell of her ear.

"We shouldn't be this close," I whisper as my heart thrums in my chest.

My fingers brush down her arm, causing goose bumps to trail across her skin.

"Why not?" she asks, pulling away to study me, but I can't speak.

She's so goddamn gorgeous that she's stolen every word from my vocabulary—everything, even the ones in different languages.

I inch closer, and I know she'd let me kiss her. Carlee

practically begs for it. I swallow hard. Her eyes close, and her breath hitches as her lips part. Fuck, I want to do this so badly that it hurts.

"You'll have regrets," I mutter as she inhales a ragged breath.

I watch her, and I hate being the one to constantly reject her.

"Just a test," she whispers, creating space between us. "You passed."

"Don't play games with me."

She repositions herself, resting her head on my thigh. Her eyes meet mine, and I want to run my fingers through her hair.

"Take your own advice," she quips.

"I *love* a smart-ass."

"You underestimate me."

"I don't," I admit.

The intoxicating sweetness of her vanilla perfume surrounds me. I gently twist a piece of her hair around my finger. Watching this movie with Carlee so close is painful, and we still have over an hour left.

Leonardo says something, but I don't hear a word as I lose myself in my thoughts.

I *almost* kissed her.

I wanted to so fucking badly as her warm breath brushed against my skin.

Would she have kissed me back or ended our friendship because it got too real?

Now, I'm unsure.

When the credits roll, I double-check that Lexi and Easton are still sleeping. Their breathing is steady. They've become the typical old couple who are in bed by ten. I knew they wouldn't make it through *Titanic*.

I take the opportunity to meet her eyes as the TV casts a blue glow in the room.

"It's the look again," she murmurs as she sits upright.

Our mouths are dangerously close once more.

"Don't test me," I warn.

She inches forward, and our breaths mix. I think she might do it, but she smiles instead.

"Right back at you, bestie."

Carlee stands, smirking, completely addicted to the chase, as if she gets high off it. I study just how fucking beautiful she is in that dress that hugs her gorgeous body.

Quietly, she tiptoes over to Easton and Lexi, then kneels down until she's face-to-face with Lexi.

"Lex, I'm gonna go," Carlee whispers, shaking her.

"Huh? *Oh.* Shit. Okay. Why are you so close to me?" Lexi backs away, and Easton tightens his grip on her.

"I love you," Carlee tells her, squeezing her tightly. "Let's have lunch soon and catch up."

"Deal," Lexi says, sitting upright. Her hair is a mess. "Have fun on your date."

"I will," Carlee tells her, standing.

"Good night," Easton says, but there's something more behind his sleepy gaze as it flicks between us. He's trying to read me again.

"Night."

I turn to Carlee, sliding on my suit jacket. "I'll walk you out."

"Thanks," she offers.

In the elevator, neither of us speaks. We don't descend to the ground floor, but to the garage my brother and I share. I turn on the lights, and her eyes widen.

"You own these?" she asks, her fingers gliding over the sleek vintage cars.

She glances admiringly at the white Mustang parked nearby, and memories of when I stole this car during our matchmaking days flood me. I pretended to be Easton then cleverly delivered Lexi to him.

"Most are Easton's, but I have access to everything," I reply as I move toward the locker, placing my fingerprint on the pad. It clicks open.

I remove the keys from the hook, but Carlee hesitates.

"It's too risky to leave together."

I smirk. "It's midnight. We're safe."

I open the gear cabinet, replacing my suit jacket with a riding coat. I pull Lexi's gear from the closet and hand it to Carlee, along with a plain helmet. They're the same size.

"This should fit."

"Weston," she whispers, but she takes the items from me.

"Do you trust me?" I ask, moving to the motorcycle.

I climb onto it, start the engine, and then lower my helmet over my head.

"If we're caught together, it could spark more rumors. That's the last thing you need," she urges, her voice laced with concern.

I flip the visor upward to meet her eyes. She hasn't moved an inch.

"Do you trust me?"

"Yes, but—"

"But nothing." I point to the bathroom door. "Change in there, then join me."

She sighs dramatically. "If I get labeled as your secret girlfriend, I'll *never* forgive you."

"I'll take my chances."

Carlee steps into the bathroom, and my phone buzzes with a text.

EASTON

The confirmation I needed.

WESTON

Go to bed, old man.

EASTON

I knew it. You were together earlier tonight.

I shake my head at the screen.

WESTON
Shut the fuck up.

EASTON
Lexi said six months. I give it four.

I glance up at the camera in the corner of the room and flip him off.

Seconds later, Carlee emerges from the bathroom, now wearing a black leather bomber jacket and fitted pants. I can't help but notice her high heels.

"You look like Catwoman."

She grins. "Does that make you Batman?"

"Considering the lore between those characters, it's plausible." I climb off the bike and grab her a pair of boots and socks. "Can you wear these? Size eight?"

"Yes," she replies.

I drop to my knees before her. Carefully, I push the pant leg up and untie the ribbon laced around her leg. Carlee holds onto my shoulder as she balances on one foot. My fingers trail up her calf, unwrapping her like she's my gift as she hangs on to me.

The moment grows heated, and she glances away. "Please tell me that's not a camera."

"It is," I say, a smirk playing on my lips.

"Weston," she hisses.

"Easton is the only one who has the feed, and he'll shut the hell up," I say loudly enough for him to hear if he's still snooping.

My phone buzzes in my pocket, and Carlee glares at me though she remains silent.

This is incriminating.

Once I lace up her boots, I stand, locking eyes with her. My thumb brushes across her cheek as I hand her the helmet. "You're so pretty."

"Hush," she whispers, placing it on her head.

We return to the bike, and I remove the kickstand before she climbs onto the back.

"Move closer and hold on."

Without hesitation, she does exactly what I said. "I've never been on a motorcycle before."

I reach behind me and place my hand on her thigh. "Don't let me go."

"I don't plan on it," she replies.

I grin, feeling an overwhelming joy that she can't see. "This is the best way to explore the city, especially at night when there isn't much traffic. Ready?"

Her breasts press against my back as she hugs me tight. "I think so."

I give the engine some gas, and then we take off. The garage door lifts, and we escape out the back entrance onto a quiet side street.

"What's the Batman and Catwoman lore?" she asks as I focus on the road ahead.

Our helmets are connected with microphones, and I can hear her clearly.

I smile. "They're two damaged individuals, trying to survive. She always brings Bruce back to reality, making him feel centered and present."

"Oh. And what does Batman do for her?"

"He inspires her to be a better version of herself. His goodness motivates her. Their relationship isn't stable because they're so different, yet so alike. The push-and-pull is intense. But don't be fooled. Catwoman is the anti-hero."

"Of course she is," Carlee responds with a chuckle.

"At its core, it's a love story about two flawed people with a very deep connection who have an even deeper understanding of the other. But they're *always* chasing their love, and they're never able to settle down."

"Catwoman is obsessed with the chase too then?" she asks, squeezing me a little tighter.

I'm so freaking glad she can't hear my heart racing.

"I guess you could say they both are," I explain.

We ride in silence. The roar of the engine bounces off the tall buildings as we zoom down the empty streets.

"How long have you been riding?" she asks.

"You don't know? That's shocking."

"I don't know *everything* about you," she admits.

"Do you want to?"

"Yes," she whispers, sending emotions flooding through me.

"And what if you don't like what you learn?" I ask.

"What if I love it?" she counters.

I hold on to her thigh as we cruise beneath the city lights.

"This is amazing," she says. "It's freeing."

"Being with you always is."

Fifteen minutes later, we arrive at Sluggers, and I pull close to the front entrance.

"Don't take your helmet off until you're inside," I instruct.

"Do you think we were followed?" She hasn't let go of me yet.

"No. But we can never be too safe. I'll enter from the back and meet you inside."

Carlee slides off the bike.

My eyes roam up and down her body, and I take the opportunity to drink her in. She places her hands on her hips.

"Are you eye-fucking me?" I ask.

She laughs. "No."

Lie.

"I'll see you in five minutes."

"Okay," she says, and I can tell she's smiling.

When she's out of sight, I drive around to the back and keep my face covered until I take the private entrance I pay the owner to use.

When I enter the bar, I remove my helmet and immediately

relax upon seeing Carlee. It's dark and dimly lit, and a group of older gentlemen are drinking pitchers of beer in the back corner.

Sluggers is safe for us for now. I'm trying to treasure it because I know it won't be one day. I plop down on the stool next to her. The bartender slides two shots of tequila in front of us, and we pick them up.

"To dating and dumping," she says, her signature motto.

We clink our glasses together, and she shakes off the booze.

"I'm going to feel like shit tomorrow." She sighs.

"For your sake, I hope you don't," I offer.

"Want another shot before we part ways?" she asks.

"No," I reply, turning toward her, not wanting the night to end. I lower my voice. "Come home with me."

She tilts her head, studying me intently. The eye contact is almost too intense.

I laugh, though I can feel the electricity streaming between us. "My intentions are *always* pure. At least with you."

She shoots me a mischievous grin. "Sure they are, Calloway."

I won't make the first move. *Ever.*

If that line is crossed, the timing has to be perfect, and she has to initiate it *without* a drop of liquid courage. Until then, we'll continue this charade.

"But I really can't go home with you. I'm sorry. I have to be at work early in the morning. Like, in five hours."

I nod, pulling my wallet from my pocket. "I get it."

"I'll see you tomorrow night," she says, twisting in her stool to face me. "But thank you. This was fun."

We hold each other's gaze.

"Always is," I say just as she yawns. "I'll take you home."

She smiles, a warmth spreading across her face. "Thanks for keeping my date-and-dump tradition alive."

"Of course. What are friends for?"

6

CARLEE

"I need you to stay a few hours over," Mr. Martin, my boss, says as he sits behind his large desk, an imposing structure that dominates the room with its wood-paneled walls.

My shadow looms across the floor of what many of us call *the dungeon*.

I glance up at the clock on the wall. My shift officially ends in three minutes. My mind races over the two-and-a-half-hour window I have before I need to be at Ambrosia.

A nagging thought reminds me of the delivery expected at my apartment, something I've been anxiously anticipating all day. Weston is dressing me tonight, and I'm curious about what he'll choose.

"Sorry, Mr. Martin. I really can't." I shove my hands deep into the pockets of my work apron, a flimsy barrier against the weight of his request.

I came in an hour early this morning because they were short-handed, which cut into my sleep. I'm running on just four hours of rest, and I'm exhausted. The first shift supervisor, Ellen—a woman with little patience—guaranteed I'd leave on time if I helped. I fulfilled my end of that bargain, and now it's their turn.

"It would benefit you greatly. Could help with a promotion." He leans forward, as if trying to entice me with unspoken promises.

The thought of that ever-elusive promotion dangles like a carrot that's always out of reach, and I'm tired of it. My blog pays me more than taking on more responsibility at the W ever could. If only I could get back to writing. I've been on a break and I'm too in my head to post again.

"Is that all?" My voice remains steady.

"Won't you reconsider?"

"Apologies, but *no*," I tell him firmly, my answer solidifying like the concrete beneath my feet.

"And if I *require* you?" he questions, the challenge sparkling in his eyes. If the *needs of the business* require extra help, there is an on-call loophole that would force me.

"You wouldn't do that to me."

"Stacy didn't answer, and you're next up on the on-call roster. You can work three more hours today. Double time, of course."

"Mr. Martin," I warn, feeling a surge of defiance, "I have an important dinner scheduled that I cannot miss. If you try to pull rank after I picked up the slack for you this morning, then you'll kindly accept my *immediate* resignation."

Today, I'm choosing violence. I glance back up at the clock, and I have a minute and a half before I can leave.

"Is that a threat, Ms. Jolly?"

"No, sir, it's not. But I'll happily let Mr. Calloway know about this conversation when I see him next." I grin.

Now, *that's* a threat.

If I confided in Easton or Weston about this conversation, either would have him fired. Their father's vast investments in the W franchise played a pivotal role in shaping it into the worldwide billion-dollar luxury hotel chain that it is today. The Calloways own forty-nine percent of the stakes, so when one of them says to jump, every employee at the W asks how high. If they wanted, they could buy more shares to take majority ownership of the company, which is always a concern.

Mr. Martin clears his throat, knowing I'm best friends with Lexi. He's very aware of who she's married to. Pushing me is the last thing he'd ever want to do because Easton would lose his shit. Weston would too. I try not to use them to pull rank, but it's necessary.

"Thank you for understanding," I offer.

He knows I'm the first to volunteer for overtime. My tireless work ethic is both a badge of honor and an end to my means. While I'm sometimes late, I'm also a diligent employee who takes pride in my work. I refuse to feel guilty about saying no; we live in a dog-eat-dog world.

His inability to staff correctly isn't my burden to bear. Nothing will interrupt my plans tonight.

I leave his office, closing the door behind me. I grab my coat and phone from my locker, then clock out. My back aches from the relentless changing of beds and cleaning up after messy millionaires and adult billionaire babies. These people navigate this world and follow different rules that were crafted solely for their social class.

Honestly, I *hate* everything about this job, and if I didn't need it for LuxLeaks, I'd quit in a heartbeat. Then again, I haven't posted in over three months. The article I wrote about Easton and Lexi remains my best work, and maybe it's a sign that LadyLux needs to fade quietly into obscurity.

The thought of quitting makes me feel sick, and a heaviness settles into the pit of my stomach. I've dedicated too much of my life to it.

I take the stairs down to the subway station, which is full of people. As I wait for the train, I stare at the Calloway Diamonds advertisements plastered on the wall. I'm reminded of Weston at every turn.

The train finally arrives. The doors jolt open, and the crowd on the platform rushes forward, a tidal wave of humanity surging out the open doors. I manage to squeeze in just before they whoosh, cutting us off from the outside world, and the car rattles down the track.

It's rush hour, and the subway is packed with commuters. Unfamiliar faces are marked by determination and fatigue; they're either lost in thought or their eyes are glued to their phone. Most of us travel to Manhattan for work, and the commute is routine.

I clutch the metal bar and stand shoulder to shoulder with strangers. Pulling my phone from my pocket, I check my notifications, and I'm shocked by what I see—a message from Samson. My ex. The only man I ever really loved.

I shouldn't be shocked, considering Lexi said his damn name, but I am.

SAM

Carlee?

After we broke up, I didn't delete his number from my phone. It's been seven years since our paths crossed, yet here he is, texting me like a resurrected ghost.

I play dumb.

CARLEE

Who is this?

SAM

It's Samson.

CARLEE

Who?

I have to give him some shit. No way I'd admit to still having him saved in my phone.

SAM

Samson Patterson.

CARLEE

Oh wow. How are you? It's been years.

SAM

I'm shocked you haven't changed your number.

CARLEE

I never will. Anyway, what's up?

SAM

I'm traveling to NYC this weekend, and I'd love to have a drink and catch up if you're available.

CARLEE

And your girlfriend would be okay with that? Or are you engaged now?

SAM

There is no one. We broke up over the summer.

I reread his text, my heart racing. Shock dances along my skin as the reality of his message sinks in. He's single again, and no one told me.

CARLEE

Oh, I'm really sorry to hear that.

SAM

And you?

CARLEE

Nothing official. Anyway, I'll check my schedule and get back to you.

SAM

Sure, no problem.

My fingers hover over the screen. I don't know what else to say, so I let the conversation fade away, the air full of uncertainty.

I message Lexi.

CARLEE

You're never going to believe who just texted me.

LEXI

Weston? I gave him your number.

CARLEE

Samson! WTF, LEXI?!

LEXI

😳 The curse is true.

CARLEE

THIS IS YOUR FAULT!

LEXI

I'm so sorry!

CARLEE

You're responsible for SUMMONING him. I told you!

Any mention of him seems to draw him back into my orbit, no matter how much time has passed. Call it superstition, but I've avoided saying his name for years. It's also helped me avoid unwanted memories.

LEXI

What did he want?

CARLEE

To meet up for a drink. He'll be in the city.

LEXI

You should.

CARLEE

I don't know if that's a good idea.

My heart races as panic grips my chest. I let out a sigh, feeling the weight of the situation press down on me.

LEXI

You should do it to see if you have any unresolved feelings for him. When I saw my ex again, I felt nothing. Cleared a lot of things up for me.

CARLEE

Hmm. Maybe you're right.

LEXI

Put it to rest so you can give Weston a fair chance.

CARLEE

Relentless.

I close out of our conversation and check my other notifications.

Weston hasn't texted me today, and the anticipation of seeing him tonight takes hold.

As I glance around, listening to the ambience of the subway, I realize how much I love New York. It was one of the hang-ups Samson and I had in our relationship, but I can't imagine living anywhere else in the world. The rhythm of the city pulses through my veins. It's my home.

When I first moved here, I was perpetually lost, navigating twisting streets and towering skyscrapers, often needing to consult my phone a few times per day. Now, I can travel the concrete maze without a second thought, each block a chapter I've memorized in the ever-evolving story of my New York life. It took a while, but finally, I feel like a true New Yorker. I'm a vibrant part of this city rather than just a Texas transplant seeking a fresh start.

I unload from the train and take the stairs two at a time to reach the bustling sidewalk above. My apartment is a few blocks away from this stop, my cozy little haven. I hurry down the snow-covered sidewalk as the crisp winter breeze brushes against my cheeks.

I don't remember it being this cold in mid-January. I shiver and pull my large coat tighter around my body. The aroma of roasted peanuts wafts through the air, mingling with the faint tunes of a guy strumming his guitar on the corner as winter's whispers greet me like an old friend.

When I finally enter my apartment, I just want to relax, but there is no time for that. As I strip off my clothes in a frenzy, eager to wash away the day, a knock on my door startles me. I stand on my tiptoes to check the peephole.

"I have something for you," Brody says, his tone laced with mild annoyance.

I was expecting this delivery, but I wasn't anticipating him. He's tall, built like a mountain, with muscles that ripple beneath his leather jacket. Tattoos snake along his arms like captivating stories begging to be told. It's clear he shares the same broody features as Weston and Easton; their family resemblance is undeniable.

"One second," I call out, rebuttoning my uniform, the fabric askew but my confidence unwavering.

I swing open the door, greeting him with a cheesy grin that feels out of place.

He sighs, unimpressed, his deep-set eyes scanning the room.

"Working for the postal service now?" I tease. A grin sits on my lips.

He doesn't respond, but then again, he's always been quiet.

Balancing a garment bag on his finger, Brody holds a large box wrapped in shimmering silver paper with a festive bow in one arm. In the other, he cradles two dozen vibrant yellow roses.

My favorite. Weston remembered.

I step aside, allowing Brody to enter my sanctuary. He sets the large box down on the coffee table with a light thud, taking up half of its surface. I take the garment bag, our fingers grazing briefly.

"Are you supposed to follow me around tonight?" I try to gauge his intent.

"Not tonight," he replies, and for a fleeting moment, I catch the hint of a smile curling at the corners of his lips.

"What does that mean? You've been following me?" I press.

He doesn't answer, but his amusement is evident.

"Is that all?" I ask, tapping my foot impatiently.

"Enjoy your *date*," he says, moving toward the door, an edge of something in his voice.

He knows.

"It's not a date! I'm going solo," I call after him as he heads toward the end of the long hallway.

"Let me remind you that Lexi said the same thing," he says over his shoulder.

It's not the first time he's graced my apartment with his presence. When Easton and Lexi first started dating, Brody and I struck up an easy friendship. It was mostly me giving him a hard time and playing matchmaker while he rolled his eyes good-naturedly.

"It's not a date! I swear," I protest until he's out of sight, my words trailing behind him like an unfinished thought.

As I step back into my apartment, I notice an envelope with my name neatly written in cursive on the outside. Intrigued, I pull out the pearly paper from inside.

C,

I personally picked out everything for you. I look forward to seeing you tonight.

—W

I tuck my lips into my mouth, feeling my heart thump with excitement as I place the two dozen yellow roses on the tiny kitchen counter. The sweet, intoxicating aroma fills my small space, and I'm full of anticipation for what the night holds.

I unzip the front of the garment bag with trembling fingers. I pull out a black A-line Valentino evening gown with a sweetheart neckline, and the fabric flutters into the air with a whisper of elegance. Breathless, I grab my phone and quickly search online.

I nearly drop my phone. It costs twenty thousand dollars.

"This is too expensive," I whisper to myself.

He shouldn't have spent this on me.

I lay the dress across the back of the couch, and then I pull the ribbon from the top of the gigantic box. It falls to the floor like a feather. Lifting the lid, I peer inside. Two gifts are both professionally wrapped; their glossy paper reflects the light and screams expensive.

I start with the larger one and gasp as I unveil silver crystal Valentino high heels. They shimmer like tiny stars captured in glass, and I can't help but think of Cinderella.

This can't be real, is the only thought racing through my mind as I lift the lid of the second box.

Inside lies a large black velvet jewelry box.

My hand quivers with nervousness as I click it open.

A luxurious blue crushed velvet lines the inside of the box, displaying a brilliant-cut diamond necklace on a delicate chain, heart-shaped diamond earrings, and a bracelet that sparkles with promise.

I can hardly comprehend the value of this jewelry—hundreds of thousands of dollars—all nestled together with a dress and shoes that cost more than I make in years.

This is too much.

Yet the Ambrosia dress code requires it. Weston's social class demands it too. I'm painfully aware that I don't belong in his world. Always the bridesmaid. Always on the outside, looking in, peering through the glass at lives more luxurious than my own.

Before I can let myself dwell on those thoughts too long, I place everything on my bed. Then, I hurry to the shower, being careful not to wet my hair. When I stand under the stream and close my eyes, Weston is on my mind.

His smile, his blue eyes, his laugh, the way he makes me feel.

After my shower, I continue preparing for the evening, putting my hair in rollers.

With thirty minutes to spare, I put on the dress, feeling the fabric hug my curves in all the right places. I put on the shoes, and they add four inches to my height, which will only put my mouth closer to Weston's if we're standing. As I remove the rollers, my hair falls into big, bouncy curls.

I move toward the full-length mirror. I pause, hardly recognizing myself. Is this the version of me Weston wants?

The black dress is pure seduction. The chiffon flows around the fitted bodice like a dream. I slide the necklace around my neck, fastening it, before putting on the earrings and bracelet.

I look like ... *royalty*.

Just as I finish my makeup and press my red lips together, I receive a text that the limo has arrived.

I grow nervous, wondering what I'm actually doing. I shouldn't have committed to this, but curiosity took over.

I make my way downstairs, and the driver quickly opens my door. I slide into the back seat, where a bottle of chilled champagne, lavishly arranged chocolate-covered strawberries, and another bouquet of my favorite roses await.

Next to them is another note with my name—written in the same script as before.

> *C,*
>
> *Lex said you require chocolate-covered strawberries and champagne. She also mentioned a trip to Paris. Might have to make that happen soon. Do you have your passport?*
>
> *—W*

I chew on the edge of my lip, my eyes scanning over his words again. With a laugh, I reread his message. Jet-setting across the world with Weston? It's too dangerous, especially with the blind items being posted about him and a mystery woman. But I'd run away with him.

The butterflies in my stomach flutter wildly as the implications wash over me.

I *can't* be her. Can I?

The thought of it sends a shiver down my spine, both thrilling and terrifying.

When I enter Ambrosia, it doesn't feel real. I've only ever glimpsed this elite restaurant through photos. It's like a fairy tale. The off-white walls glow under low lighting, casting shadows that dance across the room. Warm candlelight flickers and sways like tiny fireflies, and I'm caught in a beautiful trance, trying to process my surroundings. The who's who of the city dines here, and the atmosphere is rich with romance and promise. The wealthy indulge in simple two-thousand-dollar dinners, and CEOs close monumental deals at polished tables covered with silk tablecloths.

Among this grandeur, I can't shake the feeling that I don't belong, even if I wear the correct costume. I'm Vivian in *Pretty Woman*, an unwelcome spectacle trying to blend in with a sophisticated crowd. The thought makes me chuckle as the host leads me across the marble floor that gleams brightly.

The diamonds sparkle against my skin while curious heads turn in my direction. I can almost hear their whispered questions dancing through the air—*Who is she? Why is she here?*

Tonight, I can be anyone I want.

As I continue forward, I recognize several celebrities and rock stars but keep my gaze locked ahead, pretending not to notice. I feel a pang of longing and curiosity tugging at me, wondering if Weston has already arrived, hoping to spot his familiar face in the crowd.

I sit at a booth with a high back, and it gives me more privacy than I expected.

A server approaches, setting an extra-dirty martini with fat green olives in front of me. She hands me a menu wrapped in leather.

"I didn't order this," I say politely, my lips curving into a grin as my fingers glide over the menu.

"Yes, miss. It was ordered *for* you," she replies with professional poise. "However, I was instructed that you'd choose your meal. I'll give you a few minutes. If you have any questions, I'm at your service."

"Thanks."

As I glance over, I notice the fresh flower arrangement on my table—a single yellow rose nestled among delicate greenery, its vibrant hue a striking contrast to the restaurant's muted palette. It's *meant* for me. It's always the small, thoughtful touches with Weston that set my heart racing.

As I scan the room, I can barely contain my excitement, my eyes flitting around in anticipation of spotting him. The martini dances on my tongue.

Peering at the menu, I realize that not a single price is listed on the pages. Perhaps it's because the individuals who can afford to dine here have unlimited amounts of money.

At precisely seven o'clock, Weston enters with a stunning blonde-haired, blue-eyed woman I'm unfamiliar with. She isn't an A-list socialite or celebrity, which leaves me unsettled. I reach for my phone and quickly search his name online. The glow of the screen reveals several articles that were posted minutes ago. I can't resist clicking on the first one.

Weston Calloway spotted with Naomi Accetta at Ambrosia. His secret girlfriend?

I search her name and find her Wikipedia page staring back at me.

Who is she?

Questions swirl in my mind like autumn leaves caught in a sudden gust, and I brace myself for the answer.

Naomi Accetta is the prime minister of Italy, hailing from an influential family steeped in history and power. Her intelligence is evident. Her sharp features and commanding presence have allowed her to carve a path for her future. *She is a woman who knows her worth and has worked diligently to earn her place in a traditionally male-dominated arena, having studied at prestigious universities.*

On paper, they seem to be a match—his charm complementing her influence, their careers aligning in the public eye. Based on the candid photos captured as they exited the car together, the chemistry crackles between them. It's electric, but then again, Weston looks good with anyone who's next to him.

What if she's his secret girlfriend?

Why does the thought make my stomach turn?

With effortless grace, Weston pulls Naomi's chair out for her —a subtle yet intimate gesture—before taking his seat. I don't even have to turn my head to watch. I just flick my eyes upward, heart racing at the sight. When his gaze meets hers, a kind smile curves his lips. A pang of jealousy stabs at my heart. I wrestle with the feeling, trying to grasp why I'm experiencing this turmoil. After all, we are just friends—nothing more, nothing less.

Witnessing this is a different experience than reading about it online. Seeing him on a date makes it *real*, more tangible than any late-night conversations we've exchanged.

I shove my emotions aside, forcing myself to focus on the interaction unfolding before me. His eyes dart past Naomi, and suddenly, they lock on to mine with an intensity that makes my breath hitch in my throat. A small smirk plays on his lips, and a wave of heat washes over me, coursing through my veins like fire. I force myself to look away, the weight of our connection too suffocating to bear.

When I glance back, I catch him leaning in close to Naomi, whispering something that prompts her to laugh. It's light and flirty, the kind that dances through the air and lingers. She leans closer, as if pulled in by an invisible thread. I think they might kiss, but Weston pulls away first, revealing careful control over the evening. It feels almost out of character from his flirty demeanor.

The way she eyes him with adoration makes it clear she wants him. She's eye-fucking him and giving all the hints.

Yet the chemistry between them isn't reciprocated; Weston is clearly holding back.

Did he notice a similar restraint in me with Trever? *Probably.*

I take a sip of my drink, and jealousy brews within me. I try to steady my breathing as her finger brushes against his, a casual touch with fire behind it.

The server returns, and I realize I haven't looked at the menu. I'm grateful for the interruption; I wasn't fully aware of just how difficult it would be to witness this.

Now I'm confused. I cannot have feelings for Weston. Absolutely not.

"Have you decided what you'd like for dinner?" the server asks, a friendly smile gracing her lips.

"I think I'd like the Wagyu. Medium rare," I reply, forcing calmness into my voice.

She beams back at me. "And your sides?"

"Surprise me," I tell her, grinning.

"Easiest customer all night." She laughs, and it mingles with the classical music floating through the air.

"Can you just keep the martinis coming? And wait to put my food in for, like, twenty minutes?" I ask, knowing Weston and Naomi haven't placed their orders yet. I don't know why I feel like I might melt into a puddle of envy.

"Absolutely," she replies, and I can't help but wonder if she knows I'm with Weston.

The gin makes my head swirl, and I try to regain some composure.

Weston sips his drink and engages in a serious conversation with Naomi. Her fingertips lightly brush against his cheek—a gesture both tender and intimate—and he mutters something I can't hear. She nods attentively, her expression warm and inviting.

The server reappears, and Weston hands over his card.

They're skipping dinner. He's already taking her home.

He pulls her chair out for her, and they exchange a very G-rated hug, which confuses me. There's an innocent warmth in their embrace, unlike anything I've witnessed with Weston before. It's the kind of hug that feels purely platonic, yet there's something about the way they linger that stirs a knot of unease inside me.

Weston leads her down the long, elegant hallway, floating under the oversize chandeliers that cast a golden glow, illuminating their path, as if guiding them toward something more.

Then he's out of sight. I feel deflated.

Five minutes later, he slides into the booth beside me, the wood creaking under his weight. He checks his watch before turning to me with a blend of concern and confusion.

"Why are you looking at me like that?" I finally ask, my voice laced with uncertainty, caught off guard by the intensity of his gaze.

"Why are you here?" he counters, a serious edge creeping into his tone.

"You're joking, right?" I laugh, the sound hollow as I instinctively create space between us as jealousy rears her ugly head.

"Excuse me? Are you meeting someone here?" His eyes search mine, and I can't ignore his question.

I stare at him, the realization dawning—he's being completely serious. "Wait. *Easton?*"

"Carlee," he responds, his voice laced with concern, "are you *okay?* How many martinis have you had?"

"Two. Or three," I reply, my mind racing. "Are you cheating on my best friend?" I ask, my frustration bubbling to the surface and my heart pounding with anger.

He shakes his head vehemently. "Absolutely not. Did it look like I was cheating?"

I replay every interaction I witnessed, wondering if I was naive enough to view it through the lens of potential romance.

Naomi made every move, brushing past him, her fingers grazing his arm each time. He did seem to block her advances, though the earlier warmth between them still clings to the air. And based on how he's currently looking at me, with those captivating eyes now cold and distant, there's no way I could be misreading this.

I suck in a deep breath, the bitter taste of betrayal spilling onto my tongue as I realize I was set up. "He's dead meat."

"Who?" he asks, genuine confusion etched across his face.

"Your *evil* twin," I say, the weight of my words crashing down as I understand the implications—Weston is in this room, and he must have been watching my reactions the entire time.

I glance around the room, determined to find him.

I catch a hint of her perfume, shocked she believes I'm Easton. It's not an opportunity I thought I'd have, but I move forward since I'm presented with the opportunity. One day, she'll instantly know if it's me or my brother. We're not there yet though.

"Weston *tricked* me," she whispers, "which means he's somewhere, watching me."

That would've been smart because I could've watched her reactions. I did catch one glimpse of her, and I imagine her expression was the same one I'd worn when she was with Trever. There was nothing between them, but seeing her with him ... *fuck*. It made me primal. I was ready to rip out his throat.

"I'm confused. Please explain."

She scans the room, and I lift a brow.

"Continue," I state.

"I'm sorry, but I can't say much more."

She temporarily gives up on the search for me, then meets my eyes, and for a second, I think she might know I'm *not* Easton.

"Can you please avoid mentioning that you saw me here tonight? I don't want to have to explain anything to Lexi yet. And I won't tell her how the prime minister of Italy wanted inside your pants."

Ahh, she quickly did her research like a good girl. LuxLeaks mainly features celebrities, pop idols, and billionaires with a cult following.

"To be clear, is it because you don't want to explain that you're dating my brother?"

She scoffs, then laughs. "Trust me, I'm only here to *rate* his dating skills. What we have is platonic."

"Right," I say, checking my watch. It's an Easton trait since he's a psycho about being everywhere on time.

"I'm *not* dating Weston," she urges, making a face.

"Why not?" I ask. It's a simple question, one I know she won't answer.

"I thought you weren't getting involved."

She narrows her eyes. I might have pushed it too far.

"I'm curious."

"You know *why*. We've talked about it several times," she says. "It's like you've forgotten. You forget *nothing*."

My mind reels, but I don't react. What does Easton know? What has he said to her?

"Oh, right. *That*," I state, rolling my eyes. The reaction is the correct one.

I stare at her for a few seconds longer, unable to keep this going. At some point, it's just cruel.

I move to the opposite side of the booth. A few seconds later, a glass of bourbon is delivered, and I take a sip.

"You passed the test," I say, repeating the same words she did to me last night when we almost kissed.

She stares at me. "Don't you need to go home to your wife?"

"Last time I checked, I only have a soon-to-be *ex*-wife." I stare at her with brows lifted, but she doesn't understand. "I'm *not* Easton."

"Wait, what?" Her face contorts.

"You suck. It shouldn't have been that easy to fool you, Carlee."

"I don't believe you," she mutters.

I lean forward, interlocking my fingers, admiring her. She's absolutely stunning.

"Easton's with Lexi. I can FaceTime him right now and prove it to you. But then you might have to explain yourself, considering we're together. Or you can text Lexi and ask her what she's doing."

She pulls her phone from her pocket and begins typing. Seconds later, *my* phone buzzes.

I turn the screen to show her. "Is this the first time you've ever sent me a text without me engaging in the conversation first?"

She smirks because it's a confirmation.

Of course I noticed how she *never* texts me.

"What if you two switched phones?"

"I would *never* leave my phone near him. Face recognition can't tell the difference between us, and he'd read every word of our private conversations."

"I have nothing to hide," she tells me. "Do you?"

"Just our entire friendship," I say, lifting my glass.

However, if Easton read our texts, he'd instantly know *my* secrets.

"Maybe we shouldn't be here." She glances around the room.

"The only reason we are is because you said yes. For once."

She scoffs. "You act like I say no to everything."

"You typically do. But it seems like that's changing." I lick my lips, unable to ignore how fucking pretty she is. "You're gorgeous."

"Thank you," she says, a blush meeting her cheeks. "This dress fits like a glove. How'd you know?"

I don't dare tell her I could draw her from memory. "Lucky guess."

This morning, I called Harper Alexander—my sister's business partner at their fashion company—and asked several questions about styles. Based on Carlee's body type, she helped me pick it out. Right now, she owes me a fuck ton of favors for all the help

I've offered over the years, so she's now my personal industry expert. I could never ask my sister. She'd pry for details, and I can't explain what's happening between Carlee and me. Maybe, one day, I'll be able to articulate it.

Carlee picks up her martini. Anytime our conversation teeters on the edge of us, she avoids it. "I'm still processing that date. Wait, was it a date?"

"It was, but it felt forced. I refuse to waste time when things go off the rails. I don't have the patience you had with *Double-E*."

"Do you know her from Oxford?" she asks, well aware of my educational background. She must've quickly searched out Naomi and saw the link.

I meet her gaze. "No. We attended at different times. A-plus on the quick research because I knew you didn't recognize her when we entered."

"Guilty." Her shoulders relax. "I just don't understand."

"What?"

"You didn't try." Carlee's voice is low. "It's the *only* reason I believed you were Easton. She made every advance, and you skillfully blocked each one. That's out of character."

"Is it? How would you know?" I question.

"Your reputation precedes you," she says.

"Oh, okay," I tell her. "You assumed how tonight would go, and I proved you wrong."

She drinks her martini and empties it. The server drops another one.

"I just expected more from Mr. Playboy."

"Hmm." I replay the hundreds of dates I've had over the last year. "No one has made it past my *one drink* rule. Except *you*."

"I've *never* gone on a date with you," she confirms.

"What's this?" I ask, glancing around at the couples in the room.

"Two friends having dinner," she says flirtingly. "I'm disappointed because I thought I could tell the difference between you and Easton if we were in person. It's *so* convincing. Lexi is good."

I watch her over the rim of my glass. "It's love. My touch is cold compared to Easton's, completely void of emotions. She feels the difference. It's not based on sight, just feeling."

"Oh. That makes sense," she says.

Carlee doesn't stop watching me. I *like* being under her gaze.

"Just be careful because Easton can snap me on just as *easily* and is extremely convincing. He's smart and a professional at avoiding questions and changing the subject. After he saw us together last night, he's *very* interested in *us*, and he's convinced you're my secret girlfriend."

"How do you know?" She almost looks worried.

"Brody told me Easton cornered him and asked a lot of question about us." I lean forward, and my eyes flick down to her lips. "Now, it's time to tell me what you've been telling my brother about me. Why do you believe I'm undateable?"

"It's obvious, isn't it?" she asks.

"Clearly, it's not."

Her brows crease. "Look at me, Wes."

"I *am*. I see *you*."

Her face softens as my eyes slide from hers down to her mouth, following the diamond necklace that rests above her breasts. Her skin glows under this light, and she's pure perfection. I take a mental snapshot of her, never wanting to forget her just like this. The candle flickers as shadows dance around us. I could stay here with her until morning.

"Why are you looking at me like that?" she asks, hushed.

"Because I can. Now tell me."

She blinks a few times and clears her throat. "You only date women like Paris Hilton. Tall. Blonde. Blue eyes. Rich. It's your four requirements. Everyone knows this."

Carlee looks at me like *I'm* misunderstanding. I'm not. I want to tell her to stop being ridiculous.

"Hmm. I thought you were smarter than that," I quip.

"Huh?" She quiets like she's scrolling through her memories, searching for clues.

"Your assessment is the bare minimum. But is it true? You can't believe everything you read online concerning me, especially when the stories are sensationalized with a specific narrative about the character the media has created. Sometimes, I feed into it because it makes me feel like I have some control over what's being said."

The smile fades from her face, and her pretty red lips part. "They're decoys."

I take a sip of my drink. "Ah. There's my smart girl."

"You're an actual genius." Her eyes widen as she searches my face.

Laughter escapes me. "Now you're flirting."

"I'm shook. All this time," she says, her pulse quickening.

"Years," I confirm.

"How did I not notice before?"

"Because you choose to turn a blind eye to a lot," I explain. "One day, you'll see everything with eyes wide open. I'm just waiting for you to catch up."

She tilts her head, not fully understanding that *her* denial keeps us apart because she's not ready for a committed relationship. Not yet. I don't know if I am either.

I'm tempted to wave my hand in front of her face as she zones out. "Still with me?"

"Yes. How do you explain the Weston Calloway effect?"

"Are you taking notes so you can add this to your *How to Date Weston Calloway* manual?"

She snickers. "Genuinely curious. You know I'd *never* share any of this."

Another bourbon is set on the table, and my empty glass is taken.

When we're alone again, I speak. "When things are on the rocks with whoever I'm dating, they always dye their hair as a last-ditch effort to keep me, believing our relationship won't last because they're not blonde. It perpetuates the tall tale. I don't prefer *any* hair color. Brains over beauty. Some women have both. Most just want to fuck me," I say to her.

"Wow. I'd never dye my hair to make a man happy. That's *ridiculous.*"

"You shouldn't. You're flawless," I say, tilting my head, capturing her in memory.

She places her hands on her cheeks. "You're making me blush."

"I know, but it's also the gin at work." I smirk, watching her, loving that I can cause this reaction.

Being with her is too easy. The way it should be.

Carlee licks her lips before taking another sip of her martini. "So, you're aware of the effect you have on people?"

"Is this an interview?" I ask.

She chuckles. "A business meeting."

"A *date*," I whisper. "And, yes, I know how my presence makes some act. I'm flattered, but it usually comes from a place where I'm being overly sexualized. Purely physical and nothing more."

She inhales and speaks on an exhale. "Weston, you can have *anyone* in the world you want."

I lift a brow. "That's *not* true."

"Isn't it?" she asks, staring me down.

"If you only knew."

Our food is slid in front of us, disrupting us. Carlee picks up her fork and knife, and I glance down at my salmon and potatoes. I texted the owner my order before I arrived and had planned to have dinner with Carlee.

"That looks delicious," I tell her.

Steam rises from our plates.

"Want a bite?" She carefully cuts the steak, and the diamond bracelet reflects light around the booth. Carlee scoots to the edge of the seat, holding out her fork with a slice of meat on the end.

"Watch out for wandering eyes," I say, leaning forward and allowing her to feed me.

The eye contact is scorching, but she knows exactly what she's doing. Carlee is aware of how this game is played, and I think she understands she's more than just a pawn to me.

"Should I be concerned?" she asks.

"Considering the current rumors, *probably*," I say.

"Do you care?"

"Fuck no." I pick up my utensils. "But don't be surprised if more is posted about me after tonight."

She gasps and stops cutting. "Wait."

I raise my brows.

"You really think that was about *us*? Do you think someone knows about Sluggers?" she whispers, concerned.

"Would you like the truth or a lie?" I ask, proud that she finally put the two together.

"The truth, always."

"You're the only woman I've hung out with regularly, but I have to admit, the secret girlfriend thing is a stretch."

"Who knows about our meetups?" she asks.

"Brody. My driver. No one else," I confirm.

"Do you think they said something to someone?"

"No, they'd never. I trust them both with my deepest secrets." I don't entertain the thought. "It's nothing to worry about. As I said before, unconfirmed rumors." I cut into my fish. "Would you like to try this? It's very good. The best in the city."

"Think I'll pass," she says, avoiding my plate. "It has eyeballs, and that kinda freaks me out. I'm not used to seeing that part."

I chuckle. "You're adorable."

The server walks over. "How is your meal?"

"It's delicious, but I have a tiny request. Is there any way you can have the chef remove the head?"

The server holds back a smile. "Absolutely, Mr. Calloway. Apologies."

"No, no need for that. Thank you for accommodating me and my *date*."

"Anytime. I'll also deliver another drink if you'd like."

I nod, and the server quickly walks away with my plate. Carlee focuses on me as I toss back my remaining bourbon. She ignores my date comment.

"You didn't have to send it back. I'd have survived." She sets down her fork and places her hands in her lap, politely waiting for my plate to return.

"They'll be quick. Continue, please. Don't allow your food to get cold on my behalf," I offer.

"Now you sound like my mother," she says with a snicker, and her smile fades.

I know she hasn't visited home in a few years, and she misses her family. During one of our Sluggers meetups, we discussed it. Her work schedule hasn't allowed her the time off.

"I can't figure out why no one is speaking about going on these shitty dates," she says.

"Believe it or not, every woman I've taken out has had an incredible time. Each has wanted a second date. I set the expectation of only having one drink together. No one is ever rushed, and I give my undivided attention."

"You only commit to one drink. How long does that last?" she asks.

"Usually around forty-five minutes, but never over an hour. Dating while going through a very public divorce is ... *different*. Many believe I'm searching for a hookup or a rebound. I'm not. Within ten minutes, I know if someone is dateable or not. I'm currently on a strike-out streak."

My headless fish is slid across the table, along with a new drink. I smile. "Thanks again."

"Yes, sir. If you need anything else, please don't hesitate to ask. Chef Rallings says hello and sends his best wishes." She bows like I'm royalty.

"Please tell him I said the same."

She nods and backs away.

When we're alone, Carlee smirks. "Does everyone treat you this way?"

"Everyone except you," I mutter.

She finishes chewing. "When I was a kid, my older brothers and sister trained me not to be intimidated by anyone. There are no exceptions. Not even you."

I can't stop watching her as the candle flickers on the table.

"Does it bother you?" Carlee asks.

"Absolutely not. I *prefer* it," I admit.

Her sexy little grin returns. "What is it that Weston Calloway is searching for in a partner? Maybe I can help you find someone for real."

"I want a relationship with substance and real conversation. Someone who doesn't try to be who they think I want. I married for lust the first time. Now, I *want* patient love. It's important to me."

She pins me in place with her piercing gaze. "I hope you find it, Weston."

"I will," I confirm.

"I want to believe love exists for me, but I'm beginning to lose hope. My bad luck with dating makes me want to fuck around and find out. I've been playing it safe for the past year, and I'm growing bored," she admits.

I also know she's three martinis in, and this is how she gets when she drinks.

Invincible. Outspoken. Flirty as fuck.

"Do it," I say, wanting to take risks with *her*. "The only person stopping you is *you*."

I notice how her pulse upticks in her neck.

"I kinda miss the girl I used to be. I didn't take life so seriously. Men were disposable." Her gaze trails down my eyes to my lips and along my jawline.

"You should stop *that*." I take a bite of potatoes.

She rests her chin on her fist, batting her long eyelashes. "Stop what?"

"*Eye-fucking me,* Little Miss Tipsy," I say, knowing she needs the reminder before she takes it too far. "Don't start something you don't plan on finishing."

"Is that what I'm doing?"

The attraction swirling between us is undeniable. Dangerous, *electric.*

"What do you want in a partner?" I ask as we continue eating.

"I want to be with someone who makes me feel alive." A bright smile touches her lips, almost as if she's imagining it. "It's been years since I've felt what love carries with it. The beginning, when everything is new and exciting. The falling-in-love part—it's my favorite. I crave that." She swallows hard. "Probably sounds pathetic."

"No," I whisper. "Only someone who's experienced love understands."

She nods.

"I have a confession," I whisper. "I was super fucking jealous of Easton. Of course, I'm happy for him because I want the absolute best for my brother, but knowing he was experiencing what I wanted so badly, seeing him so damn happy, only reminded me of how alone I was. The isolation I've felt since filing for divorce wasn't something I was prepared for." I sigh. "It's difficult to explain."

Carlee chews on her lip. "I felt the same way but never mentioned it because I feared how selfish it'd make me sound. I'm stupidly happy for Lexi and Easton, and they deserve what they have. But it woke me up and made me realize life was changing. It's a reminder that I'm not getting any younger, and after all these horrible dates, I'm losing hope."

"The only saving grace for me has been our friendship," I admit.

"Same," she says.

We finish eating and continue chatting. Another round of drinks is placed on the table as our empty plates are removed.

"Dessert?"

She holds up her fresh martini. "This is dessert."

"What number is that?" I need to know what I'm dealing with.

"Five?"

I burst into laughter. "*Great.*"

She twirls the straw in her drink. "Was tonight a complete waste?"

"It never is when I'm with you," I mutter.

Our bill is placed on the edge of the table. I give the server my card, and soon, I'm signing my name on the bottom.

"Guess our night is over," she whispers.

I slide out of the booth, holding out my hand for her. She looks up into my eyes.

I lean in and mutter in her ear, "Come home with me," as I hook one finger with hers.

"Okay," she whispers with a smile as I place my hand on the small of her back, leading her through the restaurant.

"Really?" I ask.

"It's time for me to start saying yes," she admits.

My grin widens, and it's not lost on me that eyes are on us. No one knows who she is.

Carlee chews on the corner of her lip as she glances at me.

I'm so fucking happy that the night isn't ending that I can barely contain myself.

8

CARLEE

Too many wandering eyes watch *him* watching *me*. His gaze follows my every move. I keep my head down and focus on the sidewalk as we part ways. Cameras take snapshots of everyone leaving Ambrosia, just in case they can expose something later.

I'm aware pictures of me and Weston will be released eventually.

I understand how the gossip life works and navigate it as cautiously as possible. Too many rumors swarm around Weston, and he pretends it doesn't bother him. The truth is, it does when what's being said are blatant lies.

He's one of the few men at his level who can handle the truth being told about him, whether it's beneficial to his image and ego or not. It's why he's never faulted me for what I wrote about him. My words were his reality.

I slide into the car, careful not to glance over as his sleek SUV pulls away.

Those little flutters in my stomach morph into a roaring desire, and I know I should ask his driver to take me home. It's the proper thing to do, considering I unapologetically make moves on him when I've had too much to drink, and my inhibitions are down. This song and dance—it's a classic, one we both know by heart.

When alcohol mixes with my blood, I swear on unholy things that Weston Calloway desperately *wants* me. It's a heady fantasy that I remind myself of constantly, nothing more.

I'm nearly giddy from the thoughts of him, and a hiccup releases from my throat. It's a telltale sign that the five—or was it six?—martinis might've been too much.

The world outside my window blurs, and each stoplight stretches on for an eternity. The lingering taste of gin and vermouth dances on my tongue. I close my eyes and drift off, letting the hum of the city wash over me.

When the car door gently opens, I jolt awake and laugh at my ridiculousness. I forget where I am until I glance up at The Park building.

"Apologies," Weston's driver says. "Didn't mean to startle you."

"Totally my fault. Thank you," I reply as I step out.

Twenty-five minutes slipped by without me noticing, but I needed that power nap. Maybe now my head will be clearer.

I glance around the perimeter of the building that stretches across several city blocks as I search for the reflection of ambient light against long camera lenses. Paps being here isn't out of the realm of possibilities. They snapped several shots of Lexi with Easton in this very spot.

The public knows I'm Lexi's best friend and that she lives here.

If someone photographed me right now, most would assume I'm visiting her because we hang out weekly. In the articles that have mentioned me, I'm described as her longtime best friend from college. My full name is rarely used, and I'm happy to be an embellishment in her life.

I enter The Park with a pep in my step, knowing it's safe inside. Too many influential people own penthouses in this building, and privacy is required. It's on Billionaires' Row for a reason—they're the only ones who can afford it.

The lobby buzzes with activity, typical for a Saturday night, and I feel like I'm floating. A group of women brush past me, and one pauses, backing up to meet my eyes.

"Valentino?" she asks, tucking her dark brown hair behind her ears, her enthusiasm noticeable. "Love that style. Crepe Couture, I believe."

"Yes," I reply, grinning.

She looks familiar, but her name escapes me, like the final note of a song just out of reach. It will come to me.

"Excellent choice. It looks stunning on you." Her voice is bright, and she smiles.

"Thanks."

She strides toward the front door, and the sharp click of her heels echoes against the marble floor as she meets up with her friends.

I linger beside a tall potted plant by the elevators, my thoughts spiraling around Weston's date tonight. The way he interacted with Naomi was more Easton-coded than he realizes.

He made eye contact, flashed his charming smile, and devoted his full attention, but the spark—that effortless flirting I'm so accustomed to seeing during his interviews—was absent. Like he's broken.

A few minutes drift by, and I refresh the browser I had open earlier.

A new article grabs the headlines.

Naomi and Weston: Power couple potential.

Naomi had to leave their dinner early due to business. It's rumored they've already planned their second date.

The internet loves to ship Weston into relationships. Each time a new woman is mentioned, Lena gives them more content to run with. They bait her, and she goes public with her opinions, throwing as much shade as possible while trying to stay relevant. She doesn't realize she's an entire circus with the entertainment she provides. It makes me feel sorry for Weston.

When I look up from my phone, I spot *him.*

Dark hair falls above his bright blue eyes that seem to pierce through my facade. He adjusts his suit jacket like he walked right off a Dior runway. While he's polite and charming in public, he reveals a softer side in private, a side he only shows me.

His gaze catches mine, and it sends a wave of warmth through my chest. He runs his fingers through his messy hair, adding a touch of effortless charm that I find irresistible. A genuine smile spreads across his face, and I can't help but mirror it.

He's *always* happy to see me.

"Hi." He moves closer, gently hooking his pinkie with mine and pulling me with him. The single touch causes electricity to race through me as he guides me inside the elevator.

As the doors slide shut behind us, Weston releases my hand, pressing his thumb against the reader. In an instant, we shoot upward toward his penthouse.

"I've never been to your place before," I admit, my pulse quickening with excitement when I study his kissable lips.

"You're always welcome to visit," he replies, his voice smooth.

Weston easily disarms me with a single glance.

"Really? Do I get a key?" I laugh, glancing away to collect myself.

I struggle to keep my composure when he looks at me intensely. It's easy to imagine we're the only two people in the universe.

"Consider it done," he says.

"I was only kidding," I tell him.

"I'm not." He smirks. "Your wish is my command."

"Are you my genie in a bottle?"

"No, babe, because I'll give you *more* than three wishes."

"Why don't you bring this side of you on your dates? This is what women want," I say.

"You don't think I know what women want?" He blinks at me, being cocky as fuck.

Oh, he knows. God, of course he does.

I can't look at him; the urge to capture his mouth takes over.

Thankfully, the elevator doors slide open, and Weston guides me out.

"Thank you for tonight. You've spoiled me," I say as we move into the foyer that mirrors the Diamond in the Sky.

"There's so much more to come." He shoots me a wink.

This entrance has a unique charm that feels distinctly like Weston's style. Very modern with moody lighting.

I glance at him, not able to hide my smile. I could wrap my arm around his neck and taste him. Would he kiss me back?

"Don't start shit," he says, almost as if he can read my mind.

"Not sure what you're talking about," I mutter, wondering if my wants are written all over my face.

"Oh, keep playing innocent. I find it endearing as fuck." He presses his thumb onto the pad, and the main door opens.

I enter first, and I'm filled with anticipation as I walk farther inside. The glow of the city lights spills through the floor-to-ceiling windows, casting a warm halo over the space. A shiny white grand piano stands as the centerpiece, offering a stunning view of the park, covered in a blanket of snow.

"Do you play?" I ask, picturing his fingers dancing over the keys while taking in this breathtaking scenery.

"Not anymore," he replies, turning on the overhead light that floods the room with a cozy warmth.

Despite its size—two stories high, wrapped in glass, with an expansive view—the place feels lived in.

Mail is sprawled casually across the bar, and the pillows on the couch aren't aligned. There's a lingering scent of him, almost like cedar. It's familiar and comforting.

I step closer to the piano and trace my fingers along the cool, polished keys. The silence breaks as a playful sound fills the air. I lean over, plucking out the opening notes of "Heart and Soul." The melody is bright and nostalgic as I use my two pointer fingers.

"It's from *Big* with Tom Hanks. Ever watch it?"

"Yeah," he murmurs.

I can sense him pulling inward as he lights the gigantic fireplace. The flame catches and burns bright as it licks up the side of the glass. He holds his hands out in front of it, then glances at me.

"What's on your mind?" Curiosity meets his tone.

I grow quiet, a giveaway that I'm in my head, swimming with my thoughts—something I do a lot.

"Tonight, I realized there are a lot of things I don't know about you," I say, moving to the edge of vulnerability.

"How is that possible? You're a *Westoncyclopedia*," he says, smirking.

"Not yet," I admit, watching him watch me. I see an expression I'm not sure I've ever seen before. I can't read him. "What's on your mind?"

"I had the urge to paint again," he says, almost confused.

My mouth falls open. "You paint?"

"I stopped four years ago, when I stopped playing piano. But I think you've inspired me." A smile tugs at the corners of his mouth. "You're fucking gorgeous. *Wow.*"

"Weston," I whisper.

"I won't hold that back for your comfort." The confidence in his eyes is mesmerizing. "If you're told, maybe you'll start believing it."

My willpower crumbles as our eyes meet.

"What are your plans for next Friday?" he asks, changing the subject.

He sheds his suit jacket, tossing it casually on the back of a stool. I can't help but notice the rich blue silk lining that echoes the color of his eyes—the same color in the jewelry boxes. The dark gray vest and tight button-up shirt hug his body. He carefully removes his cuff links, placing them next to the mail, and loosens his tie. His biceps flex as he removes his accessories. It's casual yet somehow intimate.

"Already back to eye-fucking me." He chuckles, breaking the spell. "Didn't take long."

"Blame the suit," I reply, my heart racing as I try to convince myself it's just his clothes that captivate me. I clear my throat as the weight of anticipation floats in the air.

"About Friday, I'm going on a date," I offer.

He nods. "You are?"

"Do you remember how Lexi said my ex's name?"

"You flipped out about it, yes," he says, dropping a large ball of ice into two glasses. He fills it with an amber liquid and then hands me one.

"Sam texted me. I think I'm going to meet up with him on Friday." I wait for a reaction, but he conveniently doesn't give one. When I turn my head, my mouth falls open when I notice the shimmery water outside. "You have a pool?"

"Yes. It's heated." His voice vibrates through the space.

"Can we go swimming? Please?"

Weston tilts his head. "It's twenty-two degrees outside."

"And?"

I grab the sliding door handle, my heart racing as I step out onto the balcony with my drink in hand. I shudder under the cold breeze as I bend down and dip my fingers into the warm water. Steam rises from the top. A wave of excitement floods over me, and I can't resist.

Weston appears beside me, the bottle of bourbon in his hand. His presence radiates a blend of mischief and allure. I glance back at him. The cool night air mingles with the warmth of the pool as I set my drink down. I reach behind me to unzip my dress, letting it cascade down around my heels.

I can feel his eyes on me, and it makes my heart race. I look over my shoulder, standing in my delicate black lingerie, and offer him a teasing smile.

"Joining me?" I ask.

His eyes don't deviate from mine as I dive headfirst into the inviting water.

When I resurface, laughter dances in my chest. Weston stands on the pool's edge, the moonlight casting a silver sheen on his muscular frame.

"It feels amazing," I say, a smile breaking across my face. "You should join me."

"It's the dead of winter," he replies.

"Yep. Peer pressure," I say. "Are you scared?"

I lean back, dipping my hair in the warmth.

A heartbeat passes, and he unbuttons his shirt, revealing more of those tantalizing tattoos that cover his skin. My gaze stays glued on him.

"What are you smirking about?" His belt clangs to the ground.

"Nothing," I say, loving how warm the water is, trying to ignore the smoke show in front of me but failing.

My eyes slide down his body, and it's all curves and dips and ink like he was sculpted from stone. In those boxer briefs, he looks like a bad-boy underwear model covered with tattoos. Confidence drips off him.

"Damn," I say in a hushed whisper.

"And to think, you removed *me* as your hall pass. But don't worry; you can change your mind." He bursts into laughter, and in one smooth, fluid motion, he dives into the pool, muscles rippling as he slips beneath the surface.

His head pops up, and he slicks his hair back.

"I hate that you know that."

"I love it," he says and swims toward the edge of the pool to grab the bottle of bourbon.

"If I pulled the card right now, would you have sex with me?" I bluntly ask.

Silence.

"Oh, so you're not going to answer?" I ask.

"No, because it's a trick question."

I keep most of my body submerged and study him while treading water.

"You would," I say.

"I'm not sure what I'd do in that situation," he admits. "I haven't been with anyone since Lena."

I study him. "That's over a year."

"You sound shocked," he mutters, swigging back the liquid.

"Every date you've been on has been a decoy?" It's still hard for me to process. I'm still searching for reassurance.

"When I filed for divorce, I made a pact with myself. One I will not break for anyone."

My eyes twinkle with curiosity.

"LadyLux once wrote that I rushed things with women, and that's why I'll never be happy or find real love. I think she suggested I get to know someone first." He glares at me incredulously.

"Okay, I did say that. But I don't get how it's relevant."

"I require one year of casual dating before sex. Relationship building first. Physical second," he admits, completely vulnerable.

"Jesus, Weston." I scoff. "No woman will want to wait *that* long to be with you."

"You'd be surprised," he says with a brow lifted. "A year of getting to know someone isn't that long when you're discussing forever."

"This is a joke, right? You're Mr. Playboy. Fuck 'em and forget 'em. Bag 'em and tag 'em."

"Not anymore. Now that sex is out of the picture, other things hold more weight. Like conversations," he says.

I shake my head. "Well, I wish you all the luck in the world. And I'm sending prayers for whoever you date next. Poor thing is going to be so sexually frustrated, especially when you look like this." I shiver from the cold and smile. I'm sexually frustrated, and we're *just* friends. "I'm happy though. That means things with us will stay the same for at least a year."

My eyes trace over the ink on his shoulders and arms. I don't want to think about the things I'd do to him if we weren't stuck in the friendzone.

"Your tattoos are fascinating," I say, moving closer to him.

I've only ever studied them in photos. It's not lost on me this is the first time we've actually been alone.

"Easton drew them," he mutters as my fingers tracing over his biceps.

"It's beautiful that you're decorated with your brother's artwork. And before you say anything, I know they're different," I offer, grabbing his hand and pointing at the tiny diamond above his wrist. "This is the one I always look for in photos to see if it was you or Easton. And the diamond on your right elbow."

"Really?" He searches my face.

"They're the most recognizable to me," I whisper, knowing it's not something I've shared with him before.

The cool breeze wraps around us, soothing and refreshing as the warm water encapsulates us.

"If you could have any wish in the world, what would it be?" I ask, the intimacy of the moment inviting more vulnerability.

"I can't say, or it won't come true," he replies.

"Oh, come on. I won't tell. I'll keep your secrets."

He shakes his head, staying strong.

"Can I take a wild guess?" I plead.

"I'll allow it if you tell me when you'll write and publish again on your blog," he counters, a challenge in his gaze.

"Ah, I thought we'd avoid that conversation tonight." A sheepish smile creeps in.

"No. What's going on?" His voice is calm.

I gulp down some bourbon, and it's a distraction from the countless thoughts swirling in my mind. "I'm scared."

"Why?" he asks.

"I feel like it's going to disappear. The pressure to produce at a high quality is almost paralyzing. This was—and is—my dream, yet

I feel a sense of dread. I'm so scared of failure and letting everyone down, especially myself. And you." I take a deep breath.

He gives me a kind smile. "As long as you stay true to yourself, you'll never let me down."

I suddenly feel vulnerable and exposed. "I don't know if I trust myself with you."

"You're safe." He winks, then lazily rests his arm on the edge of the pool, the blue lights illuminating his face.

His relaxed expression is a promise of adventure. But instead of giving in to temptation, I paddle to the center of the pool, creating an ocean of space between us. I'm trying to stay on my very best behavior.

Sometimes, I hate how my mind operates after a few drinks— bold and reckless—imagining all the sweet yet dangerous possibilities with him. The thoughts wrap around me, nearly strangling me before I can push them away. The world tilts ever so slightly.

Yep, I'm definitely tipsy.

The martinis and bourbon have me captured in a dreamlike haze.

"Have you ever been curious?" I finally ask the question that has been dancing in my mind all night.

"About?" he inquires.

"Us," I say, dropping my body back into the water to face him.

"Ahh, you're at *that* point of the night," he mutters.

I raise a brow. "Which is?"

"The one where you fantasize about making out with me."

Desire and intrigue battle for dominance.

"If I actually wanted to make out with you, I would," I retort.

"All bark, no bite." His gaze locks on to mine, intense and unyielding.

"Because you reject me every time!" A laugh escapes me, airy and light. "Don't change the subject. Answer."

He swims toward me. The water ripples around us, leaving the two of us suspended in time.

My breath quickens. I'm tilting dangerously close to the edge of temptation, and I almost lean in to brush my lips against his, but I stay strong.

"Well?"

"I don't want to be another one of your statistics," he offers me. "You're not ready."

The ball is back in my court.

"Are you?" I ask, sucking in a deep breath.

I'm aware we both have our issues.

"How many of your guy friends have you dated?" he asks.

"Three. And I always think it will be different, but it never is. After the third time, I promised myself I would never do it again."

"What about friends with benefits?" he asks.

It's an interesting question.

"If there was chemistry and emotions could stay in check, I'd think about it, but it would come with rules," I say.

"Like?"

"No cuddling. No *I love you*s. No expectations. No sleeping in the same bed. No couple *bullshit*. Just fucking for pleasure only. I've also learned most men can't handle a situationship. At least not with me."

"Really?" he asks, being cocky as fuck.

"I've been in one before. It was great until he fell obsessively in love with me and got really jealous when I went on dates with other men. With the right person, it works. But usually, someone starts catching feelings, and it's never me. I can separate friendship from fucking because when I walk into something like that, I know it will never work. You never start friends with benefits with someone who has actual potential. Recipe for disaster."

He dips his hair into the water and smooths it back on his head. The tips immediately start to curl. "We should go inside and warm up."

At the mention, the air feels colder than it did seconds earlier.

Weston swims to the edge, and I can't help but admire the tattooed muscles that ripple across his back. He hoists himself out of the pool, striding toward the small room beyond, wrapping a towel around his waist while holding another out for me.

I follow his lead, pushing myself up from the edge. Each freezing step guides me closer to him. The instant he blankets me in the towel, our electric connection restarts.

The only thing that pulls me away from him is his phone buzzing in his pants pocket. It goes on for a little while before stopping and starting over.

"Is that your *secret* girlfriend?" I tease, glancing at the light flashing.

"Maybe," he replies, his voice low and husky.

Whoever is calling is insistent.

"Should you answer?" I ask, breaking away from him to fish his phone from his pocket.

I glance at the screen.

Unknown Caller.

I show it to him.

"It's Lena." His voice is steady, but the seriousness of the situation builds. "Since the blind item was posted, she started harassing me again."

My heart tightens at the thought of him dealing with this. "Are you sure it's her?"

He nods, his brows furrowing. "She used to do this *every* night in the beginning."

"This has to stop," I say, determination taking hold.

"Carlee," he warns, "don't."

I take a breath, and my gut twists as I answer. Someone breathes on the other end of the line, sending a chill up my spine.

"Yes, *please*," I moan out.

Weston's lips part as he watches me with intent.

"Right there. Mmhmm. Yes, baby." I close my eyes, unable to

look at him. "Please. *Please.* More. *Harder,*" I demand. "Yes. Yes. Weston. *Weston,*" I whisper breathlessly, my heart racing. "Oh God, I'm so fucking close. I'm—I'm co—" I end the call and return the phone to him, my pulse quickening.

I swear his blue eyes mirror the depths of the ocean at midnight. I glance down at his towel, noticing he's rock hard.

"Say something," I whisper, tucking my lips into my mouth to hold back a smile.

He swallows, his throat working nervously. "Don't you *ever* fucking say my name like that again."

I burst into laughter, the sound bubbling out of me. "Maybe that's the only way I'll say your name from now on? *Weston. Oh God,*" I moan out, my voice echoing off the tall wall of his balcony.

I lean over and grab the bourbon bottle, needing a shot to cool the heat simmering inside me. I savor it as it slides down my throat, but it tastes like water. Not a good sign.

"You should be cut off," he says, snatching the booze from my grasp.

I pout. "Oh, come on. You're *no* fun." The Southern in me says *hello* as the bourbon loosens my tongue.

The glow of the pool light illuminates his handsome face. That chiseled jaw and scruff are what wet dreams are made from.

I know it's getting late. When we're together, time always seems to slip away.

"I have to work tomorrow," I admit, hating how I always have to leave. "I should probably head home soon."

He takes a deep breath, his expression turning serious.

"What if you quit?" he asks.

"I cannot just quit my job," I insist, shaking my head. "We've both had too much to drink, and that's not logical."

"I'll give you an allowance," he offers.

"Like you're my daddy?" I waggle my eyebrows. "What's next? Grounding me if I misbehave? Spanking me?"

His brow arches. "You're really fucking intense."

Desire takes hold. "I've been told that before. By you, actually."

He holds his phone in one hand and the bourbon in the other as he guides me inside. I stand in front of the fireplace and dry my body. He sways beside me, and I reach out to steady him. Somehow, we stumble and collapse on the couch, laughing.

I remind myself of the boundaries that threaten to pull us apart just as the attraction pulls us together.

"Have you ever thought that maybe whoever posted that blind item was trying to do you a favor and end this war between you and your ex?" I whisper, laying on his chest.

"That's what my publicist believes," he says and hiccups as he stares into my eyes.

"Oh my God. Is this the first time I've actually seen you drunk?" I can't help but tease. "You're usually more careful around me when I'm tipsy."

"Shit," he echoes, amusement dancing in his eyes. "We're shit-faced."

"Uh-oh," I tell him, leaning my head back on the couch, creating space between us.

I shiver, and he notices.

Weston pulls a blanket from behind him and throws it over me. His fingers graze across my skin, causing goose bumps to race up my arm. We settle into a comfortable silence—the kind I only share with my closest friends—as we stare at the skyline.

I don't know how much time passes.

"Are you still cold?" he asks as his gaze lands on me.

"A little," I respond.

Without hesitation, he stands and taps a button. Instantly, the gas fireplace roars to life, flames dancing eagerly in their glazed glass enclosure. He returns to the couch, and this time, he's even closer. I savor the warmth radiating from him as I rest my head on his chest.

"Your heart is racing," I whisper. The thumps tug at my attention.

"Be reckless with me," he says, a seriousness creeping into his tone.

I laugh, the sound a mix of disbelief and exhilaration. I want to.

"Go all in with LuxLeaks." Challenge flickers in his bright eyes. The temptation to capture his lips is nearly overwhelming.

"I have to be responsible," I say.

"Easton paid your rent for a year because he had been an asshole to Lexi," he reminds me. "I also know your blog pays you well, so you don't have to keep working at the hotel."

"And my blog thrives on fresh content," I remind him, a reluctant grin tugging at my lips.

"You haven't posted in over three months because the information you got at the W was no longer relevant after you leveled up. If you quit, you'll have the time and freedom to be my plus-one to every social event I'm invited to."

I shoot him a glare. "That will only feed the girlfriend rumors. Everyone will think we're together."

"And?" he asks.

The thought leaves me speechless.

9

WESTON

"My publicist suggested a relationship PR stunt. I thought it was a ridiculous idea. Now I'm wondering if there is weight to it."

Carlee laughs nervously, her voice fluttering like a butterfly caught in a breeze. "Explain how it would work."

I let the words hang in the air, allowing silence to wrap around us like a cozy blanket while I think through this. It's territory I've never navigated before, yet it worked like a charm for Easton, who's now blissfully married to the love of his life.

"I don't know," I finally admit. Conversations like this are a gamble, especially given our current frazzled minds. "I think you'll need to become my plus-one to *every* social event. If people ask what we are, we tell the truth and say we're just friends. Once we're spotted together several times, the assumptions and rumors will follow."

"They'll think I'm your secret girlfriend," she says, raising an eyebrow, disbelief etched across her face.

"*So be her.*"

She shakes her head. "People will dig into every detail of my life."

"They'll find nothing," I confirm, holding her gaze with unwavering confidence.

Her suspicion flares. "Because you've already done your homework?"

I can't help but chuckle. "Yes."

"Weston, seriously?"

"Look, I had to verify I wasn't befriending someone who was a problem," I explain. "I did a background check on you and Lexi. You passed with flying colors. I mean, you're here, right?"

She sits up straighter. "What did you learn?"

"Nothing of concern, I assure you. I already knew you were smart. Your record is clean, and your credit is healthy."

"Wifey material?" she teases.

I tilt my head, a smile creeping across my lips. "You're too sharp-tongued for that."

"Ah, you prefer those who listen and obey then?"

"I only like my women to be submissive in the bedroom. Everywhere else, she needs to be a tiger. It's a requirement." I lift the bourbon to my mouth, taking a long pull. My head swims with possibility as our conversation morphs into something else.

She grabs the bottle, taking a long swig. We're teetering on the precipice, both of us daring the other to step closer to the edge. This is a recipe for disaster, but neither of us stops.

"Wouldn't it be fun?" I ask. "You could write *anything* about *us* on your blog, and the public would devour it. LadyLux could have them eating out of the palm of her dainty hand."

Skepticism is etched across her pretty face. "I don't lie on my blog."

"I'd never ask you to do that. Write the truth."

She shakes her head, and her damp hair bounces defiantly. "No one would care that we're sipping drinks in a dingy bar, swapping stories about our failed dates."

"I think your assumption is wrong," I counter. "You don't believe women everywhere wouldn't want to know what it's like to be besties with me? I'm not asking you to lie. Just write about our friendship as if you were being interviewed by LadyLux herself."

Her gaze roams over my body like she's suddenly aware that we're still wrapped in towels and sitting too close for comfort.

"It would boost your blog traffic, translating into real gains."

The intrigue in her eyes betrays her skepticism. "Always with the numbers."

"Babe, I'm the chief operating officer of a multibillion-dollar company. Numbers are my life," I reply, giving her a cocky grin.

She hiccups, amusement flickering over her features. "Are we conspiring again?"

"My partner in crime," I say with a brow lifted as electricity crackles between us.

The stakes are high, but the thrill of the chase is intoxicating. It warms me from the inside out.

"I don't know about this."

She's intrigued by the thought of teaming up with me. Damn, I am too.

"Pros and cons," I say. "Pros: *you* could steal Lena's crown, rendering her irrelevant; elevate your blog; and become America's sweetheart—without ever having to pretend to be in a relationship with me. No more hiding our friendship. We can simply be."

A mischievous expression lights her lovely face. "Okay, but that still doesn't solve the problem of everyone assuming we're dating."

"That's the fun part. They can assume whatever they want. Life continues as normal. It's just that we get to have dinner together and be seen in public. Also, it stops me from attending social events alone now that Easton ditches me to hang out with Lexi. Imagine what you'd hear."

"LuxLeaks isn't your friend, Weston. Some might say you're making a deal with the devil."

I smirk and shrug.

"What if I expose people close to you?" She studies me intently as if searching my face for clues. "I don't want you to be upset with me. These people are your friends."

"I *trust* you," I say, letting the truth settle between us like a promise. "If you hear something you believe needs to be written about, do it. I don't concern myself with what others are doing, and I know I'm not involved in anything problematic other than my ex."

Her voice drops to a whisper, almost trembling. "I'm so afraid of losing what we have." Her words are raw and achingly honest.

"Please don't be. I can't imagine my life without you. You've been my Firefly through this divorce, lighting my way when everything was so fucking dark. Not many people make me feel seen. I just want to have fun with you."

Her expression softens, vulnerability dancing in her eyes. "We'd have to make rules. This is dangerous territory."

"Of course." The corners of my mouth twitch into a half smile. "A contract."

She laughs. "Calloways and their damn contracts."

"You shouldn't expect anything less. I'll also need you to sign an NDA."

I see that look in her eye that tells me she wants to ask me something she probably shouldn't.

"What's on your mind?"

It's an open invitation to ask me anything, and she knows that.

"Why haven't you exposed Lena?" she questions gently, her eyes narrowing with curiosity.

A lump rises in my throat, heavy and unyielding. I haven't shared the intimate details of why I filed for divorce with anyone other than Easton. It's a chapter of my life shrouded in shadows.

"I'm sorry," she says, realization dawning in her gaze. "I shouldn't have asked that. It's just ... I know you're not the bad guy even though she tries to paint you like you're a monster."

Warmth floods my chest at her gentleness—a reminder of the bond we've forged in the delicate spaces between our vulnerabilities. I'm thankful for her presence, for the light she radiates into the shadows of my life. She sees me for who I am, and that's all that matters.

"Never apologize for speaking freely," I say, propping my elbow up on the back of the couch and turning my body toward her. "One of my favorite things about you is that you'll ask me what's on my mind, even if it's uncomfortable."

"Because you can handle the hard questions," she says with defiance in her eyes.

I nod. "I will share this: I should expose her because she deserves that. However, I'd much rather deny her the dirty attention she craves from me. She's been starved of my presence, and she knows it. The media is losing interest; it's been a year since she shared anything new about our past relationship. I'd rather let her unravel by her own doing. Eventually, people will see her for who she is."

"They already have," she confirms.

"Exactly. And it'll be her own words that finally ruin her, not mine. So, in the meantime, I'll spend the energy I have left to fight her in court."

"I'm proud of you. Not engaging takes maturity and willpower most don't have." She clears her throat. "Can we discuss the cons of our very public friendship?"

I'm happy for the subject change as I glance back at the flames, mesmerized as I play out our potential future together. "You being followed and watched. Rumors about us. Hate from super stans who will never approve of anyone I'm with, even if it's speculation."

She sits silent for a few minutes, inhaling deeply. I don't push her to speak, allowing her time to process what it could mean if we moved forward.

"What if someone finds out about LuxLeaks? You being tied to a gossip blog could hurt your image."

I laugh, and the sound is light and carefree. "If Lena couldn't destroy me, nothing can."

She tries to hold back a smile.

"And if your identity were ever revealed—which it *never* will be —I'd stand beside you without hesitation. I don't care what anyone thinks. I'd publicly invest in your site and help with distribution if you'd let me. I believe in what you're doing, and I say that with my full chest," I admit.

"I don't know what I did to deserve your friendship."

"Mmm. You told the truth." My voice softens. "You've been unapologetically yourself since the day we met. Most people aren't like you."

She smiles. "What do you mean?"

"You're authentically yourself. No matter the company."

Her brows furrow. "I can't imagine the type of people you constantly deal with."

"Don't pity me," I tell her, shaking my head. I'm familiar with that look. "I chose this life."

"Did you?" she honestly questions. "Or were you manufactured to be who you are?"

I smile. "You make me sound like I was harvested in a test tube."

"Nah, just a little nepo baby." Carlee licks her lips.

Our smiles pull each other closer, and I realize I never want this night to end.

"That supposed to offend me?"

"No, because it's the truth."

"I was given a choice. I chose to do what Easton wanted. He was built for this."

"And what about you?" she asks.

"I handle it, but I've imagined a different life many times," I say, knowing those thoughts often include her. "Lexi told me about you and Samson."

"I wondered if you'd mention it," she replies, her eyes close almost to shield herself from the memories. "It's embarrassing."

I offer her a gentle smile. "She said you weren't the same after that breakup."

We've exchanged countless stories over bourbon, laughing about life and love. She's glossed over her true heartaches, only sharing snippets of her recent misadventures with online dating.

"We still have a lot to learn about each other. There's plenty of time for that." Her lips curl into a thoughtful smile like she can read my thoughts.

"Lex didn't give me many details because I didn't want to hear about someone breaking you. I'm happy you healed," I say, my voice lowering to a whisper, weighed down by concern.

She seems lost in memories, deciding whether to unwrap the layers of her past or keep them tucked away. I can't bring myself to push her.

"After I graduated, we paused our long-distance relationship." She finally begins her reluctant confession. "He fell for someone he'd met at work. It started as a fling, and within a month, he told her he loved her, and they moved in together. She replaced me. Slept on my side of the bed. The frames with our pictures held theirs. Three years and a best friendship, thrown away."

"Ah, that's why you have that *I love you* rule," I nod, the pieces clicking into place.

"He moved on so quickly that it made me feel like we'd meant nothing. No one can genuinely fall *in love* within a month. The new girl gave him something new and exciting to do, so he did her. A lot. I couldn't even get on social media without seeing photos of them everywhere. I avoided going home for years just so I wouldn't accidentally run into them."

"I'm sorry he didn't treasure you," I say.

"It hurt me for a long time," she replies. The weight of her words hangs in the air. "But not anymore. I think that's why I'm ready to see him again."

I watch her. "To give him another chance?"

"To see if there's anything left," she admits, the alcohol loosening her tongue.

I admire her for being unfiltered with me.

"How long does it take someone to say *I love you* and mean it? You said thirty days is too soon? What is too long?"

She exhales. "I think it's personal. But I think I have to be the one to say those three words first because I know I'll mean them, and I wouldn't throw them around."

"What if he lies when he says it back? There are flaws to this master plan."

"Listen, I don't need you to be analytical right now." She laughs. "I wouldn't be with someone who'd lie about *I love you*. If he says it back, I'll know it's real. It just needs to feel right, or it's wrong."

Noted.

Tonight, she's shared too many of her secrets.

"Enlightening," I say with a smirk and stand. "Come on. Let's find something to wear."

She wraps the blanket around her, and then the towel drops to the floor. My hand settles lightly on her back as we ascend the stairs. She glances over her shoulder, and I raise my brows, savoring our unspoken connection. It drives me wild.

We walk down the hallway toward my bedroom, and she gasps as I push the door open. The room is bathed in the glow of the bedside lamp. She looks at the wall of windows that offers a breathtaking three-hundred-sixty-degree view of the park and the surrounding area. Carlee takes in the park that's covered in white, glowing under the moonlight.

I memorize her, almost reaching out to confirm she's not a figment of my imagination.

"It's not quite the *diamond in the sky*," I say.

"It's better. It's yours," she breathes, her fingers brushing against the glass.

I glimpse her reflection. That genuine little smile lights up her face, one I'm not supposed to see.

"Breathtaking," I say under my breath, my pulse quickening as I head to my closet. I need space before I do something I shouldn't.

"It was my idea to take a break with Samson," she says from my room, her tone thoughtful.

"You suggested it?" I slide on some fresh joggers and chuckle. "I'm glad you did."

She moves to the doorway of my closet. The light halos around her head and the air around us grows heavy.

"Why?" Her question hangs.

"Because we would've never met." The truth swirls in the space between us. "You'd have had no reason to go on shitty dates and then visit Sluggers afterward."

"You're right," she says. "It's almost like my bad dates led me to you."

"Something led me to you—that's for sure," I say while rummaging through my drawers for clothes for her.

She steps deeper into my closet, the blanket still wrapped tightly around her.

I meet her gaze. "The woman he fell in love with—are they still together?"

"No," she replies, her voice kind but resolute. "They broke up over the summer."

"Wow. So, he's single, and you're going on a date with him on Friday?" I pry, glancing back to catch her reaction.

"That's right," she admits, the flicker of uncertainty in her eyes betraying the calmness in her tone. "He was great in bed. And it's been *forever*."

"Did he get you off?" I ask, tossing the T-shirt and joggers to her.

"Yes," she hesitates, sliding the clothes over her bra and panties that are already dry. "Plenty of times."

The thought makes my jaw clench. "You just don't seem like a *second-chance romance* kind of girl."

"I'm not. But I can ignore almost *anything* for some good D." She giggles. "Might actually get some this weekend."

I turn to her with my arms crossed over my bare chest. "Closure is important."

"Is that what you believe meeting him will give me? Closure?" she asks, her eyes lock on mine.

"I hope so," I say, trying not to sound jealous. I'm blaming the bourbon.

I glance at her wearing my shirt and joggers, both too baggy, swallowing her whole. She spins around, and the jewelry I bought for her catches the light. I take a step forward, sliding my hand under the necklace.

She looks up at me. "This is too much."

"Not when it comes to you," I mutter, dropping the diamond. "More comfortable?"

"A million times." She beams, moving into my room.

Carlee settles on the edge of my bed. The comforter crinkles beneath her, and she smooths her hand across the delicate fabric. I glance at her over my shoulder as I flick on the fireplace in my room.

"Dangerous place to be," I warn, a teasing note in my voice.

Carlee smirks, propping herself up on her elbow, a glimmer of mischief in her eyes. "Is this where all the wild sex happens?"

"Believe it or not, you're the first woman in this room."

She arches an eyebrow. "You were married for three years. How's that even possible?"

"Lena declared this penthouse was a piece of shit and urged me to sell it. I refused and never invited her back."

Her expression twists into disbelief. "No way. It's great here. Feels like home."

"I know."

Our eyes meet, and time stretches as we share a moment.

It's like she's sifting through my tangled thoughts of her, of *us*.

"What were you thinking just now? Like, just seconds ago?" she probes, her tone light yet somehow serious.

Caught red-handed.

"Hmm." I raise my brows in mock confusion. "I don't remember."

But she's getting too good at seeing through my facade.

"You're lying," she declares almost gleefully. In an instant, she lunges forward and begins to tickle me.

"No," I say, wriggling away from her grip. "Fuck," I add with a laugh, but she's quicker than I anticipated, squeezing my side.

"Tell me," she insists, towering over me, her eyes gleaming with mischief as her assault continues. "Lexi told me Easton was super ticklish."

Laughter bubbles out of me as I struggle to stop her. Somehow we trip and land on the floor. Carlee topples forward, landing squarely on my chest, and I break her fall. In that instant, I realize just how close we are. Her breath catches as sparks dance between us.

"I had to test the tickle theory," she whispers, her gaze drifting to my mouth.

"And?" I reply.

Tension crackles in the air like static.

Just a couple of inches separate us, and I could capture her plump lips.

God, I want to do just that. So does she. I can see it on her face and sense it in her ragged breaths.

"Don't," I mutter.

"Why?" she shoots back. A teasing grin plays on her lips. "Scared you might like it?"

"Scared *you* might," I retort, as I settle my hand under my head.

The truth is, the image of us tangled together sends me spiraling.

"You say you don't care about rumors about us but then get weird when I'm too close," she says. Her voice carries a challenge.

I smirk, enjoying it. "I don't want *you* to have regrets."

With a dramatic roll, she flops onto her back beside me, and we both find ourselves staring at the ceiling. She bursts into laughter, and the warmth of it fills the room.

Carlee turns onto her side, and I turn my head to meet her eyes. My fingers itch to brush against her cheek. We're so close that it would take nothing to slide my lips across her skin, to whisper tantalizing secrets into her ear.

The alcohol courses through me, heightening my senses and making the temptation more potent. I'm painfully aware of every ragged breath and movement, almost as if being pushed by an invisible force to cross the line.

Her cheeks flush, a vivid pink that tells me I've uncovered too much.

"Why don't you just do it?" she whispers. "You want to."

As her lips part, the atmosphere shifts; a charged current surges between us. I've always been transparent about my attraction, yet she's never acknowledged she noticed until now. We're dancing around the truth, spinning safely in the land of denial. Or maybe it's just me.

"Fine," she hisses.

Without breaking our gaze, Carlee inches closer, but to my surprise, she doesn't stop. Her lips capture mine, careful at first, then hungry. A moan escapes her as our mouths fit together.

Heat rushes through me.

Our tongues intertwine like they were made for this very purpose. I crave more of her—*all of her*. It shouldn't feel this right. Her fingers weave through my hair, a gentle tug, encouraging me to dive deeper.

But I find the strength to pull away, my heart racing, before we lose ourselves entirely.

My logic. I can't lose it. Too much is at risk.

She places her fingers against her swollen lips—a gesture that feels like we've shattered the very fabric of space and time.

I sit up abruptly, trying to collect my scattered thoughts, while she stands, her expression a mixture of exhilaration and confusion.

The need for an explanation lingers in the air.

"It wasn't supposed to …" She doesn't finish.

I stand and search her face, hoping to glimpse a crack in her wall of denial. A sweet smile plays on her lips, but it doesn't reach her eyes.

"I should go," she says.

The tension nearly chokes me. "Is that regret I sense?"

She scoffs, shaking her head, moving toward the door. "That's the last thing I feel."

10

CARLEE

My head swims, and every inch of my body craves him.
Confidence radiates from him as he strides toward me, wearing a cocky smirk.

Weston reaches out, tucking a loose strand of my hair behind my ear, his fingers lingering longer than necessary as he twirls it. I can barely meet his gaze as the weight of our actions hangs between us.

"I shouldn't have crossed the—"

"Shh," he gently interrupts, his laughter light yet teasing.

My cheeks flush, revealing the mixture of emotions inside me—fear, excitement, and something deeper that I dare not mention or admit.

"Finish your thought. You said it wasn't supposed to … supposed to what?" He removes the little distance that was left between us.

I can sense an undercurrent of seriousness.

"You're impossible," I reply.

My body betrays me. I bite my lip, uncertainty waging war within me.

"You *crave* impossible," he says, his tone dropping. "So fucking obsessed with the chase."

His words wrap tightly around me, stirring something deep within. Weston's already figured me out.

I breathe deeply, suddenly overwhelmed by his presence, but I finally find the courage to meet his steely gaze. The spark in his eyes glimmers with an intensity that sends my heart into a chaotic dance. There's no denying the pull that tightens between us, even if it terrifies me.

"It wasn't supposed to feel *right*," I confess as desire collides with the fear of losing control.

I watch him, but his expression is unwavering.

"You didn't feel anything," I say, immediately feeling stupid.

The realization is enough to drown me alive. I'm not used to being on this side of the coin, where I'm the one who feels something. My mouth gently parts, and I check myself, tucking my emotions back in.

We really are just friends. This is proof of that.

I force a smile.

"Please forget I said that," I say in a hushed whisper.

Weston watches me fight an internal battle. He places his palm against my cheek. His thumb brushes against my lower lip as he studies it.

"You felt something?" he whispers, his voice a deep growl, as he meets my eyes.

"Yes, and I feel so stupid. I should go before I embarrass myself further," I confess.

I fall into shock as he moves forward, gently brushing his lips across mine. I'm lost with him, my willpower dissolving like sugar in water. Together, we're the perfect sweetness.

I pull him closer until I can feel the warmth of his body pressed against me. Our tongues entwine, and he threads his fingers through my damp hair, gently tugging. I hear a low growl in the back of his throat.

I moan against him, needing more—*all* of him.

"Weston," I whisper.

His hand slides up my shirt, fingers brushing over my lacy bra and against my perky nipple. His touch is dizzying.

I know we should stop, but I don't want to.

He takes my lip between his teeth and sucks and nibbles on it. We stumble over a line we shouldn't be flirting with, yet the temptation is so addictive that neither of us pulls away. I want to take that leap with him, not giving a fuck about the consequences that follow. It's a problem for future me and *future us* to worry about.

We will always be friends. Weston never breaks his promises to me.

Can we have our cake and eat it too?

We fall backward onto the bed, and he settles between my thighs, hard and rough, adding pressure to my sensitive bud as he peppers kisses along my neck and jaw.

"You taste so fucking good," he mutters against my skin, capturing my lips again.

I buck my hips upward, feeling the strain of him against his joggers. The thin fabric of our clothes is the only thing between us. The friction of grinding against him drives me wild. I thread my fingers through his hair, knowing I could crumble under him just like this.

We're tumbling, inhibitions gone, and a moan escapes me. I'm so wet for him, needing more.

"I'm so sorry," he whispers, tracing the shell of my ear with his mouth.

My eyes bolt open. "No," I mutter.

"I'm so fucking sorry," he repeats, almost pained as he presses his cock between my legs. "It's not you. Do you feel what you do to me?"

"Yes," I say, our mouths so close.

Weston places a gentle kiss across my lips, then forces himself off the bed. He stands to the side, watching me. His lips are swollen, and his hair is messy. Tattoos are splashed across his chest and arms. Weston Calloway is an archangel, beautiful and destructive.

I prop myself up on my elbows, sexually frustrated, ready to beg for him, but I don't. We stare at each other for a long while, neither of us speaking.

This time, it went too far. We lost control.

"Do you need Viagra?" I ask, trying to lighten the mood. "I swear I won't poke fun."

He bursts into laughter, glancing down at his rock-solid package. "No. My cock functions *perfectly.*"

"Am I not your type?" I ask.

"Once again." He points down to himself. I can almost see the veins through the slinky fabric of his pants. "We're just friends, Carlee."

"Friends who like to make out," I add.

"I didn't say I *liked* it," he tells me.

I take the opportunity to point toward his crotch. "You didn't have to."

"Look, you know you're gorgeous. Any man who has the opportunity to fuck your brains out is lucky. But it would complicate things between us, and I won't use you. I respect you too much," he says.

"Sometimes, I *want* to be used. Sometimes, I want to just be …" I don't finish my sentence, knowing it's full of emotions I'm not ready to face yet.

The silent conversation is so loud—or maybe it's my racing heart echoing in my head. We must break out of this trance before confessing more things that can't be unsaid. My shields have fallen, and I'm too vulnerable right now.

"I guess this is my payback?" I ask, standing and readjusting my clothes. I try to find calm in the chaos surrounding us.

"For what?" he asks.

"For replacing *you* as my free pass," I say with a laugh.

"Oh, right," he whispers, sucking in a ragged breath as if he was forced to come to his senses. "Just to be clear, you would've let me fuck you just now, right?"

His question dances in the air as I cross my arms over my chest.

"I guess we'll never know," I say, lifting my brow. My hard nipples and drenched panties say otherwise. "Was just testing you."

"Oh, okay."

He narrows his eyes, smirking, knowing I would've taken every inch of him. I'd have let him ruin me. Our lips are swollen, and our hair is a mess. While I can't speak for him, my ego is both shattered and shimmering.

Tonight, we've indulged in each other more than we should have and done things we can never undo. My skin buzzes where he touched—a reminder that we scaled the wall of our boundaries together. I search for my words or even a joke, hoping to break this charged silence, but all I can muster is a guilty smile.

"Did you feel anything when you kissed me?" I ask, not sure what his answer was because he avoided it by kissing me again.

"No, of course not," he says, lifting his brow and giving me the same energy I delivered to him seconds earlier. "Was just testing you."

"Please, Weston. Just this one time, pretty please give me the truth. There isn't a right or wrong answer. I'll accept whatever you say, and I won't mention it again."

He stares at me for a long while.

"Yes," he whispers. "Which is why we can't do that again. It's too dangerous."

Our gazes lock together, like the moon and the earth, and his eyes fill with unconfessed monologues. I know there are a million things he wants to say. But tonight, I'll fall asleep, knowing he felt something too, and that I wasn't imagining things.

"Okay. But I won't apologize for what happened," I add.

"I don't have any regrets," he offers.

As I move past him, he catches my wrist, pulling me back. I rest my hands on his chest and smile up at him.

"It's not because I don't want you," he confesses, like a whispered prayer.

"One of us has to be logical. I'm really glad it's *always* you." I pat him, moving away from him before I do something I shouldn't. I see a real glimpse of him, the part I relate with him the most.

I descend the stairs, gripping the railing as the bourbon warms my veins—or maybe it was the taste of Weston I had.

"Can you separate the two?" I ask over my shoulder.

My question pulls Weston from his thoughts.

"What's that?"

"Sex and friendship."

"It depends," he admits, trailing behind me, but just out of reach.

Once in the living room, Weston swipes his phone off the table, where he left it earlier. He types something, then sets it back down before meeting my eyes.

"The driver will arrive in fifteen minutes," he says.

All of the want and need I felt upstairs still lingers between us.

I glance down at what I'm wearing, and a wave of self-consciousness washes over me. "Do you think it's okay for me to leave like this?"

"It's your call," he replies, a smile spreading across his gorgeous face. "I wouldn't unless you want to confirm rumors."

I smile, sauntering toward the sliding door that leads to the balcony. The cool night air brushes against my skin as I step outside. He follows me.

"Tomorrow, I'll pretend like this didn't happen, just like last time you tried to make a move," Weston confirms.

"Until you bring it up because you won't be able to handle me never mentioning it. *Just like last time*," I say, finding the scattered remnants of my evening—my dress and my sparkly shoes that twinkle like stars on the balcony floor. They're both ice cold.

He watches me, and I love being under his gaze.

I turn to him. "Stop looking at me like that."

"No," Weston says, cocky as fuck. "I was your hall pass, Carlee. Your *fantasy*. The one person on the planet you would fuck without remorse if you were in a committed relationship. That says a lot about where I've been in *your* mind."

"You know, I'm actually going to murder Lexi the next time I see her for sharing that with you. And you should know I replaced you because it's supposed to be with someone out of reach, a highly unlikely reality."

"And you don't think I'm highly unlikely anymore?" he asks.

"You will *always* be out of my league, Weston. But we're friends now, and that changes things," I say, spilling truths like they're overflowing as I walk inside.

"Ah," he says, following me inside with his eyes fixated on me. "You think you're not good enough for me?"

"Let's not pretend we're the same because, on many different levels, we're not. You're Weston Calloway," I remind him. "Who am I?"

"A trusted confidant. One of my best friends," he says.

In three small steps, he could have his mouth on mine as his hand trailed up my shirt, pinching one nipple, while his other hand slid inside my pants. But even in this fantasy, the friend zone exists, and the vision vanishes before my eyes. My subconscious *always* fights back when it comes to him.

He turns his head—a gentleman, never once daring to peek at my exposed skin as I change clothes. I carefully slip out of his rolled-up joggers with practiced ease and remove my panties. The Valentino dress is cold, but I deal with it.

I move forward and place my silk panties in the palm of his hand.

"A keepsake," I whisper. "After a night we both have to forget."

"Player," he murmurs, amusement lacing his tone as his grasp tightens around the fabric.

"I just know the rules."

He laughs, shaking his head.

A smirk dances on my lips. "Have fun pretending none of this happened the next time we're together."

"What happened? I don't remember," he says jokingly.

He's too good at this.

Weston leads me to the elevator, and the corner of his mouth twitches up in a suggestive grin.

"I wish you could see how you're looking at me right now," I say.

It's like he wants to push me against this wall and fuck me on the ride down to the ground floor.

"Probably the same way you're looking at me," he mutters.

I stand straighter. "Let the games begin."

"Be careful, Firefly. I play to win," he says, looking so attractively casual as the doors slide closed.

Proof it's not the suit.

It's him.

FORTY MINUTES LATER, I ARRIVE HOME, MY MIND STILL SPINNING from being with Weston. The remnants of alcohol still dance in my bloodstream, and I can't help but replay tonight in my mind.

I undress and place my jewelry in the box on my dresser. I slip into my bed, and the cool sheets contrast with the heat simmering inside me.

Weston lives rent-free in my mind, like an uninvited yet irresistible guest. Had he not stopped us, I would have surrendered every part of myself to him. I wanted to.

My hands drift down my body, longing for his touch. I imagine his lips trailing kisses along my neck and jaw, igniting every nerve.

My fingers brush between my legs, finding my sensitive clit. It's not the first time he's been the focus of my fantasy.

My eyes shut, and my breath hitches as I dip a finger inside. His name hovers in my throat—a forbidden thought, an urging whisper. I increase my pace, need rising within me like a tide. That man drives me to lose all control as I imagine his lips on me.

The crest of my orgasm builds, and I'm on the verge of exploding, suspended in air. I'm so fucking close, my body nearly shuddering with anticipation. Right when I think I may fall over the edge, my phone rings and startles me.

The buzzing slices through the haze. Heart racing, I reluctantly roll over to see who it is.

It's Weston.

I catch a glimpse of my reflection on the screen—hair in disarray, cheeks flushed. I need to come so bad, but I reluctantly answer.

"Yes?" I'm *frustrated.*

In his darkened room, he lounges on his bed, the bourbon bottle cradled in his hand. "You look guilty as fuck." He smirks, his gaze roguish. "Did I interrupt something?"

I lick my lips, feeling as if my thoughts summoned him from the depths of my desire.

"I was thinking about you," I admit sarcastically, rolling onto my back. I squeeze my thighs together, nearly breathless.

He lifts his brow, his curiosity piqued. "Don't stop on my account."

"Can I help you?" I ask, knowing he's denied me for the second time tonight.

"Feel free to continue." His voice is smooth, like the bourbon he sips. "I don't fucking mind."

It's like he knew exactly what I was doing and timed it with precision.

A smile dances on my lips as I consider his invitation. "Would you watch?"

He picks up the bottle, pressing it to his lips as I slide my fingers between my thighs. I gasp, feeling how wet I am. My mouth falls open, and breaths escape me as I carefully work my clit.

"Carlee," he growls as my breathing increases.

"I really was thinking about you," I confess.

He needs to see what he does to me.

I'll bury it all again when the sun rises.

My breasts rise and fall, and every muscle in my body tenses. I'm right back to being suspended in air. At any second, I'll lose myself to thoughts of him.

"So, so close," I hiss, knowing I need this more than I need air.

"Come for me like a good fucking girl," he demands.

"Weston," I whisper as ecstasy washes through me. It's like I unraveled on his command.

I come so hard that I don't recognize the cries releasing from my throat. I cover my mouth, knowing my walls are paper thin, loving how he's watching me. It brought soloing to a new level. My eyes open, and I'm in a haze as he stares back at me.

Neither of us says a word.

"I told you to never say my name like that again," he mutters dangerously with hooded eyes.

"I'm not sorry," I offer, drunk on thoughts of him. "Did you need something?"

"No, I just had a hunch, and I was right. Taste yourself for me. Tomorrow, things have to go back to how they were before tonight."

"Of course," I tell him, still trying to gain control.

"Sweet dreams, Firefly."

"Good night."

I reach over, tapping the screen to end the call, closing my eyes as my heavy thoughts press down on me. I feel like I've slipped into a dream world and I don't want to awaken.

Did I really just do that? Yes, I did, but I have no regrets.

Now, tomorrow might be a different story.

11

WESTON

Six Days Later

I nearly survived the week without texting Carlee once.

Happy fucking Friday.

Five nights have passed, and we've not had one conversation. She also hasn't posted on LuxLeaks. The sabbatical continues. Meanwhile, more blind items about me have been shared.

A voice memo that I'd sent Lena years ago was passed around publicly. She's trying to spin the *secret girlfriend* rumor like we're back together, and the trashy gossip magazines have presented old images of us like it's new information. Shady as fuck.

I'm aware that Carlee is keeping up with the Calloways. She always is.

I pull on my warmest winter gear and venture into Central Park. The chill air nips at my cheeks, but snow isn't falling, so I take advantage. The scent of damp earth reminds me why I chose the penthouse on Billionaires' Row—for location alone. In the summer, the lush greens and towering trees make me feel less like I'm swimming in a sea of concrete.

The city has my heart, but the great outdoors owns my soul. It's why I love to travel.

My thoughts spiral, without pause, replaying every moment from last weekend like a movie stuck on repeat. The laughter, the side-glances, and the undeniable chemistry still linger in my mind, reminding me of what could be—or maybe what *should* be.

What would've happened had I not stopped us from going any further? The possibility of falling in love with Carlee is intoxicating, a real fantasy.

With every stride forward, I try to grasp the tangled web of emotions brewing inside me. My anxiety mingles with exhilaration, and it's a constant push-and-pull.

I don't know if I can love someone again, but I'd try for her.

A bicyclist zooms past me, pulling me from thoughts I shouldn't be thinking anyway. I breathe in deeply, focusing on the brief warmth from the winter sun peeking from behind the clouds.

Carlee's buried deep under my fucking skin. Jogging usually clears my mind, but clarity eludes me as I push westward through the park.

We shouldn't have crossed that line.

I shouldn't have kissed her.

I need a vacation, an escape to the middle of nowhere. Adventure calls.

I turn on some music, trying to drown out the intrusive camera clicks of the paparazzi, capturing every move I make as I continue down the path. I keep my eyes down, not meeting anyone who passes me.

All week, I've been followed. Easton is growing exhausted by it because he can't go anywhere without being bombarded. He hates the attention.

It's not the spotlight or large groups of people that haunt me. It's silence, intermingling with the fear of being alone.

I quicken my pace, letting my legs carry me forward. Running is my refuge. Each step an escape, and it forces the world to fade away. Or at least, it usually does. Kissing Carlee has become my Roman Empire, and thoughts of her invade my mind like a thief in the night.

We pushed our boundaries too far, and our relationship will be defined by what we do now.

Embers sizzle beneath the surface between us, and I haven't felt the same since that night.

The impulse to text her nearly takes hold, but I keep my restraint intact. I know her strategy too well. I've used it before, but I can't believe it's working on me. Maybe I'm obsessed with the chase too.

The forbiddance of *we shouldn't* tugs at me. Maybe we fucking should?

My phone buzzes when I'm fifteen minutes from home, and I blindly answer.

"Calloway," I say, breathless, pushing myself harder.

"Hi, *Calloway*. It's your favorite little sister. Ugh, what are you doing?" Billie's cheerful voice cuts through my exhaustion.

My week has been hell.

"Running," I mumble.

"Thank God." She huffs. "Didn't want to catch you with your secret girlfriend."

I ignore her.

"What do you want?" I snap, frustration edging into my tone.

"I need a brunch buddy so I don't look like a total loser. Harper canceled at the last minute because of an unscheduled business meeting. I'm at the deli around the corner."

I glance at my watch. "Is fifteen minutes okay?"

"Yep. See you soon."

The call ends.

I make it there in ten.

The warm air is a welcome relief when I enter the building. I catch sight of Billie, and she waves. Her dark hair is an immaculate bob, not a single hair out of place. Her blue eyes are obscured by oversized sunglasses that shield half of her face. The white baseball cap with our family's diamond corporation logo embroidered across the top makes her unmissable. I smile, and my little sister beams back. She's hiding her identity, but it's unmistakably her.

"Oh, I almost didn't recognize you," I sarcastically tell her.

"Shut up," she says, greeting me with a tight hug. "You always eat the same thing, right?"

I nod.

"Good. Save our spot. I almost had to fight someone for that booth." She strides confidently to the front, where she grabs a bottle of water and tosses it my way before ordering.

I'm aware of the women staring at me across the room. I glance up from my phone and grin at one of them. She nearly faints.

I down half the bottle in a few gulps. Without wasting another second, I navigate to the gossip site where the blind items are posted. My name isn't on the update yet, but I know it's only a matter of time, considering people speculated it was me in the comments.

Billie returns with a receipt between her fingers. Her eyes flick over my shoulder. "What are you looking at?"

"Just staying informed."

I shoot her a glance as she slides across from me. Her expression is a blend of skepticism and intrigue.

She smirks. "So, who is she? When do I get to meet her?"

"Who?"

"The woman you've not introduced to your friends or family," she says. "The one you're going to marry?"

My brows furrow. "Please tell me that's not what's being said now. It's all fabricated," I explain, keeping my voice low as I lean in. "Someone's stirring up trouble, trying to get a rise out of Lena. And when I find out who it is, I'm going to fuck them up."

I flash a sweet smile, but she knows I'm not kidding. This is digital warfare.

Her brows knit together in concern. "I hope you *never* find them then. That sounds like a one-way ticket to a prison cell. I don't think orange is your color," she says, shaking her head.

Since she's a fashionista, her word carries weight, and I know better than to argue.

"I'll keep that in mind." I chuckle.

"You seem different today," she says, watching me. "What's up?"

"I've had a hard week. Just tired."

"Or you're in the lovesick phase of your cycle. Easton gets in a grumpy mood at this stage too."

I smirk, wondering if she's right. Easton *does* have a cycle. Is it possible that ours is the same? We're more alike than not.

"Absolutely not."

"I'm so intrigued. Will you at least allow me to guess who it is?" she prods, leaning forward, her eyes alight with excitement. "Then you can confirm if it's true or not."

"Order for Billie!" a voice calls out from the counter.

"I'll get it!" I singsong, eager to escape the intensity of our conversation.

As I grab our food, I take the time to get my mind right. Billie is my sister and one of my closest allies, and she can read me like a book just as easily as Easton can, which is both comforting and unnerving. When one of us is in love, we act a certain way, and I'm concerned she's picked up on it.

I return to the booth, our baskets in hand, and glance at her expectantly.

"Tell me," she whispers.

"Carlee," I mutter, barely able to keep my voice steady.

"I knew it." She claps her hands together and draws unneeded attention to us.

I glance around. The women have pulled out their cell phones, and they're recording us. I'm aware this will end up on the internet.

"Stop looking at me like that. People are videoing."

"I don't care," she says, cutting into her avocado toast with a sharp knife. "I'm going to savor this moment of you falling madly in love."

"Fuck off," I mutter. I take a satisfying bite of my smoked salmon and cream cheese bagel, the flavors mingling in my mouth. "We're just friends," I assure her, the words slipping from my lips with a touch more confidence than I feel.

I shoot another woman a wink, and her cheeks immediately blush.

My sister turns and glances at her, then back to me. "Do you have to flirt everywhere we go?"

"It's called being friendly."

"Mmhmm. And that's exactly what got you into this secret relationship, right? Your charm and friendliness." She rolls her eyes.

"Don't act like you're not as bad as me, little sis. I've heard about your rendezvous."

Her cheeks heat, but her lips stay in a firm line.

I lean closer, lowering my voice to a conspiratorial whisper. "Do you think Easton could've posted the first blind item?"

She narrows her eyes, then laughs. "Easton? Why would he do that?" she asks.

I sigh. "It feels personal."

"Maybe Carlee posted it?"

My brows pinch together. "I didn't consider that."

Billie doesn't know Carlee is behind LuxLeaks. It's best no one else ever finds out.

"How well do you know her? Is she a safe person?" Billie asks.

I glance around, wary of prying ears lurking nearby. "She's Lexi's best friend. She can be trusted."

"You're positive she's not clout chasing?" my sister asks.

"I know her heart. She's not like that," I say.

I've learned everything I could about Carlee. Connections—it's so fucking nice having them.

My sister's gaze sharpens. "I saw you together in passing at my Halloween party."

"She doesn't want the attention."

"But you do." She's curious. "You're setting up the board. Stacking the odds in your favor."

The corners of my mouth lift. Maybe I am.

"Everyone will talk about the two of you. Is that what you want?" Her brow arches. Skepticism is written all over her face.

"I want to live my life," I say, somewhat defensive.

"Have you kissed?" she asks.

"I'm not having this conversation." I'm growing agitated because she's too nosy.

"You have," she whispers, giddy. "Please tell me you felt a spark. Did you?"

I glare at her.

"Why won't she date you?" she throws out bluntly, raising a brow.

A hearty laugh escapes me. "Come on. Give me more credit than that. I'm not Easton."

"It's plausible!" she counters, challenging me to refute it.

I shake my head, amusement dancing in my eyes. "No, it's not. I can have *anyone* I want. We both know that," I say, taking a bite of my food, happy for the sustenance.

"There's a reason why you can't have her—I can tell. Plus, Easton says you've been an asshole all week," she insists, her eyes glimmering with knowing. "You had dinner with her on Saturday after Naomi, right?"

I lower my voice. "Have you ever thought that maybe I'm just not ready for a relationship? Everyone seems to forget that I was married for three years, lied to for most of it, manipulated to the point of isolation away from my family, and emotionally abused. Not to mention everything else that happened toward the end. Maybe I just want to be friends, and that's it. Is it that difficult for you to understand? Please just let me live my life. No one else is."

She pushed too hard.

Her smile fades, and she removes her gigantic sunglasses. "I'm so sorry, Weston. I wasn't trying to—"

I clear my throat, diverting the conversation. "No need to apologize. How are things with you?"

Her smile widens, but I can see the cracks beneath it.

"I'm living the American dream," she says brightly, but she's lying.

My sister's company is struggling, but she won't admit it to me. Her Calloway stubbornness keeps her from asking for the help she needs, even though she knows I could single-handedly untangle any mess she's in. And I would for her.

"You're lying." I study her, and concern rises.

"I've got it under control. If I need your help, I'll ask for it," she replies, brushing off my unease with a wave of her hand.

"Don't act proud," I warn.

"I'm not, I promise," she urges.

"Okay, well, keep that same energy when the topic shifts to my dating life or friendships," I say, my tone light, yet a thread of seriousness weaves through my words.

She takes a sip of water, eyeing me thoughtfully.

Billie looks so much like our mom right now that I smile. Our mother was a famous supermodel in the '90s and married a billionaire whose wealth could buy empires. Then, twenty years later, she was traded in for a younger model ... *literally.*

My father is another reason I worry about my future relationships. Maybe I'm just following in his footsteps.

My parents' toxic relationship and my father's useless cheating were in the headlines my entire life. His divorce was covered like it was a reality television show. Now, the same toxic spotlight is on me and mine.

"Is there something you want to share?" I ask.

"No," she replies, a mystery swirling in her tone. "What about you?"

"Nope," I respond.

We share a knowing smile, a fleeting moment of connection, even in our tangled truths.

"I saw what Lena was doing," she says, her voice laced with disdain.

"It's old pictures and voice memos. Divorcing her has been a never-ending nightmare," I reply, forcing a smile that doesn't quite reach my eyes. "I'm meeting with my lawyer this week, and I'll be making my final offer."

"This is why we begged you to sign a prenup."

I shake my head, frustration knotting my stomach. "I was an idiot in love who never thought I'd find myself in a divorce, you know? When I married her, I thought it would be forever."

Her eyes are full of empathy, but then she folds her arms, bracing herself for my next words. "No one lik—"

"I don't want to hear how no one liked her, all right? I'm fully aware."

"Sorry, big bro. I hate this for you."

"Me too," I mutter, glancing at the floor. "She wants the house in Malibu, the one in the Hamptons, the penthouse in Cozy Creek, and a private jet. Oh, and half of my inheritance because I wouldn't have gotten it without marrying her."

Her expression shifts, disbelief transforming into outrage. "She's always been so greedy."

"A tiger never changes its stripes," I reply, bitterness creeping into my voice. "Lena can go fuck herself. If she were on fire, I wouldn't bother pissing on her." I give a sarcastic smile, but it's hollow. "I'm formally requesting that she drop the Calloway name immediately. I'm tired of her using it as a VIP pass and disrespecting our family."

"Good for you. Enough about that demon. I want to know more about your *friendship* with Carlee. How long have you been hanging out? Is this recent?"

Almost a year.

"Stop prying unless you want me to dig deep into your company's financials like I'm doing an audit." I instinctively lower my voice.

She rolls her eyes. "Dig all you want. You won't find anything but healthy accounting and billion-dollar projections." The confidence in her voice draws me in, but her eyes give her away. They always do.

I've shared enough laughs and secrets with her best friend and business partner, Harper, to know that's not reality. I'm trying very hard not to get involved, but I won't allow my little sister to fail either. It's not an option.

I finish my bagel, my fingertips smudged with cream cheese. I wipe my lips and my hands on a napkin, then lean back in the booth.

"What are your plans for today?" she asks.

"I don't have any. I took a mental health day," I reply with a shrug.

"Want to join me for pickleball?" she offers, excitement lighting up her features.

I'm happy to have the invitation and distraction.

A smile creeps across my face. "Am I taking Harper's place in your planned excursions?"

She laughs, a sound full of joy. "We planned to play pickleball for two hours, and then I scheduled hot stone massages at one. Pretty please?"

I shake my head, pretending to consider it, but she knows it's an instant yes. I try to say yes to everything my siblings invite me to after ignoring them while I was married. I'm making up for lost time.

"You'd better be glad I like you."

"What are you talking about? You love me!" she quips back, her grin infectious.

"Because I'm your favorite brother?"

She smiles. "Don't tell Easton."

We step outside and begin our stroll down the sidewalk.

The camera clicks fill the air, and Billie smirks, shaking her head. "Looks like we're dealing with this today?"

I chuckle, covering my mouth so no one reads my lips. "You knew that. Otherwise, you wouldn't have worn your Billie Calloway *costume.*"

Billie smirks knowingly when we enter the private fitness club. "You're *never* just friends with women. Why her?"

"She's different," I explain. A knot of confusion tightens in my heart.

"Oh, let me guess. She's not like the other girls," Billie says as we scan in.

"She's not. She's intelligent, and she can hold meaningful conversations without judgment. Her sense of humor matches mine, and she doesn't take my shit—*ever.* She keeps me humble."

Billie's grin is infectious as we grab our rackets and a ball. The two of us step onto the private court and stretch.

"You're *in love* with her," she says seriously.

"Billie—"

"And it scares you," she adds, and my heart races at the thought. "That's what this is really about."

I let out a heavy breath.

"I'm going to invite her and Lexi to hang out with me soon," she singsongs, bouncing the ball a few times.

"Why?"

"I need to get to know the woman you plan to marry. Make sure she's good enough to be my sister-in-law."

I groan, "You're really annoying."

"I always will be. But then again, what are little sisters for?"

"Being a gigantic pain in my ass."

"You're right," she says right before she serves the ball.

EXHAUSTION HANGS HEAVY ON MY SHOULDERS AFTER A LONG, unplanned day with Billie. It's nearly dinnertime, and I want a cozy evening with a bottle of bourbon, shitty TV, and a blazing fire.

As I walk into the foyer of The Park, I spot Lexi. She looks stunning in a flowy dress that dances around her knees, her makeup accentuating the sparkle in her eyes.

"Are you busy tonight?" she asks, looking me up and down.

I'm still in my running gear, gloves and all.

"I'm free. Need something?"

"You should go to Obsidian around eight."

"Why?" I ask, half joking.

Obsidian is one of the bars I own in Midtown, but I don't think Lexi knows that. My ownership is cloaked behind layers of limited liability corporations. It's a protection put in place to those who might snoop. Those who need to know it's mine do.

"I can't say. Just trust me," she offers, glancing down at her phone. "Anyway, I have to meet Easton. You know how he gets about being on time." With a wave, she rushes away.

I step into the elevator, my thoughts racing, and I text Easton to see what he's heard.

WESTON

Any idea why Lexi suggested I be at Obsidian tonight?

I own several upscale clubs around town—Diamond, Obsidian, and Quartz. Each venue boasts a distinct atmosphere with a dress code tailored to meet the vibes.

I entered the nightlife scene while reveling in my bachelor days, yearning for a taste of excitement. Obsidian, in particular, is a casual hookup haven for twenty- and thirty-somethings. Most inside is intentionally black with golden accents—right down to the toilet paper and shot glasses. It's a place to find yourself, but blend in. The dress code? Black.

In contrast, my pub, Hidden Gem, sits snugly by New York University, featuring a different microbrew weekly and an acoustic night every Wednesday. It effortlessly draws in the college crowd.

At last, my phone buzzes, and I see my brother's name. Took him forever.

EASTON

Carlee.

WESTON

What would you do?

He has always been the logical one, and I have a feeling he knows more than I do because of Lexi. I've always been known to take more risks, even if I know the odds.

EASTON

I won't get involved until you admit there is something going on.

WESTON

We're just friends. That's it. Nothing more. There will be TONS of signs if it's anything other than that. Okay?

EASTON

This text conversation is your sign. Idiot. 😊

I actually laugh.

WESTON

Rude fuck.

EASTON

If I had feelings for her and learned she was meeting her ex, who was the love of her life, at one of MY goddamn clubs, I'd make my presence very fucking known without apology.

As much as I hate to admit it, he's right.

WESTON

Want to switch places?

EASTON

If I wasn't on my way to dinner with my beautiful wife, I'd be in. The things I'd ask ...

WESTON

You couldn't handle her responses to the questions you'd ask, little bro. Trust me.

I'm fifty-five seconds older than him, and I don't ever let him live it down.

EASTON

Listen, Carlee is a genuinely good person, and she deserves happiness as much as you do, so don't fucking destroy her, Weston. Got it? You won't survive each other.

WESTON

I'm aware.

EASTON

Also was SHOCKED to learn you went on a date together last weekend.

I read his text, wondering how he knew. Maybe Carlee told him. If so, that's proof that she's been thinking about me, as I suspected.

WESTON

It wasn't a date.

EASTON

Bullshit. It was Ambrosia, Weston. You don't have dinner with "friends" there. It was a bold statement. Even Carlee knows that. Having a drink with Naomi first was clever though. Always hiding in plain sight.

WESTON

I thought so too. What else did she say?

I'm enjoying this candid conversation too much.

EASTON

You swam. Drank too much bourbon. And then she tried to take advantage of you, but you were a perfect gentleman and respected her. She's extremely embarrassed. Said she doesn't know if she'll ever be able to look you in the eye. She could barely talk to me. It was awkward as fuck!

WESTON

Hilarious.

I send the message, swallowing hard.

EASTON

Don't play games.

WESTON

I'm not.

EASTON

Watching this unfold is frustrating.

WESTON

Oh, like you and Lexi were any better. Give me a break. I think you're even more annoying now, Daddy.

I tease him every chance I get, but it's just fun and games. I love that Easton and Lexi are going to be parents. My brother will be an incredible, attentive dad, and I can't wait to be an uncle. It's still a secret, but they're almost ready to announce the pregnancy. Lexi won't be able to hide it much longer.

WESTON

I'm very happy for you. Jealous but happy.

EASTON

Thanks. Thrilled to almost have my brother back.

WESTON

Trying.

EASTON

Don't forget who you are and what you survived. I support whatever decision you make, okay?

WESTON

Thanks for the pep talk. We really are JUST friends though.

EASTON

Yeah, and I only wanted Lexi as my "fake" wife.

I walk into my penthouse and hop into the shower.

As the warm water washes over me, I try to decide what to do.

To go to Obsidian or not to go? That is the question.

12

CARLEE

As I wait to gain entry, the familiar pulse of music thumps through my veins, and I'm brought back to my early twenties. I remember what it was like to experience the city for the first time. It was invigorating, and I felt free. Those were the good ole days, when I was young and naive about how the world worked. It's been years since I've been to a club. Based on the line of people wrapped around the block, the crowd hasn't aged any.

Once I'm at the door, the big, burly bouncer checks my ID. I look past him at the vibrant lights flashing inside. The guy eyes me with a shit-eating grin—a confirmation that I've still got it. With a casual flick of his wrist, he waves me in like I'm the chosen one. No cover charge tonight—pretty girls never pay.

The night is alive with possibility, and I'm ready to embrace it. Lexi talked to me for two hours, and her voice soothed me as I hyperventilated about seeing Samson again. But I need to meet him.

Everything had felt right the last time we were together, but that was nearly seven years ago. We shared an incredible night that's bittersweetly etched into my memory. I thought he was going to propose, but he didn't. Two months later, we broke up and never talked again. Closure wasn't something I had been given. Now I don't need it.

Obsidian swallows me whole. Every inch of it, from floor to ceiling, is covered in different shades of black.

The skintight minidress hugs my every curve while the patent leather heels give me several inches. It's confidence I need. The all black dress code is required to gain entry, so everything inside is a part of the experience, including the guests.

As I step onto the dance floor, several heads turn, focusing on me. I make eye contact and grin at a few hotties as the pulsating lights flicker. If I wanted, I could take any of them home with me. I'm single, and this is the type of place where one mingles. Obsidian has a reputation.

I move through the crowd and catch glances of couples lost with one another, kissing and dancing. I take in my surroundings, knowing this will be my first and last visit.

When the crowd parts, I see Samson leaning casually against the polished wood bar, wearing a tailored black button-up and sleek slacks. I freeze, taking him in, almost disbelieving he's here.

Once upon a time, I begged him to visit me and even offered to buy his plane ticket. But his job always seemed to cage him, locking him away from us.

Gathering my courage, I glide toward him as the rhythm of the music pounds beneath my feet. We meet eye to eye, and the world narrows to just the two of us.

I smile as good memories replay in the back of my mind.

Time heals wounds, but I'll never forget how he tossed me to the side. A part of me wants revenge for him hardening me, and the other part wants closure. I should've told him no, but curiosity always gets the best of me.

In the end, that might be my demise.

"Leelee," he whispers.

A thrill rushes through me as he wraps me in a hug. It's the nickname everyone from my hometown calls me. It's one I haven't heard in a very long time.

"You haven't changed a bit," he quips in his charming Southern accent. His eyes hold the remnants of a connection we once shared.

He pulls out a stool for me, and I sit.

The truth is, I have changed—*because of him*—but I keep it to myself.

"The facial hair suits you. Have you been working out?"

I can't help but notice how fit he is. Clearly, he's taken care of himself, and time has been good to him.

"Yeah, but don't let it fool you. I'm hot-girl fit." He chuckles, his laughter warm. "Ask me to run a mile, and I might die."

My laugh blends with the club's vibrant energy. "I'll keep that in mind. How have things been at home?"

"Everything is still the same."

"I'm sure. Seeing you reminds me that I need to call and check in."

"They miss you," he says. "I still get asked about you sometimes."

"Really?" It shouldn't surprise me.

We were best friends before we were lovers, and I thought he'd be my husband.

The familiar scent of his cologne transports me back to those reckless days when our love flowed endlessly. The version of me who believed love was never-ending is long gone, replaced by a guarded and skeptical heart that can't settle but wants to.

Samson's two years older than me—the boy I crushed on throughout my freshman year in high school. I would have given him my virginity back then, but he treated me with kid gloves because he was best friends with my cousin Lucas. Everything changed the summer I came home from college. The dorms were being renovated, so I stayed with my mom for three months. That's when Samson and I fell in love under the big, open sky.

"This almost feels like a dream," he admits.

"It is weird," I tell him. "I always thought about what I'd ask you if we ever met up again. Even now, with the opportunity present, no questions form."

"It's that awkward part of the night when things are weird. We'll move past it," he says as my gaze trails along the rough scruff that lines his jaw.

I chuckle. "I think I need a drink."

"Wait, let me guess. A cosmo?" he asks.

"Extra-dirty martini with extra olives," I tell him. "No longer a cosmo girlie."

"Of course you aren't," he responds and orders two from the bartender. "I'm following your lead."

"That's dangerous," I offer.

"I'm aware." His brows lift. "You're a bad influence."

I scoff. "Please. Me, the bad influence?"

"Absolutely. You always get what you want."

"That's not true," I tell him. "I didn't get you."

"Carlee," he says, "I'm so fucking sorry."

"I know, and it's fine," I say. I twirl in the chair, my eyes drifting across the room. "Water under the bridge and all that. I wasn't ready to get married then."

The perimeter is filled with standing tables. Colorful lights dapple the space, revealing the club's second floor, where a woman is losing herself in a passionate embrace on the balcony.

Lucky her. I wonder how many of us would like to trade places.

"Have you ever been here before?" Samson asks, his voice low, intent.

"No." My thoughts trail off as his gaze roams over me.

"Obsidian has quite the reputation," I explain. "It's very ... risqué."

His curiosity is evident. "Like what?"

"It's known for finding random hookups and threesomes," I

continue. A smirk touches my lips. "Most people come here in search of a really good time. That's about it."

At the top of the stairs sits a private suite with deep black windows shrouding its secrets. But as vibrant flashes of light cascade through the open space, I catch the ghostly outline of a man standing, watching.

Our drinks slide across the polished bar top like a promise. I grasp my glass, tilting it back, welcoming the gin to wash through me. My mind wanders, and I turn my attention back to Samson.

His gaze locks on to me, and his smile falters, concern flickering in his dark eyes. "I'm so sorry. I didn't kn—"

I cut him off with a laugh, the sound carefree. "It's not a big deal. Everyone here is a consenting adult. Honestly, I've always been curious about it. Obsidian just isn't a venue for a date on a Friday night. Unless you're into sharing."

"We can leave," he offers. "There's a coffee shop just around the corner."

I chuckle, shaking my head. "We're already here. Might as well see where the night takes us, right?"

We sip our martinis.

"Fill me in. What's happening in your life?" he asks, leaning in a little closer.

"Where to begin?" I muse. "I'm still working at the hotel, trying to snatch up as many hours as I can. Living alone, navigating the dating scene when I find spare time. I've got a fantastic group of friends, and honestly, life is great. How about you?"

His smile warms me. "I'm really happy to hear that. Not much has changed. I'm working from home now and just bought a house right off the county road. Funny enough, it's close to your family's farm."

"Really? Congratulations! The Mueller place?" I ask.

"Yes, that's the one."

"Incredible. Thrilled for you," I exclaim, taking a sip of my drink. The saltiness dances on my tongue as I sway gently to the music. "How's your sister doing?"

Samson and Holiday are twins and were inseparable until she began traveling a lot after culinary school. She's one of the best pastry chefs in the United States.

"Holiday's great. Did you hear she got engaged? He's a chef too. Not my favorite person, but they're good together. I'm excited for her," he says, a hint of pride in his voice.

"I had no idea she was dating anyone. Wow, that's amazing. Please send her my best wishes!" The news brings a smile to my face.

She's the same age as Lucas, who *hates* her.

"Want to dance?" He laughs. "Like old times?"

"Sure." I grin, pulling him toward the center of the room as we venture into the unknown together.

Laughter bubbles up between us as I place his hands on my hips. The warmth of his palms sends a friendly jolt of nostalgia through me. Can't remember the last time I danced with anyone. A couple beside us are lost in their own rhythm, bodies moving in sync with the thumping dance remix overhead.

"Are you seeing anyone?" Sam asks. His breath tickles down my neck.

"Not regularly. You?" I spin around, flipping my hair over my shoulder.

"No. I've missed you," he admits, sincerity threading through his voice.

"You chose your fate, Sam," I murmur, glancing around as if the music might drown out his confession.

"Can it be changed?" he asks as I face him. His mouth is dangerously close to mine.

"I don't know," I admit.

Then I kiss him, needing to feel if there's anything left between us. As our lips crash together, I expect a flood of emotions. The kiss deepens, and he tastes like nothing more than old memories. Purely platonic. I pull away and stare at him.

He smiles. "Nothing has changed."

"Sam," I whisper, "*a lot* has changed."

The song crescendos to a close, and he gently guides me back to the bar, where I order water. I don't even have a buzz, which is probably for the best. It's a reminder that I need to tread carefully before I lose myself in the night and do something I might regret later.

"You didn't feel anything," he says.

We loved each other for three years; he knows I can't fake it.

"Maybe I need another try?" I turn to face him, meet his eyes, and kiss him again. I place my hand on his cheek, our tongues slide together, and then I replay kissing Weston. Our second kiss was a confirmation for him. I pull away as realization strikes.

He grins. "How about that time?"

"No," I exhale, shaking my head. I expected to feel something, and even prepared myself for it. I'm shocked. "Nothing. I'm so sorry."

"Are you Carlee?" the bartender asks as two water bottles slide toward us.

I chuckle. "Yes. Sorry, do I know you?"

"The owner has invited you to his private suite," he replies, pushing a golden ticket toward me.

"The owner?" No one knows who owns this bar.

"Is he really a prince?" I ask, knowing the rumors surrounding this establishment. The bartender laughs, but I continue, "Some have even called him Batman because so much crime stopped once the clubs were strategically placed around the city. His identity has always stayed hidden."

"You're right," the bartender explains. "And you're being given the opportunity to meet him."

Intrigue and caution twist in my stomach. "Is my date allowed to join me?"

"No. Only *you*," he responds, his tone serious. He sets a packet of paperwork in front of me. "Sign here, and you'll be granted full access. This is a *huge* honor."

I glance down at the document. "Is this an NDA?"

"Yes," the bartender says, handing me a pen.

I suck in a deep breath and read every page, happy I only had one drink. It's a normal document, and I hesitate before I sign my name on the glittery line that reflects light.

Sam's grin widens, but I can see the hurt in his eyes. "Go on. At least then tonight won't have been a complete waste."

"It's not a waste. I've enjoyed talking to you," I tell him, knowing his ego is bruised.

"Okay," he says. "Maybe being friends is all that was meant for us."

"We were always better friends than lovers," I remind him. "I did love you though."

"You'll always hold a special place in my heart," he confesses.

"I wouldn't hesitate too much longer," the bartender interrupts as indecision hangs in the air.

"Go," Sam says, shooing me away.

"When I return, I'll be your wingman, like old times," I tell him, waggling my brows.

"Deal. You used to always tell me no regrets," he says.

When he smiles at me like that, it stirs up a wave of nostalgia for lazy afternoons spent with him, and suddenly, I miss my family fiercely. I glance down at the golden ticket in my hand. Its embossed letters catch the dim light, as if whispering secrets meant only for me.

"No regrets," I say, needing to know who's on the other side of that smoky glass wall.

This could be the scoop of a lifetime for LuxLeaks. I'll finally solve the mystery that many have wondered about for nearly twenty years.

"Don't leave until I return, okay? Try to have fun. Meet

someone. There are plenty of single ladies here, but please wait for me."

"I will. You have my word," Sam replies, sincerity etched in his features.

"That way." The bartender points toward a private elevator at the back of the room.

My nerves take hold, but I saunter over to the two enormous bodyguards, built like professional athletes. They stand by the elevator; their imposing presence makes my heart race. As I approach, one of the guards steps forward, and I hand over my pass.

Is this a mistake?

The other nods and ushers me into the elevator.

I quickly text Lexi.

> CARLEE
>
> If I go missing, I'm still at Obsidian. Okay?

Lexi immediately sends me a text back.

> LEXI
>
> Why would you go missing?

> CARLEE
>
> I'll fill you in when I leave.

> LEXI
>
> You're worrying me!

> CARLEE
>
> I'm fine. The night was a bust with Sam. You were right. PER USUAL.

She calls me, and I reject it immediately.

"Hi," I say to the giant standing next to me, attempting to sound casual. "Do you escort women up here often?"

He shakes his head, but his lips remain sealed. I glance at my phone, realizing time is slipping away like grains of sand.

The tension in my chest doesn't ease as the black doors glide open. It's disorienting, knowing how loud it was in the club and how quiet it is on this floor.

"Are the walls soundproof?" I ask as I freak myself out. What if I scream in here? Will anyone hear me?

The guy ignores me.

I'm led down a short hallway, and lanterns with flickering flames hang above. My heels click rhythmically against the marble floor, echoing in the stillness. As I approach, another guard waits at the entrance.

The door opens, and I step inside alone.

The space is stunning and luxurious without being overwhelming. It's classic and simple. The glow from low-lit lamps creates an intimate atmosphere. The glass walls are crystal clear, and I can see everything from here.

A fireplace blazes in the corner, and an L-shaped couch faces it. The glow of the flame fills the room. That's when I notice a man with broad shoulders in a nicely fitted suit, sipping a glass of something, his back toward me.

He clears his throat and waves me forward. I take a few steps, ready to see the face of the man who's secretly made a difference in the city.

"Hi," I say. "I'm ..."

As Weston fucking Calloway meets my gaze, the world around me fades away. My mouth falls open, and he smirks, placing that bourbon glass against his perfect lips. Goose bumps trail over me as I meet his eyes.

"Is this a joke?" I whisper.

He sets down his glass and then moves toward me.

Weston grabs my hand and twirls me around before stepping back to get a proper look at me. I take him in, dressed in black from head to toe with diamond cuff links and rings. He's devilish and tempting, and I'm half convinced I'm dreaming.

"Fucking gorgeous," he mutters.

"You can thank Lex," I whisper.

"I have a lot to thank her for."

At six-two, he looms above me, his blue eyes glimmering like sapphires beneath the lights. I can't pull my gaze from him. This is a tidal lock.

"I'm highly concerned you took this invitation. What if I wasn't sitting up here and it was someone else?" he asks, crossing his arms over his chest.

"Depends on what he looked like," I say, smirking.

He narrows his eyes. "I learned something new about you tonight."

"Yes?" I ask.

"You have a *very* distinct type."

A laugh bubbles out of me. "Suits. It's *never* changed."

"We both know it's *more* than clothes. Tall. Fit. Blue eyes. Brown hair. Older than you. With a sense of style."

"That's the physical aspect of it. Now list the things that aren't obvious," I urge. "If you know me so well, there should be no issue."

He stares at me for a long while before he smiles.

"You want a man who wants you just as you are. He has to be kind but also not afraid to tell someone to fuck off, even if that someone is you. He needs to be able to laugh and make jokes but also take accountability when wrong. When you speak, he needs to listen but also hear you. You want experience over materialistic things, even though you like to be pampered sometimes. He also has to be really fucking smart. Much smarter than you."

My heart rapidly races. I open my mouth, then close it.

"I pay attention," he says.

My phone buzzes. I see Lexi's name flash on the screen, and so does Weston.

"I texted Lexi just in case the owner was some pervert and decided to kidnap me or something."

"Ah." He smiles. "She told me to be here."

"Guess *someone* is taking this matchmaking thing seriously."

I meet his eyes, remembering last week, and I lose my words. My thoughts are tumbling in confusion. Weston has that effect on me, pulling me into his orbit with his gravitational force.

I study his mouth, watching his tongue dart to lick his lips. My internal temperature rises as something bubbles beneath the surface.

"Are you okay?" he asks, noticing my demeanor change. "How many drinks have you had?"

"Not enough, clearly."

He leads me to the couch with him, and we sit. It's not lost on me that we're completely alone.

"About last weekend," I mutter.

"It was just two friends hanging out and having fun. That's it," he muses with a glint in his eye. "How'd it go with Samson? You seemed happy."

Looks can be deceiving.

"Were you watching me again?" I ask, my brow popping upward.

Weston sits back, his eyes burning into me. "Friends don't let their friends refuck their *shitty* exes, Carlee. If the roles were reversed, I'd expect you to do the same."

My brows furrow. "You are not cockblocking me tonight. That would be two weekends in a row."

"Yes, I am," he admits. "I think it will be my new hobby."

I stand. "I do not need any more big brothers to lord over me. I already have two, Weston. Mind your business."

He grabs my wrist, gently pulling me toward him. I fall onto his lap, and our faces are too close. The air is heavy as he tucks hair behind my ear, grinning as he twirls a strand around his fingers. It plays out like a movie.

"Don't go," he nearly begs, and I almost see him physically lowering the barriers between us.

I study him, keeping my hands to myself. "Why didn't you text me this week?"

"I needed time," he admits, swallowing hard.

I whisper, "I thought you were mad at me for—"

"No. Never," he says, chuckling. Leaning in, he whispers in my ear, "Watching you come was so fucking sexy."

His gaze darkens, and his breathing increases as I move even closer.

His lips part, and I wait for him to tell me to stop.

"Can I?" I whisper.

"Yes."

His fingers thread through my hair, and I gently paint his lips with mine, needing to taste the smoky bourbon on his tongue.

At first, we're gentle, but it immediately grows desperate. My world spins, and I cannot believe we're right back where we were. The pin drops, and we quickly lose control. I inch up my skirt, straddling him, feeling his thick cock below me.

"Fuck," he whispers against my throat as his mouth slides down my neck. His hands snake under my ass, and he growls against my skin, "No fucking panties."

"Just in case," I whisper, reaching for his belt.

Weston allows me to take control.

"There's no undoing this," he says as I unbutton and unzip his pants.

"I know," I say, seeing how hard he is.

His cock strains against the fabric, and I gently glide my palm against him. He groans out, the sound low and deep in his throat. It's so fucking sexy.

My mouth falls open in surprise.

"It'll fit," he murmurs.

I reach forward, ready to expose him, and he finally grabs my wrist to stop me. I narrow my eyes, somehow knowing he wouldn't allow this to go all the way. He never does.

"We need to discuss things first," he says, his eyes defiant.

"Can we talk *afterward?*"

He zips and buttons his pants, but I can still feel how thick he is below me.

"Never agree to the terms before hearing them."

"I trust you," I say, rocking against him again.

"You shouldn't," he warns, steadying me by placing his hands on my hips.

"I want as little or as much of yourself that you can give, Weston. There's no pressure with me. If you want to just be friends, fine. But it would be a whole lot more fun if we were fuck buddies too. Clearly, we're compatible," I say.

I think I feel him pulse beneath me.

"You deserve more than what I can give," he whispers.

"Isn't that my decision to make? I'm a grown-ass woman, and I know what I can and cannot handle, whether it be in a friendship, a situationship, or a relationship. I know what I want. Do you?" I narrow my eyes.

He places his hands behind his head as I continue straddling him. It feels like time stands still as a smile spreads across his lips. "I don't know what parts of myself I can give you. I'm still figuring that out."

"I just want to keep the ones I have right now," I explain. "I don't want anything more from you other than this. And maybe getting dicked down a couple of times per week. It's really that simple."

He chuckles, meeting my eyes.

I place my arms on his shoulders and twirl the hair on the back of his head. "The truth is, I don't know if I can commit to anything else. I'm fucked up too. I haven't loved someone for seven years, Weston. I don't know if I can."

"I feel the same," he admits. "I want to fall in love."

I smile. "Of course. So do I. But we don't get to make that decision. It either happens or it doesn't. Why not have fun while we search?" I lean in and whisper into his ear, knowing he's still hard below me, "If you say no this time, I'll *never* bring this up again. Now or never."

He wraps his arms around me, and his fingers trail along the back of my neck, causing goose bumps.

"Tell me the rules." Weston kisses my bare shoulder and up my neck.

"You say it like it's a game."

"But we're still playing, aren't we?" he asks, causing my heart to palpitate.

He grinds into me, creating more friction underneath me. I rock my bare pussy against him, feeling the warmth pool in the pit of my stomach.

I moan in his ear, enjoying the sensation of him below me. Weston knows what he does to me.

He runs his fingers through my hair. "You want to be friends who fuck?"

"Yes," I hiss out, feeling the orgasm build. "I want you as you are, Weston. Nothing else. No falling in love. Just this."

He grabs my ass, assisting me as I drive into him, wishing his pants were off. Wishing he were buried deep inside me.

"Your rules," he says in a deep gruff.

"We're just friends." My muscles tighten, and I know I'll unravel soon.

"I want exclusive sex," he says, grabbing my hips. "If your pussy is mine, it's mine. I don't fucking share."

"Okay," I tell him, panting, needing to feel more of him. "We should both still date other people," I add as he slides my dress down, exposing my bare breast.

He captures my nipple in his mouth.

"And if we find someone we want to pursue seriously?" he asks.

"Then we stop and pretend like it never happened," I say as he moves his hand between my legs, brushing his fingers gently across my clit.

"Treat you like an affair?" he asks.

"Fuck yes," I say as he slides one finger inside, and it's followed by another.

"Like my dirty little slut?"

"Fuck," I scream out with pleasure as his fingers curl inside of me.

"I live for moments like this with you, when you push things too far." He traces his lips along my skin.

I'm on the brink of losing myself on his fingers, and he slows his pace, not giving me what I want.

"No falling in love, Wes. We can't," I whisper.

My fingers thrust through his hair, and I think I see stars when he lays me down on my back. Weston kisses down my stomach, until he's perched between my legs.

"If that's what you want," he says, kissing my inner thigh before placing his mouth directly on my clit.

At first, I'm almost too self-conscious, but then heat pools down below. The orgasm builds quickly, and I don't recognize the sound that releases from my throat when he gently returns his fingers inside me. I sink down onto him as he brings them in and out of me. It's an out-of-body experience.

I'm high on him.

"So fucking wet for me," he whispers against my pussy, working me so fucking good that I don't know what planet I'm on.

"Always," I admit, rocking against his face.

He quickly memorizes my body, knowing exactly what I like.

"Mmm. Will you come for me?" he says, buried between my legs.

It's almost too much—the pleasure, the pure euphoria.

I look down at him with defiance in my eyes. "No. Pfft."

"Liar."

He continues to devour me like I'm his last meal, and I moan out.

I steady myself, my breathing increasing, knowing that I'm not as strong as I act, not when it feels so fucking good.

13

WESTON

"I'm in control of this pretty little pussy now. *Not you*," I growl out.

"Fine," she gasps out, her breath shaky as I take my time, driving her to the edge with my tongue.

Carlee enjoys every intoxicating second. Her thighs quiver, yet I hold her suspended, right on the brink of pure ecstasy.

Mmm. My new favorite flavor.

The sweetness of her skin dances on my tongue. Her desperate desire pulls me deeper into this heady whirlwind of passion with her.

Should we be doing this?

Probably not, but I don't have any fucks left to give.

Her back arches off the couch—a silent plea for more. The cool leather beneath her contrasts the heat radiating from her body. The tension between us is electric, and it wraps around me, nearly choking me as I enjoy her pussy. I can't stop, not until she loses herself.

"Weston," she moans.

My name escaping her sends a ripple through me. She rocks against me, her body full of anticipation. Fingers weave through my hair as she pulls me closer, anchoring me to her as if I might float away. She's hungry for me and full of desperation.

"I've fantasized about this," she admits breathlessly, her cheeks flushed.

"Making dreams come true," I say, working her back up, savoring how her body instinctively melts into my touch.

I drive her further to the edge, pulling away when her breathing nearly stops. I want her to know who's in control from now on.

The fire between us threatens to consume us both. At the rate things are moving, we'll soon be ash.

"Please," she whimpers.

"I love to hear you beg for me," I say, teasing her clit.

"Please, Wes. *Please let me fucking come*," she urges, and I can hear the anguish and need in her voice.

"You want it?" I ask, returning to that tight little bundle of nerves.

Her pussy clenches against my fingers. Her muscles constrict in response. She's standing on the edge, ready to jump, wanting to fall.

"Yes," she says in a sultry whisper.

"Come for me."

As I command her, she shatters around my fingers and on my tongue. I continue to caress her, gentle yet deliberate, allowing her to savor every wave of pleasure. She moans out her release, and something stirs deep inside of me.

"Yes, yes," she whispers, unable to finish her sentence.

Watching her body collapse is a beautiful fucking sight to see. She's breathless, her eyes sealed tight as she sucks in ragged breaths. Eventually, she sits up, her hair a wild mess and her lips swollen. She's glowing. Her aura is fucking beautiful, like the remnants of lingering sunshine at the twilight.

"That was …" A smirk graces her lips as she radiates with newfound confidence.

"Especially when you *begged* to come." I draw my fingers to my mouth, relishing her taste, the sweetness lingering on my tongue. "I already crave more of you."

"I've never ..." Carlee hesitates, weighing her next words carefully, a hint of vulnerability creeping back in. "I've never let anyone go down on me before."

"I'm your first? I fucking love that for me." I lean in closer, genuinely intrigued.

"No one ever took the initiative, and I was too shy to ask." The raw honesty in her voice does something to me.

"And? Five out of five stars? Highly recommend?" I rub my thumb across her bottom lip, ready to kiss her.

"Great service. Very attentive. Incredible atmosphere. It might have been my first time, but I would come again." She shoots me a wink.

"What I love to hear." I grin. "I want to know your wildest fantasies."

Her brow arches. "Like ... *sexual?*"

"*All* of them," I reply, watching intently as she readjusts her dress.

A delicate mix of shyness and excitement dances in her eyes. She draws me closer.

"It's your homework, so I can make your dreams come true."

"My genie in a bottle." She smirks. "Hate to break it to you, though. As of right now, you've kinda already done that."

"You're too easy to please," I say, tucking a loose strand of hair behind her ear, my fingers lingering a heartbeat longer than necessary, savoring the smell of her vanilla skin.

Her genuine happiness lights up the room, illuminating every corner with joy. My mission is to keep her just like this. Forever.

Before she can respond, a knock breaks the intimate ambience, sending a ripple of unease through the air.

"Do I look guilty?" she asks, brushing her hair back nervously, an uncertain smile twitching at her lips.

"Own it," I reply, discreetly adjusting myself, trying to mask the feelings overwhelming me.

Carlee scoots to the opposite end of the couch, wearing a playful pout.

Another knock disrupts us, and I know our intimate moment is over. They're always fleeting.

"Come in," I bark, my tone sharp.

Seconds later, the door clicks open, and Brody steps into the room, his presence an unwelcome interruption.

His eyes widen at the sight of Carlee, shock flashing across his features before he shifts his gaze to me.

"Can I help you?" I arch an eyebrow, curiosity mingling with irritation.

"I'm here," he says, glaring at me like I'm the inconvenience.

"*Obviously.* What do you need?" I look at him as if he's lost his mind, frustration bubbling.

"Ah," he exhales as he glances between us. "Easton's a bastard."

"Explain," I say, confused.

"He told me you needed my help," Brody says, his suspicion lingers like smoke. "Looks like he was mistaken."

Brody doesn't really know what's happening between us. No one does. Just us. And I'll continue to keep her a secret and call the shots. Speculation is one thing, but I'm confirming nothing.

I let out a breath, trying to mask the truth. "I'm not sure what you'd have interrupted. I've told him and everyone else today that we're just friends."

I glance at Carlee, searching for affirmation, hoping she will back me up.

"Yeah, that's weird. We're really just friends. But me and you could be a different story ..." she says, waggling her brows.

Brody rolls his eyes.

She offers him a flirty smile as she rises from the sofa. The light makes her glow like a fucking goddess.

"Anyway, I need to get back to my date. Thanks for revealing your secret identity to me, Batman."

With a wink, she glides toward the door, leaving me both amused and bewildered, along with a cocktail of other emotions.

As the door clicks shut behind her, Brody crosses his arms over his chest. "Care to explain this? Because it seems like you two were fucking."

"We're just friends," I say, the words familiar. "She's literally on a date with her ex right now."

"Why are you here if she's on a date?" he questions.

"Am I on fucking trial? Jesus, now you sound like *my* ex."

Skepticism is etched across his features. "You're transparent."

"I'm living my life," I state, following him across the room as Carlee's presence still lingers.

He stares at me for a long time. "I hope you know what you're doing."

"Goodbye, dear cousin," I say, opening the door and escorting him out. It closes with a click.

The last thirty minutes played out like a dream, and I can still taste her on my tongue.

What reckless agreement did we forge in the heat of the moment?

I turn to the wall of windows, seeking distraction in the panoramic view of the club. Music pounds below my feet, lights shimmering like stars plucked from the night sky, as an energetic sea of sex and sin fills the air.

In a crowd of unfamiliar faces, my gaze zeroes in on her.

She glides past a guy who runs his hand along her waist. My heart races and protectiveness takes over. My fist clenches at the thought of anyone touching her. But there's satisfaction in knowing that she's mine, even if temporarily.

She finds Samson, and I can't read his expression as he says something to her. She laughs, waving him off. I'm not ready for the night to end, not yet.

I whip out my phone, and my fingers fly across the keys.

WESTON

Leave with me.

The screen lights up her face, and a smile spreads across her lips. I'm entranced by her.

CARLEE

Where are we going?

WESTON

Anywhere but here.

CARLEE

Can I have five minutes?

WESTON

Absolutely. I'll meet you by the elevators.

The thought of spending more time with her rushes through me. I fill my bourbon glass and slam it back, the amber liquid burning my throat as excitement claws at my insides.

Carlee smiles as she continues chatting with Samson. They exchange a quick hug, and she lingers a second longer before walking away, wearing an expression of hope.

It's over between them. That's clear.

Relief floods through me. I *knew* she needed this confirmation. Fuck, so did I.

That's why I called in a favor.

That's why Samson is here.

It was a risk for me, knowing I could've lost her to him, but I had a hunch I wouldn't.

Now that she knows it's over, maybe *we* can finally move forward.

I'm ready to win this game and conquer the internal war waging within me.

The ultimate prize? Her.

We both need to learn how to love again. It's another risk, but it's one I'll take for her.

"THERE YOU ARE," SHE EXCLAIMS, HER VOICE SEDUCTIVE AS SHE STEPS into view.

I'm exactly where I said I'd be.

She's my friend, my greatest temptation, my ultimate secret.

"Ready?" I ask, my hand settling gently on the small of her back, guiding her toward the exit.

The simple touch sends a ripple of goose bumps across her skin, and I love how I affect her.

"You're sure about leaving together?" Her smile widens, our secret dancing in her eyes. "There will be cameras. The speculation and rumors will begin immediately."

I meet her gaze, feeling a pull deeper than I'm used to.

"We're just friends," I assure her, but her eyes linger for a heartbeat too long. "Would you prefer to wait? I'll happily—"

"No," she replies, shaking her head with a quiet determination. "I'm trusting you, Weston. You know how to play this game. I only write about it. At least, I used to."

"Are you sure?" I ask, knowing this is the right choice, one that will allow us freedom we don't currently have. I want to travel with her and experience life.

"Positive," she says, smiling back at me as we step into the unknown together.

The cool winter air is full of possibilities.

"Good girl," I mutter against the shell of her ear as the doors slide open.

A flurry of cameras flashes, and the brightness is blinding.

Carlee keeps her head down, and I gently guide her toward the car. A few people rush us, and a guy nearly knocks over Carlee.

I step forward, pushing him. "Watch where you're fucking going," I say.

I hold on to her, protecting her.

People scream my name. Several ask who's with me.

She slides in the car first, and I settle in beside her. The door thuds shut with finality.

"Are you okay? I'm so sorry. I didn't expect that many cameras," I explain. The weight of the attention presses in on us. "This is a circus."

"I'm not used to that," she murmurs, watching me. "How do you deal with this?"

"I learned to drown it out like white noise. I pretend it's a part of the scenery and try to act like they're invisible until they cross the line."

Her smile breaks through the tension. "I'm okay. You don't want people to think you have anger issues. So many are waiting for you to fuck up, Wes."

"If someone is rough with you and disrespects you, violence will be the answer. I have boundaries, and that's one of them," I state, my anger increasing. "Unacceptable. It makes me fucking feral."

She turns to me, her red lips curving into an inviting smile. "That's kinda hot."

"I'm not kidding."

The car lurches into motion.

"Oh, I know you're not," she says. "But we might as well protect your image while you're playing puppet master with your life. Please do not become a PR nightmare with me by your side. Everyone will call me a bad influence," she explains. "Tons of people are already not going to accept me."

"Because you're pretty, and they want to be you," I say, and she tries to hold back a smile.

"That's what you believe?" she asks.

"That's what I know. Anyway, are you hungry? Because I haven't eaten since brunch with Billie," I confess, meeting her heated gaze and lowering my voice. "You don't count."

Her smile spreads, radiant and infectious. "I'm starving."

My stomach growls, punctuating her words. It's loud enough for her to hear. "Do you like pancakes?"

"Love them," she replies, laughter escaping her lips, filling the limousine with ease. It's so easy being with her like this. "Coffee is a requirement though."

"I know the perfect spot," I say, pulling out my phone to text the driver, shielded from the outside world for just a little longer.

As the car makes a turn, her phone buzzes. The light from the screen casts a glow across her face, and I glance at the contact. It's Lexi.

"Sorry, I have to text her back, or she'll send a search party," she says, her voice tinged with amusement.

I smirk, leaning in a bit closer. "What are you going to tell her?"

She glances at me, the corners of her mouth twitching. "What are you telling your brother? Our stories need to be the same."

"We're just friends," I repeat, locking my gaze with hers as a sly smile curls her lips, "who fuck."

She scoffs. "Actually, we haven't *yet*."

"Smart-ass," I retort, leaning in to capture her lips, the warmth and sweetness igniting a familiar fire between us. "Do I need to change that right now?"

"I wish you would," she breathes, her voice barely above a whisper, her breath quickening as I slide closer, gravity pulling me into the space between her legs.

I smirk, teasing her. "Then what would you have left to anticipate?"

I could take her right here before we reach my favorite diner. I can hear her desperate breaths and how she instantly responds to me.

"Oh my God, Weston! You're *still* cockblocking me."

I force myself back into my seat, adjusting my tuxedo with a grin. "I'm here to please *you*. You're my focus. So are your wants, your needs, your desires, and your innermost fantasies. I'm determined to make every single one of them come true while we *enhance* our friendship."

Her smile reveals something deeper. "And what about wishes money can't buy?"

"Oh, babe, I'm fulfilling those too."

"Cocky." She bites her bottom lip. Electricity crackles between us. "But don't ever change."

"Don't plan on it." My heart jumps as her green eyes hold mine, steadying the whirlwind inside me.

I want her; I crave her.

"You're perfect just the way you are," she encourages, a quiet sincerity framing her words. She means it.

"I don't deserve you," I say, feeling so fucking lucky to be living in this lifetime with her.

"You're wrong." The conviction in her voice is fierce, full of her truths.

Despite the fractures in my heart, she sees light lurking in the shadows that haunt me. I've been truthful, fully showing her the raw parts of myself, wanting her to understand who I am now. I don't feel like the man she's written about on her blog, but she reminds me that I *am* him.

This divorce reshaped me, and I find myself wishing, more than anything, that I'd never met Lena. In my experience, it *is* better to have never loved at all. Had I met Carlee earlier, she'd have gotten all of me, the me before my heart was wrecked. It's one of my only regrets in life.

"Are you okay?" Carlee asks, her voice laced with concern as the limo glides to a stop in front of the diner.

"Yeah," I tell her, summoning a smile that feels more like a mask. "Just lost in thought."

"Stay in the moment with me." She lightly bumps her shoulder into mine. "It's a lot more fun here, I promise."

"You're right," I admit. As I shift my focus to her, tension melts from my shoulders. "Thanks for saving me from that torture again."

"I could say the same about you, especially tonight," she replies, her fingers gently squeezing mine just as the car door swings open. "Now, come on. Let's go be little piggies together."

I can't help but laugh. "I hope you never change either."

"I'm kinda set in my ways," she replies.

I want to kiss her, but it's not safe. In public, we have to play it safe.

She steps onto the sidewalk that has a mound of snow shoveled to the side. The neon sign of the diner flickers like a bright invitation. When we enter, the smells of bacon and freshly brewed coffee fill the air. Carlee's eyes light up at the sight of the checkered floor and old jukebox by the entrance. It's packed with familiar faces, but they're not friends or foes, just humans who share a space and food with me sometimes.

"Hey, Weston," Millie, one of the waitresses, says over her shoulder as we stand by the front counter. "Your booth is open. Help yourself."

She nods across the room, and I take Carlee's finger, leading her to my favorite table that gives a view of the street, but blocks me from being photographed by paps.

"You're a regular here?" she asks, glancing around. "Didn't know this was your type of hangout."

"You're going to learn a lot more about me, bestie," I mumble, and her eyes flash with delight.

Two coffees slide across the table, along with a bowl of cream.

Laminated menus are set in front of us, and Carlee's eyes widen. "You weren't kidding."

"Give us a minute," I tell Millie. "Too many choices."

She glances between us and gives me a wink.

Carlee's eyes flicker upward, meeting mine as I sip my black coffee.

"Stop eye-fucking me," I mutter.

She laughs. "Or what? Going to spank me?"

"Would you like that?" I ask.

"I'd be willing to try anything once," she says.

My eyes narrow on her. "You'd better check yourself when we're around our friends. The bedroom eyes? *Too much.*"

"Bedroom eyes?" She laughs. "Come on, Weston. I look at everyone like this."

"I hope to fuck you don't," I state.

She chuckles, adding a cream and a sugar to her coffee. "You're exactly where I want you."

It's almost as if she knows I'm already wrapped around her pretty little finger—have been for months.

"Funny, because you're exactly where I want you to be as well," I admit.

A wave of excitement crashes over me, and it feels like a new beginning, a new era of me, of us.

She licks her lips. The sexual tension is almost too much.

As I look into her eyes, wishing I could read her mind, I wonder if our endgame is the same.

Maybe, somehow, we'll both win.

14

CARLEE

I'm convinced this diner fell out of a Hollywood movie set with its checkered floor, vinyl record machine, and vintage decor. The walls are stained with nicotine, and I can only imagine the conversations that have happened at this table over a cup of coffee. It's busier than I expected, but that's perfect. It reminds me of a restaurant back home.

"What would you recommend?" I scan the menu, flicking my eyes upward to meet his deep blues.

He hasn't touched his but instead sips his coffee while watching me. "What are you in the mood for?"

I chew on the corner of my lip. "What I want isn't listed."

That smirk I adore so damn much appears on his lips.

"Don't start." It comes out like a growl, and my body betrays me.

"You started it. I was on a date," I mutter, my eyes flicking down to his hot mouth, which was buried between my legs an hour earlier.

"Hmm. If I recall, *you* started it by taking advantage of me when I was intoxicated, shoving your tongue down my throat. Give credit where credit is due. Tonight, I ended it."

Cocky bastard.

"How do *we* end, Weston?"

"We don't. *Ever,*" he confidently states, "bestie."

"I like the thought of that. However, it sounds like a commitment, and you know how I feel about that." My body is on fire, which always happens when he looks at me like that.

The server approaches and steals our attention as she smacks her bright pink gum. She glances between us, and her lips turn up into a wide smile. "Weston, you did well."

"Of course I did," he says.

Flirty is his style.

"What can I get you, sweetheart?" she asks.

Her rockabilly vibe is complete with a pinned-up hairdo. She's a tattooed grandma. The button pinned to her apron says as much.

"How many grandkids do you have?" I politely ask.

She smiles, pulling out her cell phone to show me her screen. On it are three blonde-haired little girls with ringlets wearing bright pink dresses.

"They're sisters. Sweet kids. My little pride and joys. They look just like my daughter."

I grin, feeling love radiating from her. "They're so precious."

"Thank you, honey. Thanks for asking. Weston usually does. Guess you beat him to it tonight."

I glance at him, knowing him. Of course he'd ask personal questions about her family and check in. Being personable is part of his charm.

"Now, do you need more time to peruse the menu?"

"Oh, I'd like scrambled eggs with cheese, a side of crispy bacon, and a small stack of strawberry pancakes, please." I hand her the laminated menu, which has at least fifty different items listed on each side—from steak to Belgian waffles to eggs Benedict.

"Got it," she says, writing it down with a grin. "A woman who knows what she wants without hesitation. I like that."

I'm not sure if she's talking to me or Weston. She focuses on him, but he's still watching me.

"And what about you, little Calloway?" she asks, trying to peel his attention away.

"The usual." Nonchalance coats his tone.

When he glances at her, she waggles her brows.

I wait until we're alone before speaking. "What was that about?"

He sips his coffee.

"No one has ever eaten here with me other than Easton. Not even when I was married. Millie has been here for forty-seven years and has watched me grow up. I used to call her my aunt. This place is like home. No matter what happens in the world or to me, it doesn't change." There's a touch of vulnerability behind his casual tone.

A million questions form on the tip of my tongue.

I stir my coffee and then take a sip as he continues, "It was one of my grandfather's favorites. When I was home from boarding school as a teenager, I'd sneak off and meet him here in the middle of the night. We kept it a tradition until he passed away. Now, I come here when I think about him or if I want a decent breakfast late at night." It's almost as if he's living in the memory.

This is a side of him I hope to see more of.

"Thank you. I'm truly honored you brought me here." I reach across the table and gently brush my finger against his.

His smile reaches his eyes, and he seems comfortable and relaxed.

"But ... why *me*?"

"Why *not*?" he asks.

"I'm not talking about the diner."

"I'm not either. You appreciate *it* for what it is and nothing more." His gaze bores into me as he drinks more coffee. "I don't have many regrets, but not meeting you sooner is one of them. You'd have gotten a different version of me. The version you deserve."

"What if I want *this* version?" I ask, challenging him. "The version of you who's been *humbled* by love."

His face cracks into a smile, and he chuckles.

"We can't change the past. We can only heal and learn, which takes time and perspective. On the bright side, when you find love again, you'll probably appreciate the little things more. Or at least, that's what I tell myself," I offer.

"Does it make you feel better?" he asks.

"No." I laugh. "But one day, it will. When it's true."

"Thanks." He exhales.

"I also find it adorable that you believe I'd have befriended the old Weston. I wouldn't have. He was an overly flirty asshole who had a *huge* ego. Banged anything with legs. Total douche. Camera whore. Privileged and very spoiled."

He laughs. "Seems to me that nothing has changed."

"Not really." I shoot him a wink. "It worked out exactly how it was supposed to. The wrong time is sometimes right. I have no regrets when it comes to us."

"What did you say?" he asks.

"No regrets."

He carefully lifts the sleeve of his suit jacket, revealing the watch on his wrist. It's nothing extravagant, but it shines like a golden treasure under this light. He removes it and hands it to me.

I admire it. It's old but well taken care of. In the middle is the iconic Calloway Diamonds symbol—a diamond shape surrounded by a triangle. It's *identical* to the one Lexi stole from Easton. I flip it over and read the words engraved on the back.

The wrong time is sometimes right.

"Is this a magic trick?" I ask, reading the words I just spoke.

"A coincidence." He stares at me. "Did Easton tell you?"

"No, it's something my Mawmaw says," I whisper, shaking my head as a chill runs up my spine. "You'd like her, but Mawmaw would give you a run for your money."

"Guess it runs in the family?" He laughs. "My grandfather

believed his watches were *lucky*. I think it's total bullshit, considering the awful things that have happened to me while wearing it. However, Easton firmly believes it brought him and Lexi together."

I tilt my head at him, feeling its weight in my hand. "It was the *only* reason they met that day. Had I not witnessed it with my own eyes, I wouldn't have believed it either. The scenario was disastrous, and her actions weren't logical. That's the truth. I tried to talk her out of returning to his penthouse because it was getting out of hand, but there's no stopping her when she gets like that." I sigh, remembering how she was fired immediately after. Easton is why Lexi and I stopped working together at the W. "Wait, does it have a love spell on it or something?" I place the cool metal back in his hand.

He bursts into genuine laughter, and I enjoy it.

"What if it does? Guess you're destined to be mine now." He rolls his eyes. "Touch the watch, wear the ring."

My eyes widen. "Look, Lexi held Easton's watch for as long as I held yours. Maybe it's not lucky. Maybe it's actually *charmed*?"

"If that's the case, mine might be broken," he says, sliding the watch back onto his wrist.

"Have any of your exes touched it?" I ask.

"Lena did. You see how that worked out." His eyes are unfocused.

"Did it burn her skin and leave a scar?" I ask, snorting.

"I can't wait to tell Easton your adorable little theory."

I need to distract myself from my runaway thoughts.

"Our watches are identical, except for the inside. His says—"

"*Love is always on time,*" I finish. "I know. He's shoved that personal motto down my throat since I started hanging out with them."

"And what's your opinion on it?" he asks, the conversation humming with a carefree ease.

"It's a nice thought. I'm just a little upset that we can't choose *when* we fall in love. It chooses us. If I could snap my fingers and make it happen, I'd do it in a heartbeat."

I grab my coffee mug, holding it in my hands and feeling the warmth of the liquid inside. I shouldn't drink caffeine this late at night, considering I need to be up early for work, but the experience is worth it.

He shakes his head. "I call bullshit on that statement. Without the chase, you'd get bored. From zero to love in a snap? Nah. You like the journey too much, not the destination."

"I think it depends." I smile. "If I met someone and knew deep down that we'd be really, *really* good together and my heart wasn't cooperating, that's when I'd flip the switch. Usually, my heart and my brain don't get along. The men I shouldn't want, I do."

I shrug, and I almost imagine us. The thought vanishes faster than it arrived. I swallow hard, knowing that shouldn't happen without me being three martinis deep for the night.

"I've dated several genuinely nice guys. I wish I could've reciprocated how they felt, but I can't fake it. I might be alone forever." The realization haunts me.

Weston's eyes don't leave me as steam rises from my coffee. I pick it up and drink.

"You won't be alone forever. One day, you'll find your person and be really happy."

"So will you."

Unspoken words and unfinished thoughts swirl around us.

"I don't know." His voice drops to a whisper. "I wish things were different."

A smile dances on my lips. "I don't."

The confession hangs in the air, and I can feel my own defenses crumbling. We're just another couple in a crowded diner, yet somehow, it feels like we're the only ones in the room.

He opens his mouth to speak.

I shake my head, interrupting him. "I won't stop reminding you that you're a good person who deserves to find someone who loves you exactly as you are. And, oh my God, you're going to make whoever she is *so* happy that it'll be a thousand times *more* disgusting than Easton and Lexi. Wet, sloppy kisses and all. I've already ordered barf bags, so I'm ready," I say, knowing real love is what Weston wishes for. I hope he gets it. I'd love to see him happy again, but permanently. I lean against the pleated booth seat.

He doesn't respond, so I keep the conversation moving forward.

"There's a diner in my hometown that's similar to this. The owner wears ruby-red slippers. The food is incredible. Fresh pies are baked daily and sold by the slice at the front counter by the door. I kinda miss it. Her chicken salad sandwich on a croissant is to die for."

"We should visit," he suggests. "I love chicken salad sandwiches."

"With pineapple or without?" I ask. "This is very important. It might even demote your bestie status."

"Really? Without," he states without hesitation.

I make a face, then smile. "Right answer. My hometown is very different from here. Christmas is three hundred sixty-five days out of the year. If you dislike the holidays and all things Santa, you might want to avoid it."

"What about next week?"

"My mom would love that." I smile, imagining a surprise visit. There would be fanfare, especially with Weston joining me. "My family is a lot to handle. My brothers will probably try to murder you. My sister will try to sleep with you. My mother will ask when you're putting a ring on it. And Mawmaw? She might keep you for herself and turn you into her gardener, the one she's been fantasizing about since she turned seventy."

Weston's expression remains calm and collected; his relaxed demeanor grounds me. "Only one question: is your sister hot?"

"Asshole," I mutter, tossing a sugar packet at him. "But, yes, she's gorgeous. Intelligent. High maintenance. *Blonde.* She's exactly your type. Plus, she'll turn thirty-five next month, so not much of an age gap. But there's one kicker: she's been divorced twice."

His brows waggle. "Maybe the third time's a charm?"

"I'd join my brothers in murdering you if you got with my sister."

"And what about your dad?" he asks.

"Well …" I breathe deeply. "He's off living his best life with his other family—the one I didn't know existed until I was fifteen," I say bitterly, my heart tightening. "I have siblings I've never met."

"I'm sorry," he murmurs, his voice dropping to a comforting volume as he studies me.

"Daddy issues," I say, a smile breaking through my melancholy.

"Explains a lot," he replies with a chuckle before his expression turns serious. "Thank you for trusting me, Firefly."

I've only ever shared that with Lexi, and we hardly ever talk about it. But I find myself wanting to tell Weston everything I've kept from him. He deserves to know.

I catch myself staring at his lips, lost in his intensity. My body craves more of him already.

I'm addicted.

"We probably shouldn't kiss again," I whisper, half teasing, half serious.

"Are we renegotiating?" His eyes flick around the room before meeting mine again. "Because if so, I want you to start texting me first instead of forcing me to initiate every conversation we have."

I laugh as I lean in closer. "You're a *very* busy man."

"I'm *never* too busy for you."

"You shouldn't say things like that," I reply, my voice barely above a whisper as my heart does somersaults in my chest.

"I'll always speak my truths, and I won't hold that back."

"Your truths?" My cheeks flush as his words linger in the air, charged with unspoken intensity.

"Communication is my love language, bestie. Hearing from you is a highlight. You remind me there's a whole world beyond my own. Our friendship is my *freedom*."

The weight of his revelation settles between us.

"And I know you want to text me sometimes," he adds. "So, when you do, you should reach out to me. Stop pulling moves from the player's handbook."

"Hilarious, coming from you, considering you wrote it." I try to hold back a smile but fail. "But I'll see what I can do."

His gaze remains steady, unwavering. "You know, my grandfather believed he discovered the secret of happiness while running a billion-dollar company."

"Really?" I ask.

"He believed *love* could conquer all."

"Oh, so Pawpaw Calloway was a hopeless romantic too?" I inquire.

Weston rolls his eyes.

"What do you believe?" I study the curve of his jaw as a flicker of doubt appears in his sea-blue eyes.

He contemplates my question. "I don't know if love is necessarily the key. I used to believe it was, but now I think it's friendship that's actually needed. Love is fleeting. Friendship is forever."

I enjoy my coffee as much as the conversation. "With the right person, isn't it built on the same foundation? Some say friendship is the highest form of love. Maybe that's what you've been missing in your relationships. All the *f*'s—fun, friendship, and … well, you know. The true secret to happiness." I waggle my brows.

"Mmm." He tilts his head.

A blush creeps up my neck.

I need to change the subject.

Taking a gulp of coffee, I feel my heart rate increase. I clear my throat, bringing the conversation back to the original topic.

"If love is always on time and the wrong time is sometimes right, why the contract?" I ask.

To take over the family business, the Calloway brothers were required to be married before their fortieth birthday. Weston completed his obligation at thirty-six, and Easton did just months ago with Lexi. Divorce is never mentioned, as if his grandfather never considered it an option.

"He wanted us to spend time dating and not be married to our jobs. He knew that by forty, we'd be set in our ways and less willing to change our habits. And the older one becomes, the harder it is to find someone compatible."

My phone buzzes, and I see Lexi's name pop up. I unlock it and read her message.

> **LEXI**
>
> I thought you were going home. I know you're with Weston! WTF?!
>
> **LEXI**
>
> ALSO! WHEN WERE YOU GOING TO TELL ME YOU TWO HAD DINNER AT AMBROSIA? CARLEE!

I show Weston the screen, and he chuckles as another text comes in. I catch the flicker of his reaction as he reads. The corners of his mouth twitch into a grin, but tension tightens the line of his jaw.

I read the screenshot she sent.

It's a blind item.

Blind Item #20

Mr. Playboy Billionaire was spotted at a blacked-out bar where people go for hookups, but he left with the mystery woman he'd had dinner with the other night. Rumor has it that she's his secret girlfriend. He cannot keep her hidden forever. People are beginning to notice.

LEXI

THAT'S ABOUT YOU! AND YOU'D BETTER TELL
ME EVERYTHING. EVERYTHING! EVERYTHIIIII-
IIIIIIIIING.

LEXI

I KNEW YOU TWO WERE MADLY IN LOVE!

"Oh no. She's typing in caps and now convinced we're madly in love."

"I thought you had told her we left together and were having brinner," he says.

"Brinner?" I raise an eyebrow.

"Come on. Breakfast for dinner?"

"Millennials," I mutter. "No, I told her I wasn't being kidnapped by some weirdo club owner and was leaving."

"Ah, well, now you're fucked."

"Is that a promise?" I ask, lifting a brow.

My phone buzzes again, and as I glance down, he reaches forward and locks it, setting it on the table.

"Be in the moment with me, please. Don't look at it once until you get home, and I'll reward you." He winks.

"Ah, the things I'll do for a gold star. I'll play." My phone vibrates again and again, so I turn it off. Now I'm not even tempted. I smile wide.

"Good fucking girl," he mutters under his breath.

"When you say things like that ..."

I know Lexi is probably losing her mind, and I'll have to do damage control tomorrow.

Weston's phone starts vibrating. He chuckles, pulling it from his pocket and showing me the screen. It's Lexi.

"You're fucked too," I whisper.

"I can handle her," he says, turning off his phone. "Now, back to business. Based on my calculations, you have about two weeks before photos of your face are posted, along with your name. You should probably spend this time mentally preparing for everything that will be said about us." There's an edge of amusement in his tone.

"That's all?" My voice wavers.

"Unless some *rogue blogger* who's not on anyone's payroll decides to break the friendship story first." He points behind my shoulder. "Cameras are snapping photos of us right now at the street corner. They will capture everything to purposely make it look like we're dating."

Our eyes lock, and silence hangs between us.

"You can tell the truth and take control of the narrative before the rumors begin. Before they do background checks on you. Before they dig up all your exes and start interviewing them like they did to Lexi. Even if we're *just* friends," he finally says.

A lump forms in my throat. "But ..."

"You can still back out of this arrangement," he continues, leaning closer, his gaze pinning me in place. "You look so damn pretty."

My cheeks heat. "Right now?"

He nods. "Didn't stutter."

"I'm not backing out," I confirm as our fluffy pancakes, eggs, and bacon are sat onto the table, breaking our trance.

Steam rises from the plates, and my mouth waters in anticipation. As his coffee mug is refilled, I take a minute to gather my thoughts.

He ordered what I did, except his stack is topped with fresh blueberries and whipped cream.

"Want a bite? Sharing is caring," he offers.

I nod. "Do you care?"

"More than you'll ever know," he replies, pouring warm maple syrup over the tall stack. "However, when it comes to sharing? Not so fucking much." His eyes darken, and we both know he's not talking about pancakes.

Weston picks up his fork and knife; the diamond cuff links on his wrists sparkle like little stars as he precisely cuts off a perfect sliver for me. He leans forward and offers it, the fork hovering just inches from my lips with a sweet bite of his stack.

Our eye contact is electric. I open my mouth, and he slides the food inside.

It's too intense. But maybe I'm just under his spell, intoxicated by how he looks at me. Weston gently pulls the fork from between my lips, his brow raised in anticipation.

"Delicious," I exhale, my pulse racing, unprepared for how sensual this feels.

When I look at him, I see the quiet determination etched on his face—the desire to fit in, to savor the simplicity of a shared breakfast with a friend, and to live without the spotlight. Weston craves this.

How did I miss this?

He's polished in public and more secure with himself than his brother. Their personalities are gravely different, except when we're alone, and as he lets me in, I realize how similar they are.

I pick up my fork and dig into my eggs. They taste great, and my bacon is crispy, just how I like it. I didn't realize how hungry I was until now.

"A real question: Are you really an extrovert? Or is it an act?"

"It's not an act. I love being around people, but I love having private moments too," he replies, his gaze intentionally piercing mine. "How's your food?"

"It's so good that I think I want to try other things on the menu," I confess.

"We'll *come* together," he offers with a hint of mischief.

"I love the sound of that," I say, lowering my voice.

"I bet you fucking do." His messy hair makes him look impossibly charming as he casually digs into a plate of blueberry pancakes.

It's surreal, being with him like this—at ease when everything around us feels so charged.

I glance away, half wondering if I'm dreaming.

As we continue eating, the conversation flows easily between us like a sweet melody.

"What do we do if one of us falls in love?" I venture, half teasing but also serious.

"With someone else or each other?" He pauses, lifting his coffee cup to his lips, a thoughtful frown creasing his brow.

"I can't answer that question," I say. "Just love in general, I guess."

He sets his mug down. "If our friendship ever feels threatened, we hit pause."

"You're right, which is why I don't think we should cuddle or do relationship stuff."

He smirks. "So, cuddling and kissing are a weakness for you?"

"It's not fuck-buddy foreplay. I have to reserve some things for those who I date. Oh, I'd like to also put in a request that I get you when I want you, as long as you're free," I add to the terms and conditions, hoping he's taking note.

He chews on his lip. "That goes both ways then."

"Great. I think that covers everything I want. What about you? Ready to make the deal?" I ask, holding out my hand to shake on it.

"One more thing." Weston takes a deep breath, the weight of his words hanging in the air. "Quit your job."

I stare at him. "Weston, we've already discussed this."

He takes a sip of his coffee, his gaze unwavering. "It's not for me; it's for Lux. She needs you to return. Everyone does. I won't let you forget that."

I part my lips to respond, then pause. "And if I don't quit the W?"

"Deal is off the table then," he replies, his tone more serious now.

Anxiety stirs within me. Somehow, I knew it seemed too good to be true.

My brows squeeze together in confusion. "Over that?"

"Yes." A smile graces his lips. "I'm putting you first because you refuse to do so."

"I don't think I'm ready," I admit.

The stress of posting again nearly overwhelms me. I don't know why.

"If you stand on the edge of a cliff and wait until you're ready to base jump, you'll never make the leap. Sometimes, you have to just do it or be pushed. And considering how goddamn stubborn you are, I've moved to option two." He lowers his voice. "I'll be there to catch you, I promise. Every single time."

Emotions rise in my chest. "What if I want to quit writing?"

"Do you?" he asks. "If you do, I won't mention it again."

"No," I finally say.

"Because you know quitting is failing, and that's what you're ultimately afraid of. You've got this, babe. I'll give you forty-eight hours to decide if this is what you want." He lowers his voice. "And if not, know I'll never forget how fucking good you tasted."

I glare at him. "I can't believe you're serious."

"I can't believe it's not an automatic *yes*," he teases, though his smile dims. "I'll help make all your dreams come true if you let me. But you have to be really sure *this* is what you want. If not, we should stop while we can."

I suck in a deep breath. "Two days isn't necessary."

"Once the rumors start about us being in a relationship, even if we're not, your life will drastically change. You will no longer have time for the W." He pauses, giving me time to process what he means. "Everyone in my social circle will want to befriend you. Those who I call friends will try to sleep with you. Once you're fully welcomed in, you might not have time for me. Your itinerary will be full if you want it to be."

"I'll *always* have time for you, Weston," I say, reaching across the table to brush my fingertips against his.

The contact sparks something, as it usually does, and his breath catches.

"Forty-eight hours," he mutters.

I try to speak, but he interrupts me.

"I won't accept your answer, even if you have it. Please think about it for me. Crossing this line *will* change everything—for better or for worse. *You* have to be fully prepared to navigate both scenarios."

"And what about you?"

He smirks. "I'm living in my fuck around and find out era."

15

WESTON

After finishing our meals, I pay and tip Millie generously, as is my monthly tradition. As we stand to leave, she comes over, and we exchange a tight hug.

"Keeper," she murmurs, her voice just above a whisper as she gently pats my back.

The woman is like an honorary aunt to both me and Easton. In another life, she would have been our mother. That's a story for another day.

"Thanks." I pull away, grinning as I remember how much my grandfather adored her, recalling how she'd sneak me candy when I was a kid.

Millie meets Carlee's eyes. "I really hope to see you again."

"Absolutely," Carlee confirms with a friendly wave as I push open the door.

Millie gives me a thumbs-up.

Carlee steps outside and smiles at me over her shoulder. She's picture-perfect as the snow falls around her. It feels like a dream, and I wish I had the power to freeze time.

"Promise we'll visit again?" she asks as she climbs into the car. The heat is on, but she still shivers.

"Absolutely. You just say when," I confirm.

I shrug off my coat and hand it to her. She slides her arms inside and wears it backward.

Carlee inhales deeply, snuggling into the material that envelops her. "Thanks. Smells like you."

"What do I smell like?"

"Happiness," she admits. "With a dash of torture."

"Oh wow, thanks." I roll my eyes, but I realize I'm smiling and wonder if *this* is happiness.

Nothing in the world matters when we're together. Worry seems to fade away.

She leans across my lap to look out the window. We're way too close. "The snow is really coming down now. I thought it wasn't supposed to start until later tonight."

Flurries flutter sideways as we inch down the street. I place my hand on her lower back, taking in the view of *her*. Carlee molds herself against my body, and I know exactly what she's doing—teasing the fuck out of me, seeing how far she can push it.

"You're *so* warm," she says.

"Yeah, but the inside is still *ice cold*," I warn.

She glances up at me. "You can say shit like that to everyone else, but not me. If it makes you feel better to pretend you're dead inside, go for it. But I know that's not the truth, and I'll call you out every damn time."

I lean my head back on the seat and laugh. It rings through the car. "Keep me honest."

"That's what friends do. No one else is willing to tell you the truth. They're way too busy kissing the ground you walk on."

"Excuse me? Pretty sure you've met Easton. He's the most honest person I know—to a fault—and he calls my ass out on everything every chance he gets. So, don't tell me about honesty. I've lived with *that* my entire life."

"He's family. He doesn't count."

"I can handle the truth," I say, but her smile fades as she studies my mouth.

The air grows heavy as the intensity builds between us. It would be so fucking easy to run my fingers through her silky, dark hair and capture her lips.

I want to, but I won't.

"*No kissing,*" I whisper, recognizing *that* expression on her face. I know if she starts this, we won't stop. "Your rules."

"My rules kinda suck, don't they?"

I nod. "Yeah, they do."

Thankfully, she puts space between us before things get out of control. The road noise fills the car, and we ride in silence for at least fifteen minutes. It's so quiet that I think she might have fallen asleep, but she's watching flurries float in front of the streetlights.

Thoughts of our night and conversation fill my mind as her sweet scent of vanilla and cinnamon surrounds me.

"I might try to write this week," Carlee finally says, sitting upright and meeting my eyes. Her greens glimmer like emeralds.

"That makes me so damn happy to hear," I encourage.

"I'm still scared," she admits.

"Time to tell fear to fuck off. For many, the first sight of success is often followed by self-sabotage, and if I have to push you through it, I will. Every time. The world doesn't deserve your words, but damn, do they need them."

"You say it like you're my biggest fan."

A grin slides across my lips as she studies me. "I am."

"I think I'm yours too."

I arch a brow. "You *think?*"

She reaches toward me and tickles me, forcing laughter. I wiggle away, turning my body toward her.

"Keep fucking around, and you'll find out."

"Maybe I want to," she admits.

The car parks outside her apartment. Carlee gets out, and I check our surroundings as I follow her into the building.

Our footsteps and voices echo off the whitewashed walls as we take three flights of stairs. When we reach her door, she punches in the code and the knob clicks.

She looks at me with hooded eyes, wearing a sexy little smile. "Would you like to come in?"

I contemplate the question.

Yes. Fucking yes, I would.

It's what my heart says.

My brain is more logical.

"Thank you for the invitation, but I think it's best if I go," I say.

I lick my lips, remembering how she tasted on my tongue, and I step forward. Her back presses against the cool wood as she looks up into my eyes and grabs my tie.

I grin. It's a fucking dare, and, oh, how I want to play this dangerous game with her.

I lean in and whisper in her ear, "Tonight, you test-drove the car before you leased it. Two days. You can wait, so stop testing me. Because I know this is exactly what this is."

She gently sighs. *"Fine.* You still owe me a gold sticker." Carlee holds up her phone, which is still off.

I smile. "I'll make it worth your while."

"You already did."

I step away from her, and she removes my suit jacket. I slide it on, buttoning it. Her gaze doesn't leave me. As my hands fall to my sides, she steps forward and wraps her arms around my neck, and my hands snake around her waist. I hug her until *she* lets go, wanting to keep her in my arms for as long as possible. I'll never break away from her first.

"Good night, Weston," she says, and I repeat it to her before she pulls away. "Thank you."

"For what?"

"Being yourself and not pretending."

I shove my hands into my pockets, waiting for her to say something else or make a move. She lets out a ragged breath and nods, knowing the night is over. We're undoubtedly thinking the same thing, based on how she's perpetually eye-fucking my every move.

I finally smile. "Go inside, or we'll stare at one another until morning."

"I'm going inside, but *not* because you told me to," she says, opening the door and not looking back before closing it.

I breathe in deeply, my heart racing as I take the stairs two at a time.

My mind reels as I replay the last few hours. So much has happened in such a short amount of time. Our future is spread across the table, waiting for us to place our bets. The odds are stacked against us, but the heart always wins.

Her curiosity is the devil on her shoulder.

Should she start a situationship with me? Absolutely not.

Will she? Yes.

As I walk down the stoop of her apartment, snow falls heavier and sticks to the sidewalk. Before I climb into the car, I hear my name being called from above. I glance up to see Carlee standing at her window. Brown hair blows in the cool breeze, and I smile, grateful for a final glimpse of her.

Damn, she's so pretty.

"Weston, can you come back? Pretty please? Hurry." She sounds distraught as she glances over her shoulder.

I don't hesitate. I rush up the stairs until I see her waiting at her door, worry etched across her face.

"Is everything okay?" My heart pounds.

"Someone's been in my apartment," she says, shaking her head.

I place my hands on her shoulders. "How do you know?"

"My laptop is missing." Tears well in her eyes, and it nearly breaks me when they fall down her cheeks. "I kept saying I was going to back up everything, and I didn't finish doing it."

I've never seen her like this, and it's upsetting.

"I'm so, so sorry," I say, hating that this happened to her, especially after she mentioned writing again.

"I'm scared. What if they're still in there?" she asks, pulling away.

I brush away her tears with my thumbs. "I'll check for you."

"No." She shakes her head. "I don't want you to get hurt."

"Stay here," I tell her, entering.

Nothing looks out of place or destroyed. The yellow roses I got her last weekend are on the counter in several vases. Her place is cute and cozy, exactly what I expected. On the wall, a katana hangs, and I pull it from the sheath.

She stands at the doorway, watching me. Her eyes widen, and she shakes her head.

"There are knives," she whisper-hisses, pointing toward the kitchen.

I put my finger over my mouth. "Shh."

"Men," she mutters.

I place both hands on the grip, holding it tight. The silver edge reflects the light. As I stare at the bathroom door, a burst of adrenaline rushes through me. I twist the knob and push it open, seeing the closed curtain. Carefully but quickly, I pull it back, revealing nothing but shampoo bottles and …

I blink a few times.

Are those … *tentacles*?

"What the fuck?" I mutter.

"Are you okay?" she asks.

I grab the purple dildo and stand in the hallway, holding it in the air, smirking. "This is the only monster I found."

Laughter escapes her, and her face turns bright red as I set it on the counter.

"Will you pretty please check my room?" she asks.

I nudge the door open with my knee, sword back in place. My father insisted that Easton and I take fencing in boarding school. I can't wait to tell Easton I actually used those skills.

I move into her bedroom, noticing gorgeous paintings on the walls and sexy lingerie on the floor. I open her closet door and find nothing but clothes.

"You're clear," I tell her.

Carlee rushes inside, locking the door behind her. "Thank you."

I return to the living room and return the sword to its location, laughing that she even has it. "I'm not going to ask."

"I liked how it was pink," she admits. "And it came in handy. Can't wait to rub that in my brother's face. He told me I was dumb for buying it and that I'd never use it."

I shove my hands into my pockets. "Please check to make sure nothing else is missing."

"Okay," she says, nodding as she opens a drawer in her kitchen. She pulls out a bag of money.

"Is there anything on your laptop I need to know about?"

She shakes her head as if trying to remember. "There are photos and blog articles and ..." Her eyes widen.

"Carlee?"

She exhales, and I can feel her unease.

"Hey." I give her a smile. "Whatever it is, we'll navigate it together."

Her heart rate ticks fast in her neck. She's spiraling. "I made *videos* and took pictures for my exes. They're on my hard drive. Weston, what if they get out?" Carlee's voice strains and I see tears threatening to spill over, but she fights it.

"If that were released, I'd spend as much money and resources as needed to track them down and make them pay. Anything else?"

Her eyes unfocus. "Old articles and research I've done for the blog. Most of LuxLeaks' stuff is backed up. It's just personal things that aren't. Oh God. My journal. I might be sick."

I move her to the couch and sit beside her, sinking into the cushions.

"I think it's password-protected," she whispers, placing her face in her hands. "I think I closed it."

"What did you write about?"

She turns to me. *"Everything."*

"I don't know what that means," I admit.

"My deepest thoughts."

Carlee begins hyperventilating, and I grab her hand.

"Deep breaths, okay? Breathe in through your mouth until your lungs are full, then exhale through your nose. Do it with me," I say, remaining calm. It's the only thing that used to help me when I started to spiral.

I take her hands, opening them from the balled fists they're in, gliding my fingers over her palms. "If you tense your hands, your body believes you're in fight-or-flight mode. Relax. Unlock your jaw." I rub my thumb across her cheek, keeping my voice steady. "And if you smile, it tells your brain you're safe."

She blows out a deep breath and nods with a forced smile.

"You are safe," I whisper, running my fingers across her palms. "This will pass. We'll figure it out."

"Thank you," she finally says, sounding calmer than before.

We sit in silence for a few minutes before we try to speak at the same time.

"Go ahead," I tell her.

"Do you think it's safe to stay here?"

"No," I reply firmly.

"Where will I go?"

I can see her growing upset again.

"Wherever you want. I have a beautiful loft in Tribeca that's not being used, or you can stay with me at The Park. I can get you a room at any hotel in the city. Whatever you decide, I support it, but there's no way in hell I'll allow you to stay here until we find out who's responsible. They could come back."

She's in shock, and I know she's not thinking clearly.

"I need to make a few phone calls, and I need you to ensure nothing else is missing. Okay?"

"Yes," she says, standing. "Let me do that."

As Carlee moves to her bedroom, I immediately text Brody to fill him in on what's going on.

Five minutes later, Carlee approaches me with the jewelry I gifted her. "These were still here. Not touched."

I shake my head. "It was calculated, and if I'm being honest, that concerns me."

Worry covers her face. "Do you think someone found out I'm behind LuxLeaks?"

"I don't think so. Also, Brody is on his way."

"I don't know why anyone would do this. I don't have enemies," she whispers. "Everything was going so well."

I squeeze her shoulder. "I think the time has come for you to need protection."

"I feel so violated."

"I'm so sorry."

"Don't apologize. It's not your fault," she says.

I blink at her. "What if it is?"

"Is Lena capable of this?" she asks directly.

"Yes."

She sucks in a deep breath, staring at me. "Now I'm pissed."

"Please pack your things. I'm not leaving here without you," I confirm.

"Okay," she whispers. "Come with me?"

I nod, following her down the short hallway. I lean against the doorway as she sets her bag on the bed. Seeing her like this breaks my heart.

"So, this is where the magic happens," I say to her, repeating what she said to me the first time she was in my room. I need to lighten the mood and get her mind off things.

"Actually, yeah, lots," she admits with a laugh. "Especially with this wand," she says, opening the drawer to the nightstand next to her bed and pulling out a pink toy.

"Damn, girl. How many more do you have?"

She snickers. "Don't judge me. It's the only thing that's saved my sex life this year."

"As long as you're satisfied, that's all that matters," I say, studying the artwork on her wall. "Tell me about these."

She glances at the one above her bed. It's blue and red and fades into purple. "What do you see?"

I smile, moving closer to it and studying the piece. "It tells a story. At first, it's bright and new, and then it becomes more chaotic and aggressive, before blending into a solid. I'd assume it's a dance. When two become one."

She stares at me. "It's called *Falling in Love*. It tells a story of two becoming one. Wow, you're good at this. Cultured, I guess."

"Ah." I nod, smiling as my eyes scan the imagery.

It's a painting that I can almost hear, and I want to run my fingers across the texture of the paint on the canvas.

Carlee smiles warmly as she finishes adding clothes to her duffel. "I went to this art show in an abandoned building years ago. When I saw the painting, I wanted it because it moved me. I told the artist how much I loved it but how I could never afford the price. She let me make her an offer, which she accepted. She laughed and told me it was never about the money and how she'd rather give a piece of herself to those who appreciated its complexity." She grins as if reminiscing. "Some people see splatters, and other people see the meaning. That's art. Love it," she says.

"Who's the artist?" I ask.

"Ruby Bertrand."

I repeat the name, nodding and committing it to memory.

I gesture toward the other large painting on her wall. "And what about this one?"

"I found it at a random sidewalk art sale in the park. I carried it from Madison Square to here and placed it right there. It hasn't moved in four years."

"Fuck," I say, imagining her on the subway with this. The frame alone must weigh nearly forty pounds.

I tilt my head, admiring it. The forefront is full of trees with vibrant leaves in yellow, red, and burnt-orange shades. In the distance, there's a sunrise with a subtle hint of dew and fog. Anyone paying attention would know it's a sunrise, but for those who don't see the details, it's not.

"What do you think it represents?" she asks.

"Change," I say thoughtfully. "Growth. The trees are losing their leaves, starting over, becoming bare for the winter. The scattered leaves and their colors tell a story of renewal. And in the distance, above the hill, are greener pastures and blue skies. Above the hurdle is change. It represents finding comfort in new beginnings, leaving the old behind."

Carlee laughs. "Did you pull that from my thoughts?"

"Who painted it?" I ask.

She smiles widely. "I don't know. The woman at the park didn't either. I believe a name is scribbled on the back, but I could never decipher it and haven't moved it since I hung it on that nail. It's named *New Beginnings*."

"Why did you choose a gold frame?" I ask.

"I didn't. Whoever had it before me chose it. However, the frame is what initially drew my attention. It glinted in the sunlight, and I stopped to admire this absolute masterpiece. I nearly went broke, buying it, but it was worth it."

"How much did you pay?"

"Five hundred dollars," she says, zipping up her duffel. "I used the money I was saving for a plane ticket home. No regrets though. I ended up going a few months later. And this painting has given me years of happiness." Carlee stands beside me and smiles as she studies it. "It captures you, doesn't it?"

A chill runs up my spine.

"It does," I respond, but I think she knows I'm not referring to the painting.

16

CARLEE

On the ride to The Park, my palms grow sweaty, and fear takes over. My blood pumps faster, and my breathing increases.

It's plausible someone found out I was behind LuxLeaks, though I don't leave crumbs. I'm extremely careful about keeping my identity concealed, but *maybe* I didn't cover my tracks.

People have tried to find out who I am a handful of times over the past decade, especially when I published controversial things. Every person has failed, but after Lexi and Easton, more people are reading LuxLeaks than before.

The thought of anyone accessing my laptop makes me sick, and turmoil twists in my stomach. I'm lost in my thoughts, and Weston wraps his arm around me. It's an instant comfort.

"You're safe," he mutters, giving me a small smile. "Steady breaths."

I close my eyes, mentally sorting through everything on my laptop. "I just wish I knew why someone would do this."

"Me too. You know, when I decided to divorce Lena, I stressed about things I couldn't control, and it made me physically ill. I know it's difficult, but try not to worry until a need arises."

"Okay," I say, giving him a small smile.

The car stops at the curb before the high-rise on Billionaires' Row, and my door swings open. Weston tosses my leather duffel over his shoulder and follows behind me. I move toward the door, wearing a sweater and jeans. My hair is tucked up into a hat.

"You think paps saw us?" I ask when we enter, not sure if I can take anything else right now.

"Yes, but don't worry about it. They already took plenty of pictures tonight," he says, guiding me toward the reception desk. "I'm adding you to my visitor list so you can come and go as you please."

"Mr. Calloway," a woman greets us with a kind smile and then glances at me with the same demeanor. Classical music floats through the space. "I need a few signatures, fingerprints, and an eye scan."

"Need my blood type too?" I ask with a laugh.

She chuckles.

Weston shakes his head. "No, I've already got that."

My eyes widen.

"I'm kidding." He shoots me a wink.

I fill out everything, and then we're sent on our way.

We walk toward the elevator.

"You didn't have to do that."

"I did. Unfortunately, I cannot allow you to return back to your apartment for now. You're too precious to me," he admits as we enter the elevator.

His words stun me.

"Your thumbprint. We should confirm it works."

"Oh, right," I say, pressing it against the pad and watching it light up green. The doors close, and I don't know what to say. No one has ever cared for me *this* much. "Thank you."

"For?"

We shoot to the top floor.

"Keeping me safe," I offer.

"I always will."

We enter the penthouse. Weston immediately flicks on the recessed lighting, and the space glows bright.

"Home sweet home," he says.

I look around the room, replaying the last time I was here with him and how fast things are changing between us.

"Do you want to talk about it?" he finally asks, reading me like a book.

"No. I just have a lot on my mind and need to process," I whisper as exhaustion takes over.

"I understand." He moves toward me. "Let me show you your room choices."

I nod, following him up the stairs. He takes them at my pace, staying beside me. His room is down the hallway to my right, and to my left are several doors.

I grin as we enter an oversize bathroom with gold hardware that shines. I gasp when I see the shower, then stare at the tub. It's deeper than the tiny one in my apartment that barely covers my body when I try to soak.

"No way," I say, mentally adding taking a bubble bath to my list of things to do.

"Try the one in my bathroom first, but turn on the jets."

"Yes, please," I tell him.

He leads me through another door that connects to a large room with floor-to-ceiling windows. Everything in here is white and has a dreamy aesthetic as the snow falls outside.

"You have a perfect view of the sunset. I've watched it countless evenings from right here," he admits.

I can imagine him standing here, watching the sun dip below the horizon. In this penthouse, there isn't a room with a bad view.

He's still carrying my duffel in his hand. "There are more options."

He crosses the hallway and opens a bedroom door with a tall

bed and dark blue walls, the color of his eyes. It has a gothic vibe, and I like it.

"*Moody.* This your sex room?"

"It *can* be," he says, shooting me a wink. "Want to see the office?"

I nod.

Weston leads me down the hall, setting my bag down, and I'm happy for the distraction. He pushes it open, and a large desk faces the windows. I can almost imagine him working here.

Bookcases fill the walls, and I run my fingers across the spines of books, not recognizing any of the titles. He sits on the edge of the desk, still dressed in the black tux he wore to Obsidian. Hours have passed since we were there, but it already feels like last week.

"Maybe this is a sign I shouldn't write again," I say. The thought makes me want to cry.

"I don't believe that," he says as I yawn.

"Sorry. I'm so exhausted. I've been up for nearly twenty hours."

"You should go to bed. I'll talk to you until the sun rises if you don't," he says, his eyes kind and full of something I can't quite place.

I glance at the clock on the wall, knowing I have to be at work in seven hours. "Life is better with you in it."

He meets my eyes. "I don't remember life without you. I'm grateful you spoke first."

My emotions are on overload. "I don't want this night to end."

"Tomorrow is a new day," he tells me, walking toward me. "You need rest. Have you chosen your room?" he asks.

"Hmm. I think I want yours," I say.

He tilts his head and smirks, leading me from his office. "Go ahead."

I push open the door. His bed is neatly made, and the lamp is on. This is the room where he kissed me. I glance at the place where I stood, replaying that memory, and it makes me smile.

"Where will you sleep?" I turn to him, watching me from the doorway, and I wonder if tonight was a dream.

"What side do you prefer?" He unbuttons his jacket and pulls his tie loose.

"I don't know if you're joking or not," I say as he moves to his closet.

My feet stay planted, and I hear a dresser drawer slide open.

I step into the doorway, and he looks at me as he unbuttons his shirt, revealing those beautiful tattoos across his chest. I immediately turn around, knowing it's for the best.

"I need to be completely honest. Whether you want to accept this or not, but ..."

I turn to meet his eyes. Time briefly stands still as I try to predict his next words.

"I'm a cuddler," he says with a shrug.

I chuckle, and it feels good to laugh. His shirt falls to the floor in a pile.

"And if I remember correctly, that's against *your* rules, so you probably shouldn't. Don't want to give the wrong impression."

I yawn again, knowing I need to walk away from this situation. "You're absolutely right. Good night, Weston. Thank you for everything."

"Good night. Speaking of, which room did you decide on?" he asks, undoing his belt.

I turn. "The sunset room."

"Good choice. The bed is comfy," he says as I move across his room. "Know the invitation is always open."

"I'll keep that in mind," I say, leaving.

My duffel is in the hallway where he left it, and I latch on to the handles. Once inside, I sit on the edge of the bed, staring out the windows.

My mind wanders as my ears ring from the silence. It's unsettling. I glimpse my reflection in the glass and try to process everything.

I saw Sam again, and I was with Weston.

He owns Obsidian.

I'm shocked, knowing he cleaned up neighborhoods without wanting any credit for it. Just because.

How is it possible that he keeps surprising me? Maybe I shouldn't keep the *Westoncyclopedia* title any longer. There is too much I don't know about him.

Before I get too lost in my head, I unpack my bag. I carefully remove my work uniforms and spare clothes, tucking my jeans into the tall wooden dresser in the corner. It looks old and hand-carved, stained a caramel color.

On top are a few pictures in frames.

One is a photo of him and Easton—who knows which one is which?—with an older man. Their grandfather. He's tall with kind blue eyes. Not to mention, he's handsome as hell. The Calloway gene is strong.

There are others as well, all from his childhood. Seeing toddler him and Easton in suits is adorable. I guess it's always been a part of their wardrobes.

I empty my pockets, realizing I never turned on my phone. As soon as I boot it up, I'm bombarded with text messages from Lexi.

She sent the last one thirty minutes ago.

> **LEXI**
>
> WTAF?! You both had better be having wild, incredible, amazing sex. OMG. Bet he's a freak between the sheets.

The last part of the text message has me laughing hard. I cover my mouth, knowing the sound echoed off the high ceiling.

"Fuck," I whisper, realizing I'm too jumpy.

I know she leaves her phone in Do Not Disturb mode. I always text her at different hours of the night, and she replies when she wakes up.

Right now, I don't know what to say.

CARLEE

I wish. Instead, someone broke into my apartment and stole my laptop.

LEXI

OMFG. Do you need me to come get you? I can be there ASAP. Did they take anything else? Did you call the police?

Question overwhelm is real. I suck in a deep breath and type furiously.

CARLEE

I'm at Weston's.

Her chat bubble immediately pops up.

CARLEE

He wouldn't let me stay there. Nothing else was taken. And, yes, Brody is taking care of it.

LEXI

You're staying with Weston? Yay!

CARLEE

He doesn't want to date me, Lex. That's MORE THAN obvious. But anyway, I'm stressed and going to bed. Love you! Good night.

My phone immediately rings, and the sound startles me. I drop it, and it bounces on the bed.

I put her on speaker, turning the volume down, wanting the distraction even though I'm exhausted.

"You promise you're okay?" Lexi whispers.

"Yes. I'm just upset, but it'll be fine."

"I'm so sorry!" she says in her full voice.

"Shit," she whispers. "Sorry. I'm talking to Carlee."

Easton mumbles something, and then Lexi is quiet for fifteen seconds. I hear a door click.

"I woke him up. He has an early morning meeting," she says.

I imagine her sitting at the top of the stairs at the Diamond in the Sky. I kick off my shoes and lean back on the bed.

"Tell him I'm sorry," I say.

"Not your fault." She laughs. "He'll be fine."

The quietness drowns me.

"I get so worried about you living alone," Lexi admits.

"There's nothing I can do about that since you left me," I say, giving her a hard time.

Once she and Easton started fake dating, she moved in with him. I think about their relationship and can't help but wonder if Weston and I are on the same path.

"I can't believe someone stole your laptop. Why would they do that? What the hell?"

"I don't know." I lower my voice. "There are super-sensitive things on there, Lex. I'm freaking out. What if someone finds out about LuxLeaks? That can't happen. It would ruin everything. Not to mention the videos and pictures that I used to send my exes that are stored on my hard drive. And my journal. I'm going to be sick all over again."

I close my eyes tight. If that information got into the wrong hands, they could destroy my entire reputation with one single post.

"I will help you however I can. Was anything else missing?"

"No. That was it. So calculated." My nerves take over, along with the stress. "I don't feel safe there now. It's violating, knowing a stranger was inside my apartment."

"We'll figure it out," she promises. "Maybe you can be Weston's roommate? Like, permanently, especially if you're just friends. Between you and me, I think he gets lonely. Extroverts. You have to feed them with human interaction, or they shrivel. You know how it is."

I laugh. "We both know Weston doesn't need or want a roommate. He's just being kind, per usual. But anyway, I have to be at work early tomorrow, and I'm going to try to sleep in this big room. I'm exhausted, but I'm too wound up."

She sighs. "Do you want me to come over?"

"No, please don't go through the trouble."

"It's just an elevator ride away."

"No, no, it's fine."

"I'm glad you're okay and that you weren't home when that happened."

I let out a huff. "I didn't think about that. What if they were watching me? Making sure I was gone?" A chill runs up my spine.

"I can't think about that," she says. "Can we get together soon and talk about everything?"

"Yes," I promise her.

We make some more small talk, then say our good nights and end the call. I turn on the bedside lamp and then put on a tank top and some shorts. The sheets are cool to the touch, and I shiver as I slide between them.

I set my alarm and scroll on my phone, wanting Mr. Sandman to steal me away.

I count sheep, but it doesn't work. My body is too tense to let go. I toss and turn and grow even more annoyed.

I roll over, pick up my phone, and realize an entire fucking hour has passed. Insomnia has struck—something I haven't experienced since I was a college student.

I think it's just the stress and worry of everything. Not to mention, my feet are ice cold, and I'm freezing. I pull the covers over my head and try to relax.

Frustrated, I push them off of me and crawl out of bed. I tiptoe toward Weston's room and open the door to where he's sleeping.

"Weston," I whisper, "I can't sleep. My mind and heart are racing and—"

He lifts his arm and the blanket. "Come here."

I hesitate briefly, and then I crawl into his bed. With his strong arms around me, he pulls me closer and holds me.

"Let the record state that you already broke your rule," he says in a hushed tone as his warm body presses against mine.

My breath hitches, and I roll over to face him. His eyes open. Our warm breaths mix, and he leans forward to kiss my forehead. I lift my chin, our mouths connecting, and butterflies erupt inside of me when he kisses me back. His tongue slides into my mouth, and the kiss deepens. Our breathing grows heavy.

"I'll break my rules for you," I whisper.

"You should sleep. You're exhausted," he says, and I capture his lips again.

"I don't care," I admit.

Need and want take control.

As our lips crash together, I grow desperate for him. His cock is hard against my stomach, and I slide my hand inside his joggers.

"Fuck," he whispers as I stroke him.

He's so damn thick.

My body begs for him.

His breathing is ragged as I gently rub my hand over his shaft, teasing him.

"Choose me to *be her*," I say, and it comes out as a breathless plea.

"I did the night we met," he confesses.

17

WESTON

I slide my hands into her silk panties and rub circles against her needy clit.

"You knew that though," I whisper.

She nods, and the confession makes me fucking weak. Feeling how she's dripping wet for me turns me on. Just being close to her unlocks something primal inside of me. A single look was all it ever took.

"You're so fucking sexy," I mutter against her plump lips.

She strokes me from my base to the tip. I throb against her, the sensation both overwhelming and completely consuming. I've wanted her touch for so fucking long, and while I should deny myself of her, I can't. My willpower has vanished, even if I know, deep down, I don't deserve Carlee. Not sure anyone does.

"Wes, I need to come *so* bad," she begs as if her life depends on it.

My nickname on her lips makes my heart skip a fucking beat.

"Let me worship you," I whisper, trailing my lips down her neck, sucking and nibbling her sweet skin.

She jerks me so fucking good that my eyes nearly roll into the back of my head. I get lost with her as I effortlessly rub circles against her clit.

She rocks her hips against me, and desperate pants release from her lips as we get each other off.

"Mmm. Pre-cum," she says, placing her sticky fingers in her mouth.

I brush her hair out of her pretty face, studying her.

If she only knew what she did to me.

"Can I?" She glances down at my cock with anticipation and need.

I raise my brows and smirk, then slide a finger inside her tight pussy. Curling my finger, I tease her G-spot, and she clenches around me.

"Tell me what you want." The words come out in a rough gruff.

"I want you in my mouth," she whisper-hisses as she rocks against me.

I give her two fingers and go to the knuckle. She continues working me in long, slow strokes; if she keeps this up, I'll lose myself.

No other woman has ever made me feel like she does. I'm high on her, on us, on this.

Carlee's mouth falls open, and the intensity surrounding us builds. We're finally crossing that line. We both know it; we both don't give a fuck. She rocks her hips against me as desperate pants escape her lips like sweet music.

"Mmm. You want me so bad. I see it on your face. I'm memorizing that look," she purrs, her voice low. She continues stroking me as pleasure cascades through me.

"I *always* want you," I confess, brushing my thumb across her flushed cheek.

Her eyes are wide with lust. We're lost, and logic tells me one of us has to find a way out of this. Right now, we're tumbling through space together, falling toward an alternate reality where maybe we can be together. Neither of us will admit it.

She pushes the blanket away and glances down at my cock. Her gaze is filled with hunger.

I raise my brows and smirk. The thrill of having her courses through me as I continue to finger-fuck her. She clenches around me, a gasp escaping her lips as I move from her clit to her cunt, teasing every inch of her.

"Let me have you," she whispers, her words like a seductive spell as she rocks against my hand.

A deep moan escapes her as she grips my cock tighter, keeping a steady rhythm that drives me closer to the edge. She wants me to lose myself, and I want to surrender to the intoxicating need that takes hold of us both.

It's time to give in. I can't fight myself any longer.

"You win," I tell her, meeting her eyes.

"Finally," she says, kissing me deeply.

Without losing eye contact, she sits up and removes the T-shirt she's wearing, revealing her breasts. Carlee lies back down, giving me access to her perky pink nipples that stand at full attention. I had no idea.

Dark brown hair splashes across the pillow, and my eyes soften. I want to capture her like this.

"Do you want my panties off?" she asks.

I nod.

Carlee seductively wiggles out of them. I study every curve and freckle as my fingers trail down her smooth skin.

I trace my finger around the tattoo on her hip. I turn onto my side and smile. "Is that a love potion?"

"Yep. And you can't forget this one. I had a rebellious stage," she says, rolling over to show me her round ass.

My firm palm rubs over a red pair of lips tattooed on her cheek. I scoot down and bite it, leaving teeth marks around it.

"Mmm."

My hand runs up the curve of her body.

Fuck, she's *gorgeous*.

I lift one brow, a teasing smirk playing on my lips. "You're such a *bad* fucking girl."

"You have no idea," Carlee replies, twisting her body to hook her fingers in the waistband of my joggers. My cock springs free, and she lustfully studies me before swallowing hard. "Damn."

"Think you can handle it?" I ask, my heart racing in anticipation.

"I grew up on a Christmas tree farm, Weston. I can ride *anything*," she responds, a grin dancing across her lips.

"Giddyup then, little darlin'."

I lie back and tuck my hands behind my head. She moves between my legs, licking down the shaft, her tongue exploring every ridge and contour of my length and balls.

She strokes me, chuckling. "You're not supposed to make jokes."

"Why? I find you so fucking sexy when you laugh," I say.

A heavy breath escapes me as her gaze meets mine, and I wonder if she realizes what she's always wanted is right in front of her.

"What's that look for?" she asks, and I realize she's paying more attention, reading me better than before.

"Tell me what you were thinking first," I say, licking my lips.

"I feel like I'm dreaming," she admits before taking me in her hot mouth.

Her confession causes heat to flood through me.

"Me too," I mutter.

She teases the tip as I gently run my fingers through her silky hair. Carlee takes her time like she's memorizing each inch of me with her tongue. It's agonizing how badly I want her.

"I like it when you watch me like this," she says right before taking my cock to the back of her throat.

My heart swirls with emotions—something I shouldn't feel with just a fuck buddy. This is too intimate, and the moment consumes me. I should've known better, but selfishly, I didn't give a fuck.

Carlee increases her pace, working me like her life depends on it. I give her all of me. She can't get enough as she forces me to the back of her throat.

No gag reflex.

"Give me your pussy," I whisper. "Sit on my face."

"Show me how," she says, crawling toward me.

Her lips crash against mine with overwhelming urgency. We grow breathless and needy.

"You're the only person who's ever had this part of me," she admits. "Teach me."

Knowing I'm the only man who's ever tasted that sweet pussy makes me so goddamn feral. It will stay like that from now until the end of time. Just one lick of her was all it took.

"Put your pussy right here," I instruct, hard as a fucking rock.

She climbs on top of me, hovering above me. I kiss every part of her inner thigh. Desperate moans release from her as I gently tease her bundle of nerves.

I trail my tongue down her wet slit, devouring her arousal.

"Smother me with your sweet cunt. I can't get enough." With a firm grasp, I grab her ass cheeks, pushing her against my mouth.

"Your facial hair," she says breathlessly before taking most of my cock into her mouth. "Feels so damn good."

It's ecstasy as she rides my face and sucks me. I give her a finger, and she clenches around me. Carlee's breathing grows heavy. It happens too fast, and we're both chasing our ends.

"You want to come *so* fucking bad. I can taste you," I mutter, twirling circles on her hard clit.

Her body shudders in anticipation. The desperate breaths and high-pitched pants are a dead giveaway as she steadies herself on my chest. Her back arches as she fucks my face.

"Weston, oh, oh," she screams out as the orgasm takes over, and as she shatters I shove my tongue deep inside her.

I lick every inch of her, not wasting a drop. Guttural groans release from her body, and I love the way it sounds when she loses herself.

"You taste so fucking good."

I continue giving her clit play as she returns to my cock. Carlee keeps her pussy in place as I run my hands up and down her body.

"You're close," she says breathlessly as my balls seize.

I see stars. I grab her ass, creating more friction, and seconds later, she comes on my tongue *again*.

"Mmm, fuck yes. Two," I say, knowing I'm on the brink of falling over the edge.

"I need you inside of me, Weston," she nearly begs.

"No," I whisper. "One of us has to have control. Two days. You can wait."

"You don't want to fuck my tight little cunt?" she asks, grinding her wet pussy against my facial hair.

Love that she's insatiable and horny as fuck. We're a match made in heaven—and I'd know after living in hell for so long.

I ache for more of her, bucking my hips upward, hitting the back of her throat as she strokes me with her hand. I imagine being buried deep inside of her, stretching her wide. We'll have to go slow at first to allow her time to adjust. Sure, she has toys, but they don't compare.

Her body tenses and shakes, and I slide a finger back inside her. She's coming for the third time.

"Greedy girl."

"Mmhmm," she says with her mouth full.

I can feel my orgasm building, knowing I've brought her to the end three times. Feeling her pulse around me is so fucking hot.

"Come for me. I want every drop of you," she demands. "Give me what I want, Wes."

My body tenses and the orgasm rips through me. I grunt as I pump inside of her hot, greedy mouth. Carlee massages my balls, continuing to stroke me as the world around me collapses. I can't think straight and inhale ragged breaths as she licks me clean.

"Mmm. You taste so good, baby."

"Fuck," I say, hyperaware that she called me baby, barely able to catch my breath.

Carlee lays flat on the bed beside me, facing me. We're both in a daze.

I lean forward, kissing her passionately, wanting her to taste how sweet she is on my tongue. Our pleasure mixes together, and it's confirmed that Carlee Jolly will be my goddamn demise.

"Weston, I'm …" she whispers.

There's something she wants to say, and I wait for her to continue, but before she can, the doorbell rings.

We stare at each other.

"What time is it?" she asks, the sound pulling us from our haze.

"Get dressed," I tell her, quickly capturing her lips. "Time is of the essence."

"Why?"

"Because if it's Easton, he's already let himself in, and he's making his way up the stairs."

"Shit!" she whisper-hisses.

18

CARLEE

"What the hell?" I grab my clothes and move to the bathroom, my mind racing.

"I'll be back," he says, lingering at the doorway, the playful glint in his eyes betraying his nonchalance.

"What should I do?" I whisper, glancing toward the anaconda in his joggers. "Weston."

A smirk tugs at the corners of his mouth. "Whatever you fucking want."

"You're rock hard," I whisper, the words slipping out.

His eyes dart from my eyes to my mouth, and heat swirls between us. "Because of you."

"Should I hide?" I ask, my heart pounding in my chest. The adrenaline surging through me makes me feel alive.

"That's your decision," he replies.

Just then, the doorbell rings again.

"Good. Confirmation that it's not Easton. Better check it out," he says.

I clean up and catch a glimpse of my reflection in the mirror, which seems both foreign and familiar. My just-fucked hair frames a face with swollen lips. My body sings, and I feel like I'm floating in space; it's euphoric like I've transcended to a different dimension. I let out a breath, the silence amplifying the rapid heartbeat in my ears, and that's when I notice the hickey on my neck.

Flipping my hair over to one side, I lean closer to the full-length mirror.

"What the fuck?" I whisper, my pulse quickening as I assess the damage.

I don't know if I packed the right makeup to cover this.

"Shit," I whisper to myself, remembering how it felt to be with him. I can't show up to work like this tomorrow.

I wiggle into my shorts and a shirt that clings to my body. Bravely, I crack open Weston's door and catch the sound of a high-pitched voice. A woman. I gulp hard.

Sucking in a deep breath, I remind myself I asked for a situationship only. Does he really have a secret girlfriend and lied to me?

He told me I could do whatever I wanted, so I decide to skip down the stairs, my wild hair bouncing with each step. They both stop talking when I enter the room. Weston's arms are wrapped around her, and she seems upset. I recognize her gorgeous face. She's the same woman who complimented me on my Valentino dress in the lobby. Does she live at The Park too?

"Oh," she says, noticing me. "Oh. Shit. I'm so sorry. I didn't know you weren't alone," she says to Weston, and they pull apart.

"It's okay," he says.

I feel a prick of something on my skin. Is that *jealousy*?

"Apologies for interrupting," she whispers, creating space between them. "Can we talk soon?" she asks with a pretty smile.

Her dark brown hair cascades elegantly down her shoulders, and her eyes are crystal blue, almost gray. The light reflects off a diamond bracelet on her wrist as she tucks hair behind her ear.

What bothers me the most is they actually look good together. And they were holding one another.

"Yes. We can get together this week. Just text me," he replies, stepping away to walk her out.

I make my way toward the kitchen, suddenly feeling parched as an unease takes over.

Their voices fade as they continue chatting with the door closed, but the words remain a mystery. A few seconds later, Weston saunters into the kitchen, a smirk playing on his lips, which were buried between my legs less than twenty minutes ago.

"Is *that* your secret girlfriend?" I ask, trying to keep my tone casual despite the storm brewing in my chest.

His brows lift in surprise. "You're jealous, and it's pretty fucking cute."

Am I under his spell, like all the other stupid girls who have been obsessed with him over the years?

"What? No." I roll my eyes, managing to smile at him.

The truth is, I *am*. I saw how she looked at him, that starry-eyed gaze, and how his expression softened when their eyes met. They were holding each other in a hug, and I sensed a moment that felt too personal. Like a secret was shared, and I wasn't supposed to witness it.

"And what if I said she was the woman I'd been seeing? Are you sure you'd be okay with that?" he asks, his playful demeanor evaporating, replaced by something more serious.

The mood grows heavy as emotions crawl through me. Blood floods my head, and I feel like I'm drowning. I shouldn't feel like this.

He doesn't say anything, allowing the uncomfortable silence. It's like a strong current pulling me under.

"Think about that stirring feeling. Sit in it and consider it before making your decision because *that's* what you're okay with, Carlee. That's what you're asking of me," he says.

His tone makes my stomach twist.

"I understand that. I just want you to be happy." I glance up at the clock, grimacing as I realize it's almost three.

Exhaustion quickly washes over me. The roller coaster of emotions, the dizzying highs and crushing lows, has left me breathless.

I walk past him, forcing a smile, trying to mask my spiraling thoughts. "Thanks for the reminder, bestie."

"You're welcome," he replies.

"She's gorgeous," I say. "How long have you known her? A year?"

"A *very* long time."

His gaze follows me until I slip out of sight. Seeing him embrace someone else isn't something I can easily digest. Tonight was a wake-up call. It's a loud, blaring internal siren. Maybe this is proof that I'm not emotionally capable of maintaining a friends-with-benefits arrangement with *him*.

Our attraction is more than purely physical, and that's when situationships grow dangerous. It's how people fall in love, and I don't know if we're capable of that right now. Heartache isn't something I'm searching for. My heart still feels far too fragile to risk it. And his is still in ashes.

I return to my room, crawling into the cold sheets that feel harsh against my skin in comparison to Weston's. I roll over onto my side, staring outside at the flurries—tiny flakes dancing in the dim light, swirling against the glass like fleeting dreams. When I close my eyes, the vision of the two of them locked in each other's gaze invades my thoughts.

Then, a flash of memory hits me—the diamond bracelet on her wrist, glistening like a star in the night sky. It must have cost a fortune. I can't help but think of the one Weston gave me.

Are diamonds the Calloway initiation?

Easton gave Lexi jewelry too.

My mind races, each thought more frantic than the last. Does he privately collect pretty brunettes, cycling through us like seasons? She seemed genuinely surprised to see me. Am I part of some twisted game I didn't even know I had signed up for?

Seconds later, Weston walks into my room, and before I can process anything, the covers are lifted. He slides behind me, snaking his arm around my body with effortless intimacy. I can feel the warmth radiating off him, his breath brushing close to my ear as he kisses my neck, igniting a spark that I both crave and dread.

"You're overthinking," he whispers, the words both soothing and taunting. Of course, he knew what was spinning through my mind. Weston knows me. "Just relax."

I sigh as I settle into his strong body that molds against mine. A million questions flood through me, but this isn't a conversation I can have right now. I'm too exhausted and conflicted to confront the truth.

"Good night," I finally say.

"Earlier, you were going to say something before we were interrupted."

I think back and remember I almost told him that I was afraid to fall in love with him. But I keep it to myself. Admissions like that need to have the right timing, and for some reason, it wasn't.

"Ask me later," I tell him. "Doesn't feel right yet."

"Okay," he says, nuzzling into my neck.

I could do this forever, and that alone makes me delusional. But for once, I live in the fantasy of it, wondering what could be. I let out a breath.

"Sweet dreams, Firefly." His fingers interlock with mine.

My body releases me to sleep, and I quickly drift off, hoping rest will give me the clarity I need.

I have a decision to make, and it needs to be the right one for us both.

My alarm forces me awake, and when I glance down, I realize I've already snoozed twice.

"Shit." I roll over, realizing the bed is empty. When did he leave?

The sun rises, casting an orange and pink hue across the sky. I'm not ready to face the day, but the world waits for no one.

I quickly grab my work clothes as I question everything.

Did I imagine Weston held me until I fell asleep? Or did it actually happen? Yesterday felt like a strange blend of fantasy and nightmare. I experienced my biggest fear and greatest desires within hours of each other.

I just want to know who took my fucking laptop.

As I brush my teeth, I catch a glimpse of the purple hickey in the mirror.

"Shit," I mutter under my breath.

I know I don't have time to stop by a drugstore for concealer before I need to be at the W.

I suck in a deep breath and text Lexi. Right now, she's my only hope.

CARLEE

Are you awake?

LEXI

Yep! Eating breakfast. Hungry? Easton just left. I have extra!

CARLEE

I only have five minutes.

LEXI

Perfect amount of time.

I pull my hair back into a tight bun as whispers of self-doubt take over, but I have no choice. It's either I deal with Lexi or Mr. Martin, and she's easier to handle than him. As I walk around the penthouse, I realize Weston already left for the day.

In a rush, I take the elevator to her floor. I knock urgently, and she answers with a smile. Her tiny pregnant belly is showing, and she's glowing.

"Aww, you're so cute, Mama," I exclaim.

The sight of her brings a smile to my lips.

"Aww. Thanks." She beams back at me, but her expression shifts. "Is that a hickey on your neck?"

Before I can think, I slap my hand over the mark, embarrassment flooding my cheeks. "I need makeup. I didn't pack any for this. Just have my travel bag."

"Who's responsible for that? Sam or Weston?" she asks, eyebrows raised.

"You know I don't kiss and tell," I say, refusing to answer as she guides me up to her bathroom.

"It was Weston. Those damn Calloways. Easton tagged me so many times."

Lexi rummages through her cosmetics and pulls out some concealer, dabbing it on my neck with practiced care.

"Do you know if Weston is seeing someone secretly?" I ask and almost immediately regret it.

She bursts into laughter. "He's not. Trust me. If he was serious about someone, Easton would know."

I don't know why that stings a little. Do I want Weston to tell his brother about us? What are we even?

"What's going on?" she asks.

"Last night, this very pretty woman came to visit him at three in the morning. I walked in on them hugging, very closely," I explain, my voice barely above a whisper. A creeping thought invades my mind. "What if there is someone, and ..."

My words falter. *I'm the decoy.*

"What?" Lexi looks at me with alarm on her face.

"Nothing." I force a smile, pushing the thoughts away.

Weston has always been two steps ahead of everyone. He's a master strategist when it comes to how his life is portrayed. He has a team that watches everything said about him online because his reputation is important. But would he use *me* to feed the media a false narrative that I'm not aware of? I'd like to think not, but doubt gnaws at me. I don't want to get caught up in his web.

"I can *guarantee* those blind items are about you and Weston. Why are you trying to convince yourself they're not and there is someone else?"

"You can't guarantee that," I counter, shaking my head. "Sure, it's convenient, but maybe it's a planned cover-up for something greater, and I'm just a distraction in Weston's ultimate game of chess. Lexi, there was a beautiful woman who looked like a supermodel in designer clothes, standing in his penthouse, and he was comforting her. When I appeared, her surprise was obvious, as if I'd interrupted something. It seemed serious, and she apologized and kept saying she didn't know he wasn't alone."

"What did she look like?" Lexi asks.

I sigh, my heart sinking with the memory. "About my height. Dark brown hair, light-blue eyes."

"Was it Billie?"

"No, it wasn't his sister," I reply. "She's familiar though, but I can't pinpoint her yet."

"Do you want me to ask Weston? I will," she offers as her fingers finish blending the makeup on my neck.

"Please don't. That's not my business. If people want you to know things, they'll tell you, and he didn't," I murmur, feeling the weight of this on my chest. "He's letting me stay with him out of the kindness of his heart. I just ... I just don't want to be a burden to him and his personal life."

I glimpse at her handiwork in the mirror. It's like the mark never even existed. "Thank you."

"Welcome. Also, I'd be willing to bet anything that Weston doesn't consider you a burden. Unlike Easton—that man *hates* being alone—Weston wants company and has a fun personality. You act like him being with you is out of the realm of possibility, and it's just not. Weston has the hots for you—I can tell," she confirms with a knowing glance and a slight arch of her brow.

"Shut up," I say, my face cracking into a smile. "Might need to add him to the *wannabe lovers* list."

"Oh, he's been there for a while anyway. Come get some food. You gotta go. I know you can't be late."

I steal a quick glance at the time on my phone, the numbers glaring back at me. I can still make it.

Lexi leads me into the cozy kitchen, where the aroma of freshly cooked bacon fills the air. She grabs a container from the cabinet and fills it with golden scrambled eggs and crispy bacon.

"You're doing that thing you do where you think someone is too good to be true, and you push them away. Stop trying to convince yourself you and Weston can't be together."

Is that what this is? Has my relationship trauma misplaced my mistrust in Weston?

"How well do you know him, Lex?" I ask, a hint of hesitation creeping into my voice.

We've never discussed their relationship in depth. I've known Weston longer, but Lexi has spent more time with him. Easton and Weston are always together.

"Enough to know you're his *perfect* match," she replies, her tone laced with certainty.

My heart skips a beat.

"He looks at you the same way Easton looks at me."

I stare at her. "Excuse me?"

"He's clearly in love with you," she whispers.

"Lex, it's dangerous to assume that."

"It's not an assumption. It's the truth. Something changed the night we had burgers and watched *Titanic*. I noticed it, and so did Easton."

So did I.

"I *really* have to go." A swarm of butterflies swarm in my stomach.

"Just give him a chance," she urges.

"I know I'm the problem." I place my hands on her shoulders. "Pretty please don't add more pressure on me than I already have. I don't think I can handle anything else right now."

"I do need your help with one thing. Please?" She glances at me with hopeful eyes.

"Yes?" I ask.

"I need to plan my pregnancy announcement party," she says, following me to the door, her excitement nearly boiling over. "Will you help? Thankfully, it's winter, so I can hide my bump with big coats, sweaters, and jackets in public, but that won't be the case forever."

A wide smile breaks across my face, and I hug her. "I'd be honored."

Lexi squeezes me. "Falling in love is fun. You should run toward it this time instead of away."

"Have a good day." I leave with the food container cradled in my hand.

My head spins with thoughts of Weston. Lexi thinks he's in love with me, and I think that's impossible. Isn't it?

As soon as I step out of Park Towers, I notice how the sidewalks are alive with the bustling energy of commuters. I take the stairs down to the station to wait for my train. On the platform wall across the way is a large Calloway Diamonds poster stretched out. The family logo—the diamond shape surrounded by a triangle —is simple but iconic. Immediately, thoughts of Weston flood my mind.

I quickly eat the food Lexi packed for me, then toss the container in recycling.

I snap a quick picture of the poster and attach it to a text message to Weston.

CARLEE

Thinking about you. Also, am I the decoy?

Is that too much? Am I being that annoying girl?

I don't immediately hit Send, my finger hovering over the button.

My insecurity takes hold of me, and I hate that it nearly chokes me.

He told me to text him when I was thinking about him, but I'm so fucking hesitant, and I don't know why.

Communication is his love language, the bridge he builds to connect with those around him. The years of therapy I took after learning about my dad's other family taught me that a person's love language often stems from what they didn't receive in childhood. My heart aches as I think about Weston, who listens to every word someone speaks, and how he potentially wasn't heard as a kid.

That thought makes me hit Send because he deserves to receive that, and I hope it puts a smile on his face. However, my hesitation and relationship trauma makes me contemplate my issues, and I wonder if I'll never be capable of having a healthy relationship because of it.

The only *healthy* relationship I had exacerbated my fears of abandonment that my father had caused. No wonder I don't trust men or believe anyone when they say they love me. My jaw clenches instinctively, and my body fills with tension. I try to push the thoughts away, but they're too overwhelming. The only thing that pulls me out of it is the sudden buzz of my phone.

Weston. He saved me again.

WESTON

Might consider increasing the advertising budget so you're forced to think about me anytime you're out. And decoy for what? I fucking love how your mind works.

A smile creeps across my face, and my anxiousness almost disappears. Almost.

CARLEE

A decoy for your secret girlfriend—to take the attention away so you two can continue to be together.

WESTON

You're adorable.

CARLEE

Ignore that. I'm being THAT girl, aren't I?

WESTON

It's okay to show your cards every once in a while. I'd be raging with jealousy right now if our roles were reversed. It would drive me fucking insane to see another man holding you. I thought you said you wanted to be my dirty little affair?

I imagine his smirk and find myself chewing on my lip as my heart races.

CARLEE

Weston Calloway, it is too early in the morning for all of that.

My blood pressure rises as thoughts of him fill my mind. Seconds later, a picture of him standing in his office, sleeves rolled to his elbows, comes over. My eyes slide down to his cock, rock hard in his suit pants. Damn. Memories of us last night flash in my mind.

I wouldn't last a day at Calloway headquarters.

WESTON

You've been on my mind all morning.

I swallow hard as butterflies swarm through me.

CARLEE

Are you purposely trying to make me fall in love with you?

WESTON

We both know that's not possible.

CARLEE

And if it were?

WESTON

Enjoy the fall.

My breath catches. He knows what he's doing, and I'm so easy that I fall for it.

As I glance at the time, I grow anxious, realizing the train is late. Other people on the platform shuffle restlessly, and their impatience echoes my own. Knowing I can't afford to wait any longer, I trek up the stairs, and the cold air hits me like a slap. I rush the two blocks away and wait at the bus stop. Before I'm actually late, I call the W and attempt to speak to Mr. Martin to give a notice, but I'm met with voice mail. I call back and ask for the shift supervisor, and I'm put on hold.

I overslept and spent too long chatting with Lexi this morning. I've been too distracted. That can only mean one thing.

My heart palpitates. *I can't fall in love ...*

Another few minutes pass, and frustration bubbles beneath the surface. The bus remains a phantom, and time slips through my fingers like sand. Biting back my irritation, I power-walk a few more blocks to the next stop. Just as I arrive, a bus pulls up, and it's not the right route.

Desperate for a guaranteed solution, I open a rideshare app, and schedule it for three blocks up and jog toward the corner of 6th and 51st.

As soon as I spot Radio City Music Hall, my lungs feel like they're about to burst. Every deep breath is a painful reminder of how I need to start doing yoga again. I'm relieved when the car finally arrives, but my joy ends too soon.

We make it a few blocks before we're met with traffic. Walking might've been faster at this rate. Not to mention, every traffic light seems to be against me, shifting to red at exactly the wrong time.

"Do you think you can run a few of these?" I ask with a laugh, but the urgency in my voice betrays the humor.

I have less than ten minutes until my shift starts, and at this rate, it doesn't seem humanly possible to arrive on time. Maybe Mr. Martin will have mercy on me, but I prepare myself for the worst.

I told Weston I didn't want to quit my job, but getting fired wasn't on my bingo card.

I bite my lip, anxiety swelling within me.

Taking the train close to Weston's isn't something I usually do. I should've logged in to the Metro home page and searched for information about the routes. I do it right then. Immediately, I see there was scheduled track maintenance today, causing a fifteen-minute delay.

Someone finally picks up the line. "This is the W. How may I direct your call?"

I answer, "Hotel management, please."

"Please hold."

I'm rerouted. After waiting for over ten minutes, I groan and hang up, shaking my head with frustration.

By the time the car stops in front of the W, with its gleaming windows reflecting the early morning sun, I know this is it. As I walk through the grand entrance, with its polished marble floor and elegantly designed lobby, I suddenly feel like this chapter of my life is closing.

Once I'm at the housekeeper headquarters located in the basement, I clock in and move to my locker, shrugging off my damp coat. The faint scent of laundry detergent mingles with the cool air.

A few minutes later, Mr. Martin approaches me. His serious demeanor casts a shadow over me.

"You're ten minutes late," he says.

"My apartment was broken into, so I had to go somewhere else. The subway by Central Park was delayed, there was no bus, and I had to resort to rideshare. I called and left a message, so I wasn't AWOL," I respond, my pulse quickening as I plead my case.

He shakes his head, the disappointment evident on his face. "I'm sorry, Carlee. Corporate policy is you can't be late three times in six months. Rules are rules. If you break them, you face the consequences."

I think about the rules Weston and I made, then immediately broke. I breathe in deeply, attempting to center myself.

"Thank you, Mr. Martin. I appreciate all you've done for me," I say, knowing this is out of his hands.

"I'm sorry," he says, his tone firm but tinged with a hint of something.

Is that empathy? I can tell he's upset. I'm one of his best employees, and we both know it.

"Please turn in your ID and uniform," he says, turning away.

When the door to his office closes behind him, I feel the finality of this hanging in the air.

As I pull my coat from my locker, I have the overwhelming sensation that life as I know it is changing, and there is nothing I can do to stop that.

19

WESTON

After our incredibly frustrating meeting, Easton and I climb into the back of an SUV, the scent of leather mingling with the faint traces of rain on the asphalt. The engine hums to life, and as we pull away, I glance at my watch. It's just after five.

"I'm so fucking sick and tired of playing the same song and dance where they expect a different result, knowing I won't budge on my decisions," Easton complains, his irritation evident.

Granted, it was a four-hour meeting that should've only lasted two, so I understand his irritation. I'm not thrilled about it either.

"It's a big investment for them to partner with us. That's to be expected," I remind him. "Fuck, I bet Lexi is glad you're not like this at home."

"My wife never tests my patience." He rolls his eyes dramatically.

"No, you just enjoy it and find it endearing when Lexi does it. There's a difference," I tell him teasingly.

"Maybe," he replies, a smirk breaking through.

We both know it's the truth.

My brother has very little patience in the business world. He's *always* the bad cop while I play the role of the comedic relief, the king's jester in this cutthroat arena. Often, it's necessary because he tends to go too hard, bulldozing through meetings like a freight train. Easton is a known hard-ass who takes no shit from anyone, a reputation forged in the fires of ruthless negotiations. I tend to read the room better than he does, which makes us great partners—yin and yang. We make deals happen, even the impossible ones.

"I get so fucking annoyed, having to constantly repeat myself," Easton huffs, his voice low but intense. "It's not difficult to listen *and* comprehend."

"Now it's over, so you don't have to think about it anymore," I say, fully aware he's still aggravated.

He clenches his jaw, revealing the relentless pressure he puts on himself.

"Until Wednesday, when we meet again," he mumbles. "I might let you handle that one alone."

"Whatever you need," I reply, knowing he'll rise to the occasion when the time comes.

The industry calls us double trouble because we make billion-dollar deals happen that turn heads and reshape markets. Everyone knows the diamond princes always get what they want in life. We might've been born with golden spoons in our mouths, but we've worked tirelessly to preserve what's ours, clawing our way to the top of the business world while remaining fiercely loyal to our family's legacy.

His phone buzzes with a text, and I see a grin spread across his face. I know it's Lexi. She's the only one who can successfully turn his frown upside down. She's his sunshine, breaking through clouds after a storm. Knowing I helped bring them together might be one of my greatest accomplishments.

He types something quickly, his fingers flying over the screen, and then glances back at me. "Are you attending Asher's party tonight?"

Asher Banks is one of my and Easton's friends. He also owns

one of the most successful advertising and marketing firms in the world. Tonight, he's throwing a party for his close friends.

"Is Lexi asking, or are you?" I chuckle lightly.

He shakes his head. "She said she'd only go if you *and* Carlee were attending."

"First, I haven't invited Carlee. And second, I haven't decided." My mind drifts to last night and falling asleep with her in my arms.

My brother notices, revealing a flicker of something in his expression, but he doesn't call me on it. "I'd rather stay home."

"What else is new?" I smile, knowing he prefers his alone time, enjoying the quiet moments away from the chaos of our lives. "But I do think I *have* to attend to discuss specifics about something with Asher. You should join me."

Easton's brows quirk upward, curiosity sparking in his eyes. "Regarding?"

"I can't tell you."

His brows knit together. "Are you fucking kidding me?"

I briefly glance away, feeling the weight of the secret pressing down on me. "I promised I wouldn't tell anyone."

"I'm not *anyone*." His annoyance returns and radiates from him like heat from a fire. "That's ridiculous that you'd agree to keep things from me."

I smirk, knowing this shit gets under his skin. "You know, if it had something to do with us or anything we're doing, I wouldn't hesitate to tell you, but it doesn't. And I can't fully talk about it yet without gathering more information."

He narrows his eyes, a storm brewing behind them. "Is it relationship-related?"

I chuckle, amused that he'd go there, of all places. "Not this time."

The road noise from the tires fills the back seat.

"What's going on with you and Carlee?" he asks bluntly, cutting through the silence like a knife.

"I have no fucking clue," I reply truthfully, a wave of confusion washing over me.

Easton interlocks his fingers and glares at me, his intense gaze unyielding. "I know you probably don't want to take my relationship advice, but sometimes, you just have to go for it. You're falling in love with her, and you can't hide that from me."

"That's an assumption." I flick my gaze toward him, feeling defensive.

"*Bullshit.* When Carlee is around, your whole demeanor changes, and I can tell she makes you really fucking happy. I've spent the last two weeks trying to understand how this happened. I already know the why. I'm convinced you two have been seeing each other for a *very* long time because I know you, dear brother, and I know you don't fall in love with people overnight. That's not your MO."

"Nah, that's yours. But, hey, glad to know I'm living rent-free in your head."

"How did it start?"

He's direct, but that approach doesn't work on me. I'm immune to his tactics, like a seasoned warrior on the battlefield.

I chuckle, brushing off his question. "It's not your business. However, I know you've been talking about me with her." Carlee basically admitted I'm a topic of conversation during our dinner date.

His eyes narrow, hard as steel. "I have. Many times."

"Tell me."

"What was it you just said to me? It's not your fucking business or concern."

"Don't worry; I'll find out." I grin, confident that my determination will lead me to the truth.

They've talked about me. Easton says he's not getting involved, but I don't believe him.

He clears his throat. "I'll just say this: she's looking for forever with someone. Don't waste her time."

My brows furrow. "I respect her too much for that."

"Yeah, but your reputation precedes you. And I know you get bored."

"*I* get bored? *Please.*" I roll my eyes, dismissing him. "I still have a lot of undoing to do. Oh, before I forget, I talked to our publicist today. Gabriella sent me the documentation Lena released of our text conversations this morning. Most were taken out of context, and the dates were edited to make it seem like we were still talking and that I was madly in love with her. She also wrote a seventy-five-page manifesto on why I should take her back and how good we were together, detailing private conversations and moments we'd shared during the three years we were married."

"*Fuck her.* Especially after what she did to you," Easton hisses, his voice low and dangerous. "Did she mention *any* of her wrongdoings?"

"Accountability isn't something she will ever take. Gabriella also warned me that if another one of my relationships ends like that one, it won't be good for business. The only thing that saved our company's image was you and Lexi. The foundation of Calloway Diamonds was built on love, and I won't do anything that could potentially hurt us."

"Live your life first. We will figure out everything else," he says, a serious expression etched across his face. "Life is too short, Weston. That's not a suggestion."

"So, a direct order? Got it," I reply, smiling. Warmth floods my chest as I know my brother wants the best for me. "I'm so lucky to have you by my side."

"I feel the same." He smiles back.

"Gabriella also suggested a fake engagement. Not related, but my lawyer believes he has a solution to expedite things with Lena."

Easton's brow rises in genuine surprise. "Great about the lawyer, but explain the fake engagement."

"I don't know if it's a good idea after my very public divorce." I glance at him as a sly grin spreads across my face. "We'll see."

"It worked for me. You'd ask Carlee, wouldn't you?" He smirks, leaning back in his seat as if reminiscing about falling in love.

I ignore his question.

"We're still in PR crisis mode," I continue, my voice steady but tinged with urgency, "but the public's perception has shifted significantly in my favor with the prospect of a new relationship on the horizon. The blind items actually helped."

He studies me intently, his eyes narrowing as if searching for hidden motives. "What's the plan?"

"She suggested that Carlee and I should be seen together in public several times. We need to be transparent about our relationship initially and allow the public to draw their own conclusions. That's easy." I pause, considering the implications. "After one month, she suggested a proposal, with the intention of having a lengthy engagement."

Easton holds my gaze, unamused. "And what will you do if you want to be with someone else?"

"We'll break it off and communicate to the public that we were better as friends while continuing to be seen together. An amicable split," I explain, trying to keep the tone light, though the weight of the situation is far from it.

"You won't be able to pretend forever, Weston."

"Yeah, yeah." I wave him off. "I'll invite Carlee if it means you'll be there tonight. It might be nice to introduce her to everyone, considering we'll be seen together going forward."

He struggles to suppress a smile. "And this is how it begins. I can't fucking wait. An official Carlee reveal."

"No. It's unrelated." I shake my head, shifting my tone to serious. "I need a second set of eyes and ears."

"This sounds serious. At least give me some idea of what's going on. I don't need every detail, but if you need intel, I need to understand why."

I sigh heavily as the gravity of the situation crashes down on me. "I believe Billie's fashion company is in serious fucking trouble."

His jaw tightens as something flashes in his eyes. "We spoke yesterday, and she didn't mention anything."

"And she won't," I reply, frustration lacing my words. "She's too proud and stubborn, just like us. I have to speak to Asher because he's a crucial piece of this."

"Damn," he says, exhaling sharply, knowing that Asher Banks runs one of the most successful marketing companies in the world.

Only the top-tier clients hire him and his team—a privilege that comes with a hefty price tag. His brother, Nicolas—a partner and one of the best corporate attorneys money can buy—only enhances their cutthroat reputation. The stakes are high, but I will do anything to protect my baby sister.

"What are you wearing to this cocktail party? I assume we're twinning?" he groans.

"Oh, you love it. I recently picked up my burgundy suit from the dry cleaners," I explain. "I'll probably wear that."

"Great," he tells me as the SUV stops in front of The Park.

The high-rise building contrasts with the deepening purple hues of the evening sky.

I check my text messages, acutely aware that the items I ordered have been delivered to the front desk.

Easton and I step out, entering a flurry of flashing cameras.

"Just smile," I tell him, chuckling at the absurdity of our situation.

He shakes his head. A mix of humor and annoyance plays across his face. "We're not *that* interesting."

"Eh, speak for yourself," I reply, throwing him a wink.

"Do you want to ride together tonight?" he asks, his voice cutting through the chatter of the crowd.

"That would be great. I'll let you know if Carlee is available since Lexi will only attend if she's going to be there. One second," I add, waving at the building manager, who is just within earshot.

"Mr. Calloway, I have the items you had delivered," she says, handing me a crisp garment bag and a box wrapped in shimmering paper.

Easton and I step into the elevator together, the hum of classical music surrounding us. He glances at the items in my hands, curiosity lighting up his expression.

"Gifts? I know what that means." His brow quirks upward. "If I haven't mentioned it before, I support this relationship. After getting to know her better, I agree that you two would be perfect together. Your personalities complement one another."

"Thanks. I'll keep your opinion in mind. I'll text you with a confirmation if she joins me," I assure him. "No guarantees though. Carlee has her own life."

"She'll be there." He steps out of the elevator, chuckling to himself. "You're both so damn transparent."

"Please kindly fuck off," I say with a grin as the doors slide shut.

When I'm alone, I suck in a deep breath, the weight of the evening settling on my shoulders. I know I need to play my cards correctly tonight.

I unlock the door to my penthouse, wondering if Carlee is home from work yet. My question is quickly answered when I find her asleep on the couch, resting comfortably, still wearing her work uniform. She looks so damn pretty and peaceful, her chest gently rising and falling with each shallow breath. I could watch her sleep the rest of the evening.

I quietly move closer, setting everything down, and then I kneel beside her. I place my hand on her shoulder, gently brushing my thumb across her arm, almost feeling guilty for waking her.

"Carlee," I whisper, my voice barely above a breath.

Her eyes open, and she blinks up at me with a smile. "Hi."

"Hi." I grin, warmth flooding my chest.

"I must've fallen asleep," she says as she sits up.

Her arms instinctively wrap around my neck, and she hugs me tightly. I hold her close, feeling the whirlwind of her emotions swirling around us—a connection that I cherish and crave.

"What's going on?" I ask, not letting her go, unease creeping into my thoughts.

"I got fired." Her voice breaks as she releases a ragged breath that carries the weight of her worries.

She lets me go, and I sit beside her on the couch.

"Do you want to talk about it?" I ask gently.

"I had arrived late because the train had been delayed, the bus wasn't on time, and it was just a disaster. And I was so fucking tired," she explains, her voice trembling as frustration spills from her. "My life feels like it's crashing down around me."

"I'm so sorry. Do you want me to make a phone call? I can—"

"No," she says, breathing out. "My routine was thrown off because I was here, running on little sleep. My apartment isn't safe, and I'm probably going to have to move. Now, I'm jobless. My best friend no longer has time for me, and I haven't seen my family in years. Not to mention, my laptop—with a handful of videos, along with my journal—was stolen." She lets out a huff.

I try to hold back a burst of laughter and fail, the absurdity of the situation bubbling to the surface. I wanted her to quit so we'd have more time together. Instead, she was fired. It's almost like an invisible force is pushing us together. I wish she'd stop fighting it.

"My life sucks, and you're laughing *at* me!" she mutters, annoyance seeping into her voice.

I smile, smoothing down her hair, which is sticking up in disarray, the wild strands reflecting the chaos she feels inside.

"I'm not laughing *at* you, I promise. I just find you so damn adorable."

"I'm having a crisis," she insists, her voice rising.

"Let me help you solve your problems. One can be solved immediately if you move in with me," I offer. The lightness in my tone breaks through. "I have plenty of space. We'll be roommates."

"And what if I want to bring guys home after my dates? You'd be fine with that? Because, as of right now, we've made zero agreements, Weston." Her eyebrow arches, testing my resolve with seriousness.

"I'll always respect your privacy," I assure her.

"That wasn't my question," she replies, a smirk growing on her lips as she crosses her arms.

"I want you to be happy. That's it. If you're happy, I am." I smile, shifting gears, eager to lighten the conversation. "Not to change the subject, but I did get you something."

I reach toward the wrapped box, its shimmering surface catches the light, and I hand it to Carlee. She immediately shakes it.

"Can you guess?" I ask.

"No." She shakes it again. "I used to be really good at this game when I was a kid."

Carefully, she tears the corner, taking her time, not ripping the paper, as if she were unwrapping a precious artifact. A gasp escapes her when she reveals the laptop. "Weston."

"You need this," I say, warmth flooding my voice. "LadyLux has some major shit to write about."

"Thank you. I ..." She shakes her head in disbelief; her expression is full of gratitude. "I don't deserve your kindness and support."

"You deserve more than I can ever give," I confirm. "What are your plans tonight?"

She inhales deeply, her shoulders loosening. "Eating a tub of ice cream and, well ..."

"Mmm. Sounds like fun. Can you do that after a dinner party I need to attend? I'd like you to join me."

Carlee studies me. Skepticism etched on her face, the hint of a smile threatening to break through her facade. "I don't have anything to wea—"

"Taken care of." I stand, handing her a garment bag. "I'd like to introduce you to my friends."

"Your *real* friends?" she asks, the tone I love so much returning to her voice.

"Yes," I confirm.

"Is this my first public appearance?" she asks, tilting her head with a raised brow, a hint of mischief dancing in her eyes.

"We've already experienced public appearances together. However, Easton mentioned that he and Lex would only attend if you did."

"So, I'm a pity invite?" She frowns, disappointment flickering in her eyes.

"No, babe. You're the *only* person I want by my side tonight." I smile. "But we're running out of time, and I need a shower. Want to join me?"

She licks her lips, her eyes trailing down my body suggestively. Tension thickens in the air between us.

"The invitation is open."

I begin to walk toward the stairs, loosening my tie, the silk slipping through my fingers. I can feel her intense gaze burning into my back, and it fuels my anticipation. As I glance over at her, I catch her contemplating her next move. I drift out of sight and walk up the stairs.

Carlee has always played her cards close to her chest; she's a master of poker faces and subtle hints, but lately, she's been placing big bets on us. The stakes rise each time our eyes meet, and our bodies touch.

We're standing on the edge of a cliff, and I'm reaching out my hand to her. Will she take it?

20

CARLEE

My heart races as I stand outside Weston's bathroom door, the sound of the shower running echoing through the air. The steam from the hot water leaks out, and I feel like I'm dreaming. I can vividly imagine how this will go. The anticipation of being with him again pushes me forward. I want him so badly need surges through me. I almost talk myself out of it.

Instead, I enter, my breath hitching as I take in the sight before me. He stands under the stream, water cascading over his muscular frame, droplets glimmering on his skin like tiny diamonds.

"Damn," I whisper, my voice barely audible over the rushing water.

He turns around, a smirk crossing his lips, and shoots me a wink that ignites a fire inside me.

"I knew you'd come," he says.

The confidence in his voice sends a thrill down my spine.

"Hopefully, more than once."

With a boldness I didn't know I had in me, I step closer, standing on the other side of the glass wall, feeling the heat rising from the shower. Carefully, I lift my shirt from my body, and my fingers tremble as I unsnap my bra.

Weston's eyes trail up and down me, the hunger in his gaze making me feel sexy and empowered. I remove my pants and shoes, aware of every glance as I give him a show. Turning deliberately, I slide out of my panties, my heart racing. With a deep breath, I open the shower door, drawing closer to him.

I need this. I need him.

As soon as I'm within his arm's reach, our lips crash together, desperate and frenzied. He pushes me against the cool glass, and I gasp in surprise as my back and ass connect with the cold, wet surface. My fingers tangle in his drenched hair as he pulls me closer.

"I've been thinking about this all day," he confesses, his voice low and sultry.

Our tongues slide together in a sensual dance.

"Me too," I manage to reply, my breath hitching.

Weston's hand slides between my legs and a shock of pleasure jolts through me as I nearly lose my balance.

"God." The word spills out in a gasp.

His lips and teeth find my neck, sending shivers over my body. "Mmm. I'll be your god, Carlee. Is this a hickey?" He chuckles.

"Yes, asshole," I groan, half joking. "Covering it made me late."

He kisses and sucks at the tender spot, and my head falls back. Just then, Weston sinks to his knees, a devilish grin on his face as he looks up at me.

"Looks like I'm the one getting worshipped today," I mutter.

"Every day," he purrs, a fiery determination in his eyes as he lifts my thigh over his shoulder, stabilizing me with a firm hand on my ass.

His tongue slides inside me, and it feels so fucking good that I nearly lose my footing. He catches me effortlessly, refusing to let me slip as he sucks my clit, sending waves of ecstasy through my body.

I thrust my fingers through his hair, arching my back as he devours me from the inside out, and the orgasm builds rapidly, an intense pressure ready to explode. Just as I reach my peak, I hear a voice—a voice I absolutely do not want to hear right now.

I glance toward the door just as it swings open.

My eyes widen in horror, and Weston swiftly stands, taking me into his strong arms and pulling me to his chest.

"This suit?" Easton asks.

I bury my face against Weston, my cheeks burning with embarrassment.

"Easton, are you fucking kidding me?" Weston barks, glancing over his shoulder with a mixture of annoyance and protectiveness.

Easton and Weston lock eyes, an intense stare-off occurring. Weston blocks me from view, but there's one glaring issue with this plan—my legs and feet are completely visible.

"Oh," Easton says, amusement lacing his voice. "Is this the suit?" he asks with more intent.

"Yes," Weston growls, the frustration evident in his tone.

Easton bursts out laughing. "Hey, Carlee."

"Ugh. Hi," I mumble, and I wish I could disappear.

Weston cracks up, the sound bursting from him. "Get the fuck out of here."

"See you two soon," Easton calls out, still laughing as he leaves the bathroom.

"Did that just happen?" I keep my forehead pressed against Weston's chest while he holds me under the falling stream. The warmth of the water relaxes me.

"He *usually* rings the doorbell," he murmurs, breaking the delicate silence that fills the room.

"He's so telling Lexi." I pull away from him, my entire body on fire.

"Good," Weston says firmly. "They should know I chose you." His eyes glint with a fierce intensity that makes my heart race.

"You have? What about that woman last night?" My voice trembles.

The memory of him holding her tight makes me so damn jealous that I can barely contain myself.

He lifts my chin gently, capturing my lips with his. The kiss is a slow burn, igniting every nerve ending within me.

"That's my sister's best friend, Harper. I mentor her. There is *nothing* there. She tried." His words tumble out, filled with reassurance.

"You promise?" I ask, my body temperature rises.

"Believe me when I say, you're it, bestie," he insists, a teasing smile creeping across his lips. "Now, where the fuck were we? Ah."

Weston kisses down my body, and each touch causes butterflies to flutter. His lips glide over one of my nipples, and he takes it into his mouth, sending sparks of pleasure through me. With his hands resting on my hips, Weston pulls me closer as he lowers himself onto his knees, positioning me back in the same vulnerable posture I was in before Easton rudely interrupted.

"I remember," he growls out, burying himself between my legs.

His kisses on my skin, his tongue on my clit—the combination has need coursing through my body.

"I was so close," I sigh, sinking back into him. More moans escape my lips.

He grips my ass tighter with his strong hand, humming against me as his fingers flick across my clit. "So fucking good."

"Oh, my fu—" My words choke in my throat as my teeth sink into my bottom lip, a primal growl escaping me with the intensity of his pressure and pace.

Weston slides a finger inside while keeping me upright. The steam from the hot water swirls around us like a dense fog, bringing me to a dream state. Being with him like this is pure ecstasy. I brace myself with my palms flat against the glass, fighting to remain steady as I race toward the edge.

"Weston," I hiss, breathless, "I'm so close."

"Come for me," he demands, and his voice sends surges of electricity through me.

I pulse around him instantly, a guttural groan erupting from deep within as I rock against his fingers buried inside me.

"Ride it out for me, baby. You're squeezing my fingers so damn hard."

"I wish it were your cock," I plead, feeling a wild urge consume my thoughts as he continues pleasuring me.

"Can you give me another one?" he growls, his blue eyes darkening like a stormy sea, full of desire.

I meet his gaze, heart racing, and nod.

"My horny fucking girl," he says, the words dripping with lust. "We're going to have so much fun."

He smiles wickedly against me.

"Yes, yes," I breathe, feeling that familiar, intoxicating build begin to swallow me whole.

I sink deeper into him, my back arching against the wall as my body responds to his movements. He grips my ass and slams me onto his tongue, eliciting a scream from me that echoes off the tiles.

"Weston, my God," I cry out.

He doesn't stop until I come again. After my back slides down the wall, we both end up sitting in front of each other, laughter bubbling between us.

"Now you're just showing off," I tease, leaning back against the cool glass.

"We're just getting started," he replies with a smirk, rising to his feet.

He lifts his hand, and I shake my head, determined to take control. I shift onto my knees, straightening my back as I stroke him a few times before taking him into my mouth. He leans against the wall, surrendering to the sensation as I assert control over this gorgeous man, a delicious power coursing through me.

"Fuck, you're so beautiful," he whispers, pushing my wet hair back, his thumb brushing tenderly against my cheek.

"It's hard to smile with a thick cock in my mouth," I say, sucking at his tip.

His sticky pre-cum glistens as I stroke him, and I lick it up, savoring him.

"Mmm. I love how you taste."

"I love how you taste too." He places the fingers that were buried inside of me into his mouth.

I squeeze my thighs together, almost needing more. The heat spills through me, a desperate craving that pulses with each movement.

"Touch your needy little clit, baby," he mutters, reading me like a fucking book.

Without hesitation, I slide my hand between my legs, pleasuring myself while I pleasure him.

"You're a real-life porno." He grabs the back of my head and slides himself deeper into my throat. "Now you're mine. *Shit*," he hisses, reaching down to flick one of my nipples as I tease my clit.

My pussy clenches as I bob up and down on him.

"Mmm. Taking me like a *good girl*."

I nod, returning him to the back of my throat. I stroke him so fucking slow that his legs quiver with anticipation.

"Wes," I whisper, "I'm so close."

"Me too," he mutters.

I want to milk every drop of him, needing him to see me worship and appreciate all of him. Weston is what I crave, what I've always wanted. Right now, I'm living in my own personal fantasy, where the two of us can be together.

"Carlee," he whispers, nearly begging as he fists my hair in his hand.

I look up at him, smirking, flicking my tongue on the tip, barely tugging at his cock.

"You're teasing us both," he whispers, laughing.

"Isn't that what you've been doing the entire time? Now you'll come when I say. Together," I state.

He gives me a smoldering look as I barely suck on him. He throbs hard in my hand.

"You want it?"

"Fuck yes," he whispers.

His muscles tense, and I pull away, rubbing circles on my clit. His eyes are closed when I look at him. I have him dangling on a thread.

"You're perfect."

He looks down at me. "You are."

I grab him, bringing him back into my mouth, giving him exactly what he craves. I nod, letting him know I'm coming. He screams out his orgasm as I hum mine, letting him fuck my throat. His deep voice, echoing off the walls, makes me feel like the most powerful woman on the planet. He's salty and sweet, and he tastes so good. I pull back, sticking out my tongue so he can watch the silver strands shoot into the back of my throat. I drink him down, massaging his balls with my free hand, sucking and swallowing all of him until he stops pulsing in my mouth.

Weston breathes rapidly. I stand and wrap my arms around him, and he holds me too.

He dips down and kisses me, and I can taste myself on his tongue, the remnants of my orgasm mingling with his. An unspoken conversation streams between us, heavy with the weight of our secrets.

"That felt like we just ended the world," Weston says, reaching for the body wash and a black loofah.

Everything about this man is elegant—from the way he moves to the little details he chooses.

"I felt the shift," I say, reliving it. "I think that was our trauma telling us to run."

He laughs, wrapping his arm around me, capturing my lips again. "I'm only running toward you, Carlee."

"You shouldn't say things like that," I whisper. "Unless you want me to fall in love with you."

"It wouldn't be the worst thing to happen," he replies, leaning in to plant a kiss on my nose, his breath warm against my skin.

"I literally said no kissing or snuggling," I protest, yet he brushes his lips against mine, igniting a warmth deep in my chest.

"Projection and reverse psychology. This is what you really want because you want a real taste of what it's like to be with me before you decide if it's worth going official or not. You're transparent," he states. A glint of something dances in his gaze.

"How did you know that?" I whisper, genuinely intrigued, the weight of his words hanging in the air between us.

It's the truth. He knows me too well, and he has probably predicted every single one of my moves before I made them.

"I know you better than you think," he says, his voice steady.

He washes my shoulders. The warm water glides over my skin, cascading down my chest. Then, his touch lingers between my breasts.

"Really?" I ask, my heartbeat quickening with curiosity and a hint of vulnerability.

"I've read every word you've ever written and learned a lot about you. I'm a *Carleencylopedia*," he declares, a proud grin spreading across his face like he's solved the mystery of me.

I smirk, raising an eyebrow. "You've read everything?"

"Yes. I can predict what you're thinking with a single glance. Your face gives you away every time. I know you as well as you know me. I know how your heart works, how your brain puts pieces together. I also know you overthink everything. Like the possibility of us. Right now, you're unsure. Hesitant. Trying to be careful. I'm not going to hurt you, I promise."

Weston squirts shampoo into his hands with a nonchalant ease and begins to run his fingers through my hair, massaging my scalp until I relax and my eyes close.

"You can't make promises like that. I'm too jaded," I admit, my voice barely above a whisper. "I don't know how to date anymore. I push away everyone who's good for me. I'm scared I'll do it to you too."

The electricity swirling between us begins to wrap tightly around us, binding us together.

He gently cradles my head, guiding it under the stream of warm water, washing away all the suds and the weight of my worries. I lift my head to find his gaze steady on mine.

"I'm not letting you walk away from me, and I'm not going anywhere," Weston asserts, his tone firm yet comforting, reminding me he's by my side. It's something no man has ever truly done for me. "No matter what, we are forever—friends or lovers—I promise. I will always keep my promises to you."

He conditions my hair, working the silky cream through the strands with tender care before rinsing it out. I take my time washing him, my fingers exploring his broad shoulders, tracing over his tattoos as he rests his hands on my hips. We stand, exchanging smiles that speak volumes while the silent conversations continue.

"I don't want this to end," I confess.

"I don't either," Weston whispers, urgency breaking through the tranquility as he quickly washes his hair. "But we do have to get going. This is just the beginning…"

"That a promise?" I grin.

"Hell yes," he replies, grabbing my ass. "I've had a taste. Now I want the never-ending buffet."

He steps out of the shower, wrapping a towel around his waist, and then holds up a big, fluffy one for me. I fall into his arms, and he wraps the material around me with tenderness. Taking his time, he dries me off, not missing an inch as he trails kisses all over my body. I relish being at the center of his universe, even if it's temporary. We have right now, and that's all that matters, right?

For the first time in my adult life, I understand the delicate art of taking what I can get. Whatever Weston is willing to offer, I'll accept it with my whole heart. I'll wait with bated breath, enjoying each second we have together.

My breathing grows ragged as his fingertips trail over my freshly washed skin. I nearly melt under his touch. I feel the metaphorical chains on my heart begin to snap, breaking away like fragile glass as we exchange a thousand unspoken words and promises.

"Tonight, a lot of my friends will try to get you to go out with them," he says, a teasing edge in his voice. "Feel free to bust their fucking balls."

I burst into laughter, the sound carefree. "Can do."

Once I'm dry, I add some product to my hair, hoping to achieve that effortless beach wave, the kind that dances with the slightest breeze. I slide the dress over my body; it's a velvety fabric that clings to every curve. The slit goes up to my thigh, allowing me to feel both bold and beautiful.

After I dry my hair to perfection and apply just the right amount of makeup, I meet Weston in his bedroom. I gasp when I see him, my breath catching in my throat. His suit matches my dress.

"We're twinning."

"Of course," he replies, holding out his arm and leading me to the mirror, our reflections a harmonious blend of style and chemistry. "I want everyone to know you're with me. And, damn, don't we look so fucking good together?"

My heart flutters like a trapped butterfly. "We do."

Weston leans in, holding me close to his body. "We should get going."

"We should," I agree as he slides a beautiful silk coat over my shoulders.

He leads me downstairs, hooking our fingers together as if to solidify the connection between us. As we take the final step, I spot Easton kicked back on the couch, wearing a shit-eating grin.

"Oh, you thought I'd left?" he says, clapping dramatically and giving us an exaggerated standing ovation. "The encore was *incredible*. Now, what's going on between you two?"

I glare at Easton, my irritation bubbling under the surface. "You're annoying."

"I warned you that you'd get a brother when I married Lexi."

Weston chuckles, and I shoot him an exasperated look.

"It's not funny. I hate it when you both big-brother me."

"You're clearly fucking." Easton crosses his arms over his chest, his eyes gleaming with mischief. "Try to deny it now."

I clear my throat, raising a finger in mock seriousness. "Technically—"

"Look, we're just ..." Weston starts strong but falters, unable to find the right words.

Easton glances between us, his eyebrows raised in suspicion. "Are you seeing other people?"

"No," Weston states firmly.

Butterflies take flight in my stomach as I look at him, and the sincerity in his gaze sends warmth cascading through me.

"So, you're together?" Easton presses, his tone full of intrigue.

"No," I say quickly, the word slipping out before I contemplate the implications.

"Listen to yourselves. That's not logical." Easton narrows his eyes at me, clearly unconvinced.

"Don't you start," I warn, shaking my head. "You and Lexi were so annoying with the *do we, don't we*. You need to stay out of it."

I step forward, grabbing his arm and steering him toward the door. I guide him out and shut the door firmly, rotating the dead bolt with a decisive click.

"I'm telling Lexi," Easton calls through the crack before he smugly struts away.

"No one has ever stood up to him like that." Weston bursts into laughter as he moves toward me, pulling me into his arms.

The attraction between us is undeniable as our lips almost meet in a kiss. We don't commit, and I pull away, meeting his gaze, my heart racing in my chest like a runaway train.

"This is easy," he whispers.

"That's how it should be, right?" I reply, finding solace in his touch.

"What are we doing, Carlee? Just truths." His voice takes on a serious note, and I sense the weight of the question hanging between us.

"I don't know. We have to keep our promise. One of us has to save our friendship if it starts to go downhill, okay? I might not be strong enough," I admit, vulnerability spilling from my lips, my throat tightening. "I don't want to lose you."

He licks his lips. "Just promise me, if you decide I'm not enough, you'll tell me, even if it hurts, because I want you to be happy. No matter what."

"Weston," I whisper, gripping his face gently and smiling up at him, "you're more than any woman ever deserves."

"Just promise," he urges, the intensity of his gaze almost stealing my breath.

"I promise," I repeat, rolling my eyes, "but you've checked every damn box and made me add a few extras." I laugh as my fingers pinch his butt. "If we don't leave now, I might decide I'm sick. And you won't be able to go either because you have the only thermometer."

With a cheeky grin, I glance down at his crotch and waggle my brows, delivering my best fake cough. I needed to lighten the mood, and he appreciates it.

He chuckles, a warm, rich sound. "Please don't ever change."

"Please don't make me," I reply, fully aware that I've shown Weston the rawest version of me that exists.

"Never. We should go," he says, and I follow him out.

As we descend in the elevator, a familiar song plays overhead. Weston takes my hands in his, pulling me close, and we begin to dance, swaying to the rhythm in the cramped space before the doors open. He dips me down, his face inches from mine, almost kissing me. Our breaths mix and …

"Weston!"

I hear a high-pitched voice echoing in the elevator. I look up to see the woman from last night. Harper.

Weston pulls me to my feet.

"Shit, I'm so sorry about last night," she says, sincerity wrapped around her words.

Weston takes my hand and guides me out of the elevator, the warmth of his touch lingering on my skin.

"It's fine. Just don't let that shit ever happen again, or I'm telling Billie what you told me," Weston warns, his tone light but firm as he steers us away from her.

Harper groans in exaggerated embarrassment, and I turn to look back at her, mouthing an apology. She shoots me a wink and nods—*an approval of us.*

"I like her," I say as Weston leads me through the elegant foyer of The Park. I appreciate the luxurious ambience of the space.

"Be careful," he warns, his voice low and conspiratorial. His breath tickles my ear. "She gives love prophecies that come true." He glances at me, a smile tugging at his lips.

"You're making me blush," I whisper, and our eyes lock.

He leads me outside, hooking his fingers with mine, the warmth radiating between us as I keep my gaze downward. The clicks of cameras grab my attention, snapping me back to reality.

"Head high, bestie," he says with a spark in his eye.

I can't suppress the smile that touches my lips. "You did that on purpose."

"You gotta look like you're having fun if you want them to believe it," he says, his confidence radiating off him as the limo door slides open, revealing Easton and Lexi inside.

We pile into the car together, and warmth floods my cheeks when I steal a glance at Easton, who sits across from me. Weston takes the seat beside me, wrapping his arm around my shoulders as if to protect me from the world outside.

"Wait," Lexi interrupts. "What did I miss?"

Easton smirks knowingly, and I can tell right away that he didn't tell Lexi.

"Guess Easton's keeping secrets again," Weston mutters to her.

Easton's expression grows serious. "Carlee, did Weston tell you what our publicist planned?"

"No." I shake my head, eyes darting between the two of them.

"Don't," Weston urges, shaking his head fiercely. "It's too much of an ask."

"What?" I meet his eyes, confusion clouding my thoughts, and I direct my attention back to Easton. "Tell me. Tell me right now."

Easton clears his throat. "Our publicist thinks a fake engagement would be great for business and help put a stop to Lena's shit."

"Is that true?" I ask Weston, seeking reassurance from him.

He opens and closes his mouth, uncertainty clear in his expression. "Yes."

21

WESTON

I clear my throat and meet her pretty eyes. "I thought it was ridiculous and didn't want to ask you to pull a Lexi. It's a big commitment, even if it's not real." The weight of my words hangs in the air between us.

"Do it. Totally worth it," Lexi encourages with a laugh that dances lightly in the space around us.

"What do you think my answer would be?" Carlee wears a sexy little grin, and her emerald-green eyes draw me in deeper.

"I don't know." I'm unsure of how to navigate this unexpected turn in our conversation. "Wait, *would you?*"

"Are you asking?" Carlee bats her long, curled lashes.

I stumble on my words, my heart racing.

"If your publicist believes it would work—*fuck Lena*. I read her stupid love manifesto today. I'm pissed for you," she says between gritted teeth, her frustration obvious.

"You read it?" I ask.

Carlee and I haven't had a chance to talk about anything meaningful today. We were too desperate for one another.

"It was *bullshit*, Weston," Carlee mutters, her tone sharp and fierce. "Shut her up. Enough is enough. You deserve true freedom from her."

Easton nods in agreement, his expression serious. "I agree. Enough is e-fucking-nough," he states, his voice steady.

"Carlee," I whisper, knowing this is a huge step into uncharted territory. My mind wanders with the possibility of what could be.

"How about this? If you decide *this* is what you want, I'll be ready to help. What are friends for?" Carlee's mouth turns up into a wide smile as she bumps her body against mine, and her simple touch sends a thrill through me.

Lexi watches us, her expression a mixture of shock and acceptance. "Is this *actually* happening?"

"What?" Carlee finally asks, teasingly raising an eyebrow.

"You're going to get married. That's where *this* leads," Lexi whispers. Her excitement bubbles over.

"No." Carlee shakes her head, a quick, definitive motion. "We're just having fun. That's it."

"Ah, okay," Lexi concedes, then glances at me knowingly like she sees the truth hiding behind Carlee's denial.

I shrug, already familiar with this song and dance. Carlee will not admit anything.

Easton stares at me with his arms crossed, his expression unwavering as he sees through the current situation. The only one living in delulu land is Carlee, and I wonder how long she'll stay there. She's averse to love but obsessed with finding it.

"So, we're all pretending like this isn't happening?" Lexi asks.

"I'm not pretending," Easton replies firmly, his lips curling into a smirk.

He won't speak about what he witnessed. It's brother code.

Carlee tenses beside me. I can read her like a book. Every shift in her mood speaks volumes.

I lean forward, clapping my hands together. "Okay, that's enough. We're not going any further with this discussion. Tell me how the pregnancy is going."

"Great. I'm so lucky." Lexi scoots closer to Easton as he interlocks his fingers with hers.

They exchange an adorable smile before he leans down to kiss the top of her head—an intimate gesture that makes my heart swell.

"I think I want to have the announcement party soonish. I'll be sixteen weeks along then, and I don't think I can hide it once it gets hotter. No more hiding under big sweaters and oversized coats. So, I was thinking of hosting a surprise announcement with a gender reveal."

"Yes, that would be incredible," Carlee says, nodding. "Let's get together about this tomorrow."

"Before or after work?" Lexi asks. "I'll wake up super early for you."

"I got fired," Carlee explains, her voice tinged with a mix of relief and sadness. "And I cried even though I'd hated it there."

"Do you want me to call them?" Easton sits up straighter, a protectiveness radiating from him. It's clear he's already accepted this relationship, stepping into the role of big brother without hesitation.

"I already offered," I say to him, tilting my head as a way of dismissing his concern.

Carlee exhales. There's a hint of determination in her voice as she says, "I'm returning to LuxLeaks this week, thanks to Weston. I have some things to clear up."

Lexi's face lights up. "This is the best news I've heard all week. Seems like everything is working out. I do have one request. Can you get married in two months? Any longer, and I'll be ready to burst."

I chuckle, amusement sparking in my eyes. "We're eloping. You're not invited."

Lexi gasps. "That would be *horrible*."

"That would be *payback* for doing it to us," Carlee states, glancing over at me, a hint of mischief in her eyes.

I lift a brow, and she chuckles. Memories of Lexi and Easton running away to get married flood my mind. They were desperate and didn't want to wait. I understand that urge now.

"Wait, did you already secretly get married?" Lexi asks, eyeing us suspiciously.

"No. You're acting weird. Both of you are being strange. Let it be. It's *nothing*."

I know my tongue being buried deep inside her cunt wasn't *nothing*, but she can say whatever she needs to convince herself otherwise. She's in denial, and I recognize how fucking frightening it can be to feel something after a long period of feeling nothing. Yet Carlee once told me that we don't get to choose if we fall in love. Love chooses *us*. And she was right.

"Weston? Do you agree with that? Is it nothing?" Lexi presses, her eyes searching mine for the truth.

"Lex"—my voice comes out like a warning, firm but gentle—"sometimes, we're the tortoise and not the hare."

She slightly nods, telling me she understands. I'm in this for the long haul, for as long as it takes Carlee to wake up and see I'm right in front of her, waiting.

The first time we spoke, I felt a shift—a distinct awareness that things between us were different. To know one another yet remain complete strangers was a curious paradox I'd never experienced before.

She changed my life, and I'm grateful for the chance to know her—the real her. She guards her heart, but not entirely. There are fleeting moments when her vulnerable side slips through the cracks, revealing glimpses of the woman beneath the armor, especially when we're alone, and the walls between us crumble to rubble.

Fuck. My eyes linger on her as she laughs while speaking to Lexi. A warm smile pulls at my lips, and an undeniable pang tells me she's the one. But even in this quiet connection, I recognize that if I reveal my feelings right now, she'll bolt, like she's done to every man she's ever been with since Samson.

I want to destroy that fortress around her heart and rescue the princess locked inside.

Lexi gasps, her eyes widening as she stares at me in disbelief. She saw *the look*. The problem with Lexi is her perception is razor-sharp. When she's around, nothing escapes her. She catches things that should remain hidden. I shake my head as words form on the tip of her tongue.

"Shh, Lex." I cover my mouth with my finger—a silent plea to stop pushing this topic further. She plays matchmaker too hard.

Easton glares at me, the intensity of his gaze confirming that he caught *the look* too. It's like he and Lexi have already unraveled the threads of my secret.

I'm falling in love with Carlee, and I can't help it.

All I can do is smirk.

With a stolen glance, I can see Carlee's emotions. For now, she's treading carefully, and I hope she finds the courage to allow herself to fall in love again.

I trace a circle along the outside of her arm, feeling the warmth of her skin beneath my fingertips.

Easton wraps his arm around Lexi, drawing her closer, and he captures her lips in an eager kiss. "I love you."

"Love you." Her smile brightens the car as she leans against him.

They're cute together, a perfect blend of affection and genuine connection as they talk about their day. Right now, they're lost in each other's orbit.

Carlee turns to me. "Is that our future?"

"It *can* be. That's your decision," I reply, offering her a nonchalant shrug, though inside, my heart races with the weight of unspoken feelings.

"Mine?" She raises an eyebrow, skepticism undeniable. "Are you sure about that?"

"Yes." I nod, a smirk playing at the corners of my lips as she studies me with that intense focus of hers.

She's waiting for me to crack a joke to lighten the mood, but I hold back, my expression serious.

The limo comes to a halt. When we exit an onslaught of camera flashes bursts into our faces, blinding us.

Everyone says my name, trying to grab my attention.

I hold on to Carlee as I gently guide her toward Asher's stunning townhouse in Midtown. I've tried to buy it from him countless times, but he's always turned me down. It has a charming cottage feel, complete with a quaint backyard. It's rare in the heart of the city.

"This place is gorgeous," Carlee whispers, her voice barely above a breath as we step inside.

She soaks in the intricate details of the architecture—the high ceilings, lined with elegant moldings, and the long, slender windows that invite moonlight to dance across the space. A cozy fireplace casts a golden glow that chases away the chill of the outside world. It's peaceful here. The only sound is the distant echoes of laughter and chatter drifting from upstairs.

"It has five stories," I explain.

I take her hand and lead her down a secluded hallway, the dim lighting casting shadows around us. As I glance back, I catch sight of Easton and Lexi, their faces lit up with encouragement, beaming at me.

"We'll meet you in there," I say, my voice steady and reassuring.

When we're finally alone, I stop and stand in front of her.

"What?" she asks, her breath caught deep in her chest, as if she's trying to steady herself against the wave of uncertainty crashing over us.

"You're overthinking," I say, the truth obvious. "I can see it on your face."

"I can't help it," she whispers, her eyes darting away, almost as if she fears what she might reveal.

"Talk to me," I encourage, stepping a fraction closer, hoping to bridge the gap between us. "Being with me changes everything. Is it too much?" My heart races.

What if this is what pushes her away?

"Why weren't you going to ask me about the fake engagement?" she questions as her gaze pierces through me.

"I was afraid you'd say no and …" My voice trails off. The confession shocks me.

She crosses her arms tightly. "Tell me."

"I'm afraid I'll grow too attached and not want this to end."

The admission hangs in the air, a fragile truth that could shatter everything.

"Weston, friends forever, remember?" she whispers. "Let me help you."

"I know. I haven't decided what I'm doing yet. It's a big step. Fake or not." I swallow hard.

"I'll let you make the ultimate decision," she whispers. "But I'm in."

"It could backfire. That's why you have to promise me something. Promise you won't fake it with me. I want *no* barriers. If you want to text or kiss or touch me, that's *your* decision because it's what you want, not because there's an audience. They'll write our story for us, so I don't need you to pretend." I lower my voice.

"I can do that. How long?" she asks.

"My publicist said to let it run until we want to see other people, and then we'll explain to the public that we are better as best friends. We'll give it a positive spin and do the impossible."

"That seems doable," she responds, her lips curving upward. "No dating other people?"

"Unfortunately, my image can't handle a cheating scandal right now," I explain, trying to keep the mood light despite the seriousness of what we're discussing.

"It's still a yes from me. I want you to have your life back, Weston."

Her honesty is refreshing. Her gaze ignites something deep within me.

I smirk, pulling her in closer, the urge to kiss her almost overwhelming. "Which of our original rules still stand?"

She smiles, gently shaking her head, teasing me. "No falling in love."

It's a hint, a cautious boundary she's drawing. She's not ready for that leap just yet.

"Just tell me this one thing, and I'll never mention it again," I murmur, my voice low and earnest.

"Okay." She looks up at me.

"Can you imagine it? Us? Is there even a possibility?"

The question hangs heavy between us.

"Yes." The word escapes her lips breathlessly, and it's music to my fucking ears. "I've seen it in my wildest dreams."

She gasps, her breath hitching as I slide my hand up the slit of her dress.

I cling to hope, a shimmering star in the night sky. I tread lightly, knowing that the weight of that four-letter word could crumble the delicate balance she needs.

What was it she admitted to me? She needs to say it first.

Carlee's back presses against the wall, floral wallpaper brushing against her skin in the dim light of the hallway.

I lift her chin gently, my hand seeking refuge in her panties.

"Too much denial," I whisper, my pulse quickening.

"I'm trying," she replies, gasping as I run circles against her clit.

Her body instantly responds to my touch.

My mouth trails down her neck, the rough scruff of my face grazing her skin. Her fingers thrust through my hair.

"Trust the process," I mutter against her ear, kissing her forehead. "This is your favorite part."

She nods, and a few little cries escape from her lips, soft and vulnerable. I slide a finger deep inside her dripping wet cunt and hear voices approaching, followed by footsteps. She moans as I pull myself away from her panties. She lowers her dress, the fabric sliding over her skin like a whisper, and I take a step back, creating a small distance that's electrically charged. A couple passes in the hallway, casting curious glances our way, and I notice Carlee's chest rising and falling with each ragged breath.

"You make me weak. You have too much power over me," she confesses.

"Only because you allow it, because you fucking want it," I state, leaning in closer, capturing her lips in a heated kiss that sends a chill down my spine.

Her palm slides against my thick cock, which aches for her touch. She makes me so goddamn feral.

"We both know the queen is the most powerful piece in the game." I nibble on her lip, teasingly sucking on it, feeling the warmth of her breath against my mouth.

"Apart from the king," she adds, biting down on her lip, desperately pulling it into her mouth to taste where I was.

Her eyes darken with desire, deep pools that threaten to drown me.

She'll be the end of me.

"Stronger together," I reply with a smile.

As time stretches, she holds me in her trance, and I realize that if I don't break away from her now, I might never escape her spell. Right now, I'm under it, but I somehow find my strength.

"We should make an appearance. Easton and Lexi will wonder where we are," I say, gently leading her toward the second-floor loft.

It's a large space that was designed specifically for entertaining and parties. Above us hangs a dreamy fabric reminiscent of fluffy clouds. It casts a warm light over us as a string quartet weaves a melodic tapestry through the room.

Tonight feels magical. I can't explain it.

Carlee glances over at me, her nervousness evident.

"Everyone is looking at us," she murmurs, her voice a whisper meant only for me.

I interlock my fingers with hers, grounding her. "No, babe, they're looking at *you*. You're so fucking gorgeous, wearing the Calloway crown." The words spill out so naturally.

As we hand off our coats, a server offers us glasses of red wine. Tonight's theme is Paint the Town Red, which is reflected in our maroon and burgundy outfits.

I take a sip of my wine, allowing it to swirl around my mouth, its sweetness purely intoxicating. I discreetly smell the finger that had been buried inside her.

She swallows hard, her throat constricting, and the intensity between us grows heavier.

"Mmm," I murmur.

I need her like I need air, a desperate craving I can't cure. I'm fucking addicted.

"Weston," Asher calls out, pulling my attention away from the charged atmosphere. He strolls closer, a grin spreading across his face. His presence is a much-needed distraction. He checks her out before giving me a brotherly hug; the familiarity is comforting. "I'm so glad to see you, Weston. I didn't expect you to show."

"Apologies. I've decided to start getting out again," I tell him with a light chuckle. A sense of genuine friendship surrounds us. "This is great. You know how much I love this place."

"I do. And, no, it's not for sale. When it is, you'll have first dibs," he replies, his gaze flicking back over to Carlee. Curiosity dances in his eyes.

"You own this place? Impressive," Carlee states, taking a sip of her wine.

He wants to know who she is, just as everyone in this room undoubtedly does.

"Oh, my manners. This is my gorgeous *girlfriend*, Carlee Jolly," I introduce, wrapping my arm around her possessively.

Carlee chews on the corner of her lip. My girl fucking loves being claimed. For the alternate plan to work—the one I didn't share with Easton—we can't just be friends. After Carlee made it very clear that she was a willing participant, I decided to take the extreme route my publicist recommended.

"Girlfriend? Too bad. However, Weston's a great man. Loyal to the bone. If he chose you, you must be very special," Asher states, a smirk playing on his lips. "Hmm. You don't happen to have a sister?"

"I do. She's a total brat though," Carlee responds with a light chuckle, twisting the diamond necklace I gifted her between her fingers. She's elegant without even trying.

"I fucking love brats," Asher confesses, his tone playful as he pulls out his sleek business card. He hands it to Carlee with a casual flick of his wrist. "Have her call me. They're usually great lovers."

"Ah, okay. You're the type of guy who runs directly toward red flags—got it," she teases, shooting him a wink that reveals a hint of challenge. "Not sure you could handle her."

"I'd try," he admits, and their banter flows effortlessly.

Carlee can give anyone shit and hold her own. I like watching her be herself and fit in so effortlessly.

My thoughts drift to Billie, and I remember the reason why I'm here.

"How long have you two been together?" Asher asks, pulling me from my tangled thoughts about my sister's company and the danger he imposes on it.

Carlee tilts her head, as if searching for the right words. Realization flashes across her face, her brow arching as she answers. "A year. *Tomorrow.*"

"Oh, you *did* remember our anniversary," I say, smirking. It surprises me that it took her this long to realize it.

She shakes her head as a smile spreads across her face. "It *all* makes sense now."

"You two met right after you filed for divorce with Lena? That's luck," Asher explains, leaning in, intrigued. "It took me forever to date after Emma. Still not sure I'm ready. Sucks to fall in love with someone who doesn't feel the same."

Emma Manchester is one of Billie's best friends. Asher dated her for a month and fell head over heels. Then she broke it off because she didn't feel the same. They were better friends. Emma's convinced Billie and Asher are in love, but that couldn't be further from the truth.

"It's hard, trust me," I reply, meeting Asher's gaze with sincerity. "You'll meet your person *without* forcing it. The connection you share will be undeniable. You just have to be open to falling in love again. That's the hardest part because the timing is never right."

As I speak, Carlee's steady gaze pierces through me, as if she can see the depths of my feelings and can read my thoughts.

"When it feels easy, that's when you know," Carlee admits to Asher.

"To the wrong time sometimes being right," I tell her, raising my wineglass before taking a large gulp.

This dance with her is intoxicating and dangerously exhilarating. If we keep moving forward at this rate, we might never return from it.

"So, you randomly met?" Asher asks.

Carlee nods, a twinkle of nostalgia flickering in her gaze. I take another drink of wine just as Asher turns his attention toward Easton and Lexi, who are making their way toward us. Lexi, holding a glass of wine, does her best to maintain appearances while cleverly hiding her pregnancy. I can't tell, and I know. No one in this room will notice.

"Both Calloways are madly in love at the same time. I didn't think I'd ever see the day. Looks good on you. Pretty damn jealous," Asher comments with a grin as Easton gives him a firm handshake.

As they speak, I loop my finger through Carlee's and gently pull her away, creating a small bubble of intimacy.

She jabs her finger into my chest. "I can't believe you put me on your one-year wait list."

"Why not?" I ask, smirking. "If I recall, you said no woman would wait that long to be with me."

"You *friend-zoned* me. I didn't think there was a chance," she whispers incredulously, her voice barely above a whisper.

"There always was." My tone is steady. "I did what LadyLux had suggested and didn't rush shit."

"Did it work?" She tilts her head.

"It did," I admit.

Suddenly, the quartet begins to play, their strings and slow tempo filling the air. People dance around us as we stand inches apart.

"We should dance," she says, her eyes sparkling with something I can't quite place.

The glow of fluffy clouds casts a warm light around us. I place my hands around her waist, feeling something between us shift. She runs her fingers through the strands of hair above my collar. It's a small, intimate gesture that sends my heart racing.

She glances around as countless onlookers cast curious glances our way.

"They're wondering who you are," I reply, my gaze locked on to hers. I pull her closer so there is no doubt that we're together.

"Who am I?" she mutters in my ear, a sultry edge to her words that sends a shiver down my spine.

"Mine," I say, feeling the magnetic pull between us intensify.

Our lips gravitate toward each other, and the world around us fades into nothingness. She's the light at the end of my tunnel, the one that's been guiding me forward all year long. I need to kiss her.

"Carlee," I whisper, ready to spill too many truths, but before our lips can meet, Easton interrupts.

I pull away reluctantly, knowing the opportunity has already passed me by. Disappointment takes over, and I feel the need to apologize to her.

Easton leans in, whispering, "Billie's main competitor approached Banks to help them gain majority market share because some big mergers are in the works. He hasn't decided if he's doing it yet. Said he had a lot to think about."

I glance at Easton. "I'm impressed it only took you five minutes to find out."

"Because I outright asked, and he told me," he replies, pointing his finger into my chest, firm and unwavering. "You waste too much fucking time. And I can't believe you didn't tell me it was *that* serious. If he does that, she's done."

I let go of Carlee and turn to Easton, placing a reassuring hand on his shoulder.

"We won't let that happen. Try to enjoy your night, and we'll figure it out before anything happens. She won't ask for our help, but there are things we can do. Now, your pretty wife is waiting for you," I say, nodding toward Lexi, who's chatting with some friends across the room.

"I'm leaving in thirty minutes," Easton says with a huff, his frustration lingering in the air.

I glance at Carlee. "Excuse us," I say, pulling Easton out of view.

"When we go back, switch with me. I need to know if Carlee can tell us apart yet," I say to him.

"Why?" Easton raises an eyebrow, skepticism etched on his face.

"I need confirmation of something." The words hang in the air, heavy with meaning.

He sighs but doesn't say no. "You're playing games."

"It's how I knew Lexi had fallen for you." My voice is steady.

"Really?" he asks curiously.

"Yes," I say.

"You owe me," he states. He cracks his neck and literally transforms into me, cocky-as-fuck smirk and all.

"You're so good," I say.

He rolls his eyes, then strolls flawlessly to Carlee, and I go to Lexi, who immediately sees through it.

"Pretend," I say, running my fingers through her hair.

She pulls away, her stormy expression showing her irritation, but then she relaxes against me. Not too close though—Easton would flip his shit.

"I'm testing something." I keep my gaze forward, then glance at her.

"Sometimes, I want to kick your ass. Like right now, for example, for forcing me to be in on your scheme," she says.

I pull her into my arms and dip her down.

She laughs. "You're really good at playing Easton."

I glance over at my brother, laughing his ass off with Carlee.

I grin at her, flicking my brows upward, but my voice is steady. "You're being too pushy."

Lexi looks up at me. "Are you in love with her? Because if you hurt my best friend, I swear to—"

"Yes," I mutter, cutting her off. "Yes. Stop meddling and *be* her best friend. She misses you."

Lexi's face softens. "I'm sorry I've been so bu—"

"I know you've been busy." My voice is light. "We both want you and Easton to spend as much time together. You've got so many life changes happening. It's understandable. But right now, Carlee needs *you*. These aren't conversations she will have with me. If you really want to help, do it by listening instead of questioning feelings she's trying to understand."

"Okay," Lexi responds, her voice firm. "If you hurt her, I will make your life hell."

"If I hurt her, I hope you do," I reply, seriousness lacing my words.

Moments later, my arm is forcibly tugged away.

Carlee stands in front of me. "Did you think that would work?" she asks with skepticism in her tone. "Easton isn't as believable as you."

"He's actually spot-on," I say, tilting my head and grinning wide.

"Why are you looking at me like that?" she asks.

"Because I can."

I pull her into my arms, knowing she could tell the difference between us. I lead her farther into the middle of the room, where we dance.

My brother's words echo in my mind. *You waste too much fucking time.*

Is that what I'm doing?

The song comes to an end, and there's a brief pause. I glance around the room, spotting familiar faces from various social circles mingling and laughing. Chatter fills the space, yet anticipation settles over me as I lock eyes with Lexi and then with Easton.

My brother tries to read me, and I can feel my heart pounding against my rib cage—a reminder of what's at stake. Carlee looks up at me and smiles. My thoughts are chaotic, and suddenly, the noise around us fades into a muffled hush.

I realize this is it. Urgency and need take over. I suck in a deep breath, moving forward with my plan. I steady myself before dropping down to one knee in front of her.

Her shock is real, but so is the heavy pounding in my heart as my throat goes completely dry.

"I mean every word that I'm about to say," I whisper.

"Okay," she says with an encouraging smile.

With careful deliberation, I pull the black velvet box from my pocket. As if on cue, a string quartet begins to play, surrounding us in a melody that feels both timeless and intimate. Suddenly, everything surrounding us disappears. It's just me and Carlee, and our world narrows down to this very moment.

Isn't this the way it's supposed to feel? Easy?

"Carlee Jolly," I say, my voice filling with emotion that catches me off guard, "you're so pretty."

"Weston," she whispers.

"You're one of my very best friends, and I can't imagine a life without you in it. There was a time when I thought I'd never be able to open my heart to anyone again. Until I found you. When we're together, the world fades away. There is no one on this planet I'd rather spend forever with than you. Please do me the honor and become Mrs. Weston Calloway. Marry me, Firefly."

A whirlwind of emotions sweeps across her face as they flood through me.

She smiles, and I capture it to memory.

"Yes," she whispers.

Carlee delicately extends her hand, and I press my lips to every finger and the sensitive skin of her wrist. Her pulse quickens—a reminder that our connection is real—as I slide the three-carat solitaire ring onto her finger. It fits.

The room bursts into applause as I stand and thread my fingers through her silky hair, feeling the energy wrapping around us as I capture her lips.

"That felt real," she whispers, holding my cheeks in her hands before kissing me. She steals my breath away.

"Did I mention my divorce will be finalized on Monday?" I lift a brow.

Her mouth falls open. "Really?"

"Yes," I admit as she pours every ounce of herself into me.

"You're almost free," she whispers against my mouth. "I'm so happy for you."

We're rushed by guests of the party, offering congratulations.

I glance over my shoulder, meeting Easton's eyes with a grin.

Well played, he mouths with a nod, knowing witnesses were necessary.

Lexi nods and gives me a thumbs-up. I turn my attention back to Carlee, wrapping my arm around her and kissing her hair as she chats with those who immediately introduce themselves. They all want to befriend her now.

As she politely chats and smiles, I find it hard to remember a time without her in my life.

She already feels like my forever.

This is how it begins ... with a fake engagement laced with real emotions.

One day, she'll be able to see the obvious, and I can't wait until she does.

22

CARLEE

I didn't predict him dropping down on one knee. When his hand took mine, a bolt of electricity surged between us. When our gazes met, I knew he meant every damn word.

My heart still hasn't stopped thumping hard in my chest as if trying to escape the overwhelming emotions threatening to take over. The gentle touch of his fingers along my arm makes my breath hitch. Warmth spreads through me. As I hold my hand out to meet his friends, the diamond shines in the warm glow of the lights, casting tiny sparkles that dance across our faces. It feels like I'm living in a dream.

The happiness he wears is genuine, radiating from him like sunshine. I see the promise burning behind his unwavering gaze—he will save our friendship if it's in danger.

"Carlee's my best friend," Weston admits, his voice smooth as he kisses my knuckles.

The wink he gives me nearly does me in.

He commands the room effortlessly as his friends and acquaintances greet and congratulate us as if we were royalty. The experience is different, and right now, I don't feel like an onlooker in Weston's life. The shift in the room is immediate. We exchange stolen glances and shy smiles—a language that no one else can decode.

I'm introduced to so many people that my mind spins, names and faces melting into a blur of laughter and cheer. Weston shines under the spotlight, and I'm grateful he can so effortlessly keep conversations going. His words are full of charm and charisma, and I could watch him under this light all night.

I'll help however I can, knowing he'd do the same for me.

He leans in closer, whispering in my ear, "Fake fiancée looks good on you." His warm breath sends a shiver down my spine.

"You had this planned the whole time?" I ask when he pulls me back onto the dance floor.

"I didn't," he replies with a casual shrug. "But the timing felt perfect."

"You just carry an engagement ring in your pocket for funsies?" I ask as he spins me around.

I try to wrap my mind around the sudden shift in our relationship.

He whispers, "Can never be too prepared. It was just in case I resorted to the *fuck it* plan." He smirks, his gaze flicking down to the ring.

"It's very similar to Lexi's. I shouldn't have this," I whisper. Her ring is a pink emerald-shaped diamond. The only difference is the color. Mine is crystal blue.

A sense of disbelief coats me. I'm not exactly sure how we got here.

"Agree to disagree. My grandmother would've wanted you to have this. When she thought she lost her original ring, my grandfather replaced it with this one. She adored and cherished it for decades," he states with conviction, twisting it around my finger. "It was meant for you. I didn't even have it resized. Perfect fit." His words float in the air.

After many more conversations filled with laughter, several glasses of wine, and dancing, we unexpectedly find Lexi and

Easton in the crowd. I didn't even realize they were still here. Their voices ring with laughter as they joke with Asher and his brother, Nicolas.

"There's the happy couple! Congratulations again!" Asher calls out, waving us forward with a drunken smile. "I was just telling Easton that I couldn't believe you two have been seeing one another for a year and kept it hidden for so long. Super impressive."

"It's *very* impressive. A year. Weston's *great* at keeping secrets," Easton adds, his tone laced with sarcasm as he glares at his brother before turning his gaze toward me.

Emotions fill his darkening eyes, and I've seen that same expression on Weston's face before. He's *pissed*, and I can feel the tension boiling beneath his casual demeanor.

I guess Weston didn't tell him about our weekly meetings after all. I always suspected he had or that maybe Easton had pieced it together in his own way.

Weston keeps his grin intact, effortlessly finishing his wine. The mood around him is light. "Anyway, I think we're going home. Are you staying?"

"We'll join you," Easton replies, shaking Asher's hand firmly, though I can sense the underlying edge of frustration. "We'll chat soon."

The four of us leave together, and the room's energy follows us as we make our way to the door.

"Interesting," Easton states, tucking his hands into his pockets as we walk through the cozy living room on the first floor.

Weston glances at me, his brows raised. The boyish grin I adore so much stretches across his face. When he looks at me like that, I can almost convince myself that this is possible.

"That timeline can't be right." Lexi shakes her head as she interlocks her fingers with Easton's.

"It's correct," Weston insists firmly as we climb into the

spacious interior of the sleek limo. We sink into the soft leather seats.

"You knew each other in February?" Lexi's voice comes out as a whisper, her eyes darting between us, as if she's trying to assemble a jigsaw puzzle with missing pieces. "I didn't meet Easton until the summer."

There are too many hidden truths that I'm not sure where to start. I never expected Weston and I would be discussing this with them tonight.

Weston hesitates as the weight of our reality hangs between us. "We met a year ago at Sluggers and became friends. We watched a lot of baseball and drank shitty booze together," he recounts, a nostalgic smile creeping onto his lips as he recalls the nights filled with laughter.

Easton watches us intently, his gaze piercing yet playful before his face cracks into a smirk. "You hooked us up."

Weston wraps his arm around me, proudly giving me every ounce of his attention. "We just made sure you were in one another's orbit so you could collide. You did this. It's impossible to force two stubborn people into falling in love."

He turns to Lexi and Easton.

"You wanted us to be together?" Lexi asks, her voice full of disbelief.

"Yes, after a few conversations, we knew you would be perfect together," I chime in. My heart swells when I think about them.

"We met weekly to discuss it because neither of you would've responded to a planned date," Weston admits. "You're welcome. But also, congrats. And thanks for proving us right."

"I can't believe this. You've known each other for a year," Lexi says.

"She needs to be rebooted," I say to Easton. "I think she's stuck in a loop. And, yes, when the clock strikes midnight, it will officially be a year since I spoke to Weston and bought him a beer," I answer.

The time flew by so quickly.

"You planned *everything*?" Lexi asks.

"Not everything, but a lot of things," I explain.

"The yellow roses were actually for Carlee. When you stole Easton's car and pretended to be him," Lexi interjects, realization dawning on her. "Wow, okay, you two are pros."

Weston chuckles at her compliment. His laughter is like home. "It worked out the way it should've. That's all that matters."

"Now I feel dumb. I thought I'd introduced you at your birthday party," Lexi says.

I smile. "Sorry about that. But it was adorable."

"This makes so much sense," Easton says, shaking his head. "Of course."

"That's the first night I saw the look. You've felt this way since then. I knew it," Lexi says directly to Weston.

"What is she referring to?" I turn to him, and he chuckles nervously.

"Enough, Lex," Weston urges as the limo rolls to a stop.

We get out of the car, and he grabs my hand. A teasing smile plays on his lips as he leads me into the lobby of Park Towers. Lexi and Easton trail behind us, but we're too locked in with one another to care.

"What is she talking about?" I tease. My heart throbs as we step onto the elevator. He presses the button to shut the door, so we're alone.

In an instant, his mouth is on my neck.

"You already know," he whispers, his breath hot against my skin.

"Fuck," I gasp.

Exhilaration and need wash over me as he devours my lips with a desperate urgency. The doors slide open, and in one swift motion, he lifts me over his shoulder, carrying me inside his penthouse.

"You can't just pick me up like a caveman." I laugh, my voice bubbling with joy as my body rests over his shoulder.

He holds my thighs tight, smacking my ass. I yelp, but I love the way it feels.

"Says who?"

"Me!" I retort as he pushes open his bedroom door.

The anticipation of what lies ahead has me in a choke hold.

Carefully, Weston lays me down on the mattress, and I lean up on my elbows, watching my Prince Charming loosen his tie, his fingers slipping the fabric from around his neck, revealing the muscles beneath his shirt.

"Stay right here," he mutters, his voice low.

I tilt my head, drinking in every chiseled muscle. "Okay."

The night has been a blur, and I'm living in a constant state of shock, wondering how this happened.

Earlier, everything was in disarray, and life felt chaotic and uncertain. Why does it now seem like the stars are aligning?

Weston steps out of his room, and I can hear him skipping down the stairs, the faint sounds of his footsteps echoing through the stillness. I lie back on the bed, glancing at the ring around my finger, seeing it sparkle in the glow of the lamp beside the bed. I tell myself this is fake.

Weston returns, and he's holding a cupcake with a flickering candle on top. The flame dances and casts a glow across his face. He's protectively cupping the flame with his hand as he walks toward me.

I sit upright, my heart racing.

Weston drops to his knees so we're face-to-face. The moment's full of unspoken words. "Happy one year."

I glance up at the clock on the wall, and I notice it's just past midnight. "But we weren't dating."

"Weren't we?" Carefully, he brushes my hair out of my face, his fingers grazing against my skin. "We've seen each other weekly, except for that month I was away on business." He searches my

284

face for understanding. "And you would've fucked me at least five times."

I scoff, offering a teasing smile. "Oh, it was *more* than five."

"You're all I ever think about," he whispers, his breath ghosting across my lips. "Make a wish."

Weston holds the cupcake in front of me. I meet his gaze, appreciating his thoughtfulness and how he makes the smallest thing feel special.

"Any wish you want," he mutters.

I think about my life. Uncertainty weaves through the air. I want the impossible to be possible. I take a deep breath, closing my eyes, and then quickly blow out the candle.

"Tell me when it comes true," he says with a wink, almost as if he can read my mind. "You have to taste this icing."

Carefully, he runs his finger along the frosting, and I open my mouth, allowing him to feed it to me.

"Mmm. Damn," I say, resting my arms on his shoulders as he leans in close, our faces mere inches apart. "I want you so bad, Wes."

He leans forward, tracing his lips across mine, tasting my words.

"Please," I whisper, my voice barely audible, desperate for him.

He sets the cupcake down on the table next to the bed, then unbuckles the heels from my feet, his lips trailing kisses up my leg. With precision, his strong hands slide effortlessly up to the zipper on the side of my dress. Weston hooks his fingers in the thin straps, peeling away the velvety material that clings to my body.

He tosses the dress into a pile on the floor, then stands before me, memorizing and admiring every inch of me. His gaze is intense and full of hunger.

"I like it when you look at me like that," I admit.

His need for me is undeniable. He's straining against the fabric of his suit pants.

He slides his suit jacket off his shoulders, the fabric slipping down his toned arms before falling to the floor in a puddle of dark red, and then he carefully undoes his vest and tie. I can't help but watch each deliberate move he makes as he removes his clothes. Exhilaration soars through me as he undresses for me. I sit up, my hands gliding across the contours of the muscles on his stomach. There are no more barriers between us, no more holdbacks. Our want is raw and unfiltered.

It's just me and Weston, together and alone. It's too intimate and overwhelming as passion streams between us. An intense soul connection, the same one I felt the first time our gazes met at Sluggers. That's when I knew that maybe the two of us had a chance. It was a shot in the dark, two people so opposite from one another that there was no way this could potentially work.

Or maybe it could, and I've been living in denial.

My fingers trail across his warm skin, and I lean forward, pressing kisses around his abs.

Weston places his hands on my shoulders, gently guiding me down to the mattress. I sink into it, feeling the cool comforter beneath me. My heart races when he grabs a condom from the bedside table, the sound of the wrapper crinkling a simple reminder of how far we've come. I watch him as he sheathes himself, mesmerized by his confidence as he settles between my legs. He pauses outside my entrance.

"What are you waiting for?" I gently ask, aware of the hesitation in his movements.

"We can't uncross this line," he reminds me, his voice low. "We can stop."

"Go slow," I whisper, pleading with everything I am for him to give himself to me. "Please don't make me beg anymore. I've waited a year for this."

He grips my waist and does exactly what I asked. Each thrust is deliberate, allowing me time to adjust to every long inch of him. His breath is ragged and erratic in my ear, and it nearly causes me to crumble beneath him.

The magnetic energy between us is intoxicating, and I'm being pulled under, lost in the overwhelming sensation of him. A low growl escapes me; I'm unable to contain the flood of feelings as they overtake every cell in my body.

"Are you okay?" he asks, affection mingling in his tone as he rubs his nose against my neck.

He smiles against my skin.

"It feels right," I reply breathlessly.

I am so full that I can barely handle it, but he's so gentle. I thread my fingers through his messy hair, savoring every second with him. I don't know what the future holds for us, but I'm willing to explore it further as long as he's trekking the dark woods of uncertainty alongside me.

Whimpers escape me. He's pure ecstasy.

My muscles tense underneath him.

"I want more." I can barely speak.

His movements are intentional, pushing as far as he can go, and I can't help but let out a sigh, holding his cheeks with my hands as I meet his gaze, staring into his blue depths.

"Being with you is easy," I whisper, studying him, hoping he understands what I mean.

It's not just in this moment; it's always. I never have to try when I'm with Weston; I just have to be.

Moans tumble from my lips, and I whisper his name in a breathless exhale.

His mouth captures mine, our tongues dancing in a rhythm that feels entirely natural as he slides out of me, only to plunge back in again. Emotions stream between us, and this is more than just having sex. It's not supposed to be like this. It's a connection that transcends the ordinary—something I never anticipated. I shouldn't be lost in this in-between space with him right now, yet here I am, tangled in his web. I lose all control when I'm with him. I always have, and right now is no different.

"You were made for me," I confess. The thought takes over and nearly consumes me as my back arches off the bed.

"Carlee," he breathes, each syllable of my name falling from his lips like a prayer, "you feel so good."

"Yes, yes," I say, knowing I'm on the brink of demolishment. "Keep doing that," I whisper as he picks up his pace, slamming into my G-spot.

Warmth floods through me, and I'm lost in the haze of him, wandering in a dream state.

"Oh. Oh. Oh, Wes." It's all I can manage as every muscle tightens and releases with euphoric intensity.

I growl out my orgasm, each thrust from Weston sending shock waves through my body until I see glittery stars bursting in the darkness. The room drifts away, dissolving into a blur, and I'm lost with him, consumed by the sensation. The only thing that brings me back to reality is Weston murmuring that he's close. Seconds later, he's buckling above me, groaning out his release as he sucks and kisses my neck, leaving tingles in his wake.

Our heads rest together, our breathing stabilizing, and his eyelashes tickle my cheeks as he rubs his nose gently against mine.

"It's never felt li—"

"I know," I say, my voice a murmur.

"My Firefly," he whispers.

I can't help but wonder how we found each other in the darkness. I've embraced it.

Weston pulls out, and the euphoric moment morphs into something else entirely when he stands, his posture tense.

"What?" I ask, recognizing the alarm in his expression.

"The condom broke," he whispers, and my gaze instinctively drops to the shredded rubber around his cock.

Panic rises within me. I sit up abruptly.

"Are you on birth control?" he asks, searching my face for reassurance amid the growing worry.

"Yes, but I've missed the past few days." I shake my head. "I haven't needed them. Since we met, I haven't been with anyone."

His face softens as if he's fighting a war within. He removes the broken band from him and sits next to me, anguish shadowing his features. "I'm so fucking sorry."

"I'm not freaking out," I say, waving my hands in hopes of creating some airflow to cool the sudden heat rising in my chest. "What are the odds?"

"Not zero," he replies, his expression shifting with concern.

"Do you even want kids?"

The question hangs between us. It's not something we've discussed in detail.

"The timing has to be right," he confesses in a hushed tone.

"Yes," I whisper, allowing myself to drift into a daydream.

It's easy to imagine playing with our children. It streams in my mind like a home movie as unspoken words and emotions float between us. Weston would be pure happiness. I can envision our kids, little versions of us, running around, playing baseball, delicately plucking piano keys, and splattering paint onto a canvas with him. A laugh escapes me as I picture them being cheeky smart alecks with our attitudes.

"It's a nice thought," he says, almost as if he saw exactly what I did.

I move to my room and pull my birth control out of my bag. I take the two pills I missed, swallowing them down. When I return to him, I wrap my arms around him and fall back onto the mattress with him. With my head resting on his chest, I hear the rapid thud of his heart as he draws shapes on my arm.

"It's going to be okay," I tell him, knowing I've had a scare like this once before.

"Of course it will."

A smile touches his lips as he holds me, and the weight of the world melts away. With my arm draped around his waist, I mold against him, feeling like he might disappear if I'm not touching him. Weston gently scratches my back, and I release a relaxed sigh, knowing I lost my full self with him.

I snuggle into him, our faces inches apart as he lifts the blankets over our bodies, covering us.

"I just remembered you said your divorce will be finalized tomorrow."

"That's right," he admits.

"So, I guess the thirty-day timer starts for when you can get remarried?" I ask curiously as he holds me.

His brows leap upward in surprise. "There's no waiting period in New York. I can get married the next day if I want."

"Why did she stop fighting you? I don't understand."

"After hanging out with my sister, I filed a statement with the court, detailing why I'd asked for a divorce, accompanied by the evidence I'd recently gathered that could put her in prison. She likes her freedom more than my money, so she decided to settle for the original amount I offered her." He brushes his thumb across my cheek.

His gaze lingers on me, a silent conversation unfolding.

I exhale as emotions swirl between us. "Will you tell me what happened between you two? It'll stay between us, I promise."

He's never told me any details about his divorce, and I want to know so I can support him.

Weston's eyes close tight, and I interlock my fingers with his, offering my support silently. He can take as much time as he needs.

"I caught her sleeping with her bodyguard, and then I found out she'd hired a hit man to murder me while I was with Easton."

"No," I whisper, my heart sinking as I realize the extent of her betrayal. It's much worse than I ever imagined. My nostrils flare, and nausea rolls in my stomach.

"Brody saved my life," he whispers, his voice barely audible. "If he hadn't been there, I wouldn't be here right now."

Weston doesn't say anything for at least ten minutes. "I cherish every day because I was given a second chance. Nothing like a wake-up call after facing the Grim Reaper," he continues, and I hold him a little tighter as if I can protect him from his past. "I've got the best people watching out for us."

"I can't imagine a world where you don't exist," I breathe out, the realization settling heavily in my heart.

"When we first met and I said you made me feel alive, I meant it. I was a walking corpse, haunted by knowing the woman I'd loved wanted me dead and almost succeeded. I looked past the cheating, but the death wish is unforgivable. She wanted to make sure if she couldn't have me, no one could." His voice is full of pain, and I hate that he lived this hell.

"I'm so sorry. I can't imagine." A few tears spill down my cheeks.

Had Lena succeeded, we would have never met. The thought chills me to the bone.

"Please don't. I'm still here," he says, wiping my tears away with his thumb before pressing a kiss to my forehead.

"After all that, you were still kind to her."

"You never have to meet someone at their lowest," Weston exhales. "It's almost over, and eventually, it will be in the past. My publicist did warn me that things might get worse before they get better. We should prepare for online attacks."

I watch him closely, absorbing the gravity of his words, but I also understand how this works. "I'll be ready. So will Lux."

He studies me. "You don't need to fight my battles."

"I always have," I whisper. *I always will.*

"Your words are your weapon, Carlee. Choose them wisely," he mutters, wrapping his strong arms around me.

I listen to his heart thump in his chest as his fingers thread through my hair.

"What are you thinking about?" he asks.

"Us. What are we doing?" I place my hands flat on his chest, meeting his blue eyes.

"Right now, we're cuddling," he mutters, smiling, completely relaxed. "What is it? Speak freely."

"I don't think I can be friends with benefits with you," I confess.

Weston sits up and searches my face. "Are you ending this?"

23

WESTON

"**S**hocking," I say, narrowing my eyes at her as I reach forward to gently touch her hand.

Turmoil coils tightly behind her green eyes, but beneath it lies undeniable desire.

Which will win?

Can't fucking wait to find out.

"You know, I thought we'd have at least a week minimum before you did this." I keep my tone light.

"What does that mean?" Her brows rise. Confusion and curiosity dance across her pretty face.

"The chase is over, and you're done, right? At least you can *officially* choose a new hall pass. Might have to call Jensen and warn him about you," I say, tucking loose strands of her hair behind her ear. My fingers barely graze her skin.

Her nostrils flare with a hint of indignation. "You think I'm running away from you?"

"Yes. It's what you do, but ..."

My smile doesn't fade as my gaze roams over her, pausing to linger on the light dusting of freckles gracing the bridge of her button nose. It's squished in anticipation as she waits for my next words.

Fucking adorable.

"You'll never escape me, Carlee. I've lived rent-free in your head for over a decade, and I will *always* be there. Even if you run."

Her mouth opens as if she'll refute my claim, but silence hangs heavily between us. I may have her wrapped around my little finger, but I'm chained to her. Neither of us can escape this. Tonight confirmed that for me. We're in too deep, and I think she knows that too. This is how she protects herself from heartbreak.

I tilt my head sideways, a teasing glint sparking in my eyes. "Deny it. I'm waiting."

"You know I can't," she whispers, her confession almost a plea.

"Exactly. So, we'll keep playing this game until *you* decide *you're* done. I'll pretend I don't want you, and you'll pretend you don't want me. We'll have the most incredible, mind-blowing sex while living in delulu land."

"But—"

I place my finger over her mouth.

"Gorgeous, you've got me, but know I'm not always going to give you what you want. And I will be a *total dick* about it too. Because, for some reason, you fucking love that, so we'll continue this until *you* surrender. And just know, I don't tire, Carlee. Fucking ever. We're playing a brutal game of capture the flag, but *you're* the flag."

She studies me, remaining silent.

"Oh my God. I'm the problem. I'm a *giant* red flag," she says, realization dawning on her like sunrise.

"If you're a red flag, you're the highest thread count there is," I say, grinning.

"Weston, you can do better than me. You're settling. And you're going to grow bored or exhausted of me. One day, you're going to wake up and see that."

I brush my thumb delicately across her bottom lip, feeling her breath catch. "Now you're changing tactics to try to convince me not to play the game. Sorry, babe. It's not happening."

"I'm a *brat*," she admits, a hint of defiance coloring her tone.

I tug on her hair, enjoying her feistiness. "And I fucking love brats."

"Clearly!" She shakes her head. "What are we doing?"

"Whatever you want. Look, everything doesn't have to be so serious. Live a little. Have some fun. The only decision that has to be made is what we're doing right now because the future doesn't exist. It's not guaranteed. Choose to live in the moment with me … if you want," I tell her, my voice inviting as I crawl out of bed to grab my boxers.

I pull my phone from my suit pants and set it on the bedside table to wirelessly charge. I feel the weight of her gaze lingering on me as I slide back between the sheets and pull the blankets over my body.

"Want some snuggles?" I ask, lifting the comforter, my tone casual but laced with something deeper, something both of us understand.

Carlee hesitates. "So, that's it?"

"What else do you want me to say? You're not pushing me away, even if you try."

"And if you get tired of me?" she asks.

"Not possible. I want to spend every second with you."

She crawls toward me, sliding her body next to mine. I wrap my arm around her, pulling her close, feeling her warmth pressed against me. Her presence is familiar and electrifying, and I feel a sense of comfort wash over me.

"You're the best big spoon," she admits, molding against me.

I inhale her hair and close my eyes. Exhaustion from the night —fuck, the entire weekend—crashes over me like a tidal wave. It washes away the chaos, and Carlee leaves a soothing calm in its wake.

"No contracts. No rules," she whispers. "I desperately want to live in the moment with you, whatever that is."

"Deal," I say, nuzzling into her, interlocking my finger with hers, feeling the cool metal of the ring.

Carlee ditching her rules is music to my fucking ears. The chains she keeps locked around her heart are breaking away.

"One rule still stands."

"Yes?" she breathes out. I can almost hear her heart racing.

"You're mine. And *only* mine."

"Are you claiming me, Calloway?" She tilts her head back.

I smile against her sweet skin, savoring her. "Yes, I fucking am. I play to win."

The silence drifts over us, and I almost fall asleep again.

Her voice cuts through the stillness. "I'm Catwoman, aren't I?"

This causes me to chuckle. "You are a thief in the night."

She smiles. "Yeah? What did I steal?"

"The impossible," I mutter against her ear, and she lets out a content sigh.

We both know she stole my heart, but she isn't ready to acknowledge it yet.

One day, she will.

I hold on to that thought like a beacon in the night as I drift away to dreamland with her snuggled in my arms. It feels right, the way it should be.

I WAKE UP TO THE SUN RISING OVER THE HORIZON, THE GOLDEN RAYS spilling into the room. The sky is painted with vibrant oranges and pinks, and it feels like a new beginning. A fresh canvas. I grin, tearing my gaze from the beauty outside.

I reach over where Carlee was sleeping, and the mattress is cool.

I never felt her leave.

I let out a breath, staring at the ceiling ,when I hear the distant sound of a cabinet shutting, followed by the grinding of coffee beans.

After sliding on some joggers, I go downstairs, my curiosity guiding my steps. What I find stops me in my tracks. There she is, with a steaming cup of coffee cradled in her hands as she looks out the large windows overlooking Central Park. The morning light dances across her features, illuminating her delicate shoulders. I love how my T-shirt hangs loosely on her slender frame. As my eyes trail down her body, I catch a glimpse of pink lace panties beneath.

Her laptop is open at the bar, the cursor blinking mindlessly.

I love to fucking see it; knowing that she's trying makes me so proud of her.

My eyes quickly scan over what she has.

My LuxBabies. Have you missed me?

I know you may be wondering where I've been. Where do I start?

I focus back on Carlee. Her wavy, messy hair is flipped over to one side. She's a beautiful masterpiece that I could stare at all day.

"Good morning," I mutter, making my presence known.

"Hi. Morning." She glances at me, then quickly looks away, her cheeks flushed with a rosy hue.

I smirk, moving farther into the kitchen to pour myself a cup of coffee.

Now she's acting shy. Fucking adorable. I can't get enough of her.

"How'd you sleep?" I ask, feeling proud that I held her through the night, cherishing every second of her being so fucking close to me.

"Great, actually. The best sleep I've had in literal years. You might be magic," she admits as the rich aroma of coffee fills the room.

"You're always invited to join me," I explain, leaning against the counter to watch her.

The sunlight streams in through the window, casting a warm glow on her face.

"Have you thought about your wish list? Now that we're getting married, I'd like to start knocking things off it."

"Weston, we're *not* getting married." She chuckles.

"Okay," I say, grabbing my cup of coffee and joining her in front of the tall windows.

A blanket of snow covers Central Park. Its white surface glistens under the sunlight, but it's beginning to melt.

"We're not!" she insists.

I take her hand, kissing the ring that graces her finger. "Okay."

I watch the diamond catch the light, shimmering like a distant star before I return to her gaze. "But *what if* we did?"

She snatches her hand from my grasp. "You've already had one shitty marriage. Your next one should be the real deal."

"*Okay.*" My response comes out sultrier than I intended.

She tilts her head, curiosity lighting her eyes. "Is that your word of the day?"

I shrug.

"Perfect. I want to cash in one of my wishes then," she says, shooting me a smoldering look.

"Okay?" I lift a brow, suddenly intrigued.

"Play for me," she requests, her voice enticing. "Please. I've been staring at this piano all morning, and I want to hear it."

"*Okay,*" I mutter, setting my mug on the bar with a clink.

"Pretty please?" she asks, looking up at me with puppy-dog eyes.

How can I deny her?

"You'd better be glad you're cute," I tell her.

The truth is, she's my best friend, and I'll give her *whatever* she wants.

With a smirk, she hooks her pinkie with mine, then guides me to the grand piano in the center of the room. "You haven't forgotten how to play, have you?"

"No."

I place my hands on her hips and lift her effortlessly to sit on top of the polished surface of the piano. Carefully, I pull the bench seat forward and part her legs, revealing her barely there panties clinging to her delicate curves. Her tiptoes balance on the edge of the keys, teetering with anticipation.

"Mmm. I'm suddenly feeling extremely *inspired*," I say, licking my lips.

"Really?"

Carlee hooks her fingers in the hem of her T-shirt, removing it and revealing herself to me. Her perky little nipples stand at attention, exposed to the air. I breathe deeply as I place my fingers on top of the keys.

"What would you like to hear, gorgeous?" I ask, looking up into her eyes, pressing my face against her, inhaling her essence. The only barrier keeping us apart is the thin fabric of her panties. I grab the material gently with my teeth and tug until it pops back onto her.

She keeps herself propped upright with a glint in her gaze. "Anything. I'm not picky," she whispers.

Für Elise. A classic.

At first, I start slow, my fingers hesitant, knowing I haven't touched the keys in over four years, but it's a skill that lies dormant, never forgotten. I pause, cracking my fingers to shake off the rust before I return, sitting up straighter, my body awakening. At one point in my life, I thought I'd never play again. Lena hated every note I struck.

With renewed confidence, I continue, my fingers flying over the high notes, the twinkling reminding me of a music box.

"Beethoven wrote this song for a woman he wanted to marry," I say, my voice a low murmur as I stop to peel her panties to the side, needing to taste her.

She's already so fucking wet for me as anticipation simmers between us. My fingers fly back to the keys, the song growing more intense as she greedily chases her orgasm, the melody intertwining with the mounting tension in the room.

Carlee moans, a sound that resonates deeply within me, and I hum against her, relishing in our sweet symphony. I only withdraw my tongue when I feel her tense beneath me. Her panties are drenched with her arousal.

"It wasn't published while he was alive, only discovered forty years after his death," I offer, my eyes closed as I lose myself in the melody surrounding us. "You taste so fucking good," I whisper, my voice husky, before returning my mouth to her.

I dive deeper into the intoxicating rhythm of her body, enjoying that I have so much control over her, even though she pretends I don't.

"Wes," she breathes, her head falling back in surrender, exposing the delicate curve of her neck as she arches toward me.

The notes ring through the penthouse, their vibrations dancing off the walls, mingling with her sweet moans.

It's literal music to my motherfucking ears.

"I think you'll get the extended version today. Panties off for me, gorgeous," I command, kissing the inside of her thighs, my fingers dancing across the piano keys.

Carlee does as I said, wiggling them off her body, allowing the fabric to drop to the floor like a forgotten note.

"Ass on the edge, like a good girl. Steady yourself for me."

"Keep playing," she hisses, surrendering to my tongue, giving me everything she has to offer.

I suck and lick every inch of her as I match the song's tempo. I fucking savor her, savor this.

"Mmm," I growl, aware that she's right on the brink of losing herself. "No, no," I mutter, kissing her clit gently, feeling her pulse beneath my lips. "Not yet. We've got at least three more minutes left."

With a smile, I pull away, my fingers pounding harder into the keys.

"You want me to beg?" she pleads, her breath hitching as I tease her with my breath before I plunge my tongue inside her, claiming her.

"Mmm. My greedy fucking girl," I mumble between sucks and kisses.

"Wes, please."

Her body trembles with anticipation. I close my eyes, continuing the song by memory, lost in the allure of her as Carlee screams out my name. The encore continues, the crescendo rising as she slides off the lid of the piano, her ass landing against the keys with a beautiful, jarring sound.

I can barely focus, my concentration fraying as I lift my hips so she can remove my joggers and boxer briefs. She pushes them to my ankles. Carlee straddles me. Her movements are deliberate as she slides onto my cock.

"Fuck," I gasp, looking up into her eyes, shimmering with need as she guides me deep inside her.

"Play until the end," she demands breathlessly as she slides up and down me. Her fingers tugging roughly through my hair as she rides me.

"Take what you need," I whisper, the words slipping from my lips. Then I capture her nipple in my mouth.

"Yes, yes," she urges.

I lift her ass, slamming her into the keys with each thrust as we frantically chase our ends. Together, we're lost in each other's magnetic pull.

As I raise her leg, driving deeper inside, she wraps her arms around my neck, her breath hot against my ear as she whispers, "I'm so close."

With an earth-shattering gasp, I pull out, losing myself on her stomach as she leans back against the piano, surrendering completely.

I stare at her, barely able to catch my breath. The aftermath of our passion swirls around us.

We lost control.

She glances down at my release dripping down her body, desire still flickering in her eyes.

"I wanted you inside of me," she murmurs.

I meet her gaze, and the silent conversation between us is loud and clear, each unspoken word hanging heavily in the air.

"Fuck," I breathe out, realization dawning. "You *want* me to give you a baby?"

Her mouth opens and closes, but I see her hidden desires written on her face. Her expressions always give her away.

Carlee turns and moves to the kitchen to clean herself up, her shoulders tense. I pull up my joggers and follow her, the air thick with unsaid words.

"It was a moment of passion," Carlee admits.

The thought of putting a baby inside her puts me in a fucking choke hold.

Our eyes stay locked until I pull her into me, holding her. "The day you say those three words to me and mean it, I'll keep you pregnant," I mutter in her ear, my breath warm against her skin.

A small gasp escapes her as she holds me tight, not daring to let me go. "I don't know if I can, Wes." Vulnerability laces her words.

"You will, and when you do …" I stop mid-sentence, not having to finish my thought. The weight of this revelation lingers tightly between us.

Carlee glances over at her laptop, and uncertainty washes across her features. "There's something I have to tell you."

I search her face, waiting as the seriousness of her mood takes hold.

"Whoever stole my laptop knows about our friendship, along

with every time we've met up, and I think they're aware that I run LuxLeaks too," she confesses, her voice shaking.

"How do you know?"

"Lexi texted me this morning about this brand new website that was just created," she says, reopening the screen and typing the address into the browser. Her face pales.

"*Obsessed with Weston Calloway dot com?*" I say, sitting on the stool in front of her laptop. I chuckle, trying to lighten the mood. "Love the address."

She shakes her head. "It's cheesy! Whoever came up with this sucks. I guess your name has better SEO than Carlee Jolly though. Anyway, they've published every single journal entry here that mentions you. All of my most private thoughts about *you*."

I can hear the worry in her voice and see it etched on her face.

"Carlee. It will be okay." I grab her hand and pull her closer.

"My thoughts weren't for anyone's entertainment," she whispers, and I wrap my arms around her, holding her tightly as if to shield her from her own confessions. "People are saying I'm obsessed."

I chuckle lightly, trying to ease the tension. "Are you?"

"No," she hisses, looking at me incredulously.

I smile, unable to resist the pull of her energy. "You sure about that?"

"I'm being serious. Not everything I said about you was great and glowing. And my biggest fear is you'll read it and *hate* me." Her voice drops to a near whisper.

"Never," I say firmly, swallowing hard against the knot in my throat. "Were you honest and truthful?"

"Yes." She glances away from me, unable to hold eye contact.

I tilt her chin upward with a single finger, forcing her to meet my gaze. "Your truths are yours regardless of how it's delivered. I can handle your criticisms. I've been doing it for *years*."

"I think you should read it so you're not blindsided if someone mentions it to you," she says, sounding defeated, her shoulders sinking. "I'm so sorry."

I lean closer and read the top of the website.

Alleged journal entries from Weston Calloway's new fiancée, Carlee Jolly.

Read her private thoughts from when she met Weston and leading up to their recent engagement.

"I've got my team on this. They're doing whatever they can to find out who's behind this. Might take them about a month, but when I learn who it is, because I will, they will pay," I say between gritted teeth, feeling an overwhelming surge of anger from seeing her so upset.

Carlee pulls up the LuxLeaks website, her fingers trembling. "They used the same layout as my LuxLeaks website. It feels like a clue. Like whoever is behind this knows the truth. What should I do? Let them continue to monetize us? Deny I wrote it? I'm freaking out. I'm worried about the videos getting leaked or them exposing that I'm LadyLux. I have a lot on the line."

She starts to hyperventilate, and I stand to wrap my arms around her.

"I'll text it to my publicist and legal team and see what we can do," I assure her firmly, wanting to comfort her. "We'll figure it out, I promise. I also know some people who can hack the website and get it shut down."

"The damage is done. You won't be able to erase everything." Her face turns bright red. "They've structured our friendship like it's a modern-day love story. It already has thousands of views in hours. The world has already written our story."

"No. *You* wrote our story," I say, smiling as I glance at the screen. "Right here. These are your beautiful, powerful words that are setting the stage for us. No one else's. Not even LadyLux's. *Yours,* babe. Thousands of people are reading Carlee Jolly right now. Kinda jealous, to be honest. You're my favorite writer."

She swallows hard. "Spoken like my number one fan."

I shoot her a wink. "You know it."

"Always finding the bright side of things. How do you do that?" she asks, smiling.

"Just proving that I'm not the evil twin," I say, easing the conversation away from her anxiety.

"Thank you," she whispers. "You always save me before my thoughts have me crashing."

"I always will." I press my lips against hers. I gently move her hair over her shoulder and meet her eyes. "I'm suddenly in the mood for pancakes."

I shut the laptop and turn my full attention to her.

"I don't like you being exposed like this," I say. "Whatever you said about me doesn't matter. I'm really sorry you're going through this, and I somehow feel like it's my fault. Someone must have been watching us to know we'd been meeting and targeted you to get to me."

"Or maybe they found out about LuxLeaks and want to ruin me personally for all the things I've written about. You were just a bonus. My journal is the juiciest thing they've found so far. And I can't point blame anywhere but at myself for being so careless. Neither of us asked for this." She lets out a frustrated huff. "Weston, I called you a pretentious asshole. A cocktease. I wrote in detail about how you were frustrating and stubborn."

"And? I *am* all of those things. So are you."

Her face cracks into a smile despite the circumstances. "That's fair."

"When you're with me in any capacity, whether as friends or lovers, there will *always* be some publicity stunt to wedge us apart. I can't keep people in my life because of it." I grab her cheeks gently in my palms, looking deep into her eyes. "Only the strong survive. Do you understand?"

"Yes," she whispers, her conviction unwavering. "I'll be okay. I'm spiraling, but I don't crack under pressure."

"Diamonds are formed from pressure. And, oh, how you shine,"

I say, brushing my thumb across her cheek. "It will take more than you calling me an asshole or stubborn or frustrating to upset me. I hear that from Easton daily."

Her eyes twinkle, and a hint of resilience returns as her shoulders relax. I refuse to be the cause of any more of her stress.

"Thank you," she says.

"If it's your truth, fuck it. I will always support your truth over my feelings." I gulp down the rest of my coffee, now barely warm. "I think I'd like chocolate chip pancakes today with whipped cream. Need to change."

I head out of the kitchen, but she doesn't directly follow behind me.

"You're joining me today, fiancée. Get dressed," I call back over my shoulder as I take the stairs.

"Fake! You forgot the word *fake*," she hollers back, but I can tell she's smiling.

"Okay," I yell, my voice echoing off the walls upstairs.

Carlee Jolly will be the fucking end of me, and I *want* her to be.

24

CARLEE

I'm mildly aware there are paps across the street as we eat breakfast.

"Showing off that ring," Weston comments, and I realize I'm sipping my coffee with my left hand fully visible.

"Not on purpose," I reply, noticing how it sparkles in the winter sunlight. "But maybe I should give everyone something to talk about when it comes to us."

"Am I watching a villain be born?" His eyes soften at the edges, almost as if he's lost in a daydream.

I wish I could see what he sees. Maybe, one day, I will. I hope.

"If you keep looking at me like that, they'll say *you're* obsessed with *me*," I joke, smiling over the rim of my cup.

"I have a secret," he whispers, leaning in closer. "I *am*."

"Oh, stop." I shake my head.

"Still not convinced? Okay," he says with a nonchalant shrug, grinning as our pancakes slide across the table.

I ordered pumpkin while he opted for chocolate chip, topped with whipped cream, just as he had mentioned.

"Want a bite? They smell amazing," I offer, cutting a chunk of my pancake for him. He does the same for me, and we feed each other. "That's delicious. Very chocolaty."

As we eat, our eyes flick toward one another, but neither of us feels the need to fill the silence with words. It's a comfortable quiet where conversation flows naturally when needed. His presence is enough, an entire experience in itself.

My mind drifts as I gaze out the large windows of the diner. It may be in the upper forties, but the streets are bustling with people soaking up the sun. A steady stream of hungry couples enters the building, and the bell above the door jingles each time.

Low chatter fills the air, mingling with the aroma of bacon and freshly brewed coffee. Our gazes meet once more, and just as I'm about to speak, my phone rings.

"Shit," I mutter, glancing down at the display.

Weston's brow arches. "Who's that?"

"No one," I assure him, but he reaches forward and answers.

"Hi, Carlee Jolly's future husband," Weston says.

I can hear a deep voice on the other line.

"Who the fuck is this?" Weston snaps back, continuing to eat, then laughs. "Oh. Hilarious. Yes. One second."

My anxiety spikes as he hands me the phone.

"Oh, so you're just going to get engaged and not tell anyone in your fucking family? What the fuck, Carlee Jean Jolly?" my older brother Matteo says.

My teeth grind together at the use of my full name as he scolds me like a child. "The last time I checked, I was a grown-ass woman with grown-ass problems who can make grown-ass decisions. For the last time, stay out of my life. It's not your business."

"Yes, it is," my brother yells.

"I'm not arguing anymore." I end the call with a frustrated sigh. "Older brothers are a pain in my ass. I feel sorry for Billie."

Weston smirks. "He cares about you."

"He needs to chill," I state as a text comes in.

I unlock my phone and read it, quickly realizing it's a group message featuring my mom, both brothers, and sister.

> MATTEO
>
> Are you fucking kidding me? That conversation wasn't over!

There's a picture attached of Weston and me leaving Asher's place. The ring on my finger is circled, and he drew arrows pointing to the headline, *Weston Calloway Engaged Again!*

"Oh God." I seethe, my eyes widening.

It was rude of him to send this to everyone.

Weston leans forward, and I turn the screen around for him to see.

> DEAN
>
> Who the duck is this guy?
>
> DEAN
>
> Duck.
>
> DEAN
>
> DUCK!
>
> ABBI
>
> Is this an AI image? I can't tell. I don't think it's real.
>
> MOM
>
> Can you please watch your language, or I'm leaving this chat?!
>
> DEAN
>
> FUCK!

I lock my phone and continue eating, trying to push the anxiety away. "He's being a drama queen."

"What will you do?" he asks.

"Ignore them until I can't." My heart races.

I thought I would have a few days to get my plan together and properly announce it to the family. I was wrong about that. My phone continues to buzz, and Weston turns it off.

"Thanks. I guess we should've planned this better," I say with a laugh.

"Is this a good time to tell you I'd like to invite you on a family holiday with my parents?" His eyes meet mine.

Butterflies flit in my stomach. "Can we not?"

"It will be fun. Plus you do need to meet my parents. They're a lot, but they mean well." He smirks. "I'm looking forward to my mother's reaction since I vehemently swore I'd *never* get married again."

"But you're not," I say, taking a sip of my coffee.

"Okay," he replies, moving his empty plate aside.

"Not that word again."

His gaze slips down to my mouth and lingers a little too long.

I finish chewing my last bite and gulp it down. "You're openly eye-fucking me now?"

"What will you do about it?"

He leans forward, reaching toward my face. His thumb brushes against the edge of my mouth, and when he pulls away, there's whipped cream on his finger. I blush as he pops it into his mouth.

"Mmm. You always taste so good."

His words set my entire body on fire.

Millie walks over with a bag of to-go boxes and takes our empty plates. "Tell Easton and his wifey I said hello."

"I will," Weston says cheerfully, handing over his card like he wasn't just lost in a fantasy with me.

When she returns, she squeezes my shoulder. "So good to see you again, baby. How was the pumpkin?"

"Great. The powdered sugar and whipped cream were top notch," I say as we stand and move toward the door.

She shoots me a wink.

"I'll see you again," I tell her with a wave.

"I know," she says. "I like her, Weston."

"Me too," he says.

We load into the car and return to The Park. It's still early, and I've experienced a full day of emotions. I grow quiet, wondering how Weston and I ended up here together.

"I think you're right about me needing to read your journal, even though I don't particularly want to," Weston finally says, placing his hand on my thigh and gently squeezing it, drawing my attention back to him. "I was thinking you could read it to me one day. Not right now, but when you're ready."

"Absolutely not." I shake my head, laughing at him like he's lost his mind. "I can't do that."

He smirks, closing the distance between us, eliminating any space that once separated our bodies. "What if I told you I'd make it worth your while?"

I stare at his mouth, wanting to taste the coffee on his tongue. "How?"

"As long as you read, I'll keep pleasing you," he whispers, his head resting on my shoulder as he peppers kisses along my neck. "I just want to desperately hear your inflections, your breathless pauses, and the cadence in your voice as you string your beautiful words together."

It's just the two of us in the back of this car, and right now, I'll do anything he wants, especially when he gives me all of his attention. His hand slides down my body, settling between my legs. I'm relieved the partition that separates the driver from the passengers is up. Right now, we are entirely alone, speeding down the road, and I desperately want him.

"Deal?" he whispers, applying pressure to my clit.

My entire body springs to life.

"You *promise* to make it worth my while?" I ask, moaning out as he rubs gentle circles against me.

"Fuck yes," he breathlessly says, working me up so fucking quickly that my body quivers in anticipation.

He knows exactly what to say and how to touch me until I'm

putty in his hands. A pant escapes me as every fiber of my being begs for him, for more. I'm so fucking greedy for him.

"Didn't hear your answer, gorgeous," he murmurs.

"Yes," I say breathlessly. "As long as your hands and mouth are on me."

"Happy that's settled then."

He pulls away, leaving me breathless and burning with desire. Let's not mention that my panties are drenched.

My breasts rise and fall as disappointment crashes over me. "Wait. You're not finishing what you started?"

"Nope." The cocky bastard checks his watch and smirks.

"I'm going to get you back," I breathe out, my nipples hardening, my heart racing. "Oh, just you wait."

His laughter spills out, a sound that only ignites my frustration further.

"Love seeing you so undeniably desperate for me." A raging fire simmers in his blue eyes, matching the swell in his jeans.

Before I can protest, his phone rings, and I see his sister's photo flash across the screen.

"Wow. It seems like the news about us is getting around," he says, placing a finger over his mouth before answering.

First my family and now his.

"Calloway," he says.

She immediately starts in on him.

While he chats with her, I readjust myself, trying to calm down. My body wants every inch of him.

Weston places her on speakerphone and lifts his brows at me as I unbutton my shirt, revealing my bare breasts. I position myself, giving him a better view of me as I slide my fingers inside my jeans. I bite my bottom lip, feeling how slick with need I am.

His eyes are zeroed in on me as I continue to touch myself.

"*We're just friends*," his sister mutters mockingly.

He mutes his phone, glaring at me. "You'd better not come."

I sigh out. "Or what?"

He unmutes. "Don't you have enough to worry about?"

"Not really," she tells him.

I haven't comprehended anything she's said. I work myself closer and closer, and right before I completely lose myself, I remove my fingers from my panties, nearly gasping for air as I squeeze my thighs tightly together.

Weston mutes his phone, taking my fingers and placing them in his mouth. "Don't break my only rule. You're mine, Carlee. Every orgasm that pretty little pussy has is mine. For me. By me. Do you understand?"

I meet his eyes, mesmerized by his undeniable need for me. "They're yours," I confess.

"Weston?" Billie asks. "Are you still there?"

He stares at me for another few seconds. I glance down at his bulging cock as he unmutes.

"Sorry. Yes. I need to go soon."

"I was just saying, you gave Asher Banks major friendship credit for proposing at his damn party. Everyone believes you're the best of friends now," she says.

"We *are* friends. Asher is a good guy when he wants to be." He laughs. "I thought the two of you would grow out of this nonsense. The animosity is ridiculous. You might need him one day, sis."

"*No. I. Will. Not.* He's rude, and he thinks he's smarter than everyone in the room. He loves the sound of his own voice and believes his stupid jokes are hilarious. Annoying as hell," she replies.

I button my shirt, but he smoothly continues the conversation. "Are you more concerned about where I got engaged than about the fact that I'm engaged? Am I reading this conversation properly?"

She sucks in a deep breath. "I was just trying to eat my bagel in peace when I was blindsided by questions regarding *your* engagement. I was speechless. I wasn't even given a text or a heads-up. Absolutely nothing from you or Easton. I was approached in public, and they videoed my reaction."

"I'm sorry. I should've considered you. It wasn't planned, I promise," he says.

"So, you expect me to believe you just carried our grandmother's engagement ring in your pocket as backup?" Billie asks.

I focus back on him because I thought the same thing.

"That's right," he responds. "I didn't know when the opportunity would present itself, but I was *always* ready."

"Always? What does that mean? You'd been planning this for months, just waiting for a good time to ask the question?" She sighs.

"Harper told me to be ready and to trust my gut," he admits.

My mouth falls open because he mentioned Harper gave love prophecies that came true.

"Great! You got a love prophecy from Harper. It's over. If you pull an Easton and elope, I'll never forgive you," she warns.

"Are you finished?" he finally asks.

I mindlessly scroll through the text messages my family sent. I'm furious because Matteo decided to invite our grandmother into the discussion. What's next? The rest of the Jolly cousins? I can feel my anger rising, hating that I'm thirty years old and they're still meddling.

Billie sighs. "Congratulations. You seem very happy. I just want to make sure you're not putting yourself in the same situation as before. I worry about you, Bubbie."

"Aww," I whisper.

He winks at me.

"I'm happy and safe," he comfortably confirms as he twists the ring on my finger. "We'll plan something soon, okay? You, me, and Carlee."

"Good! I still need to plan a girls' weekend with her and Lexi," she says.

"I'm sure she'd love that," he repeats back to her. "Anyway, we'll chat soon."

"Soon," she says and ends the call.

"Didn't want her to know I was here?" I ask.

"I didn't want her to bombard you with five hundred questions that you're not ready to address yet," he replies, watching me. "What's up?"

I shake my head.

"Come on. Something is bothering you."

"Are you sure I can make you happy?"

Weston chuckles. "I'd be a lot happier if you were sitting on my face, but this will do for now."

A smile slides across my lips.

"Get out of your head," he says. "And to answer your question, yes. You have no idea what you do to me."

We arrive at The Park and head to Easton and Lexi's place. As we walk in, music drifts through the air, and the delightful aroma of baking cookies fills the space. Easton is settled in an armchair, carefully drawing in a little black book.

"Breakfast," Weston announces, holding up several takeout bags.

"Amazing!" Lexi replies from the bar, her focus glued to her laptop, where she's typing away.

She has been honing her playwriting skills for the past five months while navigating her pregnancy. Easton has already secured a production company for when her project is complete. From what she's let me read, I think her work is nothing short of incredible. With the right actors, it could be Broadway huge.

As she takes a sip of tea, Weston carefully sets the bags down on the bar.

"What have you two been up to today?" Lexi asks, her gaze flickering to the hickeys on my neck and my swollen lips.

"Just been working and had breakfast. Oh, Weston played *Für Elise* for me," I offer casually as I meet his warm gaze.

He shoots me a wink.

"Really? *Für Elise* is an interesting choice." Easton closes his book and strides over to us. "You played again?"

Weston's perfect teeth graze over his bottom lip. "Yes. I was very inspired. Anyway, we brought pancakes, sausage, and eggs. Do you need anything else before we head out?"

Easton pulls Weston aside, their voices low as they share a quiet conversation. Though I can catch fragments of their words, I don't have enough details to piece it together. Neither of them sounds happy.

Meanwhile, Lexi and I chat in the kitchen as she slices into her sausage links. "What if I held a surprise costume party here? I could order amazing food and adorable little cupcakes. And before anyone can bite into their cupcakes, we'll reveal it's really a pregnancy announcement, and the color of the cake will be the expected gender."

"I think that's a very cute idea! The inside of the cupcake is such a nice touch. Get everyone involved," I respond enthusiastically.

"Even Easton and I have no idea. We'll learn with everyone else," Lexi says, her excitement growing. She gently places her hand on her belly. "I'm so happy, but I'm scared to death."

I smile wide. "I'm so happy for you. You're going to be an incredible mom. Plus, you have the best doctors on the planet. Everything is going to be perfect with no complications. And I'll babysit as much as you need. I love babies. Did I cover all your fears?"

"Yes." She snorts. "Thank you." She barely gets the words out before she bursts into crocodile tears.

"Oh my God," I say, immediately hugging her. "What's wrong?"

"It's hormones." She shakes her head, sniffling. "On top of all of that, I just want you to get your happily ever after too. And I've been way too pushy. I'm sorry. I can tell you're stressed, and I don't want to add to it."

"Hey, it's fine. Please don't apologize. I find it endearing that you're not great at playing matchmaker. It's just part of your personality to try to set me up with your husband's identical twin brother," I tell her, trying to understand. "If you keep crying, I'll start too, and we don't need that. I'm a very ugly crier. My brothers made fun of me for it! Plus, you're not supposed to be under any stress at all. Cross my name off your list."

She sniffles, sucking in a deep breath. "I just remember how we dated that same jerk in college and how we have the same taste in men," she says with a laugh, even as tears stream down her face. "I read a few of your journal entries. It made me so sad, Carlee. I'm really sorry. I feel like I abandoned you after everything you did for me."

"No, no. You did not, Lex. Seriously. Those entries weren't for anyone to read. They were just for me to get my thoughts out of my head. I don't even fully remember what I wrote," I say truthfully. "No pity parties, okay? Weston and I are *great* friends. And when things seem too good to be true for me, they usually are, so I'm being careful. Even though I *want* to lose myself with him, I don't know if I can. I'm trying to give this a chance," I confess, and she listens to every hushed word.

"A chance is all Weston needs." Lexi wipes away her tears.

"Uh, everything okay?" Easton asks, moving toward us, concern etched in his brows. "Darling?"

"She's fine," I say, smiling, loving how much Easton cares.

"Just overwhelmed with joy! I think we planned the surprise baby reveal party," Lexi says, recovering quickly, sniffling as she squeezes my hand.

"Great," Weston says, walking toward me. "Anyway, please enjoy your breakfast. Millie wants you to visit her."

"Maybe. Have fun." Easton gives us a wave as Weston walks past me, grabbing my hand and pulling me away.

"I'll text you some food ideas," Lexi says, waving with a smile.

We take the elevator to the penthouse, and he seems lost in thought.

"Easton just forced me to take leave from work," he mumbles.

"Why?" I ask.

"Because he pulled rank like an asshole," he says, shaking his head. "He said I needed to spend time with you."

"He'd also said he wasn't getting involved." I shake my head, somewhat annoyed.

"Yeah, well, he changed his mind and wiped my schedule for the next two weeks."

We step off the elevator and walk inside.

"If you could visit anywhere in the entire world, where would you go?"

A smile touches my lips. "Home."

"Anywhere, and you choose Texas?"

"There is a caveat." I laugh. "You have to come with me. My grandma said she'd remove me from her will if I didn't visit."

"Damn. Your grandma is tough." Weston smirks.

I narrow my eyes. "She didn't give me a contract to get married at forty."

"Touché." He crosses his arms over his chest.

"How about we trade? I'll go on vacation with you and your parents, and you can meet the Jollys. Deal?"

He holds out his hand, and we shake on it.

"What was with the hesitation?" he asks.

"It's just … I know everyone in my family will get attached to you. And if we break this off, they'll never let me live it down."

It's the truth. Mawmaw will love Weston for his gentle heart. They all will. Even my asshole brothers.

He exhales, smirking. "You said *if.*"

My mouth opens and closes. "I meant when."

"No. No, you didn't," he mutters.

We tumble through unspoken words, lost together in thought.

"Stop looking at me like that," I whisper, feeling my body temperature rise.

"Not a fucking chance, Little Miss Denial." Weston shrugs off his coat and hangs it by the door. "*Not a fucking chance.*"

I kick off my shoes and move to the kitchen to grab some water, my throat feeling parched. As I glance at the piano, heat rushes through me, and *Für Elise* drifts into my mind.

Weston watches me closely.

"Easton seemed shocked that you'd played again," I say.

"It'd been a long time. Lena had forced me to stop."

"You stopped painting because of her as well?"

He nods, a shadow crossing his face. "Love, combined with mental and emotional abuse, is fucking wild, isn't it? I would have given up *everything* to make her happy. She isolated me from anything that had brought me even a semblance of joy. That woman was only smiling when I was miserable. She fed off my sadness and anger. When I caught her cheating on me the first time, it was in our bed. The second time, it was against my piano. The third time, well ..."

"In your art studio," I whisper. "You caught her three times?"

"Love makes us blind. I gave too many chances."

His expression changes, and my heart breaks for him all over again. Even though he shows me his softer side, I think about how much this divorce has hardened him.

"I'm so sorry, Wes." I move closer, wrapping my arms around him.

"Don't," he says, leaning his head to kiss my hair. "I don't want your pity."

"It's not pity; it's admiration," I tell him, holding him tighter, repeating the same words he said to me not too long ago.

"You inspire me to reclaim those parts of myself that I thought I'd lost forever," he admits, and I don't let him go.

"I guess all that's left is for you to paint me." I smile, pulling away just enough to meet his gaze.

He kisses my forehead. "I already have."

25

WESTON

I interlock my fingers with Carlee's and guide her up the stairs. The wooden steps creak under our weight, the sound echoing in the quiet house. I open the door to my painting studio and lead her around the corner. Windows line the wall, filling the space with golden beams of sunlight that dance across the floor. She's fascinated by the studio while I'm captivated by her.

"I didn't realize this room was so big," she says in awe. When I gave her the tour, we never entered this room.

She follows me to the opposite side, where my supplies are neatly stacked. It includes tubes of colorful paints, different-sized brushes in jars, and large blank canvases waiting for inspiration.

The easel is set up in the middle of the room. I've escaped here, spending countless hours pouring my heart into the fine details. I've been working on it since the night we first kissed.

Carlee meets my gaze before walking around to the other side of the easel. I follow closely behind.

Her hand covers her mouth, and she gasps as she sees it.

My eyes sweep over the image I painted of her, her serene beauty forever captured. She's standing at the window in my T-shirt, her silhouette framed by the swirling snow outside. Her face isn't fully shown, just a glimpse of a smile reflected in the glass. That expression of hers lights a fire in the dark corners of my heart.

"Gorgeous," I whisper.

This is the image of her that haunts my thoughts, the one that floods my mind when all is quiet. She causes the noise of the world to fade away.

"This is how you saw me?" she questions, a note of disbelief in her voice.

"Yes," I say. "And when I close my eyes, I can still imagine you standing there, wearing a smile that wasn't meant for me. *True Happiness.* That's what I named it."

"I'm speechless," she says, her hand resting over her heart, her breaths coming a little quicker now. "You're *so* talented. This is brilliant."

I laugh. "I'd hope so, considering how much my father spent on private instructors. At age three, I started art classes and piano lessons. I could've attended Juilliard. Instead, I chose business school."

She's still staring at the painting, her head cocked to one side. "There's something very familiar about this."

I breathe in deeply, watching her eyes scan over my strokes. "It's just a memory captured in paint."

"Maybe so," she says, turning to me, her eyes sparkling with excitement as if she discovered something new. "Do you have anything else? I'd love to see more."

"They're in storage. More than one hundred paintings," I explain, my voice tinged with a hint of regret. I removed them all.

"Promise me. Please. Let's hang them on your walls. You have tons of blank space," she encourages, giddy with excitement.

I love that she's supportive, but I'm not used to this. Our deep connection sends a rush through me.

"That's what you want?" I tuck loose strands of hair behind her ear, my fingers brushing against her skin.

"Yes," she replies, her voice sincere.

"Okay," I say, knowing Carlee craves the things money could never buy—a shared human experience with *me*. And, fuck, do I want to give it to her.

"If I'm moving in, we might as well make it feel like home," she encourages. "Until I figure out what's going on with my apartment," she adds, a hint of vulnerability creeping into her tone.

"You can stay as long as you want," I express, never wanting her to leave.

"You make me feel safe, and you're like human melatonin. I instantly fall asleep when you hold me close. I don't think I want to give that up just yet."

I can see the layers of her thoughts as she shuffles through them. I wish she'd let the cards fall.

I chuckle, pulling her gently into my arms. "Where do you want to hang this one, roomie?" I ask, a grin breaking across my face.

She tilts her head up at me. "Above *your* bed."

"You already poison my thoughts. Isn't that enough?" I tease, unable to hide my amusement.

"No," she admits, her tone serious, but her eyes betray her. "I want under your skin too."

"You're already there," I say, wearing a cocky-as-fuck grin.

Carlee tries to kiss me, but I only barely brush my lips against hers. Her frustration with me simmers just below the surface.

"Are you going to deny yourself me the rest of the day?" she asks, grabbing my shirt, desperately clenching the fabric in her fists.

"Maybe," I reply with a nonchalant shrug, enjoying the tension building between us. "I might let it go on for a week."

The flash in her eyes and the blush creeping to her cheeks tell me everything I need to know. She enjoys this more than she'll ever admit.

"You want me begging," she whispers. It's almost desperate.

"You wanted to play games, gorgeous. So, we're fucking playing."

THE PLANE WAITS FOR US AS WE GET OUT OF THE CAR. CARLEE STOPS mid-stride, her eyes widening as she gazes over the jet, taking in every polished detail. She studies the Calloway Diamonds logo on the tail, and when she meets my eyes, I can't help but smirk.

"I can't believe this," she whispers as I place my hand on the small of her back.

"You should," I say as we board the aircraft.

I guide her to the window seat, wanting to experience everything with her.

She curiously glances.

"What are you thinking?" I ask, intrigued by the emotions that cross her face.

"Mile-High Club?" she suggests, blushing, a grin spreading as she runs her fingers through her hair, attempting to deflect attention.

"Are you a member?" I ask, my brows rising.

"Not *yet*," she admits.

Her eyes lock on to mine. It's a challenge.

I lean in and whisper in her ear, "So fucking tempting. But we're still playing unless you're giving in."

Soon, we're speeding down the runway, the wings lift, and then we're soaring. Carlee looks out the window, her eyes wide with astonishment as we curve around the city, revealing a breathtaking view of Manhattan. The sun glimmers off the river, casting glittery reflections across the water.

"I love New York," she whispers, pure wonder in her tone, "so much."

I catch a glimpse of another smile I'm not supposed to see. My heart skips a beat, and I snap the moment to memory right next to the other one. She turns to me, and the eye contact is intense. It holds us both in a prison of unspoken connection.

"It's been a long time since I've felt this way," she admits, her voice barely above a whisper.

I remember holding her last night as she drifted to sleep, how her smile lit up the room at breakfast, and how she's looking at me right now.

"Me too," I confess, smiling brightly. "Feels so fucking good, doesn't it?"

"Yes."

Carlee removes her laptop from her bag, and I hold on to the magic happening between us.

I smile. "Such a good girl."

"Don't start something you don't plan on finishing, Calloway," she says matter-of-factly. Leaning in, she whispers in my ear, "My panties are already drenched."

The warmth of her breath sends a thrill through me.

"Mmm," I respond. "Love that for you."

She smirks. "Want to take advantage while I'm feeling very inspired?"

As she begins to type away, the rhythmic tapping of keys fills the cabin. I close my eyes, letting my thoughts drift back to what Easton told me earlier. Somewhere between reality and dreams, I start to doze off, but a sudden whisper jolts me awake.

"Weston," Carlee murmurs, concern etched on her face, "are you okay?"

"Yeah," I reply, my voice raspy.

The cabin lights are dim, casting shadows across her face. The glow of her laptop illuminates her eyes, revealing a hint of worry.

"You seemed like you were having a nightmare," she says empathetically. "Are you sure you're okay?"

"My anxiety is elevated with the divorce and traveling. Routine keeps me grounded," I admit, lifting the armrest between us.

She returns her laptop to her bag, wrapping her arm around me. "I understand. I'm always here if you ever want to talk about it."

"I know." I hold her a little tighter, feeling the tension in my body begin to dissipate as she comforts me. "Thank you."

I inhale her perfume and the faint scent of new leather and close my eyes, allowing myself to relax.

"It's almost over," she whispers. "It's almost all behind you."

"Us," I mutter against her hair.

The unknown stresses me because Lena is unpredictable. Easton is right. Leaving the city is for the best, at least until the dust settles. The thought hangs heavy in the air.

Time slips through my fingers like sand, and a sense of peace washes over me. I fall asleep with Carlee in my arms, knowing I could stay like this forever.

I wake when the plane rolls to a stop. The pilots greased the landing with such skill that it hardly felt like we touched down. Our pilots are Brody's ex-military friends, who now work for our company, flying us safely across the globe.

Carlee sits upright, the remnants of sleep still lingering on her face. "I wasn't even tired. You're just too comfortable."

"It's you," I reply as we deboard the plane.

An SUV waits for us just outside, and standing next to it is my cousin—the man who saved my life.

He grins, meeting Carlee's eyes before turning to mine. We exchange a brotherly hug, the weight of unspoken history hanging between us. He is always by my side when I need him.

"I showed up early to ensure everything was safe for your arrival," he explains, his voice steady, reassuring.

Carlee slides inside, and I move next to her, feeling the comfort of her presence. Brody takes the front passenger seat, keeping his focus ahead, not turning to acknowledge her presence.

"I'm happy you're here," she says, patting his shoulder.

Brody doesn't respond, his demeanor guarded. He's grumpy, quiet, and all business, especially on trips like this—outside the city, where threats can linger in the shadows. His eyes dart around the vehicle, scanning the surroundings, constantly flicking to the side mirror. I know he carries a collection of firearms just a breath away, ready in case of trouble.

We pull out of the airport, rolling through the private gate, and Carlee opens the group chat where her huge family is now eagerly waiting for updates.

"Take a picture with me?" she asks.

"Sure."

She holds her phone, snapping a photo. She quickly types a message and turns the screen toward me.

CARLEE

Get ready to talk crap to our faces.

"You're starting shit," I mutter.

"I should apologize in advance. They're really going to adore you, Weston. Just hope you're ready to be initiated into the family."

I lean over and kiss her cheek. "I look forward to it. Seriously. Easton fought Lexi's brothers. He even gave one of them a concussion. I think I'll be fine."

She shakes her head in disbelief. "My brothers are rodeo champions. Grew up working on the farm and are built like brick houses. Please do *not* fight them. Matteo and Dean would enjoy it way too much. Why do you think Samson wouldn't date me in high school?"

"I'm not afraid of your brothers," I admit.

"You should be," she confidently replies. "And my cousins—Jake, Lucas, and Hudson—are even scarier. They're *very* protective of me, Wes, and they're going to put you through the paces. I hope you're prepared."

Brody snorts, barely containing his amusement, and I glare at him.

"I'm not concerned."

"Good. It's settled then."

With that, she pulls her laptop from her bag, and the familiar click of the keyboard soon fills the air. Her eyes scan the screen while she rereads what she wrote on the plane. I lean over to steal a peek, but she quickly covers it with her hand, a grin on her lips.

"You can read it tomorrow when I post it," she whispers.

"Fucking proud of you," I tell her, my voice full of sincerity.

"Thank you. I'll take my gold star now," she replies teasingly as she returns her fingers to the keys.

We zoom away on the long road, which opens to rustling brown grasses and the occasional tumbleweed. There's nothing on either side, except rustic Texas mountains and pastures that go on until the horizon. This place is untouched by the concerns of city life. When I imagine small towns, Merryville comes to mind.

An hour later, we're merging onto the main drag of the town, cruising at a leisurely twenty miles per hour. I roll down the windows when we're in the heart of downtown.

Around us, the smell of fried food fills the air, and colorful carnival rides have sprouted in the heart of the town square. The bright lights that lace the streets twinkle like stars against the dusky sky. Food trucks line the perimeter, and my stomach grumbles in response. I catch a glimpse of the grocery store and a cozy coffee shop nestled among the other small businesses. As we slow at an intersection, my eyes zero in on Glenda's Diner, and it's exactly how I imagined it. The parking on the street is packed. As we drive by, chatter and laughter, mixed with country music, floats from inside.

"Oh, there's Glenda's," she says, glancing from her screen with an excited glint in her eye. "I think it rivals the diner in the city."

"Guess we'll see," I reply, excited to experience it with her.

Soon, we're leaving city limits. Text messages flood in, making Carlee's phone buzz nonstop.

"Everything okay?" I ask.

"Perfect. They're fighting over where we're staying right now."

We turn onto a road, the tires crunching over gravel, and then we slide under a freshly painted sign for Jolly Christmas Tree Farm.

"My mom has space, even though my sister is currently living with her after her divorce. My grandma and aunt have room too. I'm going to have to let them duke it out." She laughs lightly, and the sound warms something in me.

"Oh, turn right here, and it's at the end of this road," she says to the driver. "I have to introduce you to my grandma first. Otherwise, she'll never forgive me."

"Are you nervous?" I ask, trying to read her expression as the woods on either side of the road start to thin out.

We're coming to the end.

"A little," she admits, a hint of vulnerability slipping through. "I haven't been home in three years. And I'm returning with a fiancé. Not how I imagined it."

"Would you change it?" I ask.

"No," she whispers, studying my lips.

We finally roll to a stop in front of a charming log cabin. Vehicles are parked haphazardly in the field beside it. The warm glow of lights spills from the windows inside. We have an hour before the sun sets.

"Shit. They must've all known what I'd do," Carlee whispers, her voice barely audible. "Looks like we already have a crowd. Hope you're ready to steal the spotlight."

"I was born for this." I get out and stride confidently around to the other side, then open the door for her.

She steps out, and our eyes lock, and an unspoken connection flows between us. She reaches out and clasps my hand, our fingers interlocking. It's electric and grounding. A pang of anxiety greets me because I want her family to welcome me with open arms, to embrace me like I'm marrying Carlee. Because I am.

She takes a deep breath as I rub my thumb gently across hers.

"Relax, gorgeous. It's going to be fantastic. Promise."

I'm used to purposely stealing attention from Easton, doing my best to make him comfortable in social situations. Carlee isn't much different; she wants to be seen by *me* and no one else. It's difficult to balance, but I understand.

"You can do this," I assure her.

Carlee steadies herself, taking a deep breath as her fingers brush the doorknob. Before she can twist it, the door swings open with a smooth creak. Standing before us is a silver-haired woman, her green eyes sparkling in the golden hour of the evening. Her brows lift as she appraises me, a smile breaking across her face.

"Well, you did real good, Leelee," she says, reaching toward me and giving my biceps a hearty squeeze that feels like a warm welcome.

"Mawmaw," Carlee whispers, hugging her tight. "Please meet Weston Calloway. The man I'm going to marry."

I fucking love hearing her say that. "Hello. It's very lovely to meet you."

"That voice," Mawmaw exclaims, waggling her brows as she steps onto the porch, the door closing behind her with a thud. She crosses her arms over her chest and a glimmer of mischief darts in her eyes. "Who are you staying with while you're here?"

"We haven't decided yet," Carlee explains, casting me a cautious glance.

"Great. You're boarding with me," Mawmaw declares, her tone leaving no room for argument. "Your sister is currently camped at your mother's, and she's been acting like a complete *you know what*, now that she got that new job. She needs dead silence during the day because she's doing virtual interior design consultations or something. Driving us all insane."

"Mom's gonna be pissed," Carlee whispers.

I can't help but smile.

"I'll deal with her," Mawmaw tells us, her voice firm yet warm. "So, it's settled then. You're both my guests of honor."

I glance at Carlee, who gives me a nervous smile. I play it cool. "I'm honored. We appreciate your hospitality."

"I like you already, Weston. Now, you two come in out of the cold. Brace yourselves. They're feisty," she says, leading us into the living room, which is bustling with people.

I quickly take in the scene—a woman who must be her mother, two brothers, and another guy I don't recognize, but their shared green eyes tell me they're all family.

Carlee squeezes my hand tighter, and I respond by squeezing hers back—a silent promise of support.

The TV plays in the background, setting the mood while the fireplace roars passionately. Crocheted blankets are draped artfully over the back of the couch. The aromas of freshly brewed coffee and baked cake waft through the air, creating a cozy atmosphere that feels like home.

"Hi, y'all! Wow, I didn't know you were throwing a party," Carlee exclaims, her smile bright. I can tell she's nervous. "It smells incredible."

"I hurried and whipped up a strawberry cake for you. It's got about ten more minutes to bake. Everyone, this is Weston Calloway, Carlee's fiancé. The two of them are staying with me while they're here," Mawmaw adds warmly.

Sly woman.

"Excuse me?" Carlee's mother interjects, her tone laced with surprise. "I thought you'd stay with us."

"Sorry, Mom. You know Mawmaw makes the rules round here," Carlee replies.

"That's right," her grandma asserts, a proud smile stretching across her face. "Would you two like some coffee? I've got a pot brewing in the kitchen."

"That's a great idea after our long flight. We'll be right back," Carlee says, guiding me down the hallway.

She takes a deep breath, and I can sense her trying to shake off the lingering tension.

The walls are covered with a mix of family photos and school pictures. There's one of her with braces and bangs, tucked between two other high school mug shots of her brothers.

"Who's this cutie?" I ask, and she tugs me into the kitchen with her.

Once we're in the kitchen, I move close, sliding my lips against hers. She immediately relaxes in my arms, drifting away with me. Carlee groans against me, running her fingers up my shirt. I know her hands on my stomach is a silent plea for more. I laugh against her mouth, wanting her so fucking bad that it hurts.

"Ahem," I hear from behind us, and we break apart.

Carlee wasn't exaggerating about her brothers' sizes. They loom over me, muscles jacked and expressions unreadable. If I were the type to feel intimidation, I might have. However, I'm Weston motherfucking Calloway.

"Matteo and Dean," Carlee mutters, her fingers brushing over her swollen lips, "this is my fiancé."

"How old are you?"

Matteo reaches out to take my hand, his grip firm. It's a threat, and I reciprocate, squeezing back just as hard.

"Forty," I say.

Dean steps forward and takes his turn, mirroring his brother's scrutiny. "Aren't you a little too old to be dating our baby sister?"

They gauge me, sizing me up, which is fair. I'd do the same if this were Billie.

"Stop it," Carlee says, stepping between us, glaring at her brothers. "Seriously, cut that shit out. I'm not a baby."

"You'll always be our baby sister," Matteo tells her, glaring at me.

The silent warning is clear. Hurt their sister and get hurt.

"Do you love him?" Dean demands, his glare fixed firmly on Carlee.

"Of course," she replies without missing a beat, confidence radiating from her. "Weston's my best friend. Other than Lexi, he's the only person who has been there for me the past year. Where were either of you? Not giving a fuck about your baby sister or what she was doing. So, back off." The warning in her voice is undeniable.

Zero hesitation or intimidation. She wasn't joking when she said her brothers had trained her.

Damn. She's fucking hot when she's mad.

Carlee shoots them a fierce look, and I think she might clock them. But before she can make a move, Mawmaw walks into the room. Her presence is like a tornado and shifts the air around us.

"Leave them alone," she commands. Her tone spares no room for argument.

They exit the kitchen, and she gives us a wink before leaving us to ourselves.

"Why did you kiss me," Carlee asks, her expression shifting from curiosity to something deeper, "when we first walked in here?"

"Because you needed it. Kind of like right now," I whisper, brushing my lips against hers again, pulling her out of her head.

"You always know," she admits.

The admission lights a spark of satisfaction within me.

"Let's get this over with so we can be alone," she whispers. "Please. I forgot how intense they are."

"It's almost over," I say, offering some encouragement.

My phone buzzes with a text, and it's Brody.

"One second," I tell her.

BRODY

Are you staying here?

WESTON

Yes.

BRODY

I'll put your suitcases on the porch. See you tomorrow.

WESTON

Tomorrow.

"Everything okay?" she asks.

"Yeah, Brody is putting our suitcases on the porch."

"Great," she tells me, leading me back into the living room. She does proper introductions. "My mom. My brothers, who you just met. My Mawmaw. And this is my cousin Lucas."

"Her favorite cousin," he chimes in, standing to greet me with a friendly smile and a firm handshake. "Nice to meet you, Weston. Welcome to the family."

"Thanks," I tell him, happy for the instant approval.

We sit next to her grandmother on the couch with Carlee in the middle. Before anyone can ask us any questions, a pretty blonde rushes into the room, breathless.

"Sorry, I got caught up," she says, her voice bright. Her green eyes lock on to mine, brows arching in surprise. "Uh, hi. I'm Abigail, but you can call me Abbi. I'm Carlee's older sister," she introduces.

Her gaze lingers on me with a boldness that almost feels like an invitation. I don't like it.

"Weston Calloway." I stand, giving her a smile and a handshake, but also reading her like a book.

"Oh, and you're tall too," she says, really turning on the Southern belle persona. "Pleasure is very much mine."

When I sit again, Carlee interlocks her fingers with mine. I smile at her, but I can see her anger flaring behind her gaze. As if her sister would ever have a chance with me. I know exactly what kind of woman she is after being married to the queen of them for three years.

I rub my thumb across Carlee's, finding it cute she's so worried when I only have eyes for her. No one in the world fucking matters. Since we met, it's only been her, and it will only ever be her. I think she's the only person in the room who doesn't see it.

26

CARLEE

I meet Weston's eyes, noticing how my sister is drooling over *my* fiancé.

"Would you like to sit?" I ask her, standing to offer my seat next to Weston as I settle onto his lap.

Mawmaw immediately senses the tension in the room.

I've never been able to understand Abbi; she has always tried to get under my skin. It's impossible for her to be genuinely happy for me, and even now, she seems intent on awkwardly flirting with the man I'm going to marry.

Fake marry.

She has always been competitive with me and has tried to one-up me since we were kids.

"I heard you were divorced," she remarks as Weston wraps his arms around me.

He laughs like it's no big deal. Keeping the energy high as she tries to bring it down.

"Actually, I heard the same about you," he responds cheerfully. "But I think you've got me beat on the number. Twice, right?" He sounds way too enthusiastic about this.

Abbi scoffs.

"It's really not a big deal, is it? Sometimes, we marry people who aren't meant for us. Some of us do that more than once," Weston offers, chuckling lightly. He put her in her place without hesitation and without even trying. "I won't make the same mistake twice," he mutters matter-of-factly.

"Damn," Dean whispers under his breath.

Weston is used to dealing with presidents, CEOs, and world leaders. My sister is a fly in comparison.

"Third time's a charm," she says. "Hopefully, the second is yours."

My sister glances at me, and I offer her a sweet smile.

She's enraged. I can see it in her eyes.

No one ever dares to talk back to her, and Weston establishing that boundary early on is smart. If given an inch, she will always take a mile. Not with him though.

"How's the new job?" Mawmaw asks Abbi, successfully steering the conversation in a different direction.

When the focus moves back to her, she lets out a relieved sigh.

"Fantastic! My boss is incredible. She works me hard, but we click. I even invited her to visit this weekend. There's a possibility of her sponsoring the Valentine's Day event next year. If you're still here, you might all get to meet her."

I study Abbi, aware of her constant need for validation. This is one of the main reasons we clash.

Weston tilts his head, locking eyes with me. I can't help but smile. Our silent conversation continues as I lean back against him, feeling him grow hard beneath me. He interlocks his fingers around my waist to keep me in place.

"Stop it," he mutters against my ear, nibbling on my lobe.

My brother glares at us, and I shoot him an evil eye in return.

"You're pissing Matteo off," Weston whispers.

I turn to him, gently placing my palm on his cheek before

meeting his gaze. It's just the two of us. Everything in the room fades away, and I'm completely lost in his eyes.

"Wow, you two really are in love," Mawmaw comments, jolting me back to reality.

My heart races as I become aware of the chatter around us, realizing I was too lost with Weston.

"Love to see it," my mom adds.

A wave of guilt washes over me, knowing I'm lying to everyone about this engagement.

Weston notices my shift, and his fingers lightly brush against my back. The family continues to steer the conversation back to Weston and me. He shares bits about himself and briefly touches on his work without sounding boastful. My mom seems genuinely intrigued, and so do my brothers, who ask questions that aren't really their business. Lucas adds in commentary where necessary and makes jokes.

Weston responds thoughtfully, revealing just enough without getting too personal. He works the room effortlessly, commanding everyone's attention as they lean in to listen. He shines like a diamond in my grandmother's living room. My sister watches him with an intensity like she wants to eat him for dessert.

"Cake, anyone?" Mawmaw says, almost as if she read my mind. "I'm going to go ice it."

Weston sips the last of his coffee, his fingers grazing my wrist. "Carlee's incredible. I honestly don't know what I'd do without her by my side." He leans in to whisper, "I mean it."

I believe him.

Ten minutes later, Mawmaw serves the cake, alongside enormous glasses of milk.

Once the sun sets, she unapologetically ushers everyone out of the house. I feel a wave of relief wash over me as silence fills the room.

I relax on the couch beside him, my eyes scanning over the space. I've missed being home so much.

Mawmaw changes into her nightgown and silk cap, then comes into the living room to bid us good night. "Leelee, I assume you'll be in your favorite bedroom, and Weston will be in the other?"

"That's right, Mawmaw."

Weston glances at me with his brows knitted together.

"If you need more firewood, the storage shed is full. Hudson took care of it for me yesterday. Good night, lovebirds."

"Good night, Mawmaw," Weston replies with a warm smile.

"See y'all bright and early," she says, squeezing our shoulders.

Moments later, she shuffles down the long hallway in her house slippers. Her bedroom is on the opposite end of the house, and I barely hear her door click shut.

My mind buzzes from family overload.

"So, we're *not* sharing a bed?" Weston asks, his disappointment evident.

"I completely forgot about that," I admit, feeling annoyed by the idea of him not being by my side while we're here.

The fireplace roars, and we both stare into the flames. His arm wraps around my shoulders, pulling me closer against him. I find myself lost in thought, entranced by the dance of the flames as the fresh wood crackles and pops.

"They like you," I whisper, relaxing into him.

"I hope so." His fingers gently trace the outside of my arm as he holds me.

"Weston," I say, turning to face him.

No more words escape me. His lips crash against mine with a hunger that feels both exhilarating and inevitable. We're losing control, and I want to embrace it. He lays me back against the couch as I wrap my arms around his neck, fingers tangling in his hair. I laugh against his kisses. We're breathless and alive. It feels like I've been born again.

"You smell so damn good," he murmurs against my skin, his cock hard against me.

"She's still awake," I mutter, tugging his lips between my teeth, craving him more than I crave air. "If she catches us …"

"I *need* you," Weston confesses, his voice low and urgent.

"I need you too." My eyes roam over him, and I realize we're on the same page, our desires intertwining like words in a shared story.

"You drive me crazy." His cock grinds against me.

"Weston," I gasp, "please."

He chuckles, kissing my jaw and claiming my mouth. "Not on your Mawmaw's couch. I'll meet you in your room in twenty minutes. Does the door lock?"

"Yes," I whisper as he presses hard against me. "You're actually going to give yourself to me?"

"Fuck yes," he mutters. "I need you like I need air."

A minute later, he's standing, his cock at full attention. "Good night, Carlee. See you in the morning," he says in his normal voice, just in case Mawmaw is listening.

"Good night. Sweet dreams. I'm going to stay up a little longer," I tell him, watching as he stalks down the other hallway.

There are two spare rooms and a sewing room, where Mawmaw does most of her crafts.

I lean back on the couch and sigh, giddy, finding it ridiculous that we're sneaking around like this.

Maybe Lexi's right. Maybe all Weston needs is a real chance. I'm giving him one.

I stare at the spackled ceiling, letting the minutes tick down. Five minutes later, I go to my room and leave the door cracked. I stand just inside it, looking at all the snow globes my grandmother and her mother collected over the years when she was growing up. This was my favorite place to be as a kid because it always felt like a fairy tale.

I set my laptop on the desk and open the top drawer. I see a pair of handcuffs with keys next to it. I place them on the bedside dresser.

After, I slide out of my jeans, and as I take off my sweater, the door quietly opens. When I turn around, I see Weston standing in front of me.

"Getting started without me?" he asks, reaching over to lock the door as I toss the heavy fabric onto the floor.

"Why waste time?" I whisper, placing my hands on my hips.

Weston saunters over to me, and as soon as we're close, it's over. We're hands and mouth and teeth, losing ourselves in each other's touch. I'm desperate and oh-so fucking wet for him.

"It hasn't been twenty minutes," he confesses.

"I don't care. I've waited all day for this," I tell him.

"Proof that there are still things to look forward to when you're in a relationship," he says, kissing my shoulder and carefully peeling my bra strap down my arm. His fingers graze across my skin, causing goose bumps to form. "Ah, love that I can do that to you," he whispers.

He undoes my bra with a simple snap. It falls to the ground between us. Weston dips down, capturing one of my nipples in his mouth, swirling his warm tongue around the peak.

"You always have," I admit, relishing how his mouth feels against my skin.

Weston slides his hands into my panties, and the sensation feels so fucking good.

"Mmm, you weren't exaggerating earlier."

"I want you inside of me," I confess, guiding him to the twin bed.

His long legs barely fit, but there's just enough room for both of us.

He leans against the wooden bed frame, one leg propped up. I crawl onto the bed, sliding his joggers from his body before removing his boxers as well.

"Condom in the pocket," he whispers.

"Love a man who's prepared."

I snatch and rip it open, sheathing him. He's hard for me.

Carefully, I straddle him. His hands find my waist, guiding me as I adjust to his size. I hiss; he stretches me so fucking full.

"You feel incredible," he huffs.

"You do too," I barely cry out.

I take his face in my palms, studying his gorgeous features, drowning with him. We share slow kisses, our noses brushing together, the intensity growing.

"Wes …" I slide up and down on him, our bodies meeting rhythmically.

Being with him is an out-of-body experience. I feel like I've been transported to another dimension, lost in his touch, in the warmth that floods through me. Our labored breaths fill the silence as he kisses my chest and wraps his arm around me.

My head falls back on my shoulders as he pumps deep inside me. I cover my mouth, stifling the cries threatening to escape from the intense pleasure he brings. When my eyes open, I catch a glimpse of the silver handcuffs glinting in the light. Smirking, I reach over and grab them.

His eyes don't leave mine as I slide one cuff around his wrist and loop it through the bed frame.

Weston shakes his head, then cuffs me to the other side of him. "We're in this together."

His free hand runs through my hair as our movements grow more ragged, more intentional. His deep grunts have me shushing him against his lips as we chase our releases together.

"So close," I whisper as we race toward our end.

We're losing control. The world around us disappears as every inch of my body seizes. I slap my free hand over my mouth while he slams inside me. The bed squeaks beneath us, and I kiss and nibble on his neck, barely managing to hold on as I ride out my orgasm, feeling him empty inside me.

I collapse on top of him, breathless. The world tilts on its axis as I get lost in the fog of being with him. We're both too stunned to speak, our pulses racing. He holds me in his arms, still buried deep within me, his fingers lightly brushing over my skin.

"Mmm," he murmurs. "Unlock us, gorgeous," Weston says, glancing at our wrists.

"Right here," I whisper, my chest rising and falling as I reach for the keys on the bedside table.

He sits upright. "Babe, those aren't it. They go to a filing cabinet or a safe. Look at the shape."

I twist my wrist, glancing at the keyhole. "Shit. This is not happening."

Somehow, I slide off of him, relieved to see the condom still attached after the last scare. I haven't missed a pill since then though.

I stretch and barely manage to grab my panties with my toes. As I slide them on, I realize my shirt won't go over my body—not with both of us cuffed to the bed frame. My heart rate increases, and I start to feel overwhelmed.

"It's okay. I might have a solution," Weston finally says as I attempt to cover myself.

"And?" I sift through possible options, but nothing comes to mind.

"Brody."

I shake my head, glancing at the condom that's still attached to him. "No way. He can't see us like this."

"Your brothers then? Or would you prefer I call a locksmith to meet us at nine on a Sunday night, handcuffed to your grandmother's bed while both of us are naked?"

"Okay, okay, you make a good point. Brody is the *safest* option. What's he going to do, saw it off our wrists?"

"He carries a cuff key on him at all times," Weston confirms. "He's prepared for anything."

"Even this?" I glance at our predicament. "How do we explain ourselves?"

He chuckles, pulling me close to him and kissing my lips with a laugh. "Look at us. We won't have to."

SOMEHOW, WESTON AND I MANEUVER OURSELVES INTO A POSITION where we can slide open the window.

He starts with a light chuckle, then falls into full-blown laughter. I join in.

"This is ridiculous. How can I be so smart and also dumb as hell?" I glance at him.

"Don't forget cute," he says, and I elbow him. "But I wouldn't want to be handcuffed to a bed with anyone else."

I smile. "I'm glad you're here."

"Me too."

Fifteen minutes later, Brody lightly taps on the glass. He lifts the screen and pokes his head inside, only to find us covered with blankets as our arms dangle above our heads.

"I don't want to know," he mutters, holding up his hand. "Unbelievable."

He tosses the key inside, and it lands on the mattress. Weston snatches it, unclicking my wrist first before freeing himself.

"Thanks," he tells his cousin, returning the key to him. "I'll *never* give you crap for that again."

"Good." Brody walks away, his leather jacket fading into the night.

I never heard an engine or saw any lights against the front window so he must've taken the trails that are cut between everyone's properties. If he was on the farm during tree season, he might know this place better than I do right now.

I fall onto Weston's chest, and he holds me close, kissing me.

"That was close," I say, laughing as I listen to his heartbeat while he runs his fingers through my hair.

"Always an adventure with you."

"Always," I whisper, feeling my eyes grow heavy. "I can't fall asleep. I need to schedule my post for the morning," I tell him, sitting up to meet his deep blue eyes. I want to swim in them.

"Do it now," he replies, kissing my forehead before releasing me. "Join me right back here."

"I'll be quick. Less than five minutes."

"No need to rush perfection. They're going to love your words," he encourages, pulling the blankets over himself.

"They're going to love you," I tell him, sitting on the edge of the bed.

"Are you?"

My breath catches in my throat, and I stare at him. "I think so."

His fingers thread through my hair, pulling me back down to him. Our mouths and tongues dance together, growing too desperate.

"I'm not giving up on you," he whispers.

"Please don't." I steal a kiss, tempted to stay right here.

"Schedule your post before I distract you," he whispers.

I grin. "You're right."

Somehow, I pull away from him and move to the small desk in the corner. I place the cuffs in the top drawer, where I found them, almost tempted to leave a sticky note nearby to prevent anyone else from making the same dumb mistake I did. Those keys are tossed in a different drawer.

I slide my laptop out of my bag and set it on the flat surface. The chair has been in this room since I was a kid, but I somehow manage to perch my ass on the edge. I open my browser and review the post I wrote while traveling here.

FROM THE DESK OF LADYLUX

LuxBabies,

Did you miss me? I'm back after a longer-than-intended sabbatical, and there's much to discuss.

Today's topic is one I know you've been clamoring for:
Weston Calloway and Carlee Jolly.

I've sifted through your emails, waded through all the juicy rumors and outrageous speculation surrounding these two after the big announcement on Saturday night. It's like Weston was urging me to come back, just for him.

Many of you are eagerly awaiting my detailed analysis of why I believe this couple won't survive. Considering how I've successfully predicted the endings of each of Mr. Calloway's relationships over the twelve years, I should be able to do the same for this one. Yet here I am, perplexed by this news. It has me questioning if I truly know Weston Calloway as well as I thought.

Currently, three rumors are swirling about this couple, and I anticipate that number will only grow as we learn more about her—especially now that they are publicly engaged. As of now, I refuse to use the word officially. More about that down below.

Allegedly, Weston's divorce will be finalized later today, which means we could hear wedding bells as soon as Tuesday. That would be shocking to everyone.

Before we delve deeper, let me clarify: this post is based on speculation regarding public figures, utilizing information that is readily available online. My opinions are my own, and they are for entertainment purposes only.

Please don't sue me, Weston.

Rumor #1: The couple met while Weston was still married. Carlee is a home-wrecker.

Based on Weston's track record of committing to women without any cheating scandals, I find this claim hard to believe. He's many things, but a cheater isn't one of them. I genuinely believe he loved his ex-wife and would have done anything for her, even at his own expense. He didn't start publicly dating anyone until a month after filing for divorce, but we know that the marriage was over before it started. He may be a serial dater, but he fully invests himself when he commits.

Rumor #2: Carlee is a gold digger.

Based on the interviews Lexi Calloway has given, discussing her friendship with Carlee, I find it hard to believe the claims being made. She could have easily monetized their relationship months ago and engaged in clout chasing, which would have allowed her to make a fortune from her connection to Weston. While many of us have read her journal, I'm left here questioning what she hasn't documented.

What other secrets about Weston is she currently keeping? We have seen plenty of gold diggers attached to Weston Calloway, but her actions are unlike anyone we've witnessed in the past. Unfortunately, I disagree with this narrative being pushed.

Rumor #3: C & W are in a fake relationship to help his image.

This is plausible.

However, we know Weston doesn't need assistance with his image. He's

America's sweetheart, one of the sexiest men alive, and he possesses incredible charm. His fan club is global, and even though his ex has attempted to initiate smear campaigns, she hasn't been successful. His popularity has only increased since his divorce became messy a year ago.

I'd be shocked if he faked this because he doesn't need to. I suppose time will reveal whether this rumor is true or false. I'll keep my eyes and ears open.

I SINCERELY HOPE WESTON FINALLY FINDS WHATEVER IT IS HE'S SEARCHING FOR.

Right now, I fear we may be asking ourselves the wrong questions about this relationship.

Many of us want to know why her, *but maybe we should be asking ourselves,* Why not?

She's one of us, a "normie," just like Lexi Calloway. It gives me hope that perhaps love can transcend the boundaries of social class that keep us separated.

On a serious note about love: I used to believe that falling in love was hard, but now I'm convinced the real struggle lies in maintaining it. Love can be kind, but it can also be oh-so cruel. Most of us desire it, but very few manage to keep it for a lifetime.

Sometimes, I question love itself.
What is it exactly?

I believe love is about holding space for someone and accepting their messy parts. Love teaches us to be comfortable in silence because just their presence is enough.

It's laughter, shared vulnerabilities and a deep connection that feels like it can move mountains. Love is that bubbling deep inside after a single glance. It's unimaginable intimacy and compassion and understanding. It's feeling safe in their arms. Sometimes, we find love when we're not ready, when we're weak, but that's when we need it the most. To love and be loved takes courage. Which brings us back to the age-old question: Is it better to have loved and lost or to never have loved at all?

Weston deserves to be in a relationship that truly fulfills him. I wish him the very best.

What do you think? Are there any other rumors I haven't addressed? Leave me a comment down below. I'll be back next week with more juicy celebrity news and drama, served with a side of honest opinions.

Until then, sending my love,
LadyLux

A SMILE LINGERS. I'VE STILL GOT IT.

I schedule the post to go live in the morning, then close my laptop. While I still feel anxious about it, I push the thoughts away. It's not easy to rise again after losing my self-confidence, but I did it, even if my legs shook.

I move toward the bed and crawl under Weston's arm. He wraps the blanket snuggly around us. My emotions begin to take over because I really didn't know if I'd ever be able to post again.

"You inspired me," I admit.

Weston holds me a little tighter. "So fucking proud of you," he says, kissing my neck and my ear. "Can't wait to read it in the morning."

"Sneak out of here in about an hour, okay?"

"Okay. Good night," he says.

"Night," I tell him.

The silence lingers.

"Wes?"

"Mmhmm?"

"Is this what falling in love feels like?"

"Yes," he whispers, kissing my neck as butterflies swarm inside of me. "Yes, it fucking is."

27

CARLEE

"Carlee," Weston whispers in my ear, his arm still wrapped around me.

"Yes?" My eyes bolt open, and I roll to face him, realizing the sun is rising. "You shouldn't be in here. My grandma will lose her shit if she catches you."

"She's already awake. I just heard her in the kitchen, making coffee."

"You have to go," I whisper urgently. "Put on your clothes. I need to sneak you out of here."

"You can't be serious."

"I am!" I hiss, sliding out of bed. "Don't get on her bad side this early."

He chuckles, standing to grab his joggers.

"They all treat me like I'm a delicate flower. I'm not even the youngest in the family." I slip on my shorts and the oversized T-shirt.

Just as Weston moves toward me, he slams his mouth against mine, leaving me breathless. I want to stay here just like this for the rest of the day.

"I can't get enough," he says.

As we pull away, the door cracks open, prompting me to push Weston behind it.

"Hi, Mawmaw. Good morning!" I call out, holding the door with my foot to keep her from pushing her way inside and discovering him.

I let out a fake yawn and suddenly feel like a teenager again, sneaking around so Mawmaw doesn't lose her shit. Weston remains frozen, his gaze locked on me.

"Mornin', honey. Making coffee. Should I wake Weston?"

"No, no. Just let him sleep in. I'm sure he'll join us soon. He's a light sleeper," I say, lowering my voice to a whisper.

She nods. "I had a dream that you got married."

"Mawmaw, we've been engaged for a day and a half," I reply, trying not to roll my eyes.

I know how she loves meddling in relationships. She's the matchmaking queen. I learned from the best.

"No time like the present, Leelee. Besides, I'm not getting any younger, and traveling to the city is tough on my old, weary bones. You two are clearly in love, so why wait?"

She winks at me before walking toward her sewing room, pausing at Weston's door. When she walks past it, I let out a relieved breath, then quickly close the door.

"Want to get married soon." He waggles his brows.

"Stop." I glare at him. "If you didn't know after last night, Mawmaw is one hundred percent Team Weston."

"So are you," he mutters, smirking.

He leans in, stealing another kiss.

As he moves away, I pull him back to me. "You make me weak, Weston. This wasn't supposed to happen."

"It goes both ways," he replies just as Mawmaw whistles, walking past the bedroom door and back toward the kitchen.

"I have to go. Wish me luck."

"Good luck," he says.

I study him, taking in the sight of him standing in my grandma's house, looking like a daydream.

"This doesn't feel real," I say, still half asleep.

"It is, I promise."

"I think that's exactly what someone in a dream would say." I narrow my eyes at him suspiciously.

"Would *dream me* do this?" He pushes me against the door, his leg parting my thighs, adding a slight pressure.

"Actually, yes," I admit with a gasp. "Fantasy Weston isn't tame."

"I'm not either." He lightly kisses me, pulling away as I lean in for more. "If you don't go now, we won't leave this room until lunch."

"So tempting." I force myself to step away. "I want a rain check."

"You fucking got it."

Once in the hallway, I take a deep breath, checking my pulse. My heart races, and I try to calm myself. Mawmaw doesn't know. I just have to pretend he didn't sleep against me all night long.

Weston drives me wild and makes me want to risk it all.

When I enter the kitchen, Mawmaw pours me a mug of coffee. She removes a container of vanilla creamer from the fridge and sets it on the counter. I move closer to her.

"How'd you sleep?" she asks, brows raised as she watches me.

"Fantastic," I say, remembering Weston was snuggled against me.

I brace myself for the onslaught of questions I've been waiting for.

Before she can speak, I hear the front door open and close as I pour and then stir in the cream.

"Are you expecting someone?" I ask, glancing over my shoulder as light footsteps echo down the hallway.

Whoever it is, I owe them a thank-you later. Mawmaw wanted to discuss something, but she won't forget. She never does.

A red-haired woman appears, wearing a big grin as she enters the kitchen, bright-eyed. It's just past six in the morning, and in her hand is a basket of fresh eggs. With her voice and pretty looks, I'm convinced she's a real-life Disney princess.

"Morning, Mawmaw," she says, setting the basket down on the counter. "The chicks have been busy."

"Hi, sweetie. Thank you," Mawmaw replies. "Oh, this is Carlee, my granddaughter. But we call her Leelee."

"Hello. I've heard about you in passing," the woman says, immediately pulling me into a warm hug. She's a natural beauty with high cheekbones. Her brown eyes sparkle. "I'm—"

"Emma?" Weston's voice rings out behind us.

"Weston?" she asks, puzzled.

"You know each other?" I glance between them, witnessing a flood of memories flash through their eyes.

Emma chuckles nervously. "Uh, yeah. *This* is strange. What are you doing here?"

They exchange friendly side hugs, both clearly surprised.

"What are *you* doing here?" he asks, shoving his hands into his pockets.

"I live here." Her eyes study us with a curious wonder. "Are you two—"

Mawmaw hands her a cup of coffee just as my jealousy flares like crazy. Every insecurity I have boils to the surface. I have nothing to worry about, right?

"Actually, yes," Weston says. "We're getting married."

He shoots me a wink.

"Is Brody with you?" she asks.

"You know Brody?" I try to piece it all together, but nothing makes sense.

"Yes, he sometimes works for my dad. He stayed here during the holidays and took residence in Jake's little cabin behind his house. You know, the one that's used for storage for old holiday decorations."

Jake is my cousin who's six years older than me.

"Wait, Brody stayed here during tree season?" I turn to Weston, not sure how I didn't know this.

"He was on a special assignment because neither of us needed him. I had no idea where he was, and he never mentioned it," Weston confesses.

He interlocks his pinkie with mine. It's a small gesture, but it instantly calms me when my heart races a little too fast. Weston notices my tiny anxieties and always does this.

When our eyes meet, I see his are filled with compassion and admiration. I wonder if he has always looked at me this way.

Yes. The word echoes in my mind as the blindfold shrouding our relationship falls away.

Mawmaw clears her throat, breaking the silence that streams between us.

"Emma married Hudson last week. She's also last year's Cookie Queen," Mawmaw announces. "Come on, sit."

"Cookie Queen? What an accomplishment," I say, intrigued. "It's a cookie contest held in town every year. Super competitive," I explain to Weston, filling him in on the details.

"It's a very special town tradition. I never could've done it without Hudson though. I needed my Cookie King."

The four of us pull wooden chairs from under the kitchen table, following Mawmaw's lead.

"Sorry, you married Hudson?" I ask, just realizing what she said.

A stack of newspapers lies haphazardly in the middle of the table. When I see the familiar font of the *Merryville Gazette*, it brings a smile to my face.

Then I catch sight of the headline about the wedding—"Hudson Jolly Marries Emma Manchester." It was featured on the front of last Sunday's paper. I open it, my eyes scanning the words that detail how happy they are together.

"Wow. Congratulations! I didn't even realize he was dating

anyone," I say, struggling to recall the last time I saw him genuinely smile. She must be sunshine in human form.

"Emma's also best friends with Billie and Harper," Weston explains.

"I was at Billie's Halloween party. I saw you two chatting," Emma admits.

"Really?" I ask, trying to recall her from that night. But it's a blur. I attended with Lexi. Weston and I acted more like acquaintances than best friends. "Oh, wait. Are you the Emma that Asher was in love with?"

Emma chuckles. "Yeah, sorta. I dated him for a month, but there was no spark. I'm convinced Billie and him would be perfect together. But you know how stubborn those Calloways are," she says, glancing at Weston.

"It's a lost cause with those two. Anyway, congratulations. Had I known you got married, I'd have sent a gift and congratulations," Weston says. "My sister didn't mention it."

"It was a quick turnaround, and she's been preoccupied with her business and being in yours." Emma shrugs nonchalantly.

"This happened fast," I say, still processing the fact that my cousin Hudson is married.

"As soon as Hudson's divorce was finalized, we thought, *Why not? What do we have to lose?* I was never letting him go. And I knew he wouldn't let me go either. We were like two galaxies colliding. I realized I couldn't imagine my life without him," Emma explains, blowing on her hot coffee. Steam rises from the cup like delicate tendrils. "You two know what I mean. Clearly."

I glance at Weston. Is it really like that with us?

"*Emma Manchester,*" I whisper, finally realizing *who* she is.

It clicks in my head. Emma's family is incredibly wealthy, but instead of joining the family business, she opted for the influencer route. The Manchesters own a very upscale hotel chain that rivals the W.

Of course they know one another.

Emma's not problematic, so she's never been on my radar. LadyLux has never once covered her.

"I'm Emma Jolly now," she says, proudly displaying a cheesy smile.

"I'm trying not to fangirl. It's very nice to meet you. Wow. I can't believe you married my cousin. He's so ..." I struggle to find the right words.

"Grumpy?" she suggests, snickering.

Over the last six months, I've been intensely focused on Lexi and Easton's relationship, leaving little room for anything else, whether it be celebrity gossip or family matters. Now, I feel out of the loop—something I never wanted. I've been a terrible daughter, granddaughter, sister, and cousin, completely avoidant.

"This is six degrees of separation from Weston Calloway. Do you know everyone?" Emma asks him, breaking me from my thoughts.

"Feels like it," he replies with a laugh. "Small world. We're all connected in some way."

"Yes, we are." Emma grins wide. She turns to me. "Funny story: I used to have the *biggest* crush on Easton and Weston back in the day—mainly Easton. I probably should've realized I was into moody men from the start."

She shares that like she's trying to ease my concern. Maybe I'm more transparent than I think. Nervous laughter escapes me.

Weston raises an eyebrow. "When I say *all* of my sister's friends tried and failed, I mean *all* of them."

Emma shrugs. "Weston's a tough one to capture. You must be really special."

"My Leelee is so special," Mawmaw interjects proudly. "When she was younger, she was so shy. My big-hearted grandbaby. Don't have many like her without an attitude. She loves deeply and is compassionate, empathetic, and a great listener."

"Just admit I'm your favorite, Mawmaw. They won't tell anyone," I say, and she shoots me a wink.

Weston brushes his fingers across mine. Electricity surges through me, and I force my attention back to Emma.

"You know Hudson swore he'd never get married again or even date anyone until Colby was older. Can you share the recipe for your love potion?"

Mawmaw sips her coffee, glancing from Weston to me. "Honey, you don't need it."

"You don't," Emma agrees, and I can't help but wonder how well she knows Weston.

"You don't," Weston adds with a smirk while drinking his coffee.

"Glad we're all in agreement." Mawmaw stands. "Now, what would you kids like for breakfast?"

"I thought we were going to Glenda's?" Weston questions.

"No, sir," Mawmaw scolds. "I'm feeding ya today. My treat."

Emma stands. "Just wanted to come by and say good morning and bring in the eggs since I was nearby. Need anything else while I'm in town? I have to head home and get Colby ready for school." She chugs her coffee, then sets the mug in the sink.

"No, sweetie. Have a good day. Come back over later, and we'll play some rummy," Mawmaw tells Emma.

"Maybe." She leans over, giving me a side squeeze. "Nice to officially meet you. Bye, Weston."

He shoots her a wink as Mawmaw smiles at us.

"Now, are bacon and eggs with some toast good? Or do you want sausage?"

"Either one. I'm not picky." Weston stands to help.

"No, baby, let me," she insists, gently forcing him to sit back down. "Now, let me know how you take your eggs."

"Choose wisely," I mutter to him. "Or she'll never trust you again."

"Over medium," he replies without hesitation, resuming his seat and scooting his chair closer to me.

"Correct choice. You can never trust a person who orders them over easy." She returns to the stove, setting her cast iron skillet on the gas burner.

Weston snickers.

Moments later, Mawmaw slaps a slab of bacon onto the hot iron. The aroma and sizzle fill the kitchen.

My eyes wander over the flowered curtains that have been hung since I was a child. It feels like a nostalgic little time capsule. The space brings back unforgettable memories from my upbringing and makes me miss my grandpa. He was such a kind, loving man.

"What are your plans this week?" Mawmaw asks.

Weston clears his throat. "Not sure. Carlee mentioned a Cupid carnival."

"The town is expectin' record crowds, so parking might be awful. Just be prepared. But the weather is supposed to be really nice. Supposed to warm up some," she says, skillfully flipping the bacon.

Mawmaw taught all the grandkids how to cook when we were barely old enough to walk. After grabbing another iron skillet and adding spoonfuls of butter, she cracks open the eggs. Mawmaw hums a little melody.

"I read what you wrote this morning," he mutters.

"Yeah? And?"

"I'll have my lawyer get in touch," he mutters, his gaze fixed on my lips.

I'm acutely aware of how he's looking at me. "Yeah right. What did you think?"

"Loved it. And I agree; it does take courage."

He steals a kiss, and I let him. I know I shouldn't melt into him, but I do. Right now, I'm fully immersed in this fantasy. I want to play this game.

Mawmaw sets plates in front of us. "Eat it while it's hot. Don't wait on me."

I grab my fork and cut into my eggs, knowing better than to argue with her over this. She gets offended.

The whites of the egg and the bright yellow yolk are cooked perfectly. It oozes into my plate, and I realize just how hungry I am this morning.

"Wow, this is amazing," Weston says. "Thank you so much."

"Yes, thank you, Mawmaw."

"Farm-fresh eggs—with lots of butter—make all the difference," she explains. "Don't y'all have them in New York?"

I chuckle. "Sometimes, I can find them at the farmers markets, but I haven't had eggs this fresh since the last time I was home."

"Don't wait so long to come visit next time. I'm getting older, and I want to see you more," she scolds.

"Okay, I promise I won't wait so long. I'll try for every six months."

"Join us for Christmas this year. Both of you."

"It's February!" I tell her. "I can't plan that far in advance."

"And? Plan it now so there are no excuses for not making it."

"She does have a point," Weston says, then grins at her. "We'll be here."

"Fantastic!" She claps her hands together. "You're staying here too."

"Already staking a claim?" I ask, shaking my head.

"Yes, but you should come and surprise everyone. We'll plan it and keep it a secret from the family."

Weston chuckles, shaking his head. "Your favorite."

I smirk.

A minute later, she joins us at the table and reaches for the strawberry jelly.

"How have things been with you two? I heard you've been seeing one another for a year," she says, holding up her hand. "And before you get worked up, I didn't read your journal. Matteo summarized it for me after *he* read it."

"I'm mortified." My adrenaline spikes because I wrote some

very personal things about Weston. Many are sexual things I never wanted my older brother or the entire world to read.

Weston takes a sip of coffee, focusing on her. He doesn't seem worried. "Things have been going great. We've had a lot of fun. No pressure."

"Is she in denial?" Mawmaw asks.

"Excuse me? Denial about what?"

"Honey, I know this engagement is fake." She smiles as she cracks open her eggs. "It's just not like you to get engaged without us all meeting him first. You may not live here anymore, but you care about the family. It matters to you if we like your significant other, no matter where you live." She glances at Weston. "If you're wonderin', we do like you."

Weston smiles, and I shake my head.

Mawmaw's eyebrow rises. "Am I wrong? Now, don't you be lyin' to me."

I let out a huff, knowing I can't feed her stories. "Mawmaw."

"You can pull this scheme on anyone else but not me, sugar." She smiles. "It's okay if you do things backward. I'm not judgin' as long as it ends with the same result. It's obvious you've both got it bad for each other, so the lie works. Don't stress about it."

Weston clears his throat, but Mawmaw interrupts him before he can speak.

"It's hard to play tricks on an old dog. The emotional connection you share is real, and it's difficult to overlook. You two are like the fireworks show on the Fourth of July. I can see it in the way you look at each other. I'm just trying to figure out why you're not moving forward."

How did Mawmaw know it wasn't real?

Weston turns his attention toward me, smirking. "I see where you get your spunk from."

"No comment," I state, keeping my mouth shut, not giving her any more ammunition.

Mawmaw wipes her mouth with her napkin, grinning. "Okay, so we're not talking about it then?"

She may look prim and proper, but she woke up and chose violence today.

"How's the weather supposed to be today?" Weston changes the subject as we finish eating, expertly steering the conversation away from the topic of us.

"Will be in the lower sixties around lunchtime. Lots of sunshine."

"I heard you have an identical twin brother. Are you two alike?" Mawmaw asks.

"Yes, but he's quiet and reserved. I think you'd like him," Weston replies.

"Didn't he marry your friend Lexi?" Mawmaw asks, and I nod. "Maybe they can visit for Christmas too."

"You'd love them." I chuckle nervously. "However, Lex is pregnant, and I'm sure they'll want to spend their first Christmas with the baby at home."

"Welp, the invite is open since you two will be here."

I smile, then glare at Weston, who seems to be enjoying this way too much.

Once our plates are cleared, we volunteer to clean the kitchen while Mawmaw calls her friends on her brand-new cell phone. It's part of her morning routine to catch up on all the town gossip—a habit she's maintained for decades. If someone needs to know something, Mawmaw is the source. And if she's ever out of the loop, she has those who do know on speed dial.

As we scrub the dishes, I say, "I have a bone to pick with you."

"Don't be upset. It's ten months from now," he replies.

I open my mouth to respond but then shut it. "But ..."

"But what? You don't see me in your life then?" he questions.

"What? Of course I do! If I think ahead ten years, you're there. It has nothing to do with that; it's just hard for me to predict my life that far in advance. Tree season in Merryville is intense. You'll see when they put you to work."

"I'm looking forward to it." He laughs. "How did she know it was fake?"

"I think she just knows me that well," I whisper. "It had to be a lucky guess."

"Oh, so she's as perceptive as you? Got it. I need to watch myself around her then," he offers, studying me.

"What?" I ask.

"Your words are haunting me. *To love and be loved takes courage.* Fucking powerful. Spoken like someone who's survived true heartbreak."

"Really?" I ask, turning to face him, leaning my hip against the counter.

"Yes. You amaze me." Weston dries his hands on a kitchen towel, looking at ease in my grandma's kitchen like he's supposed to be here with me.

"Thank you," I say, clinging to his words.

As I dry my hands, an alarm on his phone suddenly goes off.

"Shit." He pulls it out of his pocket. "Outside-the-courthouse coverage is starting."

Weston opens the page, and the cameras are already rolling. My heart races as a car pulls to a stop. Out walks Easton, sporting a pair of Ray-Bans and a smug smirk. People in the crowd shout questions at him, truly believing he's Weston.

"Tell us about your new fiancée!"

"She's incredible. Carlee is the love of my life," he responds confidently.

"When are you getting married?" someone presses.

"Very soon," he replies, waving with a grin that feels almost like it's meant for Weston.

I chuckle. "He's an asshole. But, wow, he's good at playing you. Shocking," I say.

The camera pans out, and Lena emerges from the car, dressed

in all black, as though she were attending a funeral. It's dramatic, just like her.

"Lena, Lena!" someone yells.

Weston swiftly closes the feed and locks his phone. "Guess I'll officially be divorced in an hour."

"We should celebrate," I tell him, wrapping my arms around his neck.

"Yeah?"

"I've got the perfect idea," I reply, bubbling with excitement. "But you might want to wear some jeans."

28

WESTON

Carlee parks the side-by-side in front of a tall red barn. She smiles at me as I fall in line beside her. "Can you horseback ride?"

I meet her gaze. "Yes, I've played *a lot* of polo in my life."

"How did I not know that? You should consider rescinding my Calloway crown," Carlee remarks, her tone teasing.

"It might be permanently attached at this point," I say, glancing at the top of her head, almost envisioning the jewels adorning it. Diamonds and emeralds for my girl.

We walk toward the barn, and she intertwines her fingers with mine. A light breeze blows, sending strands of her hair dancing in the wind. She leads me into a room filled with Western saddles and colorful pads. The air is rich with the scent of leather and fresh hay and dirt.

Carlee moves past me to grab a rope from the wall. Her perfect ass, in those tight jeans, grazes against my cock.

"Still playing games?" she asks, returning to me.

"Have been for a while, gorgeous. You know that," I respond, my lips hovering close to hers. "Are you ready to give up the chase?"

"Not sure," she replies, a spark of determination in her voice.

The early morning sunlight streams through the slats above, casting warm rays throughout the room.

"Soon though?" I whisper, gently tucking a stray strand of hair behind her ear.

She blinks at me challengingly, then smiles sweetly, stirring something deep within me. My hands rest on her waist, and my mouth finds hers.

"Yes, soon," she whispers. Her tongue slips into my mouth.

She's so fucking greedy for me.

I lean her against the saddle rack and sink to my knees before her. My hands glide to the button of her jeans, and I unzip them. With my fingers tucked in the waistline, I slide the material down to her ankles, making sure her panties go too.

"Give me that pretty little pussy." It comes out deep and husky.

Carlee leans back, resting her elbows against the saddle rack to steady herself better. I dive my tongue inside her, savoring the desperate gasps that escape her lips. She grinds against my face as I flick my tongue gently across her swollen clit.

"Wes," she whispers when I slide a finger deep into her cunt.

She's so fucking wet for me already. It feels religious, being here, worshipping every inch of her. I should, though. She saved me from the hell I had been living in.

Just as her body begins to seize, I pull away.

"No, no, no, you're not coming yet," I growl, my eyes darkening with desire. "Too soon."

It's an exhilarating game of cat and mouse with her, where we constantly switch between predator and prey.

"You always know what I like," she hisses breathlessly, suspended in time with her back arched and mouth open.

With just a flick of my tongue, I could bring her to the brink and have her crumbling.

My gorgeous girl wants to come so badly. I can see every

muscle clenched, including that cute little cunt. I kiss the insides of her thigh, relishing in her intoxicating scent and taste.

"I'm in love with you," she confesses, her voice nearly ragged.

I feel as if I'm dreaming. I stand to meet her gaze, and a smile touches my lips. "What did you say?"

She's breathless, nearly frantic. "I'm in love with you, Wes. I don't know how this happened. I realized it last night and then again this morning and—"

Our lips crash together.

I gently cup her face in my hands to calm her racing heart. "I'm so damn glad you're joining me. It's fun on this side of things."

My fingers thread through her hair as our tongues twist together in a passionate dance.

"I've been in love with you, Carlee," I confess, hoping my honesty doesn't send her running.

She needed to be the one to make any sort of confession that included the four-letter word. She opened the door though, and I'm walking through it.

Carlee grabs my shirt in her fists, pulling me closer. "Say it again," she says, kissing me so passionately that she steals my breath.

"I'm in love with you, Carlee Jean Jolly. Leelee. My Firefly. My gorgeous, smart girl. I can't deny it anymore. I don't want to."

"Please don't hurt me, Wes," she nearly begs, peppering kisses on my eyes and cheeks and mouth.

It's an emotional turn of events I didn't expect. But it's music to my fucking ears.

"Never. I promise," I say, returning to my previous position, kneeling before her, worshipping her.

I want to scream to the world that she feels the same as I do for her.

My tongue dives into her drenched pussy, giving her everything she needs and desires. Her fingers weave through my hair as she grinds against my stubble.

"Yes, yes," she says. "Keep going."

In the distance, I hear the unmistakable sound of an engine roaring. Carlee hears it too.

"I'm so fucking close. Please. Don't stop," she urges, sinking into my mouth.

I coax her to the very edge.

Just before she comes, I plunge two fingers knuckle deep inside her, and she screams my name, lost in her pleasure. Her body shakes with ecstasy, and I hold on to her tightly, feeling power surge through me. As she rides out her orgasm like a good fucking girl, a grin spreads across my face.

Carlee's head falls back on her shoulders, laughter spilling from her lips—light and free. That sound is addictive.

Seconds later, a deep voice calls out from behind, "Hello? Who's here?"

Carlee stiffens, glancing over her shoulder as worry etches itself onto her face. Her lips are swollen from our kisses, and her cheeks are flushed.

"Shit," she mutters under her breath.

She quickly pulls up her panties and jeans, then shoots a glance at my still-hard cock straining against my jeans.

"Do something about that." She winks suggestively.

I adjust myself as a smirk spreads across my face like wildfire. "Better?"

"Not really," she replies confidently, chewing on the corner of her lip. "Stay here."

She turns back to face me, one eyebrow raised in challenge.

"How do I look?" Her voice drips like honey mixed with whiskey as she runs her fingers through her messy hair.

"Guilty as fuck," I growl in response, channeling every ounce of dominance within me. I want her so fucking bad.

I cross my arms over my chest and shake my head. There's no denying what we just did. Her face gives her away every time.

Carlee strides toward the deep voice with purpose, hips

swaying subtly under the weight of my gaze. She knows exactly what she's doing, knowing she's completely irresistible to me.

Carlee steps into the middle of the barn, and I watch her face transform. "Hudson."

"Hey, little cousin," he says, moving forward to hug her. He glances over and catches sight of me. "Ah, didn't realize you weren't alone."

He stalks over to me. An air of confidence surrounds him, and I understand precisely why Emma married this man. It's the no-fucks-given attitude he exudes.

"Weston Calloway." I stand, offering my hand.

"Hudson Jolly. Nice to meet ya," he says with a firm grasp.

We stare at one another, standing eye to eye.

"I assume I don't have to threaten you?"

I shake my head. "Nah, Dean and Matteo took care of it."

"Did it work?" he asks.

"No," I admit.

He grins, but I see the underlying meaning behind it. "Ah, well, you know the drill. I'll fuck you up."

I nod. "You have nothing to worry about."

"I know," he replies. "Emma told me."

Hudson turns back to Carlee. "So, you and this guy?"

Carlee smacks him, and he pulls her into a hug.

"Missed you. Been staying out of trouble?"

"Always," she says, laughing.

He releases her, grinning. "What are you two up to?"

"Thought we'd go for a ride. The weather is nice; the sun is out. It's a great day to be free from shitty exes," she says, winking at me.

"Yes, it fuckin' is," Hudson agrees. "Dakota and Thor are saddled and ready to go. They're in the trailer right now."

"You're a literal angel," Carlee says, waving to me to follow her. "We'll take them off your hands."

Hudson's eyes remain fixed on me as I approach Carlee. When I'm close, I wrap my arm around her and kiss her forehead.

She chuckles, pulling me along with her. "He really will kick your ass."

"Oh, I don't doubt that," I say.

A truck with a gooseneck trailer attached is parked outside the barn. Inside the trailer are two horses, patiently waiting, fully saddled.

"Where've ya been?" Carlee questions Hudson as he steps out of the barn.

"Lucas and I checked the fences on the other side of the property. We rode for about an hour," Hudson explains. "Anyway, have fun. Unsaddle when you're finished, please. I'm havin' lunch with Emma."

"Tell her I said hello. We'll see ya," Carlee tells him.

"Nice meetin' ya, Weston. You two should come over for dinner," he says.

"Maybe," I tell him. "I'll have to check our schedule."

"Sounds good."

He climbs into his truck and backs the trailer in place. After he unhooks it next to the barn, Carlee grabs a pack from the side-by-side and ties it to the saddle strings.

"Are you sure you know how to ride?" she asks when we're alone.

"Babe," I mutter.

"Look, Dakota loves to run and spooks easily." She shakes her head. "No, you should take Colby's horse. You're used to proper little ponies because of your polo playing." She bursts into laughter.

I scoff. "Was that a burn?"

She winks, trading reins with me. "You're not a cowboy."

"And you are?"

"Damn straight," she says, lifting herself onto the saddle with ease. Carlee clicks her tongue, glancing at me over her shoulder. "Come on."

"Okay, that's hot," I tell her, climbing onto Thor.

He doesn't seem to give any fucks as we move along leisurely down the trail.

I catch up to Carlee, trotting behind her, unable to take my eyes off of her.

I fucking adore seeing her in her element like this.

She glances around at the rolling hills and woods. Sunshine beams down on us, and she closes her eyes, soaking it in.

"Home," she says, smiling. "I've missed it so much."

"I can see why," I admit. "The weather is great for February. It's an oasis here. Your family is incredible, and I can tell how close you are with everyone. They love you."

She smiles. "Yeah, but they tend to forget about me too. It's the out-of-sight, out-of-mind type of thing. If I could, I'd have a place here and my apartment in the city, splitting my time between the two. Writing my blog. Just loving my life."

"So, let's do it. We can search for property while we're here."

A cool breeze blows through the tall grasses as we follow a trail that leads into an opening in the trees.

She turns to me. "Weston."

"Would it make you happy?"

"Property here is *very* expensive and hard to come by." Her hips rock forward as she rides. "Things don't get listed for sale often."

"Everything is for sale with the right price." I study her. "Also, our definitions of *expensive* aren't the same."

"You know I don't care about any of that, right? Money, fame— none of that will ever make me happy. I just want you." Carlee smiles so sweetly as we continue to mosey down the dusty trail. "I can just imagine *us* here, escaping the weight of the world together, breathing in fresh air, enjoying the sunshine. It brings me comfort."

I lose myself in thought as we continue into the dense forest. The temperature drops in the shadows, and the horses follow the trail without guidance. I reach out and take her hand, kissing the ring. Sunlight leaks through the branches, and I inhale the fresh scent of earth and dirt.

"This ring—it was your grandmother's?" Carlee asks.

"Yes," I admit. "You know, I always said I'd give that ring to the woman I'd spend the rest of my life with."

She licks her lips, glancing at it. "I shouldn't have this."

"You absolutely should," I say.

"Why doesn't Lena have it?"

I give her a small smile. "She refused to accept a secondhand diamond."

Her happiness fades. "When I thought I couldn't hate her more."

"There were big flashing signs that it wasn't going to work out. I should've known then."

"Like you said, touch the watch, wear the ring." Carlee shoots me a wink.

Fifteen minutes later, we approach a clearing with a running stream. Carlee slides off the saddle and leads Dakota to the water. I follow her lead with Thor lazily walking behind me.

Once the horses have drunk their fill, we tie them to a post fifty yards away. Carefully, she unhooks the pack and carries it into the clearing. On her knees, she unties it and lays out a checkered blanket. Carlee sits on the blanket and pats the space next to her, and I join her.

"I should've brought cake," she tells me. "Next time."

"You are the cake, babe," I tell her, pulling her into my arms and sliding my lips across hers. Knowing she's in love with me makes it feel that much fucking sweeter.

We fall back on the blanket. I meet her gaze, my finger brushing her cheek, feeling so grateful for this moment with her.

"The look," she whispers.

"I have something to tell you," I say.

"Okay."

"I paid Samson to see you in New York," I blurt out.

She smiles. "I know."

"What? How?" I ask.

I prop myself on my elbow. She's so breathtakingly beautiful, lying like this, her dark hair spilling around her head.

"He told Lucas because they're best friends. My cousin called me and spilled the tea. Small-town rumors spread wide and far. Knowing you wanted me to be there was the *only* reason I agreed. Now, you being the owner? I didn't see *that* coming. I was surprised," she admits, chuckling, and I love the sound of it. "It was a respectable move. Impressive, actually."

"You didn't say anything," I whisper.

She shakes her head. "I wanted to see how long it would take you to tell me. You passed the test. I guess I can trust you after all."

Carlee pulls me down to her. She tastes like cherry lip balm. We pull apart.

"That cloud looks like a drumstick," she says, pointing.

I burst into laughter. "Okay, I see it."

She moves closer to me, relaxing in my arms as we enjoy the meadow. The breeze blows, and fresh air surrounds us. Being with her like this feels like home, and I could do this forever. I don't remember the last time I felt this at ease. My fingers brush along her skin.

"Did I ever tell you how I originally learned about your blog? Years ago?"

She shakes her head, and I catch the sweet scent of her shampoo.

"No, you haven't."

"Lena," I state.

I watch Carlee's expression harden.

"She was enraged with fury over articles that LuxLeaks had posted about us. She decided she'd find your identity and destroy you for hurting her ego. Nothing was going to stop her."

She sits up and faces me. "What are you talking about?"

I have to get this out right now. I can't wait any longer.

"Lena hired a hacker who found out who you were. I paid a lot of fucking money to him to feed her a lie and to keep your identity a secret. Then I paid for your site to become more secure than the goddamn Pentagon. Why do you think people believe LadyLux is a divorced late-forties socialite? Just because?"

"You started that rumor?" She glares at me, but I can see concern wrapped tightly around her. "Why would you do that?"

"To protect you," I state.

"Why are you telling me this?" The carefree girl who was just with me is now gone. Her face hardens.

"Because it matters. We both know this is more than just friendship. There is more I have to share with you. And I'm fully aware you might not like what you hear and might never want to speak to me again. But if I don't tell you the truth, it would make me a piece of shit. I respect you too much to keep this from you," I admit. "The truth sets *us* free. I want to be free, Carlee. With you. No more secrets."

"What if I don't care?" she asks, worry etched across her face. "I don't want to think of you any differently than I do right now."

"We can't move forward without us discussing this. Please," I whisper, not wanting her to fully push me away. I can already see her rebuilding that fortress around her heart.

"I don't like this," she says, her voice cracking. "It feels very much like you're breaking this off."

I catch a glimpse of the woman I fell in love with, the one who doesn't have walls built from earth to heaven.

"I'm not breaking this off." I shake my head. "But I'm so fucking scared you might."

29

CARLEE

M y mind is spinning.
      My thoughts are out of control.
I might crash. This seems too serious for my liking.

I wish I could predict the words that will come out of Weston's mouth, but he's unreadable, and he's completely blocked me out of his emotions. If he told me he was really Easton, I'd believe it.

"Is this something that can wait?" I finally ask, wanting to enjoy the sunshine, the sound of the trickling creek, and the cool February breeze as the wind travels through the brown grass. "We don't have to ruin today. We're supposed to be celebrating."

"This conversation is unavoidable, gorgeous." His thumb brushes across my bottom lip, a featherlight touch that sends goose bumps racing over my skin.

"You told me things don't have to be so serious," I remind him.

"Yeah, but this can't wait any longer. If I don't tell you, Easton will. He's already threatened me and said you deserved to know."

"I don't like the look on your face," I whisper.

I'm so scared this protective bubble we've been living in is about to burst. I don't want everything around us to crumble. Is this proof that when things are too good to be true, they usually are? I push away those thoughts.

"I'll be right back."

His brow lifts in question as I walk over to the saddlebag. I shove my hand deep inside the pocket, fumbling until I find the familiar bottle of Fireball. It's something Hudson always keeps stashed in his pack. The seal has been broken, but it's full. I take several big gulps. The cinnamon burns going down, a sensation I welcome. It tastes shittier than I remember.

I return to Weston's side, resting my head on his stomach. "I just want to watch the clouds a little while longer."

"Is day drinking a good idea?" he asks, a hint of concern in his voice.

"This is doomsday prepping. And if you're concerned, I can ride a little tipsy," I admit, forcing a laugh to keep my tone light as I meet his eyes. "Want some?"

Weston props himself up on his elbow and takes several large gulps.

"You're lost in your thoughts." He passes the cinnamon liquor back to me.

We take turns, the bottle gleaming in the sunlight like a promise or maybe a warning. It goes down fast and steady. This strangely feels like a goodbye.

"That cloud is shaped like a heart." Weston points up at it with one hand while his fingers thread through my hair, loosely twisting strands. "It's a good omen."

I smile, listening to the calming water. Am I enjoying our last time together?

I hiccup, realizing I'm headed to Wastedville. The bottle is over half empty.

"Oh no," I whisper, sitting upright, my head spinning.

"Exactly my thoughts," Weston says, glancing at it. "This tastes like shit."

"Does the job," I say as we drink it like we're parched.

When my face grows numb, I know it's time to finish this unavoidable conversation.

"Okay, it's showtime. You were at the part where Lena wanted revenge and you hid my identity from her," I tell him, meeting his gaze.

"Oh, right." He gives me a small smile. "After LuxLeaks was on my radar, I read every article you'd published. Your words became my refuge and made me realize I was being manipulated. So many were too damn afraid to speak the truth. But not you. LadyLux gave no fucks and backed claims with receipts. It started spreading around our social circle, and everyone eventually turned on Lena."

I let out a ragged breath. "Wow."

"While I protected your identity, I learned everything I could about you. I had Brody follow you to ensure you weren't dangerous or *in* danger. I learned you worked at the W, and that was how you gained access to so much private information. Genius, actually."

An eternity passes between us.

"Say something," he urges.

"How long was I followed?" I ask.

"Years," he admits.

I stare up at the clouds. "Was it all a lie? Did you trick me into falling in love with you?"

Deep blue eyes bore into mine. "Do you feel that way about Easton and Lexi? Is their relationship any less real because we planned when they'd meet?"

The question catches me off guard, but I contemplate it, knowing that neither of us could've *made* them fall in love. We knew they were compatible. It made our job easy. Their love is the real deal. Undeniably so.

Weston continues combing his fingers through my hair. "We don't get to choose who we fall in love with. You know that."

I sigh. "Damn you and your logic."

"Also, my goal was *never* to date you. And I wasn't supposed to fall in love with you." Weston's fingers trail up my arm until his palm rests on my cheek. He sits up, keeping my head propped in his lap. Sunshine beams behind him, and he looks down at me like he's the angel of death.

When he smiles, my heart does a pitter-patter, and I know I'm in too deep with him. There is no life jacket, and I've been treading water since we met, hoping I'd survive him. I will, won't I?

The question lingers in my gaze as I stare at his beautiful face. "Why were you at Sluggers?"

Weston swallows hard, the moment growing too intense. "I needed closure. I needed to see the face of the woman who had saved my life. Just once. But when our eyes met, time stood completely still. Once you spoke to me, I imagined an entire lifetime with you. Being strangers was no longer an option."

"Weston," I whisper, looking up at how beautiful he is.

"You dared to be honest when you could've lost everything. You risked it all for me. I was no one to you. And I didn't understand why you cared until I got to know you and your heart. I'm here with you right now because of you," he says.

"I'm glad. I'm glad I could shake you awake. I was worried you wouldn't survive her. You lost your spark. It was depressing to watch," I admit.

"I know." He nods. "There was one article you wrote—'When Egotistical Narcissists Marry Rich.' It was the single thing that woke me up and made me realize I was living in a nightmare. I didn't understand how I'd let it happen. I was a shell of a human, Carlee. You saw *me* when the world didn't. I wasn't invisible to you."

My voice gets caught in my throat because that was the last article I wrote about Weston. I tried to save him. There had been too many red flags, but he'd married her anyway. I stopped mentioning him until he filed for a divorce.

"I'd pushed away everyone in my life who cared about me.

Easton. Billie. Brody. Asher. Harper. They'd warned me, but somehow, *your* words reached me. You saved me," he says.

I move closer, brushing my lips across his. He tastes like cinnamon and spice.

"Thank you." He kisses my forehead and eyelashes as he holds me tightly in his arms like I'll vanish if he lets me go. "Your beautiful words set me free."

I never realized how much he believed in my work and how it resonated with him. My words always held a deeper meaning for him. He wasn't just being kind and giving random compliments.

A roller coaster of emotions rushes through me, and I'm not able to comprehend the hell he lived in for three long years. My heart aches for past him. She tried to destroy him, to *kill* him.

"Please don't cry," he says, gently wiping my tears away.

"I'm angry for you," I admit, shaking my head.

"Don't be. It's over," he says, grinning. "Officially."

I fall back on the blanket, and Weston follows me. We stare at the clouds as my eyes grow heavy.

"Your wife hated my blog, so you protected me from her. You stalked me for actual years while you divorced her, learned about my hangouts and where I worked, purposely befriended me, slept with me, fell in love with me, asked me to be your roommate, and then decided to come home with me to meet my family? Oh, not to mention, we hooked up your identical twin brother with my very best and only friend in the entire world, who's now carrying your family's DNA. Did I miss anything?" I blink over at him and hiccup. "Sorry, blame the Fireball. Truth syrup."

Weston narrows his eyes. "You make me sound like a fucking psycho."

"Did I exaggerate?" I ask, blinking at him. "Did you take my laptop to help orchestrate this?"

"No." He laughs. "That would have been evil. I'd have asked for it if I wanted it, and you'd have willingly given it to me. And you'd have been my roommate without the drama."

My mouth falls open when he smirks.

"I'm not the villain. I can't force you or anyone to fall in love with me."

"Somehow, the Calloways *always* get what they want." I tilt my head at him.

I pick up the Fireball, take a long drink, and then burst into laughter as I return to my cloud watching.

"You're not upset?" he asks.

"No. She probably would've killed me! And I kinda like the thought of you stalking me in the night," I say.

"That *never* happened."

"Fantasy Weston will now do that," I reply, meeting his eyes. "You really were my secret admirer. Go ahead and admit it."

He smirks. "Fuck, I was."

I roll over on my side and face him, leaning my head against my hand. "That's what I want to see. This. You being happy."

"You promise you're not upset?" he asks.

"No. I know your heart, so I believe you. And I appreciate you making sure I was safe. However, it could still be very bad for me if she learned I was behind LuxLeaks. That entire scenario is how a villain is born, Weston. It was never supposed to go *real life* with us."

"She'll never know it was you," he confirms. "No one ever will. That's a guarantee."

"Except for whoever stole and hacked into my laptop," I mutter, becoming more paranoid with each passing second.

"I'm working on tracking it down."

He kisses me, and I hiccup, breathing cinnamon that feels like fire. Weston twists the ring on my finger. Everything has more meaning than it did this morning.

I meet his gaze. "I choose you, even when it's messy. You said last night that we're in this together. Are we?"

"Yes. If you want to be," he breathes out, and it makes my heart skip a beat.

"No more secrets."

I crawl into his lap, settling against him as his hot breath brushes against my cheeks. Our faces are so damn close.

"Okay," he promises. "No more secrets."

"That night at Sluggers, when our eyes met, deep down, I *knew* you were there for me," I confess, my voice barely above a whisper.

"You wanted me to find you?" he asks, a smile threatening to take over his lips, his eyes twinkling with an intensity that suggests something deeper.

"Yes," I whisper against his mouth, daring to close the distance between us. "And now that you have, what's your next move?"

Weston's eyes close as he kisses me with such passion that we both become breathless. The world around us briefly fades away, leaving only the warmth of his lips and the intoxicating scent of his lingering cologne.

Each kiss feels like a promise, like this could last forever. The fantasy of us that's lived in my mind could become a reality if we let it.

"Tell me your intentions, Wes," I nearly beg. "I need to know."

"I plan to make you my wife," he whispers.

His lips brush across mine, and the world blurs around us.

"Prove it," I mutter.

30

WESTON

Carlee straddles me and forces me onto my back. I run my fingers through her hair, the intensity increasing as she kisses me so desperately.

"You want me to prove it?" I ask.

"You want to do this forever with me?" Her lips brush against mine.

"Yes," I breathe out.

"They say only fools rush in."

"I'll be foolish with you any day of the week. I don't give a fuck as long as we're together." I crisscross my fingers behind my head, watching Carlee. Big, fluffy clouds float behind her as the cool breeze surrounds us. "You're a dream."

"Let's make it a fantasy." She smirks, her lips curling upward like we're sharing a secret.

I don't protest as her hands slide under my T-shirt, pushing it up over my chest. Her fingers graze down my abs, teasing, fucking taunting me with how close she is to my cock that's rock hard for her.

Her eyes lock on mine like she's daring me to stop her but fuck that. I'm not stopping shit. I'm letting her do whatever the hell she wants to me. I'm Carlee's fucking fantasy, and that expression on her face tells me she's about to worship me like the god she believes me to be.

She pops the button of my jeans, slides down the zipper, and pulls them just low enough to free me. I'm throbbing for her, and she fucking admires me like she's never seen a cock so perfect in her life.

"Beautiful," she whispers, her cheeks flushing as she wraps her delicate fingers around my shaft, giving it a slow, deliberate stroke.

I hiss through my teeth, my hips jerking upward like they've got a mind of their own.

She smirks up at me with that fucking devious look in her eyes that I love so much. Without warning, she leans forward to take me into her wet, hot mouth.

Jesus Christ.

I groan, my hands gripping her hair as she sinks down on me, her lips stretched tight around me. She swallows me down like she's starving. Her tongue slides against the underside of my shaft like she's memorizing the shape, and I let out a ragged breath.

She pulls back, sucking so damn hard that I think she steals my fucking soul. My gorgeous girl is not holding back, not even a little. Her mouth works me over like we're living out one of *her* fantasies. Fuck it; it's mine now too.

Carlee's cheeks hollow as she sucks, her tongue flicking against my tip before she takes me deep again. She works me up so fast.

I'm so fucking helpless, my hips thrusting into her mouth as she takes every inch I give her. Her hands grip my thighs, her nails digging into my skin as she moans around me.

"Fuck, Carlee," I growl, my voice rough and strained. "You feel so good."

She smirks around my cock, her eyes flicking up to meet mine, and then she pulls back, letting my dick slip from her lips with a filthy pop. I'm a ticking time bomb, and if she keeps this up, I'll explode.

"Mmm. You're mine, Weston," she says with swollen lips that are glistening with spit.

She doesn't waste a second before she's leaning back in, her tongue lapping up the pre-cum that's pooled at the head of my cock like it's the sweetest fucking thing she's ever tasted. Her lips close around me as she gently sucks, teasing me, fucking driving me insane.

Her fingers dig into my hips as she takes me deep again, her throat opening up to swallow me whole. If she had a gag reflex, she'd be choking on me. I still feel her throat tightening as she forces herself to take every thick inch.

It's the hottest goddamn thing I've ever experienced.

She pulls back again, gasping for air with swollen and pouty lips, before returning to me. Carlee changes her pace, head bobbing up and down. High-pitched moans release from her, and I can tell she's enjoying herself. I love a woman who takes pride in her work.

She strokes me with the rhythm of her mouth, and I'm so fucking close that I can't think straight. Her tongue swirls around my tip, her lips sucking hard as her hand works me over, and if she doesn't stop, I'll be fucking gone.

My body tenses as pleasure surges through me.

I'm teetering on the edge, ready to spill over, ready to pump my hot cum into the back of her throat.

"Fuck," I groan, my fingers tightening in her hair.

My cock pulses. I'm so fucking close ...

"You come when I say," she mutters, backing away from me.

With a racing heart, I'm left gasping as I stare up at her. I've never given any woman such control over me.

"Carlee," I hiss, teetering on the edge.

"Mmm. So fucking greedy for me," she whispers.

This is easy with her. It always has been.

With rosy cheeks, she rubs her palms up and down my shaft,

working me back up before pulling away. Carlee stands, kicking off her boots, and removes her jeans and panties.

"Come here," I say, sitting upright.

She hovers over me, then slides down onto my cock, adjusting every few seconds until I meet her end. We're face-to-face, breathless but oh-so fucking desperate as our mouths meet. I soak inside her hot cunt, loving how tight she is and how she throbs around me.

Carlee rolls her hips in a sensual rhythm. I grip her waist, guiding her movements as our kiss deepens. The trees and creek around us fade away, leaving only us lost together, but even now, I feel found with her.

"Thank you for seeing me. The real me," I whisper, kissing her neck, tasting her skin.

Every inch of her body is absolutely intoxicating.

I can barely think, not with how I'm stretching her, filling her completely full. Her legs wrap tighter around me, and I growl, a low, feral sound that makes her cunt clench in response.

"That's the you I crave," she says. "All the time. The you that you don't give to everyone. The you that's reserved just for me."

We're falling into the abyss together, and right now, the connection we share is deeper than I ever imagined. I'm full of emotion, fully lost with her.

"You have all of me," I mutter against her neck, trailing kisses along her collarbone.

Her head lazily falls back, exposing more skin for me. A moan escapes her swollen lips.

"I'm so in love with you," she confesses with a gasp.

I slide my hands up her sides, underneath her shirt. I push the fabric over her head, revealing her perky nipples. No bra. The sunlight filtering through the branches dances across her skin, highlighting every gorgeous fucking curve and dip of her body.

"You're breathtaking," I whisper. "You're going to be *my wife*."

"Soon." She laughs against my mouth, then pulls away.

I stare at her, smiling, buried deep inside of her. The future I imagined with her the first time our eyes met replays so vividly in my mind. Right now, it's becoming a reality.

I tuck her hair behind her ears, wondering what I did to deserve her. I'm the luckiest man in the fucking world.

"I don't know how to say this," she whispers as we continue to make love. "I love you, Weston. I can't spend another second not telling you. I'm tired of denying it. I just want this, and I'm so scared of losing you. Every man I've ever loved has left me." The mood grows serious, and her bottom lip quivers.

"Fuck, Carlee. I love you too. I'm not going anywhere. I promise. Best friends *forever*," I confess, my thumb tracing the curve of her cheek.

I kiss her like tomorrow isn't promised. It's not. I will protect her from any heartache and won't be the cause of it.

Her fingers are in my hair as our bodies press together, and this moment threatens to consume us both. I can feel her heart racing against my chest, matching the frantic rhythm of my own.

"Promise me this is forever," she says.

"Forever, I promise," I breathe against her lips. "Until my dying day."

A whimper escapes her lips as our bodies move together. I lose myself in her and know I can't live in a world without Carlee.

Right now, it's only us. This is the way it's supposed to be.

Our kiss deepens, and my gorgeous girl rides me, increasing her pace. A moan releases from the back of my throat. It's raw and primal. I trail kisses down her neck and across her collarbone. She arches her back, and I take one of her perky nipples into my mouth, teasing it with my tongue.

"Oh God, Weston," she gasps.

Her nails dig into my shoulders, causing a mixture of pain and pleasure that I revel in.

I flip us over, laying her gently on the blanket. Hovering above her, I pause to drink her in. Flushed cheeks, swollen lips, emerald-green eyes sparkling with desire.

Fuck, she's never looked more beautiful.

"You belong to me," I whisper, pushing back into her tight little cunt.

I grip her hips tighter as I thrust to meet her end. The pleasure is overwhelming, threatening to consume us both.

"More, Weston," she commands.

"Carlee," I growl, slamming further into her.

"Yes, yes, it feels so good," she barely says. She looks into my eyes, her gaze filled with love and lust.

I slide my hand between us, finding her sensitive spot with practiced ease. I circle it with my thumb.

"I want everything with you, Wes," she confesses. "I'm tired of pretending I don't. I do."

"Yes, fucking love this confession," I mutter against her.

Carlee's breath hitches, her eyes fluttering closed as she nears her peak. "Oh God, Weston … I'm so damn close."

I increase my pace, driving into her with renewed determination. The sounds of our bodies meeting, our breathless moans, and the trickling creek surround us. It's beautiful.

"Come for me, gorgeous," I urge as my release builds. "You need this."

Carlee releases a cry of ecstasy as her inner walls clench around me when the orgasm rips through her. "Keep *all* your promises. Please."

I briefly pause, studying her, knowing she's referring to the promise I made her.

The day you say those three words to me and mean it, I'll keep you pregnant.

The sight of her coming undone pushes me over the edge, and I follow her, pumping and emptying deep inside her. She pulses around me, gasping as our foreheads rest together. A content sigh releases from her.

"Marry me. Tomorrow. You're it for me, Carlee. You're the woman I've been searching for my entire life, and I found you, and I don't want to waste any more time. A future doesn't exist without you in it. Please be my wife."

"Really?" She smiles, running her fingers through my hair.

I nod as her pretty eyes sweep over my face. "It would be my honor to be your husband."

"Yes, yes, of course." She giggles as I pepper kisses on her cheeks.

"Let's fuck around and find out," I say, grinning. "For the first time in my life, I understand why Easton and Lexi ran away. I know you're the woman I want. I can't imagine my life without you, bestie."

Our lips meet in a passionate kiss, sealing our promise. We break apart as an intense wave of happiness takes over.

"I love you so much," I whisper, my voice thick with emotion as I hold her.

"I love you." Carlee smiles. "This is happiness, isn't it?"

"This is love," I say, stroking her cheek. "I'm looking at the future Mrs. Weston Calloway."

She smirks. "Mrs. Weston Calloway. I could get used to that. How did we go from friends to this?"

"It's been a year in the making. Hasn't it?" I ask as she falls into my arms.

"You're right," she says, drawing circles on my stomach. "I got you something."

"Really?"

She grabs her jeans and pulls out a braided bracelet. There are two of them. She grabs my wrist, the one without my watch, and ties it around. "Best friends forever. Mine matches."

"A friendship bracelet?" I ask with a laugh. "You're the first person to give me one of these."

"Ever?" She's shocked.

"Yes," I say, admiring the different colors of the braided strings. I help her tie hers onto her wrist.

"Now, you'll always be reminded of me."

"Oh, babe, you live in my heart. But thank you. I love it," I tell her as we fall back on the blanket together, holding one another.

I'm glad she's no longer in denial. However, I'd have waited years for her. She has no idea what she's always done to me. I kiss her forehead, and she sighs against my chest. Being this content and relaxed should be illegal.

"We should go," Carlee says, and I realize we drifted asleep.

"You're too comfortable," she tells me as she puts on her clothes.

I pull my zipper up and button my jeans. Carlee folds the blanket back into the pack and attaches it to the saddle. When she walks, she stumbles a little.

We drank too much, too fast, which is probably why we fell asleep.

"I'm riding on the back of you. No way I'm letting anything happen when we have a very important wedding to attend tomorrow."

She laughs. "Sure you can handle riding double?"

"Babe, I was riding horses before you were born," I tell her, helping her up and then climbing on the back of the saddle. "Cute you think otherwise."

She gasps. "You really are the whole package."

"And somehow, you underestimate me." I click my tongue, taking the reins from her hands.

Thor follows behind us as we trot through the forest. Our only goal is to return to the barn in one piece.

"Did you have a good day?" she asks, her hair blowing in the breeze.

Carlee leans against me, and I hold her steady to my chest. The booze is getting to me, too, but I didn't drink nearly as much as her.

I kiss the back of her head. "It's been the best day of my life."

Until tomorrow, when we make this official.

As we approach the barn, I see the side-by-side is where we left it. I chuckle to myself, imagining how Billie and Easton will react to this news.

Billie will be shocked, but Easton won't be.

"What's funny?" she asks, placing a kiss on my cheek.

"Easton texted me earlier and bet me that I'd be married before the end of the week."

Carlee chuckles, her body shaking against mine. "Remind me never to bet against Easton when it comes to you."

"I guess he does know me better than anyone," I say, steering the horse toward the barn. "But I think everyone can see I'm head over heels for you."

"That's why you weren't worried about the fake engagement," she mutters.

"It was never fake for me," I admit as we near the barn. "I knew I'd make you mine."

"Cocky as fuck," she says as I help her dismount.

Once her feet are on the ground, I swing off, joining her.

"That will never change," I admit.

The world tilts a little as my feet hit the gravel, reminding me how much booze we actually consumed.

"Whoa there, *cowboy*," Carlee teases, steadying me with a hand on my stomach. "Just a few more chores, and we're free."

Carlee takes Thor's reins, and I follow her inside the barn, where we unsaddle and brush the horses. Before placing the gear in the tack room, Carlee grabs the booze. When she returns, she takes a swig.

"I have the overwhelming urge to have you again," she whispers, glancing up at the hay loft.

"Up there?" I ask.

"I've always wanted to." She chews on her bottom lip.

The adrenaline from our earlier confessions mixes with the liquor swimming in my blood.

Carlee backs me up against the ladder, greedily crashing her mouth against mine. Her eyes light up, and she bites her lip as she climbs up to the loft. I look up at her, smiling.

"Come on."

I waste no time and join her.

She leads me to the back of the loft, where stacks of fresh hay are stored.

"You're insatiable," I murmur, sliding my hands up her thighs.

She undresses me frantically. "I want you nonstop. I can't get enough. You're my addiction."

"Fuck, gorgeous, you're mine too," I admit as my hands roam her body.

"Don't be gentle with me," she demands. "Do you understand?"

The air is heavy, thick with the scent of sweat and skin and something primal. My cock twitches in anticipation.

"Take off your shirt and jeans." My eyes pierce through her.

She undresses. Her tits are on full display, nipples hard and begging to be in my mouth. I watch her rib cage rise and fall as a shaky breath escapes her pouty lips.

"How bad do you want me?" I slide one hand around her body, rough and possessive, then cup her pussy through those soaked fucking panties with my other.

"Desperately," she gasps.

She arches into my touch, but I don't fully give her what she wants. At least not yet. I press harder, grinding the heel of my palm against her clit until she's squirming, her hips jerking uncontrollably so she can feel more friction.

"My greedy girl," I mutter.

She whimpers, and it's goddamn music to my ears.

My other hand is in her messy, windblown hair, pulling her head back so she's forced to look at me. Her pupils are wide, her cheeks flushed, and I can practically see the thoughts racing through her head. Every last one of them is about me, about what I'm going to do to her.

"Beg," I command, my voice a fucking earthquake. "Beg for my cock like a dirty little slut."

"Fuck, that's so hot. It's making me so wet," she breathes out. "Please. Please stretch my little pussy wide, Wes. Please. I need you so fucking bad; it hurts. I want you so deep inside me."

With one swift movement, I rip her tiny panties off her body; the sound of fabric tearing makes her gasp. Her pussy glistens, swollen and ready for me. I slide two digits inside her, curling them just right to make her scream.

"You didn't specify what you wanted," I growl against her skin.

Her walls clenching around me as she rides my fingers.

"You're dripping for me, gorgeous," I mutter, pulling my fingers out and placing them in her mouth. "Taste yourself. Taste how fucking wet you are for me. How fucking wet you always are for me."

She sucks on my fingers obediently, her tongue swirling around them.

"Fuck me. I want your cock inside me," Carlee whispers.

"Louder," I state. "I want everyone on this farm to hear *you* begging for my cock."

"Now!" she cries out, her thighs quivering as I tease her clit with my thumb. "Fuck me, Weston Calloway! Fuck me like I'm your slutty little wife."

That was all I needed to hear.

My cock is ready to destroy her exactly how she wants. I lead her over to several bales of hay that are stacked, turning her to face them before I bend her over onto all fours. I'm hard and fucking throbbing, needing to be buried inside her again.

I line myself up with her dripping entrance and slam into her with one brutal thrust. Her nails clawing into the dry grass as I sink myself balls deep inside her.

"Wes," she says, her body quivering as she grinds against me.

"That's it," I grunt, my hips pounding into her with a rhythm that leaves no room for mercy. I grab a fistful of her hair, my hot mouth close to her ear. "Taking my fucking cock like a good girl."

She'll be sore tomorrow, and she'll know exactly where I was.

"Harder," she screams out breathlessly as I continue to slam into her.

Whimpers and moans continue to escape from her. Her ass jiggles with every thrust, her tits bouncing, followed by the sounds of our skin slapping together.

We're ravenous, dirty, and fucking obscene. It's full-on fucking with one goal in mind—to lose control again. She's tight—so fucking tight—and her greedy cunt clenches around me like she wants to suck me dry.

"Wes," she gasps, her voice broken and ragged, "come inside of me."

I grip her ass, my fingers digging into the flesh as I lift her higher, slamming her down onto me with enough force to make the floor of the loft shake.

Her pussy is soaked, her juices running down my shaft. The filthy, wet sounds of our bodies slapping together is a beautiful symphony. She screams out my name like a good little slut. Her hips grind against mine as I hit that sweet spot that makes her eyes roll into the back of her head.

"You feel that?" I growl into her ear, my voice rough as I wrap my hand around her stomach, continuing my assault on her perfect pussy. "That's me claiming you, Carlee. Every inch of your tight little cunt belongs to me. Only me. Forever."

"I'm going to be your wife," she mutters.

Her body trembles as she clenches around me, her orgasm crashing over her like a fucking tsunami. Her pussy pulses around my cock, and I'm not far behind.

"Fuck, gorgeous. You're squeezing me so tight," I say with a roar as she squirts all over me and the floor.

I slam into her, my release exploding inside her in hot, sticky bursts. I pump deep in her, the orgasms leaving us both panting and shaking.

We collapse together, our bodies slick with sweat. Hay sticks to our skin.

Her breathing is ragged, her heart pounding against mine as we lie in the aftermath of what might've been the best sex of my fucking life.

"I've never come so hard in my life," she says breathlessly, as if she can read my mind. "I love it when you talk dirty. A fantasy."

Carlee's small frame curls up against my chest as I wrap my arms around her.

"Oh, then we're just getting started," I admit, kissing her forehead. "I want to make all your sexual fantasies come true."

"Shit, I'll write you a list tonight." She smiles wide with hooded eyes, completely satisfied.

Pure happiness stretches across her beautiful face as sunlight streams through gaps in the weathered wood, illuminating specks of dust dancing through the air.

She squeezes her thighs together.

"You feel where I was?" I say, stealing a sweet kiss. "What's mine and only mine?"

"Yes," she says, holding me tight. Her finger slides under the bracelet she attached to my wrist, and she smiles. "Do you think it will always be like this with us?"

"Fuck yes," I tell her, my hands roaming over her bare skin. "I'll never be able to get enough of you."

She lifts her head, gazing at me with those big green eyes that seem to see right through me. "I'm so scared you might."

"Not going anywhere, bestie," I say, checking the time. "However, we should get back before your family sends out a search party. We've been gone for hours."

"You're right. Just know I could stay with you all day like this."

"We will. Soon. Just me and you," I promise. "We should do something fun tonight."

She smiles wide. "You're not supposed to see the bride the night before the wedding."

"Fuck traditions," I tell her. "They did me *no* good."

"Thankfully," she says as we reluctantly gather our scattered clothes.

She watches me pull up my jeans and zip them.

I smirk at her. "You like that?"

"Damn straight," she whispers, her eyes sliding from my eyes down to my cock and back up again. "You're really mine?"

I move to her, capturing her lips. "I have been for a while."

"How long?" she asks.

I swallow hard. "You had me at, 'Hi. Can I buy you a drink?' "

31

CARLEE

Weston drives us back to Mawmaw's in the side-by-side, and we take turns passing the bottle of booze even though he mostly denies it. As we park on the side of the house, I grab the bottle, taking it with me. My head swims, and we're both giggly as he hooks his pinkie with mine. The gesture feels more intimate than before.

Our eyes meet, and electricity swarms through me. His gaze drops to my lips. Just one look—that's all it's ever taken for him to make my heart beat a little faster.

I swallow hard, aware of Weston's intense gaze. The booze buzzes through my veins, lowering my inhibitions. We move onto the porch, and I take a step closer to him, our pinkies still hooked together. The air is full of hope and excitement.

"You make me so fucking happy," he says.

Weston's gaze darkens with an intensity that makes my breath catch.

I bite my lip, my heart pounding as I close the distance between us.

"I was so jealous of Easton and Lexi because I wanted that to be us," I admit.

He reaches out with his free hand, his fingertips grazing my cheek. The simple touch sends shivers down my spine.

"Yeah? And look at us now," he whispers.

"Are you happy?" I lace my fingers behind Weston's neck, my eyes drifting shut as I tilt my face expectantly toward his.

"So fucking happy."

When he captures my lips, the world instantly falls away. Our tongues twist together hungrily. One hand is in my hair while the other grips my hip, pulling me against him.

A needy moan escapes me as his body presses against mine. I've wanted him like this, without any barriers or unscalable walls, for so damn long that I can hardly believe it's happening.

"We should go inside," I whisper.

He freezes, then crashes his lips back to mine in a sort of frenzy. We kiss like we're drowning and this is the only way to breathe. He walks me backward until my back presses against the front door.

"I can't wait to be alone with you again," he whispers against my neck.

I'm breathless as the door opens from behind me, and we topple over onto one another. We land on the floor, both of us looking up at my grandmother, who's very confused.

"Oh, you startled me!" She places her hand over her heart. "I was just gettin' ready to run some errands."

Weston laughs into my hair before he pushes himself from the ground and holds his hand out for me. With too much strength, he pulls me upward, and I crash against him with an *oof*.

It's official. I'm drunk.

I pick up the bottle of alcohol from the floor and step inside.

Mawmaw tears the bottle from my hand.

"Hey! That my Fireball!"

"No, honey. This is Jake's homemade cinnamon moonshine. His giggle juice! It will give you the shits!" She looks at us with wide eyes.

"Oh no." I burst into laughter, knowing the two of us nearly finished the bottle.

I glance at Weston, whose eyes are as wide as saucers.

"Please tell me you're joking." His voice is low. "I'm physically prepared."

A big grin touches her lips. "I'm jokin'. But seriously, that's the worst moonshine on this side of the Mississippi. I've got the good stuff in the cabinet."

Mawmaw moves to the kitchen while we stay in the living room.

Weston's mouth brushes against mine. "You're so fucking pretty."

"I want you again," I whisper, breaking away from him when my grandma returns with a bottle full of liquid the color of honey.

"After a while, the cinnamon burns your throat until you can't taste a thing," I tell her with a hiccup.

She hands me a fresh bottle of booze. "If you're gonna drink, drink the good stuff. Life is too short to consume nasty alcohol and sleep on cheap pillows." She glances between us, green eyes sparkling. "Okay, what's going on with you two? Something's different."

I meet Weston's eyes. Things *are* different.

"I've stopped being in denial," I admit. "No more fighting my feelings."

She smiles. "Wait, you were fighting feelings?"

Weston chuckles and then happily announces, "We've decided to get married tomorrow."

It feels right, like an adventure.

She glances between us. "You gotta get your marriage certificate, and then you have to wait for seventy-two hours, sweeties. Unless you already filed your paperwork down at the courthouse and I didn't know about it."

My smile fades. "Three days? That's *ridiculous*."

"That's the law, honey," Mawmaw says.

Weston interlocks his fingers with mine. "We can wait seventy-two hours. Gives us a little time to prepare."

"Or we can fly to New York and get married in the morning," I suggest.

Mawmaw shakes her head. "Absolutely not."

I stare at her.

"What's the hurry? Are you pregnant?" she blurts out.

"*Absolutely not*," I state matter-of-factly. "And it wouldn't matter if I were."

"Okay, don't get worked up. Three days is hardly enough time for me to plan to go grocery shopping. And you're gonna get together a whole wedding? Out of the question."

"Mawmaw, a courthouse thing would be fine. I don't need a production."

She sighs. "Location won't matter if you don't get your butts down there today and fill out the paperwork. Y'all aren't in any position to drive." Mawmaw shakes her head. "I'll take ya. I was just gettin' ready to return some books. You're gonna need your birth certificate, Social Security card, and driver's license. We leave in ten minutes."

Weston smiles. "Luckily, I have everything I need."

"You do? You were prepared for this?"

He shoots me a wink. "Always prepared, gorgeous."

Mawmaw turns to me. "What about you?"

"Mom has my originals in the safe. I'll text her so she can get it together," I explain, pulling out my phone and doing it right then. I can't believe any of this is happening.

Weston steals a kiss, causing my emotions to swirl.

"You two are … *wow*." Mawmaw glances between us, smiling wide, before walking down the hallway. "I need to change shoes. Meet you in the car."

"You make me feel like a teenager again," I say to Weston, taking several big gulps of the moonshine in my hand.

The world shifts on its axis, and Mawmaw wasn't joking about hers being great. It's sweet like honey, and it slides down like water.

Weston steadies me, and we're lost in the haze together as we dance in my grandma's living room. The lamplight casts shadows across the walls, and the glass bottle becomes a prop in our dance as we pass it back and forth.

"Three days," he whispers against my ear. "After last night, it feels too far away."

Our mouths are inches apart.

"I'm impatient too."

"You always have been," he says, gently sucking on my earlobe. Weston brushes my hair over my shoulders, meeting my eyes. "I thought it would take us longer to get here."

"I'm glad it didn't," I admit. "Just be patient with me. I don't know how to be in a healthy relationship, Weston. Especially not a marriage."

"Uh, based on my track record, I don't either." He laughs, holding me tight in his arms. "We'll figure it out together."

Before I can respond, Mawmaw meets us in the living room.

"Good news," she says, grinning wide. "I called in a favor from Judge Robinson. He'll sign a waiver for you to get married tomorrow."

"What?" I ask, shocked.

My arms swing around Weston's neck, and he lifts me up. His hands hold under my ass as my legs wrap around him.

"Okay, okay," Mawmaw says modestly. "We still gotta make it to the courthouse, and you know how the traffic gets around this time. We gotta get goin'. Chop-chop." She pushes open the front door and steps outside.

The screen door snaps closed, and Weston sets me down.

"I can't believe this," I mutter. "Tomorrow."

"Meant to be," he says, kissing me. "We should get going."

"You're right. Grab your stuff. I'll see you in the car," I say, stepping out.

I climb into the back seat and buckle, making sure to text my mom. The moonshine has made my head woozy. The smile on my numb face right now might be permanent.

Mawmaw's eyes meet mine in the rearview. "I can tell you two really care about each other."

"We do. He's incredible, kind, and compassionate. He has a good heart. Weston is the man of my dreams," I admit, leaning my arm on the back of the seat so we can chat easier. I hiccup, and Mawmaw knows I'm three sheets to the wind, but she likes to drink as much as everyone else. "How did you know Pawpaw was the one for you?"

She smiles fondly, like she's replaying old memories.

My grandfather passed away years ago, and Mawmaw never moved on. I don't think she ever will.

"I knew he was the one when I couldn't imagine my life without him. Marrying him was a risk because we were so young—barely twenty—but he was all I wanted. Back in my day, I could've married rich, but I chose to marry for love. God's favorite gets both," she says, winking.

I smile wide. "Thanks, Mawmaw."

"You're real good together. Sometimes, couples have it, and sometimes, they don't. The two of you are actual fireworks on the Fourth of July," she says as Weston walks out of the house.

His hair is messy, his lips are swollen, and his eyes are sparkling.

"And he's good-lookin'," she confirms.

"Yes, he is," I say.

A minute later, he joins me in the back seat. The cab fills with the faint scent of his cologne and sweat. We rolled around at the creek and in the loft, and the sun hasn't even set. It's been a day of us just spending time and being with each other. It's not something we've ever had. I'll cherish today for the rest of my life.

Weston buckles and opens his arms for me to fall into. "You have hay in your hair."

"So, Weston, do you want kids?" Mawmaw asks.

"That's a loaded question," I warn him.

"Lots," Weston tells her as we approach my childhood home. "I'm letting Carlee decide."

Her brows rise. "Really?"

"I used to tell Mawmaw I wanted ten kids," I say.

Mawmaw is giddy with excitement. "Yes, you did. I want all the great-grandbabies. However, I think that means you need to move back to Texas so I can give them Mawmaw's special kisses."

I smile. "Weston was discussing buying property."

"Honey, no. We've got a slice of heaven for you on the farm. You can build here. Be close to family."

"Really?" I ask.

"Every Jolly has ten acres reserved for them if they want it," she explains. "I'll sign off."

I grow emotional. "I didn't realize ... since Dad left ..."

"Oh, honey. Just 'cause he was cut out a long time ago doesn't mean you were. Hudson has the farm maps with the land divided. Just choose a plot."

Weston's fingers interlock with mine, and he kisses my knuckles. "See, proof it always works out."

I grow a bit overwhelmed, and a few tears stream down my face. "Sorry. I've had too much to drink," I tell them.

"Don't apologize for happy tears," Mawmaw says, parking outside of my childhood home.

The two-story log cabin is the same layout as the others on the property. The green shutters look freshly painted, and I can see how hard Mom has worked to keep up with the place. My brothers help a lot too. I haven't been home in years, but nothing has changed.

"I'll be right back," I say.

My mother steps out onto the porch with a folder in her hand, and I meet her halfway.

"You're getting married?" She's excited and happy—I can see it on her face.

Mom pulls me into a tight hug.

"Yes. Tomorrow, hopefully. Mawmaw is pulling strings."

I flip open the folder, seeing my birth certificate and Social Security card. "I'll text you all the details once I find out what's going on."

"You'd better," she warns, pulling me back into a hug. "So happy for you, Carlee. If your father had looked at me the way Weston looks at you, we'd still be married. Cherish that, honey. Love like that only happens once in a lifetime."

"Thank you, Mama. I'm so in love with him," I whisper, voicing my thoughts.

"I know. I could tell the first time I saw you together," she says.

Everyone has always been able to see the chemistry we share.

Mawmaw honks, growing impatient, and Mom laughs.

"Tell her to call me," she says when I break away.

"I will." I return to the car.

"Ready?" Weston interlocks his fingers with mine, kissing my knuckles.

"Yep. Let's get a marriage license," I say.

Mawmaw turns on some country music and hums along as she backs out of the driveway.

"I wonder what Dolly Parton is doing these days," Mawmaw says, tapping her fingers on the steering wheel as we get on the county road. It's an endless highway that leads straight to downtown Merryville. There is only one through road, and we're on it.

Weston unlocks his cell phone and opens his text messages to his sister.

He tilts his screen so I can see what he's typing.

WESTON

Be in Texas tomorrow for my wedding.

He chuckles as Billie's text bubble immediately pops up.

> **BILLIE**
>
> What if I told you I was already here? So are Easton, Lexi, and Harper.

His brows furrow, and so do mine. He continues to type.

> **WESTON**
>
> Excuse the fuck out of me?

"That's what I was thinking," I whisper.

She sends a photo of them, including Brody, Emma, and someone I don't recognize. They're all flipping us off. "Who is that?" I ask.

"That's Claire Manchester, Emma's sister. I think she's married to your cousin Jake," he explains.

Carlee's eyes widen. "I'm so out of the loop."

> **BILLIE**
>
> Mom and Dad and their "baggage" are on the way.

> **WESTON**
>
> Right now?!

> **BILLIE**
>
> Yep! Thank you for inviting me first. I love you, Wessy. So happy for you and Carlee. We're at Jake's place, hanging out with Claire and Emma.

She sends another picture of them sitting out by a gigantic firepit, drinking.

> **BILLIE**
>
> We're partying without you.

My heart races. "How did they know before us?"

Before he can answer, a text from Easton pops up.

EASTON

> We flew here as soon as I left court. When and where is the wedding?

Weston laughs. "I can't believe this."

EASTON

> I know you. And I know what I'd do. So, Lexi and I rounded everyone up to be here. We've been waiting for an announcement.

I smile wide. "Easton really does have you figured out."

"Apparently," he says.

WESTON

> Speaking of, how did everything go today?

EASTON

> No issues. Glad she didn't try to fucking murder me afterward. For about an hour, I was concerned and paranoid. Lena is a PSYCHO! She wanted to talk to me. I refused.

WESTON

> Let's get together tonight.

EASTON

> That was already the plan.

My cheeks heat. "I'm suddenly super nervous."

"It's excitement. I feel it too," he whispers, leaning his head back.

Our faces are close. The late afternoon sunshine leaks through the back window of Mawmaw's Cadillac.

"I love seeing you smile like this," I say just loud enough for him to hear.

"I'm smiling because you chose me," he mutters against my ear.

His confession has goose bumps trailing over my body.

The past year, I told myself we would never work. I was

convinced neither of us would ever be happy in a relationship. That's partly true. I don't think we'd be happy in a relationship without the other.

"I don't deserve you," I say.

"But you do," he tells me, kissing my forehead.

My eyes close, and I feel safe and free. An overwhelming amount of joy takes over.

I'm living in a reality that I wasn't sure could be possible for us. But it is.

When the large courthouse building with its turn-of-the-century architecture comes into view, Mawmaw slows. Carefully, she pulls over to allow us out by the front entrance.

"I'll meet you here in twenty minutes."

I immediately feel twelve again as we give her a wave goodbye.

WE FIND THE CLERK'S OFFICE AND FILL OUT THE PROPER PAPERWORK. Once Weston pays the sixty dollars, we're sent on our way. I can't stop grinning, and neither can he as I hold the certificate that will make *us* official.

We pass by a few court officers, and before we exit from the side door of the building, Weston pulls me into a closet. An empty bucket and mop are inside, but I barely notice because his lips quickly devour mine.

"Mmm," I moan against him. "Are you trying to break my daily record?"

"What's your number?" he asks, his fingers sliding down my body, teasing and taunting me.

When he adds pressure between my thighs, I can't help but bite my bottom lip. I'm so needy as he slides one hand inside my panties.

"How many, gorgeous?"

"Six," I breathlessly say when his fingers brush against my swollen clit.

A moan escapes me, and my body arches toward him. My pussy throbs for him, begging for more, but he wastes zero time.

"Solo?" His eyes almost darken.

"Yes. And I was thinking about you," I gasp out. "No man has been able to bring me there except you."

"I had no idea it was like that," he growls out. "I love making you come. Those little whimpers that release from your throat? So goddamn sexy. Like right now."

My eyes roll into the back of my head as he teases me.

"Shh. Don't want anyone to hear." He covers my mouth with his other hand.

He slides two fingers down me, spreading my wetness along my slit before pushing two digits back inside. Weston moves at a tortuous pace as my cunt clenches around his big fingers. My legs nearly go weak, and he catches me, chuckling.

"You work me up so fast," I sigh, knowing I'll spill over at any second.

Weston pumps his fingers in and out of me so damn good. I can hear how wet I am for him, and it only turns me on more.

He curls his fingers inside me, finding my G-spot, causing me to see stars. He finger-fucks me harder and faster, adding his thumb to the mix against my clit.

"You know what I love?" I mutter against his lips.

"Fuck yes," he mutters. "You love my fingers buried deep inside of you, filling you up."

My heart races when I hear a voice coming closer. Footsteps click against the marble floor, but Weston doesn't give a fuck as he continues to give me what I want. I'm so close. My body tenses and my breathing grows ragged. The orgasm builds like a storm in the distance, but I miscalculate.

My eyes slam shut. "Wes."

My pussy clenches around his fingers, and I come so hard that my legs tremble. I cover my mouth, not allowing a single moan to escape. He doesn't stop, knowing how horny I am for him, and he continues to rub my clit. His fingers stay buried inside me as I fully ride it out. When he tries to remove his hand from my panties, I shake my head, holding him there.

"I want another one. Make me come again," I demand, barely down from my current high.

His presence looms over me like a dark cloud on the horizon.

"Your greedy cunt can't get enough." His voice is low and gravelly.

"Never," I say, barely able to speak and form words.

His fingers return, circling my sensitive nub, and I grind against him.

"Such a good fucking girl," he purrs, and I know he's smirking.

My body hums with anticipation as he pushes my jeans and panties down to my knees.

"Spread your legs wider for me."

Without hesitation, I obey his command.

Weston removes his jeans, pushing them down to his thighs. He slides his cock up and down my slick pussy.

"You're dripping, gorgeous," he mutters. "Look at you covering me."

His tip brushes against my clit. Carefully, he bends his knees and holds my thigh, slamming into me in one hard thrust. He stretches me so wide that I nearly scream out with satisfaction. I adjust to him as he fucks me up against the cool brick wall at a relentless pace.

"This is what I wanted. What I craved," I hiss.

"Taking every fucking inch of me," he says into my ear.

I feel him everywhere, in all the places he was earlier. His cock hits my sweet spot as he claims me.

I'm his, and he's mine.

I'm pinned to the wall, completely at his mercy, as he fucks me so good that I nearly lose my balance again.

"You belong to me, Weston," I say as I cling to him like he will disappear.

"I'm yours," he confesses.

His thrusts grow erratic. His breath is hot on my skin, and I feel the pressure building. Without hesitation, his thumb returns to my clit, giving me everything I need.

I come hard; my pussy clenches around him. He groans against me, pumping deep inside me. Warmth spreads through me as pleasure takes over.

We're breathless and sticky with sweat. He possessively kisses me.

"I lose control with you," I admit breathlessly when our eyes open.

"Because it's easy," he says.

Weston helps me clean up with a few paper towels in the closet. Just as we button and zip our jeans, the door swings open. It's a security guard.

Weston takes my hand, and we run down the hallway, laughing, guilty as fuck. We turn the corner, and Weston pushes me up against the wall, kissing me.

"I love you," he says, taking the extra few seconds to meet my eyes.

"I love you," I repeat, meaning it with every fiber of my being.

I hear footsteps moving closer, and I grab his hand, pulling him away.

"Hey! Y'all come back here," the guard hollers.

We bolt out a side exit door and move around the side of the building, and he kisses me again.

As he laughs against my mouth, he says, "I can't fucking wait to make you my wife."

"Tomorrow," I say, seeing my grandmother's car in the distance. "You're absolutely sure you want to marry me?"

"Never been surer about anything in my entire fucking life," Weston says, kissing my nose.

I smile, but then my brows furrow. "Did you hear that?"

Weston turns around, and that's when I spot a pap across the way with a lens.

"Fuck," he hisses, taking my hand and leading me away.

"It's okay," I say, interlocking our fingers, hoping to ground him. "We have nothing to hide."

He smiles. "No, we don't."

"Can you drop us off at JJ's?" Carlee asks as we turn onto the Christmas tree farm.

"Sure, honey," Mawmaw tells her, steering in the opposite direction from her house.

"Does this road make a big loop around the property?" I ask, glancing out the window.

"That's right. You can't get lost as long as you're on the gravel road. Just follow it, and it'll always lead you home. Eventually, you'll have the land memorized like the rest of us," she replies as we curve deeper into the woods.

Trees surround us on both sides until the sky opens up and reveals a grassy clearing. Mawmaw rolls to a stop in front of a log cabin with a wraparound porch. It's rustic and charming. In front is an oversized fire pit that crackles with fresh wood. Everyone I adore is gathered around it, chatting and sipping drinks. Seeing my friends mingling with Carlee's family feels surreal. I glance at her, noticing she wears a similar expression of disbelief.

I smile to myself. More proof that our worlds are colliding.

"Seeing everyone here tells me small-town rumors travel fast," Mawmaw teases.

"What's the rumor?" I ask, intrigued.

"That you two came to Merryville to get hitched. I knew it wasn't just gossip when I saw you two on the porch together."

"What? That is *not* why we're here," Carlee insists, her cheeks flushed.

Mawmaw looks at her, puzzled. "But you're getting married tomorrow."

"Yes, but it wasn't planned," Carlee explains, turning to me with a questioning glance. "Or was it?"

"I have *nothing* to do with this other than sliding that ring on your finger," I say, glancing at the bracelet tied around our wrists. "Lucky guess from my family."

Carlee unlocks her phone and types in the website where the blind items are posted. Right at the top, the latest one was uploaded three hours ago.

Blind Item #83

Mr. Playboy Billionaire and his secret girlfriend have escaped to her hometown to get married now that his divorce from that demon was finalized earlier today. He was spotted leaving New York in one of his private jets directly after being seen at the courthouse. His plane was tracked at the airport close to her hometown. He's not wasting any time to be with this woman. Wedding bells will ring before the weekend ends.

She gasps. "Who posted this?"

"I have no idea," I say, placing my hand on her thigh and feeling the warmth radiate from her skin. "Don't worry about it, gorgeous."

Mawmaw chuckles. "What's it say?"

Carlee reads it out loud.

"And? Someone must know how serious you two are." Mawmaw shrugs.

Carlee types my name into her internet browser, and pictures from the night I proposed flood the screen.

Weston Calloway finds love at last.

Weston Calloway's friends say he's a new man.

Weston Calloway and his secret girlfriend, Carlee Jolly.

Carlee Jolly ... her exes wish they had more chances.

"Great. They've contacted my exes. Guess we're at that stage of this," she grits out, locking her phone. She leans forward and hugs her grandma tightly. "Thanks for everything, Mawmaw. Good night."

"You need me to come back and pick y'all up?" she asks.

"Nah, we'll catch a ride with Lucas or Hudson," she replies.

Mawmaw rolls down the window to talk to Carlee as she gets out of the car. "Now, y'all don't stay out too late. I'll call Judge Robinson and confirm when he can fit you in tomorrow. Last I heard, it was two."

"Thanks again for everything," I say, and she smiles wide.

"Thank you," she responds with a wink. "That's the happiest I've ever seen my Leelee."

I meet Carlee's gaze, placing my hand on her back. She glances over at me, and I interlock my fingers with hers.

Mawmaw honks, and Carlee waves.

"My brothers and cousins might try to pull something. They always do when I'm dating someone," she tells me.

"Noted."

As we approach, everyone bursts into *woo-hoo*s and applause.

"Y'all stop," Carlee says, laughing.

I meet Easton's eyes, and he smirks before I glance at Lexi. She's wearing that *I told you so* smile. Brody sits beside my brother, and on the other side of him is Hudson. My eyes scan over her two brothers, Lucas, and a guy I haven't met yet.

"Hi. I'm Weston," I say, giving him a firm shake.

"I'm Jake, but my friends call me JJ."

Moments later, Claire Manchester approaches me. "Weston, wow. You still look exactly like that asshole."

Easton chuckles.

I give her a side hug.

"JJ is my fiancé," she says proudly.

"And if one more person gets married before us, I'm going to lose it," JJ tells her.

"Sorry," Carlee says to him.

Once all introductions are out of the way, we're handed bottles of the same shit we drank earlier.

"We've had enough of this. And by the way, Mawmaw is telling everyone it gives you the shits," she says to him.

Hudson and Brody howl with laughter.

"It does taste like total shit," Brody says.

Carlee walks away and grabs us some drinks from inside. I stand by the fire, waiting for her to return.

"There's something about those Jollys, isn't there?" Emma says, patting me on the back.

"Both Manchesters in the same vicinity. Have I finally died and gone to hell?" I joke.

Emma snorts as she sits on Hudson's lap. As I look around, everyone seems happy. No drama. No business conversations. Just living, enjoying a hot fire and open sky. This is freedom.

Carlee returns with a bottle of tequila.

I raise a brow at her and smirk. "Dangerous."

"Just how I like it," she says, taking a swig before handing it to me.

"Time to chug," Matteo tells us.

He stabs a beer can with his key, then cracks it open before shoving it into Carlee's hand. She gulps it down, and then he does the same for me.

"Fuck, we can't keep doing that, or we'll be trashed," I warn.

She giggles and kisses me. "Live a little. That's a problem for future us."

The large group of my friends and her family sit around the blazing bonfire. Her cousins must've worked tirelessly throughout the day to set this up, and I'm genuinely grateful. An hour or two passes as we shoot the shit and hang out. The temperature begins to drop, and Carlee leans against me as we watch the flames.

Laughter echoes off the surrounding trees as country music floats in the background.

"Dance with me," I say, flashing her a smile.

"I'd love to," she replies, and we stand.

I take her hand and pull her close. Our bodies sway together as the fire crackles beside us. Sparks fly and flutter into the night sky.

"Did you think it could be like this?" I ask.

I run my fingers through her silky hair, admiring how flawless she is.

"I hoped," she admits, her green eyes sparkling brightly. A sweet smile graces her lips.

The world around us fades until it's just the two of us, lost together.

We linger in this embrace, stealing another brief kiss as the song fades into another one.

"Get a room!" Lucas yells, and Brody gives him a high five.

Carlee flips them off and captures my lips with a laugh.

"I called it. I knew they'd get married," Lexi says to Easton.

Easton pulls her into a kiss. "You were right, darling."

Billie and Harper can't stop whispering about something. They both look pissed. My sister's eyes meet mine, and she smiles, lifting her drink. Harper turns and grins at me. They're faking it though. Right now, they're discussing business. Billie is wearing the same expression Easton does when finalizing a deal.

As the song comes to an end, I spin her around, dipping her down and stealing a kiss.

"Don't let me fall." She giggles.

"Only in love with me," I say, bringing her back to her feet, then leading her over to where we were sitting.

As soon as I sit and Carlee takes my lap, all eyes are on us.

"What?" Carlee asks, glancing around.

"Anyone going to explain how this happened?" Claire finally inquires. "No one can give me a clear answer, and I don't have time to piece it together. I need the TL;DR version."

I chuckle. "You can take the girl out of the corporation, but ..."

"Very true," JJ says with a laugh. It earns him one Manchester glare.

Carlee explains how we met and became friends without divulging any extra details. It takes her a few minutes, and I replay everything that's happened over the past year. We went from being friends to becoming lovers. As I watch her laugh and talk about us, it's impossible for me to imagine my life without her. She's my soulmate.

"After being friends, you just one day randomly decided to date each other?" Claire asks.

"Yeah, basically. I went on a handful of horrible dates and realized I was searching for what I had with Weston," Carlee says.

I wrap my arms around her.

"It was just easy being with you," Carlee says, leaning in for a kiss.

Everyone looks at us with awe, even her brothers.

"Make my little cousin cry, and we'll all fuck you up," Lucas warns, narrowing his gaze.

"Count us in on that too," Easton adds, grinning.

"Okay, I'm feeling ganged up on," I say, biting Carlee's arm.

Goose bumps trail up her skin—something I've always been able to trigger since the beginning.

I hope we never change.

"Everyone is Team Carlee," she teases.

"So am I," I admit. "What will you do about it?"

Suddenly, Carlee's phone buzzes, and she pulls it from her pocket to answer. Clearing her throat, she raises her hand.

"Mawmaw confirmed we're getting married at two!" She brings it back to her ear, laughing. "Love you too. Bye!"

Her stomach growls loudly, and Claire hears it.

"Are you hungry? We have plenty of food," Claire offers, standing.

"I'll be right back," she says, kissing my hand before following Claire.

Once we're alone, the guys glare at me.

"Ah." I smirk. "This is what I was waiting for."

Lucas stands, crossing his broad arms over his chest. "You're coming with us."

"Are we fighting?" I ask, glancing around.

"No," Matteo states firmly. "We're not animals."

Easton snickers and everyone turns to him. "Sorry. Lexi's brothers made me fistfight them."

Dean lifts his sleeves. "We can arrange for that."

"I kinda beat the fuck out of her brother and gave him a concussion," Easton explains. "I'd probably *not* do that. Weston has more pent-up anger in his pinkie than I do in my entire body."

"Thanks," I say. "Always honest."

Easton laughs.

Carlee walks onto the porch, noticing her cousins and brothers surrounding me. "Excuse me? What's going on?"

The screen door slams behind her.

"Weston's gonna be busy the rest of the night," JJ says with a sly grin.

"No, he's *not*," Carlee insists, taking deliberate steps toward us. I think she might fight them all. "He's coming home with me."

"I'll be okay," I tell her, seeing she's growing pissed. "It's just family fun. You know how this goes."

"Yeah, family fun, Leelee," Matteo says, wrapping his arm around his sister and leading her back inside, trying to calm her down.

I can't hear what she's saying, but she argues the entire way.

I turn to Brody, Matteo, Dean, JJ, Hudson, Lucas, and Easton. "What are we doing?"

Seconds later, I'm being blindfolded. My arms and legs are tied together, and I don't resist. The seven of them carry me across the pasture. They lift me into the back of a truck, where I lie on my side. I stay calm, trying to focus on the direction we're driving while trying to guess the speed. I expected something like this, especially after what Easton dealt with when he met Lexi's brothers. It's almost like a Southern tradition, an initiation full of hazing to become part of their family.

I'm not sure how much time passes when the truck comes to a stop. I'm lifted from the back and placed face down on the ground, still bound.

"Okay, now what?" I ask.

"Find your way back," Hudson replies.

"And if I don't?"

He bends down close to me. "Then you won't marry my little cousin."

The truck drives away, leaving me lying on my chest. Carefully, I work my wrists, twisting them to try to undo the knot. It takes every second of ten minutes, but I manage to loosen my hands and remove the blindfold.

It's well after dark. The moon rises over the horizon, and it illuminates my surroundings. I reach into my pocket, hoping they were stupid and didn't take my phone, but I'm not that lucky. I close my eyes, recalling the direction of JJ's house relative to their grandmother's, which is north. Using the night sky, I locate Polaris.

"They're fucked." I grin, both relieved and determined.

After doing some quick math, I calculate I might be two miles from JJ's house. I look for the smoke from the fire, but I can't see anything in that direction over the tree line.

Easton and Brody must have known dropping me in a random pasture wouldn't work. In my twenties, I'd go backcountry backpacking every summer in Europe. I've hiked some of the most dangerous trails in the world alone, and Merryville is a joke in comparison. They should've tried harder—much harder.

I set off at a steady pace, the earth crunching beneath my shoes. Time becomes fluid as I walk, kept only by the gradual shift of constellations overhead.

Suddenly, the landscape changes.

Rows upon rows of Christmas trees materialize, their silhouettes stretching endlessly into the darkness. The branches rustle gently in the breeze. I can feel the bracelet on my wrist—a gentle reminder of my gorgeous girl. As soon as I make it back to Jake's, we're leaving. I want to take a shower and give her the queen treatment before tomorrow.

If I can make it to the main gravel road, I'll follow it to where they are. I cut across the tree farm and navigate through the rows. When I take another step, that's when I faintly hear my name being called.

"Weston." The woman's voice slices through the night, freezing me in my tracks.

Every hair on my body stands on end—a primal response to that familiar tone.

I turn and see a silhouette in the distance, long hair blowing in the breeze.

"I found you. You've always loved games."

Lena.

My blood runs cold as I dart out of her view and hide.

She growls out with annoyance.

What the actual fuck is she doing here?

How did she know I was here?

The blind item.

Adrenaline surges through me as my heart pounds so hard that I can feel it in my temples. I open my hands, forcing myself to relax, knowing I have to stay calm. The trees are like a maze, but I navigate through them, away from her.

The click of a gun being cocked echoes in the night, and it sends a chill down my spine.

She came here to finish what her hit man couldn't do last year after I filed for divorce. I should've known she'd seek her revenge once it was finalized.

"It's so sad that your little fiancée will find you bleeding out on her family's Christmas tree farm tomorrow. Actually, it might take them a few days to find your body." Lena's voice drips with mock sympathy.

I stay silent.

"I followed Easton here. I fucking knew that wasn't you at the courthouse today. That was your second mistake. The first one was divorcing me."

Her footsteps crunch against the walking path.

"It's time to end this," she screams. The fury in her voice is undeniable.

My muscles tense; I'm ready to spring into action at any point. I close my eyes tight, and the only person that comes to mind is Carlee. I have to escape this because an entire future waits for me. I focus, refusing to be manipulated by Lena. She knows my triggers and uses them against me. Carlee made me realize that.

"I'll *never* let you go, Weston. As long as you're alive, I'll *always* be watching you and that little bitch. Gotta give it to you—she's very pretty. I can't help but notice that she's nothing like me." A gust of wind carries Lena's voice.

My heart nearly stops. The thought of never seeing Carlee again is too much. Not surviving Lena isn't an option.

"Then again, you'll make her miserable too. Like you do to everyone in your life. Eventually, the spark will fade from her eyes, and she'll be nothing but an empty shell. And when you see it, you can blame yourself. Or maybe I'll track her down after I take care of you," she mutters.

My jaw clenches, and I remind myself that she's baiting me. She's trying to get under my skin so I'll reveal myself.

Fuck that. Fuck *her*.

One thing about my ex: she's never been the smartest. She's always allowed her emotions to control her. Right now is a great example.

My jaw clenches hard.

"Weston," Lena coos in that sickeningly sweet voice. "Until death do us part. That's what you said, wasn't it?"

I ball my fists tightly at my sides. My fingernails dig into my palms.

She moves closer. She's less than a few feet away.

My breathing slows, and I know it's my life or hers.

Just as I'm ready to pounce, a dark figure explodes from the shadows. In one fluid motion, he grips Lena by the throat. Her startled yelp echoes through the night as she stumbles forward. Her eyes meet mine, and I see moonlight glint off the metal of the gun. She points it directly at me, and I lunge out of the way as a shot rings out.

The sound is deafening.

I get up as the two of them fight desperately for survival. Grunts and cries release from them as they struggle for control. Lena fights with a ruthless intensity.

The gun lies just out of reach.

I sprint forward.

As I close the distance, I know those broad shoulders.

Brody.

I dive forward.

The three of us reach for the gun.

A shot rings out.

I see blood.

33

CARLEE

"Honey," I hear Mawmaw say at the bedroom door. I stir, reaching for the lamp, realizing I fell asleep while waiting for Weston. I'd had a long day full of big emotions and realizations, so it's not surprising I was exhausted. Not to mention the ridiculous amounts of booze we drank. I lift my arm, catching sight of the bracelet attached to my wrist, knowing Weston is wearing one too.

I like seeing it and thinking about him.

Mawmaw's hair is up in rollers, and I can't read her expression. I can feel the energy is off though.

"Mawmaw? Everything okay?" I ask, half asleep.

I glance at the clock on the table and see it's just after nine. It's earlier than I thought. My hair is still damp from my shower, so I haven't been asleep for very long. I just crashed hard.

She sits next to me on the bed. "Leelee, there's been an accident." Her voice is comforting, but it doesn't stop my heart from racing.

"There's been an accident with Weston and—" Her bottom lip quivers.

"Mawmaw," I say, my voice trembling as I turn to her, "Is Weston hurt?"

"I don't know. I could barely understand what Lucas said."

I stand, growing desperate as adrenaline courses through me. "I need to know if Weston is okay."

"I don't know. Lucas said there was a gun involved."

I want to understand. With each passing second, I grow more upset. "It was supposed to be family fun. No one was supposed to get hurt. My brothers and cousins were playing a joke on him."

"Let's drive out to the tree farm. Lot D—that's where they are. Ambulances are already there. We can go right now."

Tears immediately stream from my face as I grab my phone and call Weston. I call again and again and again. When he doesn't answer, I grow hysterical. The surge of hot blood pumping through my body makes me feel like I need to throw up. The terrible thoughts make me sick. I drown in them, struggling to breathe. I think I'm hyperventilating.

"Come on. Deep, calm breaths," she says. "It will do neither of us any good, sitting here, waiting for someone to give us an update."

I call Lucas, but he doesn't answer. I make my way down my family Contacts list, starting with my brothers and then moving to the rest of my cousins. I consider calling Easton, but I can't tell him something bad might have happened. It would be too difficult to hear his voice.

Mawmaw and I get in the car and drive to the tree farm lots. She can't see well at night and blasts the high beams, but she's driving too slow.

I text Weston.

CARLEE

Weston, please call me back. I'm so worried something bad happened. Mawmaw is driving me there.

CARLEE

I don't know what I'd do without you. I'm so scared.

Tears stream down my face. Mawmaw prays for ten minutes straight.

CARLEE

Weston, I love you so much.

CARLEE

Please call me! I'm freaking out.

The flashing lights of the ambulance and the spotlight of the police car make me panic. My heart pounds so hard in my chest that I feel like I'm dying.

When Mawmaw finally parks, I unbuckle and run toward the small crowd of officers gathered. As I approach, I freeze because nothing makes sense.

Lena. Why the fuck is she here?

My face contorts as her cold, dead eyes meet mine. Then I notice the blood covering her white shirt. I rush toward her, pushing her with all my strength. Seconds later, she falls backward. With my fist clenched, I'm ready to bash her face in, but an officer pulls me away.

"Ma'am, you keep this up, and you'll be going with her," he warns.

I don't care what he says.

"If you hurt Weston, if that's his blood on your shirt, I will fucking kill you," I scream at her, my voice full of vengeance.

She laughs like I'm the crazy one. It sets me off again, and I bolt forward. Strong arms wrap around my waist, pulling me away.

"Don't let her make you a villain too."

Just his voice has me bursting into tears. I frantically turn around, grabbing Weston's face, searching over him for cuts or bruises.

"You're okay?" I ask.

"I'm safe. She broke the restraining order and attempted murder," he whispers against my mouth, kissing me.

I hold him tight. Emotions take over as I realize how tragic this night could've been.

Lena's here. She's in Texas.

How long has she been watching us?

"None of this makes sense." I'm panicking, stuck in a spiral. I can barely get the words out as I wipe tears from my cheeks.

"I'm here, Carlee. We're safe. Shh. Baby, it's okay. I was going to call you, but your brothers had taken my phone."

My mind spins. "She had a gun?"

Weston squeezes my shoulder, but my attention is torn away when I see the body resting on the gurney. My nostrils flare, and my heart drops when I notice it's Brody.

I rush to him. "Are you okay?"

"Yes, yes." He smiles, and then I notice his blood-soaked shirt. "Bullet grazed me. I'll live."

"Do you want us to meet you at the hospital? I can keep you company," I offer.

"No. *No.*" He shakes his head. "I don't even want to go, but Weston is *forcing* me. Enjoy your night together. Tomorrow's important. Worth risking my life for."

I bend over and hug him. "Thank you. Thank you for being there."

"Don't get sappy. I was doing my job," he says, but I know he cares about Weston. They're like brothers, the three of them.

"If you need anything, please text me. I'll get my phone from whoever has it." Weston looks pale like he's seen a ghost, as he talks to Brody. "Thank you."

"I'm fine," Brody states, growing frustrated.

Lena screams something, and the officers shove her into the back of a car. It only muffles her.

"I don't understand," I say, shaking my head.

"She stalked Easton here after the courthouse. Lena said she'd never let me go," he says roughly. I can hear the frustration in his tone. "Hope it was worth the years she'll spend in prison."

Easton rushes toward us and pulls Weston into a tight hug. Easton says something, but I can't make out his words.

"I'm not hurt," Weston tells him, squeezing him. "Brody saved my life. *Again.*"

Easton breaks down while holding his brother. Seeing them both so vulnerable, knowing what was at stake, has my anger level rising to an unhealthy level. When my cousins and brothers approach me, I finally lose my cool.

"You could've gotten him killed," I say, pushing Matteo. "I'd have never forgiven you, any of you."

"Leelee," Lucas says, reaching out for me.

I push his hand away.

"No. Grow up. I could've lost the love of my life. And for what? So you could have had a laugh? Think about that."

I walk away, but Lucas doesn't give up.

"I understand how pissed you are, but none of us knew his psycho bitch ex was hunting him. If we had known, we'd never have done that. As soon as we heard the first shot—"

"The first shot? There was more than one? You'd better be glad he's walking away unscathed," I warn.

He hands me Weston's phone before I storm away from him.

I find Weston and give him his device just as Mawmaw approaches.

"Can we get out of here?"

"Yes," I say, overwhelmed by the surge of emotions that travel through my veins.

"It's probably for the best," Weston says, taking my pinkie. "I've already given my statement."

Tears stream down my cheeks again. We climb into the back of Mawmaw's car and drive home in silence as I hold on to him.

"Shh. I'm okay. Everyone is okay."

As soon as we step into my grandmother's house, Mawmaw gives Weston a hug. "Glad you're safe, baby."

"Me too," he tells her as they break apart.

"Good night. Y'all get some rest. Big day tomorrow. The wedding of the century."

"Yes," I whisper. "Good night."

I lead Weston to my room, both of us shaken, almost too stunned to speak.

As soon as the door closes, I face him, searching his eyes.

"Are you really okay?" I ask, reaching up to stroke his cheek. "I was so worried." My voice cracks, and tears threaten to spill over again.

Weston pulls me into a tight embrace, burying his face in my hair. "I'm okay. Really. Brody took the bullet that was meant for me. Your brothers held her at gunpoint until the sheriff arrived." His voice is filled with emotion.

Images of what could have been flash through my mind. I clutch at Weston's shirt, needing to feel every part of him to reassure myself that he's unharmed.

Pulling back, I tilt my chin up to look at him through watery eyes. "I don't think I would've survived losing you like that. I'd have lived the rest of my life angry."

"Let's not think about it." He takes a shuddering breath, holding me tight in his arms. "I was unprepared. It felt like a nightmare."

My eyes scan over him, and I notice he's dirty. "You should take a shower."

"I don't want to be alone," he admits.

"I'll join you," I whisper.

The two of us sneak into the bathroom, and I lock the door. Something primal and untamed swirls between us. My heart pounds hard as he steps closer.

"Fuck, Carlee," he whispers against my neck, placing deliberate kisses up to my ear. "You're all I could think about. The bracelet on my wrist was a reminder of you."

Weston sucks on my earlobe.

That's all it takes, and I'm putty in his hands.

With messy, dark hair and hunger in his eyes, he pulls away. His pupils dilate as my fingers push up the hem of his shirt, helping him remove it. My hands slide over his tattooed muscles and down to his jeans, which I unbutton and unzip. I want to drop to my knees and worship him like the god he is.

"Love it when you look at me like that," he mutters.

He smirks that fucking devilish smirk that makes me want to beg for him.

"I need you," I whimper. My panties are already soaked, clinging to me; I'm damp and desperate.

Weston grabs my waist, and his fingers gently dig into my hips. I gasp, my breath hitching as he pulls me against him. He's hard against my stomach.

"You're my guardian angel. Brody saved me, but so did you." His lips brush against my ear.

"Weston …" My voice breaks.

"I stayed calm, knowing if I didn't, I'd never see you again," he admits, kissing me.

He lifts my shirt from my body, then removes my pajama bottoms. He admires my naked body like it's a precious sculpture in the Louvre.

Weston gently cups my breast, his thumb grazing over my nipple until it's hard and aching. I finish undressing him, leading him into the shower. Every inch of me is on fire as hot water falls over us.

"Fuck," he breathes out, his voice strained as he presses my back against the wall. *"You're perfect."*

One hand slides down my stomach, leaving a trail of goose

bumps in its path. He drags his fingers through my folds, teasing my clit with a firm, deliberate touch that makes me cry out.

"Shh," he says with a laugh.

It's the first time I've seen him smile all night.

I nod. "It just feels *so* good."

"Mmm. Don't want your Mawmaw to hear us," he growls, his voice dripping with lust as he continues to rub circles against my clit.

I can't think. I can barely breathe as pleasure washes over me.

Another deep moan escapes me when he presses two fingers inside me. Weston curls them, and I nearly lose my balance. Just as his mouth brushes against my ear, a knock taps on the door.

My eyes widen, and I hold on to him for dear life.

"Carlee?" Mawmaw says from the other side of the door.

"Yes?" I ask.

"Everything okay? I thought I heard something," she says.

Weston's fingers are buried knuckles deep inside my soaked cunt. His thumb rubs relentless circles on my swollen clit, and I'm so fucking close to screaming, but I bite my lip instead.

"Honey?"

"Oh, sorry." I swallow hard. "I didn't hear anything." My voice is somehow steady.

His other hand grips my thigh, spreading me wider, and I bite down on his shoulder to muffle the moan threatening to spill out. His skin tastes like salt, and I can't get enough. Gently, Weston brushes his scruff against my neck and chuckles. The vibrations send shivers down my spine, and I swear I can feel his smirk burning into my skin. He knows exactly what he's doing and knows I'm teetering on the edge of oblivion.

"Oh, okay then. Good night," Mawmaw says, and I can hear her shuffling down the hallway.

"Night!" I choke out., my voice strangled as Weston's fingers hit that fucking spot that makes my vision go white.

My body tenses, and then it happens. The orgasm rips through me as my back presses against the cool shower wall. My pussy clenches around his fingers, milking them like they're the only thing keeping me alive. The ecstasy of him nearly shreds me into pieces.

"So fucking sexy." His words send another shudder through me.

Weston doesn't stop. He keeps finger-fucking me, working me until I'm gasping and begging for more like a greedy little whore. I am a whore for him. Proudly.

"You're coming for me at least two more times before bed," he instructs, his tone leaving no room for argument. "We have a record to break."

I hold back a moan as he kisses me. My thighs tremble, my cunt pulses around his fingers, and I come again. I wrap my arms around him, holding on for dear life as my knees buckle. With ease, he holds me, but Weston's not close to done with me.

My lips find his. We're all teeth and tongue. He'll never be able to satisfy my intense hunger for him. I break away from him, kissing down his body. My tongue and mouth trail over his chest, and his abs, until I reach the thick, throbbing cock.

The tip glistens with pre-cum, and I don't waste time teasing him. My mouth is on him in an instant, taking him deep. My tongue swirls around the head before I plunge down again. As I hollow my cheeks, sucking him like both our lives depend on it, Weston groans.

"I'm so in love with you." He swallows hard. His head falls back on his shoulders as he props himself against the wall. "If I wasn't already marrying you tomorrow, I would," he whispers.

I take him deeper, my throat relaxing around him. What I can't fit in my mouth, I stroke in rhythm with my hand. As he climbs to the edge, he grows harder, and his balls tighten.

"Fuck, I'm so close."

I suck him slower, moving to a crawling pace with my lips stretched around him. I edge him until he can't take it anymore.

Hot cum spills down my throat in hot, salty bursts. I swallow every drop as he shudders beneath me.

Deep blue eyes meet mine. "Such a good girl."

The praise sends a spark of heat straight to my already-dripping cunt.

When I finally pull away and stand, his lips crash against mine. His chest heaves, and his cock is still twitching. The hunger in his eyes matches my own.

"I'm not done with you yet," he says again as the water falls over us.

I lift a brow. "You take this job pretty seriously."

A smile touches his pouty lips. "I can't let you keep your own record. After tonight, it belongs to me, gorgeous."

"There it is," I say. "Your sparkle."

Wrapping his strong arms around me, Weston holds me against him. I don't know how long we stay like that, but when we break apart, I wash every inch of him. My hands run up and down his body, paying extra attention to his cock. Just as he finishes rinsing his body, the water turns cold.

Weston dries me off, and then I do the same for him. With a towel wrapped around his waist, he cracks open the door and sneaks into my room with me.

The glow of the lamp spills throughout the room. The shift is obvious. It feels both intense and intimate as we drop our towels.

Weston moves me back to the bed, and I lean on the pillows. His breath is warm and heavy against my skin. Light fingers trace the curve of my body as his lips slide all over me. His touch is electric and sends shivers down my spine. Want pools in the pit of my stomach, and I don't understand how I can need him this much.

I can't get enough.

I'll never get enough.

Weston fucking Calloway is addictive.

And he's mine.

Right now, I have to feel every inch of him deep inside of me. Our lips brush together in a kiss, and it makes me ache for even more.

"You're so fucking beautiful," he whispers against my mouth, his voice full of need.

His hands slide over my hips, and he parts my thighs. Light fingers skim over my sensitive pussy. Somehow, I keep the moan buried deep in my throat.

"Make love to me," I whisper, reaching for him.

"Is that what you want?" he asks, his breath hot against my ear as his fingers tease my hard nub.

"It's what I need," I say. My mind spins, my body is on fire, and every nerve ending in my body screams for him, all of him.

"It's the closest I can be to you," I breathe out, barely audible, but he hears me. He always hears me.

Weston moves between my legs, kissing and licking up my pussy before hovering above me. I part my thighs wide, and his cock already eagerly waits at my entrance. Reaching forward, I wrap my hand around him, feeling the thick, hot weight in my palm. I guide him to where I need him most.

In one long, slow thrust, Weston pushes inside me, making my toes curl.

"Wes," I whisper, my breath catching in my throat as he pushes deeper.

My head falls back on the pillow as he rocks his hips in rhythm with mine. I grow overwhelmed with pleasure as I hear his ragged breaths in my ear. Together, we're utterly perfect.

His hands and mouth are everywhere like he's memorizing me with admiration. His hand slides down to grip my hips as he fucks me with a tenderness that makes my heart ache.

This isn't just sex. It's raw and real and so intimate that it leaves me breathless.

I wasn't prepared to feel this with him.

"I love you," he whispers against my skin, his lips brushing against the curve of my neck as he thrusts into me again.

My body tightens around him as pleasure builds deep inside me.

"I love you too," I gasp, my nails digging into his back as I get closer and closer to the edge.

He shifts his hips slightly, the angle changing just enough to make me see stars. I whimper, knowing I need to stay quiet as the orgasm pulls me under.

"Wes, more," I whisper, my back arching. I need him deeper.

He keeps fucking me as I pulse and clench around him, his own release building.

And then he lets go.

His cock pulses inside me.

His face is buried in my neck, his breath hot and ragged against my skin.

"I want to have babies with you," I admit.

"Yes," he says, nuzzling against me.

We stay like that for what feels like forever. His body pressed against mine, his cock still deep inside me.

This is easy, I think to myself, *and oh-so fucking right.*

THE NEXT MORNING, I WAKE UP NAKED IN AN EMPTY BED. AT FIRST, I'm not sure where I am. The sun is high in the sky, and birds are chirping like they're spreading Merryville gossip. I listen for the sound of a TV in the living room or Mawmaw chatting on the phone to her friends, but all is quiet.

Last night felt like a dream. The only indication that it wasn't is my towel lying in a heap on the floor where I dropped it. As I sit up, the door opens. It's Weston, carrying a cup of coffee, dressed in a collared shirt and slacks. He closes the door and then sits on the edge of the bed.

"How'd you sleep?" He hands me the cup.

"Great." I squeeze my thighs together.

He smirks, his brow lifting. "That's what I like to hear."

I set the coffee down on the bedside table, then slide the comforter down, showing him I'm still naked. With a lifted brow, he slides his hand down my stomach and between my legs. His fingers trace down my slit, brushing against me. A moan nearly escapes me, but I bite my lips to stifle the sound.

"Wes," I whisper, knowing my grandmother is awake.

"Mmhmm?" he asks, teasing my clit.

As my mouth falls open, I spread my legs wider for him. "*Fuck.*"

He slides a digit inside of me, and I'm so needy as he quickly works me to the edge. Right before I lose myself, he pulls away, placing his finger into his mouth and sucking it clean.

"The next woman I make come will be my wife." He stands, smirking.

"Weston, finish what you started," I say.

He kisses me. "It will be worth it, I promise."

I wrap my arms around his neck, pulling him back to me. "Already miss you."

"I'll see you later today," he explains.

Sadness sweeps over me, and he returns to me, sitting on the edge of the bed.

"If you keep looking at me like it might be the last time you see me, I'll never be able to leave."

"Can't help it. Especially after last night."

He pulls me into a hug. "I'll be with Brody, and he's like a cat. He's always watching, and he has nine lives."

I can't help but laugh. "I guess the next time I see you, we'll be tying the knot?"

"That's right, gorgeous. And I can't fucking wait for it to be official. See you soon."

Weston steals another kiss before he leaves me.

I fall back on the bed and sigh, wearing a smile.

Today, I'm marrying Weston Calloway.

After I drink my cup of coffee, I get dressed. The smell of freshly baked cookies floats through the house, and I follow it to the kitchen. Lexi and Mawmaw are sitting at the table, laughing.

"There you are!" Mawmaw says, her eyes lighting up with happiness that makes me feel instantly at home. "How'd you sleep?"

"Good, after I fell asleep," I admit.

"I was just asking Lexi about the pregnancy," she adds, a knowing smile on her face.

"Oh." I move toward them. "Sorry, Lex. I only told her because sh—"

"It's fine," she reassures me. "Now, come on. I have something to show you."

I follow her to the living room and see several garment bags folded over the back of the couch.

"What's this?" I ask.

"Wedding dresses," Lexi explains, moving toward them with excitement. "Billie and Harper brought them, just in case."

"That was so kind of them." My smile widens at the thought. "But I was actually thinking I might wear your dress, Mawmaw."

Her face lights up, eyes sparkling with pride. "Sweetie, I'd be honored, but I think you're way tinier than I was when I got married. Let's see."

As soon as she disappears into the other room, Lexi pulls me into a tight hug. "I heard about last night. I was already asleep, but Easton told me this morning over breakfast. He spoke to Brody. He was sent home last night after a few hours."

"Good. I'm happy to hear that." The memory of seeing Lena's dead eyes is still fresh in my mind. Her coldness is unsettling. "It was scary. Mawmaw said a gun was involved, and I thought …" I want to push that feeling away. "Brody saved Weston. I don't know if I'd have survived a different outcome."

"Here it is," Mawmaw calls out, returning with a silk garment bag. I'm happy for a change of subject. She carefully unzips it, revealing a stunning sleeveless A-line dress with a full pleated skirt that sways. With pride, Mawmaw hands it to me. Her smile is sweet and encouraging. "Go try it on. Don't keep us waiting."

I grab Lexi's hand, dragging her with me. "No wonder you eloped," I tease.

"It was great," she says, her happiness contagious. "Was just us."

She follows me down the hallway into my room. With care, she removes the dress from the hanger. Her fingers gently brush the fabric as I search for a strapless bra in my suitcase.

"Oh my goodness," Lexi gasps. "This is a vintage Dior dress."

I glance at the tag in disbelief. "This must have cost a fortune."

"I think it will fit you," she insists, holding it up against me with a smile.

Excitement bubbles in my stomach.

"You're going to make Weston so happy," she says.

"I hope," I admit as she helps me slide the sheer material over my head.

She carefully zips it. The flowy fabric hugs my shape and cuts low in the back.

When I turn to face her, she's in tears, her eyes shining.

"Wow," she whispers. "You're a *beautiful* bride."

"You approve?" I ask, knowing this is our tradition.

"He's going to be obsessed with you. But we both know he already is," she encourages.

I turn toward the full-length mirror, my heart racing as tears start to fall. I run my hands over the silk, realizing this is my dream. "This is how I always imagined it."

"Oh," Lexi says, digging into her pocket with a cheeky smile. "I have Weston's ring for you."

My eyes go wide. "Shit. I forgot."

Her laughter is light and airy. "It's all good. Mawmaw took care of everything you could ever think of. That woman should be a wedding planner."

"She's only been planning our weddings since before we were born." I pull Lexi in for a tight hug, feeling so grateful. "Thank you for being my best friend."

"Thank you for becoming my sister, little Mrs. Weston Calloway. You two are made for one another. I'm not just saying that."

"That means a lot to me. I couldn't keep pretending. I tried."

She pulls away, giving me a knowing look. "You weren't very good at it anyway. Neither was he. Weston is friendly and flirty, but not *that* friendly and flirty."

"I love him, Lex. I loved him before you knew Easton," I admit.

"I don't know how you survived him that long. Now, can you please get knocked up so I don't have to do this pregnancy bullshit alone?"

Laughter spills out of me. "When it happens, do you want to start a moms club?"

"Oh my God. We totally should. Now"—she lifts my hair and places it over my shoulder—"let's get you ready to marry the love of your life."

34

WESTON

I stand in front of the little white church perched on the hill. Its bright white siding shines under the afternoon sun. The large windows on each wall allow natural light to flood inside.

This morning, over coffee, Mawmaw explained why a courthouse wedding wouldn't cut it for her precious granddaughter. With a sparkle in her eye, she transformed into a wedding planner, as if she'd been waiting her entire life for this. The budget was unlimited, and Mawmaw took care of everything. This woman had a whole wedding planned before Carlee even woke up. Mawmaw isn't her grandmother; she's Carlee's fairy godmother.

Hudson, dressed in a crisp tuxedo, takes the steps to greet me. We exchange a firm handshake, but he gives me a warm smile. "Nice friendship bracelet."

I glance at it, smiling. "My bestie gave it to me. Thanks for officiating."

"It's an honor. Truly," he says, guiding me inside.

The church is decked out with a stunning display of yellow and white roses. Their sweet, flowery aroma fills the room. Each flower seems to glow in the sunrays. White pews line both sides, and dark hardwood floor covers the room. It's beautiful. I see why Carlee dreamed of being married here as a little girl.

"Son, come here," Hudson says, and a miniature version of him runs toward us. "Colby, this is Weston. He's marrying Leelee today."

"Hello, sir," he says, holding out his hand to shake mine. "Welcome to the family. My dad got married a few weeks ago! Where is Emma?"

I chuckle and check my watch. "Emma's helping Carlee. She'll be here in about ten minutes."

"Okay!" He jumps, then runs away to meet up with his friends.

"Kids," Hudson says.

"Do you enjoy being a dad?" I ask.

"Love it. While it's not always easy, it's rewarding." Hudson watches his son fondly.

When I turn my head, I see Easton enter with Brody.

"You know, Mawmaw has already talked to me about the two of you choosing a plot of land on the farm."

I grin. "I'm leaving it up to Carlee."

"The property next door to my place is vacant. Would be nice to have you as a neighbor, even if only temporarily throughout the year. Could watch things while you're in the city."

"Thanks for the offer," I say, giving him a firm handshake. "That would be amazing. Merryville seems like a good place to escape to."

He laughs. "There's a reason why Claire and Emma never went back."

"Why's that?" I ask.

"The magic of Merryville, of course." He gives me a pat on the back and moves to the front of the church.

I shake my head, making a mental note to ask Carlee what he means by that.

As I glance at the time, Billie approaches me. She's wearing a gray dress that matches my tie. Not a single hair is out of place. I meet her blue eyes that are the same color as mine and Easton's.

"Are you nervous?" she asks, adjusting the tie.

Thankfully, my brother arrived with everything I'd possibly need to get married.

"I'm excited," I reply truthfully.

Anticipation crackles around us.

With her hands firmly on my shoulders, she smiles again. "Last time you got married, when I asked you the same question, you told me you were terrified."

"I did?"

The memory flickers like an old film reel, but it barely hangs on. Most memories with Lena are like that now—distant. I've buried them and moved on.

"That's when I knew she wasn't the one for you. But Carlee? She's the missing piece," she says, pulling me into a tight hug. Her words cause a chill to run up my spine. "I'm so happy you've found your person."

"Me too. Thank you, sis," I whisper. Before she walks away, I grab her hand. "You know I will help you with anything, right? I always have your back."

"I know," she says. "But today is about you, not me."

"Your busi—"

"Weston"—she shakes her head—"This conversation can wait."

"Okay," I breathe out.

Easton approaches me. "Are you ready?" he asks, checking his watch.

"So fucking ready," I say, turning to Brody. "Everything okay?"

"On light duty for the next month. It's nothing," he says, playing it off like being grazed by a bullet is no big deal.

"I can never thank you enough," I tell him, pulling him into a tight hug.

"I've got you." He pats me hard. "Now stop acting like that."

As I glance down the aisle, the sunlit church buzzes with

excitement and joy. I scan across the familiar faces of my friends and her family. Every smile from the pews pulls me deeper into this moment as we wait for Carlee to arrive.

With every passing second, my heart races a little faster. I take a deep breath, knowing she will be here, but the anticipation is almost too much.

I spot my father, his wife, and my little brother, who's throwing a terrible-three tantrum in the middle of the aisle. His nanny allows him to do it. Behind them are my mother and her third husband—or it might be her fourth, but I've lost count.

I sigh, hoping this is the last time I get married.

Easton sighs too. "They're a hot fucking mess."

"An example of what not to be," I mutter just as Carlee's mother enters.

She blows me a kiss and waves.

At two o'clock, the church bell rings.

"She'll be here," Easton says, grabbing my shoulder. "I texted Lexi and asked them why they were late."

"Of course you did." Laughter erupts from me, and I realize just how much I needed it.

Matteo and Dean give me a tight handshake, followed by JJ and Lucas. Almost everyone is here now.

Just then, Mawmaw strides in with Abbi, and they're both wearing yellow. Mawmaw's presence grabs everyone's attention.

"Sorry. We're almost ready. I had to blindfold her," Mawmaw announces. Her enthusiasm is contagious as she whispers loudly, "Everyone, remember, she has no idea we're doing this here, so be very quiet."

Suddenly, Lexi and Emma lead Carlee up the steps. An electric energy flows through the room as it grows completely silent.

As soon as I see my bride, the world stops spinning.

The sunlight pours in behind her, causing her white dress to glow. Everything fades into the background, and she's all I see. Her dark hair cascades around her in curls, and I can't miss the smile on her pouty red lips.

"You're not gonna tell me what we're doing? What about the time?" Carlee asks, blindfolded. "We cannot be late! Seriously, if I'm late, Easton will complain."

Lexi bursts into laughter. "He'll survive."

My brother shrugs. It's not a lie.

Laughter bubbles from Emma. Her giggles dance through the church like happy little notes. I glance at Hudson and can see the admiration he has for her.

"Don't you think the blindfold is a bit much? Don't you trust me to keep my eyes closed? Where did Mawmaw go?" There's a hint of uncertainty in her voice. "Do I smell flowers?"

My heart skips a beat when she steps further into view. My gaze rests on the woman I'll spend forever with.

As the pianist, handpicked by Mawmaw, starts to play "Für Elise," I see Carlee's breath hitch. Each note resonates in the sacred space, but it's a special song only we share. One of many. A smirk appears on her lips as the melody shifts into Canon in D. The notes float lightly through the air.

Lexi carefully removes Carlee's blindfold, revealing the smiling faces of family and friends.

My gorgeous girl is in awe, her emotions swelling as tears of joy roll down her cheeks. A wave of warmth washes over me, and time stands completely still.

Emma grabs tissues, dabbing at Carlee's teary eyes. Easton beams at me with pride. Beside him, Brody gives me a nod.

I'm overwhelmed with happiness, overjoyed by what's to come. For the first time in my life, I'm looking forward to the future and what comes with it.

Colby and the flower girl toss petals along the path, each tiny splash of color marking this moment.

As Carlee is handed her bouquet, I can't help but notice the jeweled crown I had made for her. She's my queen, shining with grace and beauty. Right now, I feel as if I should bow down to her. Tears stream down my face, and I quickly wipe them away. Deep down, I know without a doubt that this is the happiest day of my life.

Carlee greets her uncle, who's waiting to walk her down the aisle. He leans in, asking her if she's ready. With a smile that could light up this whole town, Carlee nods. Her excitement matches mine, and it's ready to bubble over.

When her eyes finally meet mine, visions of our entire life flash before me. Carlee is stunningly beautiful, her presence so captivating that I can't find the words to fully describe how she makes me feel. We're locked together, sharing a novel's worth of unspoken words. Her eyes glimmer, and it tugs at my heartstrings as she moves down the aisle toward me.

"How did you pull this off?" Her voice trembles with disbelief as I take her hands.

"Mawmaw," I whisper in her ear. "You're so beautiful."

Carlee kisses me. "You are too."

The afternoon sun pours through the stained-glass windows, creating bursts of red, blue, and yellows that dance around us. Our love is a kaleidoscope of colors intermingling together, always changing and shifting.

Her gaze shifts to Hudson. "Oh my goodness," she says, hugging him.

"Sorry, y'all!" Carlee calls out to everyone in attendance. A blush touches her cheeks. "I wasn't expecting any of this."

"It's fine. Time to get married!" Mawmaw exclaims, clapping her hands. I think she's growing as impatient as Easton.

"Let's get married," I say to Carlee with a smile.

Hudson starts the ceremony, but my focus is on Carlee. Everything else fades away. It's just us as we exchange a silent conversation.

"The couple has decided to say their own vows," Hudson says, his voice suddenly formal. It breaks the spell around us.

Carlee's eyes go wide, her brows shooting up in panic. "I didn't prepare anything," she says quietly, a hint of worry creeping into her voice.

"I didn't either. No script. It's just us." I give her a reassuring wink. A warm feeling fills my chest because this isn't something I expected.

"Weston." Hudson's voice brings me back, grounding me.

I take a deep breath, studying her. "No one's ever looked at me the way you're looking at me right now. You have so much love and admiration shining in your eyes for me and only me. I don't think you or anyone in this room understands what you mean to me. You are the love of my life, and I'm so lucky and grateful to have lived at the same time as you. My little Firefly, you were the spark in my heart. You woke me up and freed me. You saw me. And to be seen—to really be seen—is one of the most intimate experiences I've ever had with another person. I see you too, gorgeous. I will always take care of you and make you laugh, even when you don't want to. Loving you is so easy, and I'm ready for our forever. You're proof that the wrong time is sometimes right."

Tears stream down Carlee's face, and I wipe them away, kissing her forehead and then her lips.

I think to myself that this is how it was always meant to be.

Me and her. Just like this. Together. Forever. This is our new beginning.

35

CARLEE

I kiss Weston deeply, pouring every emotion I have into him.

"I love you too. So fucking much," he whispers.

"Ahem," Hudson interrupts. "Just a few more things."

I chuckle, still surprised that we're getting married in the chapel on the hill. When I was a little girl, I told Mawmaw this was my dream location. Somehow, she made it happen, even though the church is closed for events from January through March. It wasn't on my radar. I would have married Weston in her living room without a second thought.

"Carlee, your vows," Hudson mumbles, wearing a kind smile.

"Right," I say, holding Weston's hands and peering up into his blues that swirl with love for me. "The first time our eyes met, I knew you were my other half. That night, we both felt the invisible string that pulled us together, and there was nothing either of us could do. I won't go through the details because—let's be honest—everyone in here probably read my journal."

The crowd laughs, and so does Weston.

He hasn't read it yet, but one day, I will read it to him. I want him to understand everything he does to me.

"Wes, you give me purpose, and I look forward to adventures

444

with you. Your voice, your smile, and how you laugh bring me so much happiness. I've lost count of how many times you've made my heart pitter-patter. Being with you is easy, and my greatest honor is being your friend and loving you. Thank you for making me laugh, for waiting for me, and for bringing so much love into my life. Best friends forever. No matter what," I whisper.

Our mouths crash together, and Hudson doesn't try to stop us this time.

"Exchange the rings when you come up for a breath," he says.

Lexi hands me Weston's ring, and I tremble as I slide it onto his finger. He kisses me, then slips a diamond wedding band onto mine. We laugh as our mouths frantically slide together, and I wait for someone to wake me from this dream.

"Do I even need to say it? Ah, I guess I should. You may now kiss your bride." Hudson chuckles and rolls his eyes.

"Should've started with that," I mutter as Weston dips me back.

"My wife," he says against my mouth, claiming me.

"My husband," I whisper, tugging on his bottom lip with my teeth.

There's a fire in his eyes that I want to explore. Weston Calloway can burn me to ash.

Hudson grins wide. "I'm thrilled and oh-so honored to present to you, Mr. and Mrs. Weston Calloway."

The small room fills with applause as the music plays. I even catch a glimpse of my sister and mom crying. Mawmaw is too. Billie and Harper smile, and Lexi wipes away tears. Love like this makes me cry too.

Weston picks me up in his arms and carries me out of the church. Carefully, he walks down the wooden steps to where a sleek black limo waits for us.

He sets me down on my feet. I thought we were staying in Merryville.

Our friends and family meet us outside. We exchange thank yous through tears of happiness.

"Carlee," Weston says, grabbing my hand. His mother and father greet us with smiles.

"Welcome to the family," his dad says, introducing his wife, who's dealing with a cute little boy who looks just like Weston when he was a kid.

"I'd have thought my son would've introduced us before the wedding, but alas," his mom says. Both of his parents and their new spouses are beautiful.

"Thank you so much," I tell them.

"Family vacation in the Bahamas," his dad says. "Both of you are joining us this summer."

"Can't confirm that yet," Weston admits with a laugh.

My mom pulls me into a tight hug, and then she does the same to Weston. "You kids should get going."

"We should," Weston confirms. Lexi and Easton offer congratulations and goodbyes.

The limo door opens, and we climb inside. When we're alone, his mouth captures mine.

"Are we going somewhere?" I ask, confused.

"We're going on our honeymoon," Weston says as I admire him in that tailored suit.

"We're going on a honeymoon?" I ask, semi-shocked.

"Of course we are. Also, you're so fucking adorable to think I wouldn't spoil my wife," he says, creating just enough space between us to really study me. "I'm so fucking lucky to be with you."

"I'm the lucky one," I whisper against his lips before I kiss them.

The private jet lifts into the air, and the cabin lights dim.

"You still won't tell me where we're going?"

"No," he replies.

Once we're at a safe cruising altitude, Weston stands and pulls me with him. I glance, amazed by the pure luxury surrounding us. He guides me to the back of the plane and pushes open a door.

I step inside, seeing a bed, television, and closet. "You have a room in your plane?"

"*We* have a room in *our* plane," he corrects.

I can't suppress the smile creeping across my face as he steps closer. My back presses against the cool wall.

"Mrs. Weston Calloway," he whispers.

My heart pounds like a fucking drum. My skin is flushed with a heat that has been building all day, all week, all *year*. Now, this man is my husband.

My husband stands before me, his eyes dark with desire. His plump lips part, as though he can already taste me.

With confidence, Weston reaches for the zipper of my dress, his fingers brushing against my bare back. I shiver; his touch drives me wild.

"This was my grandmother's wedding dress," I manage to say as he unzips me.

Weston steps back, fully taking me in. "You're perfection, Carlee."

Torturously, he pushes the dress down until it pools around my feet. Every inch of my skin is revealed. My tits spill out of the white lace bra, and the panties are more for decoration than anything. He groans, and the sound goes straight to my core, making my clit throb like it has a goddamn pulse.

"Fuck," he breathes out, his voice vibrating against my neck. His hands grip my hips, pulling me closer until I can feel his hardness pressing against me through the fabric of his suit pants. "Gorgeous."

He leans down, his lips trailing along the curve of my neck, shoulder, and collarbone. With precision, he reaches behind my back, unsnapping the bra. A sigh escapes me as his tongue flicks out, tracing a hot path down to my nipple. Every inch of my body aches for him while wetness pools between my legs, soaking through my panties.

"We're married," I whimper, barely above a whisper, but he hears me. Of course he fucking hears me.

"Ready to join the Mile-High Club, wifey?"

"Yes." I smile as his strong hands slide down to my ass, gripping me as he drops to his knees.

After moving my dress out of the way, he levels his face with my pussy. Weston looks up at me, worshipping me as we lock eyes. He hooks his fingers into my panties and guides them down until they fall to the floor.

I'm fully exposed and in desperate need of my husband.

His mouth finds my heat, his tongue sliding through my slick folds like he's fucking starving for me. I cry out and grip his shoulders while he licks me from slit to clit and back down again. When his tongue circles my sensitive nub, my legs shake like a fucking leaf.

"*My God*," I moan as I roll my hips against his face.

"Yes, I am," he replies, his tongue flicking over me again and again until I teeter on the edge.

My muscles tense and tighten, but he never gives it to me on the first try. *Never.*

He pulls back, blue eyes sparkling up at me. He licks those swollen, wet lips, then smirks.

"That look," I say. "Damn."

Weston stands and catches my mouth with his. "See how good you taste?"

Not wanting to waste any more time, I fumble with his belt and zipper. Weston helps, and with one swift movement, he releases the leather around his waist. The belt makes a pop sound, and I gasp.

"Okay, that was sexy."

"Yeah?"

448

He knows it was.

Right now, I need to feel him buried deep inside me so much that I can barely stand it. Weston lifts me effortlessly onto the bed, pressing my back down on the mattress. With strong hands, he scoots my ass to the edge, taking his time devouring me.

Labored breaths release from me, and I'm so damn close, and I want it so fucking bad.

"Come for me, gorgeous." He smiles against my pussy. "I know you want to."

Heat pools in my belly as I rock my hips against his scruff. His tongue and mouth lick and suck every inch of me. I grab the comforter with white knuckles, my back arching off the bed as I release on his tongue.

He slides his pants down just enough to free his cock. It's thick and heavy and *perfect*.

Weston spreads my legs with urgency, positioning himself between me and pressing against my entrance. His eyes are filled with love and lust, an intensity that makes butterflies swarm me.

"I love you," he whispers. before pushing inside me, slow and steady.

He fills me completely until I can't tell where I end and he begins. I moan, my nails digging into his back as he moves, his hips grinding against mine in a way that's both tender and filthy.

"I've never felt this way about anyone," I admit. "Just you."

"Only you," he replies.

Weston is everything I've ever wanted. He's every dirty fantasy.

And when I come, I scream his name. When my pussy clenches around him, I know I married the right man. No one will ever satisfy me emotionally, mentally, or physically like my best friend does.

He follows me over the edge, burying himself deep inside as he spills into me.

Warmth floods me as a wave of peace washes over me.

His hand gently strokes my hair, his touch soothing my soul.

We lie together, bodies entwined, hearts beating in sync, and I think this is heaven on earth.

As I gaze into his eyes, I can tell he feels it too.

"I'll love you forever, Wes," I whisper.

"Forever, gorgeous."

"PARIS?" I GASP WHEN I SEE THE EIFFEL TOWER.

"Lex said it was on your bucket list," he explains.

I meet his eyes. Weston has many properties around the world. This is just one of them. "I thought you sold your French townhouse a decade ago. I remember reading an article about it."

"You're so fucking cute. I never get rid of the things that make me happy. You also shouldn't believe everything you read about me. I considered listing it but never did," Weston says, stealing a kiss as the car door opens for us.

Paparazzi wait outside on the stoop and on the sidewalk. Signs are propped up near the door, each congratulating us on our marriage.

Weston takes my hand, protecting me from the cameras, and leads me up the steps.

"You're the people's prince," I tell him.

"That makes you the princess," he replies with a wink.

It's easy for me to forget his importance when we're alone, but in public, it's impossible to ignore.

Weston Calloway is *the moment*. He always has been.

When we step inside, our lips crash together.

"How long do we get to stay here?" I ask.

"As long as you want," he says. "But Lexi's baby announcement is in two weeks. We can't miss that."

"Two weeks," I repeat.

He grabs my hand, guiding me through the house and giving me a tour. It's surreal to be standing here. Weston bought it when he was attending university.

"You're the first and last woman I've ever brought here. I can't wait to share everything with you," he says.

We climb the stairs and enter a beautiful bedroom with a wall of windows. He opens a patio door that leads to a balcony that overlooks the Eiffel Tower.

"Wow. The perfect view," I whisper, admiring it.

"I agree," he says, admiring me.

My face softens as I lean toward him, kissing him.

"Tell me about the magic of Merryville," Weston says.

I snicker. "It's an old wives' tale about finding true love in Merryville and never leaving the town because of it."

"Did you take me home to finalize your love spell?" Weston asks with a chuckle.

"Did it work?" I ask.

"Yes." He chuckles against my lips, pulling me up into his arms.

He carries me inside and lays me gently on the bed.

"I'm madly, deeply, obsessively in love with you, *Carlee Calloway*. Damn, even your name is sexy."

"Because it's yours," I say. "Just like me."

His palms slide against my hips, waist, and breasts. A moan escapes me as his mouth trails down my neck, his teeth grazing my collarbone.

I reach for his shirt, fumbling with the buttons. He pulls it off so quickly that it makes me laugh. My hands greedily explore the contours of his muscles, tracing the intricate designs of his tattoos before trailing my fingers down to the button of his pants. He groans as I press my palm against him.

Weston undresses me with careful urgency, and somehow, in the blink of an eye, we're both naked. His sculpted body hovers above mine, and he kisses me with an intense passion. He starts on my lips, my breasts, and even sucks along the curve of my stomach. Every place his lips roam is his.

When he finally sinks into me, it's slow and deliberate. His gaze locks on mine, and it steals my breath away. I instinctively wrap my legs around his waist, drawing him deeper. Each thrust rocks through me. With his hands in my hair, he whispers my name like a prayer. This man is intoxicating.

I cling to him, my nails digging into his back as pleasure builds within me. Weston continues to give me everything I need, stoking the fire of desire until I can't hold on any longer.

With a cry, I scream out his name and the orgasm washes over me, spiraling into bliss.

He's everything.

He leaves me breathless and dizzy, and I'm lost in the haze of him.

Quickly after, he follows me over the edge. His body shudders against mine, and he whispers the words I'll never get tired of hearing.

"I love you, Carlee Calloway. My gorgeous wife."

36

WESTON

Two Weeks Later

As soon as Carlee and I hop out of the car, camera flashes explode around us. Bright lights temporarily blind us, but I guide her forward. Paparazzi swarm like bees, snapping photos and calling out our names. It's five in the morning; the sun will rise within the next thirty minutes. My fuckup was not expecting them to be here, waiting for us. Oh, how wrong I was.

Carlee grabs my hand, and I lift her knuckles to my lips, placing a kiss on them. It's a little promise that we're together in the chaos. In Paris, we weren't followed very much, but now that we're back in New York, that will change.

Our gazes connect, and I shoot her a wink. She blushes, a light hue spreading across her cheeks. I hope she always responds to me like this.

Right now, pictures of us are flooding the gossip sites, gaining attention that usually goes to A-list celebrities. The public's view of us is positive, and for once, life feels so fucking good.

"Weston! Did you hear about Lena?" a deep voice calls out from the crowd, snapping me back to reality.

I shake my head, curious.

"Twenty years in prison. She got what was coming to her," the person says, giving me a thumbs-up like I had anything to do with it.

Once inside the foyer of The Park, I hook my pinkie with Carlee's. Touching her feels purely electric and something I crave constantly. We step into the elevator, still riding the wave from spending time together for two weeks.

"Ready to leave again?" I say, my mind drifting back to the peaceful days in Paris.

"I'd go anywhere with you," Carlee replies. She means that.

The elevator ride up to the penthouse is filled with stolen glances and silent conversations. I smile, knowing I'll never get tired of her looking at me like I'm the only thing in the world that matters.

"It feels like we've been gone for a lifetime," she admits as I unlock the door.

"It does," I say as we step inside.

Boxes are piled in the living room, chaotic but with neatly written labels. The sun will soon break over the horizon, and the early morning light will stream through the windows.

"Um," she says, eyes wide, "what's all this?"

"Your apartment," I explain. "Your furniture is still there. I didn't know what you'd like to do with it."

"Let's donate it. Everything was given to me," she replies, moving toward her beloved paintings, leaning against the wall like old friends. "I only ever paid for art. Oh, can you help me with something? I want to see what's on the back of this one. I can never remember."

"Sure."

I lift the painting and spin it around to face her. She tilts her head, studying it with an artist's eye, and snaps a picture with her phone. I smile and pose.

"Did you get it?"

"Yep." She glances at me as I set it down. "Still can't figure out what it says, other than the title. I guess the artist was too tired to sign their name after making this masterpiece."

I chuckle. "You're probably right. Something like this must've taken a few months."

"Maybe longer," she says. "Oh, speaking of paintings, I'd like to see the ones you have in storage." She looks up at me with sparkly green eyes like she adores the shit out of me.

"Whatever you'd like, gorgeous."

She grows giddy. "Today?"

"If that's what you'd like. And you can pick the ones you want pulled, and I'll have them delivered here next week."

She tilts her head. "Can you have them *all* delivered here?"

I laugh. "No room. I have over a hundred framed paintings. That means you'll need to be strategic with wall space."

Her mouth drops open in disbelief.

"Oh, come on. Don't act too shocked. I've been painting most of my life. If anything, there should be more." I kick off my shoes, enjoying being back home.

The stack of unopened mail that was delivered while I was away is a reminder that my honeymoon is over. Tomorrow, I return to work.

"You impress me," she says with admiration in her tone.

I tuck loose strands of hair behind her ear.

"Can we look at your paintings after we take a nap?" She grabs my hand and leads me up the stairs, her steps light.

"A nap? Or *a nap*?" I ask, raising an eyebrow.

"A *nap* and then a nap. That's the *only* logical order." She smirks.

When we reach the second level, I pull Carlee closer. The smell of her vanilla-cinnamon skin is intoxicating. Our mouths slide together, and her arms loop around my neck. In one swift motion, I lift her, holding her ass to steady her. Instinctively, she wraps her legs around me.

"I can never get enough of you," she confesses in a hushed tone.

Her soft lips brush against my neck before returning to my mouth. "I'm addicted."

I nudge open the bedroom door and gently lay her on the mattress. Her hair is splayed around her, and she smiles up at me.

My wife is gorgeous.

She glances at the wall and spots the painting of her above the headboard. It's where she wanted it. The colors pop, and the image is full of life and love.

"Oh wow," she says, totally captivated by it while I'm completely captivated by her. A smile tugs at her lips as she turns her gaze back to me. "I can't believe you see me like that."

"You're my gorgeous girl. Now"—I wipe my hand over my scruff—"sit your pretty pussy on this face."

"Mmm." She gives me a smoldering look, chewing on the corner of her lip. "You don't have to ask me twice."

FOUR HOURS LATER, I'M UNLOCKING THE CLIMATE-CONTROLLED space and flicking on the lights. Carlee walks in first and freezes.

"This is an art gallery," she whispers.

"I guess you could say that," I explain, glancing at the neatly organized space. "I own a few of these around the city. All of my artwork is hosted here."

"Really? These are all yours?" she asks.

Classical music plays in the background, creating a calming vibe.

She reaches her hand out for me and interlocks our fingers. "Can I take the tour?"

"Yes, please." I lean over, kissing her forehead gently, loving being able to share this with her.

We start at the first room, and she studies each painting with wide-eyed wonder. I wish I could see this through her eyes as she takes her time with each piece. Her expression shifts from joy to deep thought, her feelings written on her face.

After we've seen half of the paintings, she narrows her eyes at me. There's a flicker of intensity in her gaze.

"What?" I ask with a laugh, feeling the lightness in the air.

"Nothing," she singsongs as we step into a larger area.

Her brows knit together as my artwork shifts to a more intense tone. The colors are darker, each brushstroke full of emotion. I think I catch her wipe away a tear. She squeezes my hand tightly, grounding me.

"I feel your pain and sadness in this," she mutters.

"It's all a part of the story. Without the storms, we'd never enjoy the sunshine," I say, brushing my fingers against her cheek and sliding my lips across hers. "You're the sunshine, Carlee."

An archway leads us to a big, empty room, and she takes a deep breath. It's the final showpiece. Two overhead lights illuminate the large white wall. Under one display is nothingness—a blank wall. Next to it is a lone painting, off-center.

As we approach the exhibit, our shadows flicker across the floor.

She reads the plaque before we enter. *"The Missing Piece."*

Her gaze lingers on the empty hook, then shifts to the painting beside it. It's a green pasture dotted with rolling hills and lush forests encased in a thick golden frame. The scene breathes with new life. It's peaceful and inviting.

As I stare at it, a chill races up my spine. It looks *exactly* like Carlee's family Christmas tree farm in Merryville.

I watch her expression shift, the colors of her emotions changing like paint on an artist's palette. Her breathing grows uneven. It's like she's finally putting the pieces together.

"Wes," she whispers. There's a storm brewing in her pretty green eyes.

"Yes, gorgeous?" I ask, keeping my gaze on her.

"Will you please take that painting off the wall?" Her voice shakes, and I see goose bumps form on her arms. The hairs on her neck stand as electricity fills the space between us.

I reach forward, lifting the artwork off the wall, and turn it around for her to see. The weight of the moment feels as heavy as the golden frame in my hands.

She covers her mouth, and tears start to flow, tracing paths down her cheeks like streams.

"*The Other Side,*" she says, reading the original title inscribed on the back of the canvas. "I have *New Beginnings*. It's this painting's match."

"You have the missing piece." I carefully place the painting back on the wall. "I've been looking for it for five years."

In an instant, our mouths collide, an explosion of raw emotion, and tears stream down both our faces.

"How did it go missing?"

"Lena stole it and I never knew what she did with it. Honestly, I thought she destroyed it because I loved it so much. Instead of removing the display, I renamed the feature out of spite. When I saw you had my lost painting, it took my breath away …" I trail off, shaking my head in disbelief.

"Invisible strings. A confirmation of us," she says as she looks at me in a different light. "You're one of my favorite artists."

I chuckle, and my heart swells. "*This* is what it took for you to *finally* fangirl over me?"

Her hands glide down my chest, and she smirks. "Artists are hot. Especially the ones who wear tailored suits and slide diamond rings onto my finger."

Our lips meet again, and I lose myself with her beneath the soft, low-lit lights of the gallery.

"My painting belongs here," she whispers. "It's only right that it returns home."

"And what will *you* name the exhibition?" I whisper across her lips, savoring each second.

Her eyes drift from my eyes to my mouth. "You want me to rename it?"

"Yes, of course. It's your painting," I say, barely leaning forward to kiss her.

"*Together at Last*," she says. "Like you and me."

Eight Hours Later

"Sorry I missed the memo about your wedding," Asher says as we share a whiskey, the amber liquid glimmering in the dim light while we play pool at his place.

"Oh, don't worry about it," I say casually, sinking a ball into the pocket with a satisfying thud. "It was short and sweet. Very last minute."

He takes a sip. "I can tell you've finally found *her*. Now I'm convinced the Calloways have all the luck." Asher calls the far pocket like a pro.

"Not *all* the Calloways," I say, thinking of my sister, but he makes a face. "Ah, so you still can't stand her either?"

"Billie can get fucked," he replies with a smirk.

"I'll never understand it. You two are practically the same heartless person—impossible, hardheaded, stubborn, with anger issues. And soulless. Can't forget that. Holy shit, don't get me started."

I grab my whiskey; it swirls in my glass as I stroll around the table. My only goal right now is to help my sister.

His slightly older brother, Nicolas, bursts into the room, whistling a catchy tune that I recognize but can't place. In his hands is a vintage bottle of bourbon. "To celebrate your nuptials."

The two of them are a force to reckon with. Co-owners of a

marketing empire that can make or break anyone. Billie's company is still in the infant stage. The foundation is too shaky to handle the onslaught of seasoned competitors that, if merged together, would ruin her in months.

"How's the wifey?" Nick asks, his voice warm.

"She's great. Just what marriage is supposed to be like." I smile at the thought of her, of us, and our future.

Right now, Carlee's helping Lexi prepare for tomorrow night's costume and baby announcement party. I would be there, too, but Easton forced me to do recon for Billie instead. So, here I am.

"Love to hear it, man," Nick says, casually handing me a glass, pouring the bourbon with ease.

So, now I've got two drinks. Whiskey in one hand and bourbon in the other. The perfect combination for the tough conversations that will happen before I leave.

"Did you decide if you'll work with Lustre?" I cut straight to the point, slicing through the casual chatter.

Nick freezes in place and glares at Asher, who brushes off the tension. He's not intimidated by anyone, unfortunately. It's one thing that makes him dangerous. No one gets in his head.

Lustre is my sister's main competitor, ran by her shitty ex. The rumor spreading in the investment world is that Lustre offered Asher a billion-dollar contract to represent them. It would be devastating to Bellamore, Billie's fashion company.

"Actually, I think I might," Asher finally replies. "The money is great. But we both know it's not about that."

I stare at him. "What would it take for you to work with Billie instead?"

He chuckles sarcastically. "She'd have to kiss the ground I walk on."

I roll my eyes. "You know that'll never happen."

"That's because Billie Calloway is too stubborn to ask for help, even when she desperately needs it. The Ice Queen will rescue herself, won't she?" He shoots back the rest of the whiskey in his glass. "I don't need Billie and her constant bullshit."

"Careful. You might eat those words one day," I warn, breathing deeply, already knowing I'll need to speak to Harper as soon as possible. The stakes are higher than any of them are aware, but I stay calm. "Seriously, what would it take?"

He pours some aged bourbon into his glass, his eyes narrowing. "I think I'd like for her to beg."

"Now you're just being a facetious asshole," I throw back at him, laughing but also knowing this conversation is over.

After a few more drinks, I kick his ass at pool, and then we decide to call it a night.

"If you need anything, you can always call me," Asher says as I climb into my car.

"Only if it has nothing to do with my sister, right?" I throw back at him.

"Correct." He crosses his arms over his chest and smirks.

My driver takes me the short distance home while my thoughts swirl like the bourbon I drank.

When I walk into the penthouse, Carlee is lying on the couch, wearing nothing but a T-shirt and panties. As soon as she sees me, her face lights up. I sit beside her, and she climbs onto my lap, straddling me.

"I missed you," she says as she tastes my lips. "Bourbon."

I lean in, kissing her again more eagerly, growing hard underneath her. "I missed you so damn much."

"What's wrong?" she asks, leaning back to get a better look at me. "Don't say nothing. I can tell."

"Billie's company is in bigger trouble than I thought," I explain. The weight of it is heavy on my shoulders. "Asher will ruin her since she's too stubborn to ask him for help."

Carlee laughs against my lips. "You're such a good big brother. But I think I know how we can fix this."

"How?" I ask, hoping she has the answer.

"Let's hook them up. We're awesome matchmakers. Harper could help us," she suggests, her eyes sparkling as she bites her lip.

I tilt my head. Skepticism paints across my face. "I don't think you understand, babe. They want to gouge each other's eyes out. If Asher was lying in the middle of the road, waving for help, my sister would take him like a speed bump, going thirty miles per hour. It's not the cutesy *oh, they like each other* kind of hate. She fucking despises him. And it's mutual. They can't even be in the same room together."

"That just means the sex would be scorching hot," she says, rolling her hips.

My girl is becoming a love optimist. A few months ago, she was the biggest pessimist I knew.

"I've heard hate sex is *so* good."

My thumbs dig into her hips, and I groan as she continues rocking against me.

"We have an incredible track record." The way she says it, with that mischievous look in her eye, makes me wonder if she might actually be onto something.

"He has joked about helping her if she'd fake date him," I reply, caught between how ridiculous the idea is and the possibility of it working. "They'd destroy one another."

"Maybe it wasn't a joke, and there's some truth to it?" she urges. "Most people don't just say things to say them. Could be what he really wants."

"Fuck," I hiss out, needing her like I need air. "You might be right."

Carlee leans in, and her warm breath sends a shiver down my spine.

"Are you thinking what I'm thinking?" Her voice is a sultry whisper.

"The only thing on my mind right now is the thought of being buried deep inside my wife," I mutter in her ear, my fingers gently massaging her scalp.

"You must be a mind reader," she says, wiggling out of her panties.

When she climbs on top of me and I slide deep inside her, everything fades away. And it's just us, desperate and breathless.

37

CARLEE

"We'll turn around on the count of three, okay?" I say to Weston.

Tonight is Easton and Lexi's very exciting party, and Weston and I decided to surprise each other. While we were in Paris, we ordered our costumes. Tonight is the reveal.

"One. Two. Three," we count together.

We spin around, and his face lights up.

"Mmm. Marilyn Monroe. Love it." He bites his lip.

"You know what they say—blondes are Weston Calloway's favorite." I pop my hips, lifting my skirt and letting it float down. It's my best attempt at her iconic pose.

He bursts out laughing, and it sounds so perfect. "Actually, *you're* my favorite. But, yeah, they do say blondes have more fun."

His hand slides up my thigh, and his finger sneaks under my panties.

"By fun, do you mean sex? Because I'm totally down for that."

"Mmm. I do mean sex."

The pad of his thumb circles my clit. I sigh, holding on to him for dear life as he slides two digits inside of me. It feels so good that I cry out for more.

"And let's not forget, Queen Marilyn says diamonds are a girl's best friend," I say as he places his fingers in his mouth and tastes me.

Everything about this man is a fantasy, and he's mine. All mine.

"You're my diamond, gorgeous," he mutters against my lips.

I love that he's dressed as a young Elvis, complete with slicked-back hair. I take a step back, admiring him as I grab my phone.

"You know I've always had a thing for twenty-something Elvis."

He gives me a smirk. "Mawmaw told me."

I gasp. "Cheater! What other childhood secrets of mine did Mawmaw share?"

"I'll never tell." He kisses along my collarbone. "All good stuff, I promise."

"Keep kissing me like that, and we won't make it to this party. Then we'll lose our godparent status! That would be the worst!" My head rolls back as he sucks along my skin.

"Fine," he whispers, then checks his watch. "Please save me before Easton mansplains the importance of punctuality again."

I laugh, loving the playfulness between them.

Weston hooks his pinkie with mine, and we take the elevator to the Diamond in the Sky. The penthouse is packed with friends. Even though some faces are unfamiliar, everyone seems to know who I am. Now, I guess I'll never meet a stranger. Not after my face was plastered on the internet and on the front of magazine covers.

A string quartet begins to play in the corner. The energy is joyful and vibrant, and I couldn't be more impressed with how beautiful it is in here. Long, flowing pieces of fabric and pretty lights hang from the fifty-foot ceiling that stretches across three stories. *the diamond in the sky* is gorgeous—a centerpiece for The Park and Billionaires' Row.

"The newlyweds!" Harper exclaims, pulling us both in for hugs. "How was Paris? Are you even more in love than before? I've heard it's pure magic there."

"Spending Valentine's Day there was a dream. Seeing the Eiffel Tower lit up at night …" I smile, remembering all the times we made love as that iconic structure sparkled just for us.

Weston's gaze meets mine, and we share a smile, a little secret passing between us. He's thinking about it too—I can tell by his expression.

Billie grins, moving closer. "Cute. Elvis and Marilyn. Both icons. You two *are* the main characters."

"And who are you?" Weston asks. His eyes slide over her black pantsuit and stilettos.

Billie looks like she's dressed to kill—probably Asher, if what Weston said is true.

"I'm every billionaire's worst nightmare." She holds up a card that reads *IRS AUDIT TEAM*.

Weston howls with laughter. "Your humor is dry as fuck, but hilarious."

"I'm Cher," Harper chimes in, swinging her long hair over her shoulder and striking a pose. "This is one of her touring costumes."

My eyes widen as she spins around, showing off the purple pants. "Oh my God. Now, that's iconic."

A server walks around with tiny quiches.

I snag one, glancing back at Billie and Harper. "How's work been since the mini vacation? Did being in Texas spark any ideas?"

The question freezes them both in place. Weston notices their odd behavior but doesn't stop smiling. Somehow, I catch the subtle flash in his eyes. I think Billie sees it too.

"How *has* work been?" Weston repeats, crossing his arms over his chest.

I can feel the big-brother vibes radiating off him, and I know I need to rescue them before he starts digging for information. Since we returned, helping Billie without her knowing has been a priority. I understand. I'd do anything for my family too.

As I scan the room, I find Lexi and Easton dressed like Sandy and Danny from *Grease*. Seeing Easton's and Weston's hair slicked back exactly the same is hilarious. They both look like young Elvis to me. The long-sleeved nightgown totally hides Lexi's belly. She's so good at this.

"Excuse us," I say, pulling Weston with me, not giving him the chance to protest. "We need to say hello."

I glance back at Billie and Harper, who whisper a thank-you.

Time reveals secrets, and apparently, the two of them are keeping some.

When Weston and Easton approach each other, they step off to the side and chat privately. Lexi and I pretend we're discussing something important while we eavesdrop.

"What's going on?" I ask.

Lexi glances around. "Billie's company is in trouble."

"We can't help her then," Easton says loud enough that we hear. "She would never."

"I know." Weston sighs.

Lexi leans in and whispers in my ear, "Asher Banks plans to destroy her company and make snow angels in the ashes."

"This is worse than I thought," I admit.

Easton's voice lowers, and I can't catch what else he says.

"This can't be good," Lexi explains.

"Do you think *we* can help?" I ask, glancing over at our husbands.

Easton's jaw is clenched tight, and so is Weston's.

"I don't know," she whispers.

"What if we played matchmaker?" I ask, and her brow lifts.

"It would never work. They hate each other," Lexi explains. "They act like they've already gone through an awful divorce together."

I burst into laughter. Weston moves close, hooking his pinkie with mine. I smile at him, and he returns it.

"That looks good on you two," Easton says, taking a sip of wine.

"What does? Our costumes?" I ask.

"Being in love," he confirms.

Lexi smiles wide and agrees.

"Looks gorgeous on you," Weston says, his eyes scanning over me.

"Don't make me blush," I say to him.

Easton interlocks his fingers with Lexi's, turning his attention toward her. "Ready, darling? It's about that time."

"Yes." She takes a deep breath and smiles.

"Do either of you have any final guesses?" Easton asks.

No one in the room knows the gender, not even them. It'll be a surprise for everyone in attendance.

"A girl," I whisper, grinning.

"A boy," Weston says.

I hug Lexi quickly and squeal, "We'll love whatever you have!"

The two of them move to the center of the room, standing in front of a table full of beautifully decorated cupcakes draped in chocolate and topped with sliced strawberries. They've been waiting for this for a few months now.

Weston wraps his arm around me, pulling me close. "You're so pretty."

"You are too," I tell him, loving that smile. The real one.

Servers walk around, handing cupcakes to everyone, and a tiny card on the plate says, *Wait to eat.*

Weston grabs the card and pops it into his mouth. My eyes widen in surprise.

"It's white chocolate," he whispers, smirking.

"Is it?" I ask, amazed, then do the same. It melts instantly, teasing my taste buds. "Bad influence."

He shrugs. "No regrets, bestie."

I glance at the friendship bracelet that's still wrapped around his wrist. Neither of us has taken it off since we decided to get married. He notices me staring at it. BFFs.

Lexi and Easton are given wireless microphones.

"Hey, everyone! You all look so adorable. Thanks for keeping the spirit of the party alive and for following instructions. I know some of you might be wondering why we're having a costume party in March." She radiates confidence when she speaks to the crowd.

"It's because we have a super-special announcement," Easton says, meeting Lexi's gaze.

They announce together, "We're having a baby!"

The room fills with, "Aww," and I hear Billie scream from behind us.

I turn to see her overcome with emotion.

"And you say she doesn't have a soul," I say to Weston, grinning.

"Only when it comes to babies and mimosas." He laughs.

Our eyes meet, and I lose myself in his gaze.

"We don't know the gender yet, so we thought it would be fun to share that moment with our closest friends and family. Inside these cute little delicious cupcakes is a surprise filling. We'll count down, and then everyone will take a bite to reveal the secret together. Pink is for a girl, and blue is for a boy," Lexi says.

The two of them each grab a cupcake and then face each other while low chatter fills the room.

Weston and I hold our desserts, grinning, and count along with them. "Three, two, one!"

Everyone takes a bite. I look inside mine and see it's filled with pink. My eyes light up, and then I notice Weston's is blue. I glance up at Easton and Lexi, and they're both in tears.

"Twins?" Easton asks, struggling to hold back his emotion.

"Twins?" Weston echoes, eyes wide in disbelief.

"Twins!" I exclaim. "A boy and a girl!"

Someone asks, "What does green mean?"

Lexi and Easton look shocked as a third color is introduced.

"Triplets?" they say at the same time, shocked.

An envelope is propped up beside the dessert table, and they tear it open to read the results aloud.

"Everyone"—Easton clears his throat—"we're having *triplets*."

"I think Easton might faint," Weston says, bursting into laughter.

He grabs my hand, and we weave through the crowd toward them.

"Triplets," I whisper in Lexi's ear, hugging her tightly. "Congratulations! I'm so damn happy for you. You went from having one baby to three."

"I feel like I'm having a litter! Please hurry and get pregnant with me. *Please*." She laughs, her excitement infectious.

"We're trying," I mutter. "So happy for you."

"Thank you," she says as more friends and family quickly surround them, all eager to congratulate them.

Weston and I step back, letting Lexi and Easton enjoy themselves. We've been quietly celebrating their journey for months, and I'm excited they don't have to hide anymore. It will be a night to remember for every person here.

We separate ourselves from the group and face one another.

Weston grabs my hand and twirls the wedding ring around my finger. "One day, that'll be us, gorgeous."

I pull him closer, brushing my lips against his. "It could be right now."

He pulls away, searching my face for any hint of doubt.

"I think I'm late," I admit. "I was never regular, but I've lost track."

Weston links his pinkie with mine and leads me upstairs to Easton and Lexi's room. He bursts into their spacious bathroom like he owns the place. Without skipping a beat, he opens the cabinet under the sink and digs through it.

"Aha. I knew Lexi would have one," he says, revealing a pregnancy test.

Weston locks the door and opens the box. With a sexy smile, he places the stick in my hand. "Neither of us will be able to think about anything else until we know."

"You're right." I take a deep breath. "But I just got really pee shy."

He turns on the faucet, wraps me in his arms, and grins. "Think about flowing waterfalls. Gushing tidal waves."

I close my eyes, trying to imagine it while the sound of running water fills the room. He turns on the shower, and steam fills the space.

"It's hard for me to take you seriously, dressed as Elvis."

"All righty, Marilyn."

I raise an eyebrow. "When we get home, I can't wait to show you the other costume I ordered."

He bites his lip, looking excited. "Really? Give me a hint."

"Meow," I say, making a claw motion at him.

"Catwoman. I love it," he replies, then twirls me around. "Think about rushing rivers and trickling streams."

I give him a kiss. "Read the instructions, and I'll try."

Weston tilts the box. "It's one of the early ones. Over ninety-nine percent accuracy."

"Numbers, of course." I chuckle, settling onto the toilet with the stick between my legs, focusing on relaxing.

"Pee on the stick, then wait three minutes. Sounds like a microwave meal. Okay, so two lines mean pregnant, and one line means not." He grins just as I tinkle.

I set the test on the counter and wash my hands.

"Three minutes?" I ask, starting a timer on my phone.

"Yep," he confirms, stepping closer to pull me into his arms. He hums as we dance in the bathroom.

"Whatever happens, happens," I say, looking into his eyes. "I won't be disappointed either way."

"Same here, gorgeous. You're enough for me, even if I can never get enough."

He spins me around, and our lips almost touch.

"I picked the property near Hudson and Emma," I say.

Our noses brush together, and excitement floats through the air.

"I can't wait to start building our home together."

Before I can speak, my alarm buzzes. Our eyes meet, and Weston laces his fingers with mine.

"We'll look at it together," he says with a grin. "Happy either way."

As we lean over the counter, I spot two faint lines. I blink hard, wondering if I'm imagining things. "Two lines is …"

"Pregnant," he whispers, his voice full of amazement.

Weston drops to his knees, wraps his arms around me, and kisses my belly. Tears stream down his face, and I can't hold my emotions in either. I sink to my knees, holding and kissing him as intense feelings wash over me.

"Easton must have super sperm, which means you probably do too," I whisper, laughing as I snuggle against his chest. "*I'm scared.*"

He gently cradles my face, brushing his lips against mine. "You've made me the happiest man in the world, gorgeous."

"This is a dream," I say, laughing and crying at the same time. I can't stop kissing him, but I somehow pull away. "We should probably keep this on the down-low for a bit. Let Easton and Lexi have the spotlight."

"You can choose when we share the news," he says, tucking a strand of hair behind my ear and taking me in. "It's our little secret."

"Why are you looking at me like that?" I ask.

He breathes me in. "Because I don't know how it's possible that I fall more in love with you every day."

"I love you, Weston. You've made all my dreams come true."

"I love you too, gorgeous." He grins wide, twirling my hair between his fingers, admiring me like artwork. "It's because you started saying yes."

I laugh against his lips. "Touch the watch, wear the ring, right?"

"Steal my heart, wear the ring," he says.

"I didn't steal anything, Weston. You gave it to me."

"Because it belonged to you," he admits, his lips brushing across mine. "You were my missing piece."

"You know, during our one year anniversary of meeting, how you told me to make a wish?" I ask, meeting his eyes.

He nods.

"You are what I wished for."

EPILOGUE
BILLIE

One Week Later

In my corner office, I stand at the far wall of windows. The early morning sunlight glimmers off the surrounding structures, creating a dazzling display of reflections. Bursts of yellows and pinks stretch across the skyline, painting the horizon with the hues of a new day.

In the distance, I can see the corporate office of Calloway Diamonds. It looms there—a stark reminder of the once-in-a-lifetime opportunity I refused. Instead, I started a clothing company with my best friend. We're self-made billionaires. Behind my desk is Banks Advertising and Marketing firm. I refuse to look that way, knowing Asher Banks' office is directly across mine. That asshole purchased the property just to troll me, a reminder that he exists.

My office building stands tall in the center of Lower Manhattan. Its sleek, modern design is a sharp contrast to the more traditional architecture around it. The building gives the illusion of a crystal palace, which is why it's nicknamed that. Its shimmering surfaces evoke a sense of sophistication and luxury, just like Bellamore.

We're one of the fastest-growing fashion companies in the world, and expansion comes with pains. In this industry, the ones who aren't afraid to pivot and take risks survive.

Before I drown in my thoughts, I move to my desk and open the bottom drawer. I pull out the laptop and slide it into a padded envelope, along with a letter I wrote.

I open it one last time and read over my words.

Carlee,

I had Lexi let me into your apartment because she still had a key. I took your laptop. She also gave me the password, so I didn't have to hack it. Now that those questions are answered, you and my brother needed a push in the right direction. I knew he'd save the day once this went missing. And look at you now.

I'm sorry for the stress I caused you. Please don't hold that against me, and don't be mad at Lexi. She just wanted what we all did—for you two to find true love.

I adore you. I'm so happy you're a part of the family.

Billie

P.S. I don't know who submitted and posted the blind items to the gossip site. That wasn't me.

P.P.S. Weston, you owe me one giant favor.

After I seal the package, I call my assistant, Hannah. She enters wearing a gorgeous vintage miniskirt and fuzzy sweater.

"Please address it to Carlee Calloway," I reply with a faint smile. "Have it delivered ASAP."

"Will do," she says, her heels clicking against the polished floor as she leaves.

I pick up my coffee mug and take a sip, feeling warmth spread through me for what I orchestrated. They're together and happy—proof that love conquers all.

After chatting about Carlee with Weston, I sensed that something deeper was simmering between them. It was evident how much they cared for one another, even in secret.

Discovering Carlee was behind LuxLeaks was a surprise I'd never anticipated, but it didn't compare to the revelation that they'd hooked up Lexi and Easton. *So sly.* It was as if fate had twisted their paths together so they could find love for themselves and others. It's serendipity.

As I continue to watch the sunrise, golden light spills into my office.

My door opens, and I turn to see my best friend and business partner, Harper.

"Good morning!" she singsongs.

She gives off orange-cat energy, while I hold the temperament of a black cat. The two of us are complete opposites, but we've been best friends since we played New York Fashion week with our Barbie dolls.

"You're in a good mood," I comment, raising an eyebrow as she makes herself comfortable in one of the chairs in front of my desk.

"I had the best sex this morning. He's a bartender. Young but gorgeous. Huuuuung," she explains as she delicately applies a layer of lip gloss.

I glance up at the clock on the wall. Its ticking reminds me that our first meeting of the morning will start in less than fifteen minutes.

"You should try getting laid. It helps with anxiety."

I glare at her. "I don't have time for that. Last thing I need to do is fall in love."

"What about a situationship?"

I type my password into my computer and open my email. "This is my focus. I don't need any distractions."

She leans back in the chair, watching me. "Are you worried?"

I study her as my mind spins. "Not yet. We have passion, and that's the most important ingredient for success. I'll keep surviving, even if it's out of spite."

"I'm in this as long as you are," she says, determined. "I'm concerned though."

If we don't pivot, Bellamore won't survive through the end of the year. Everyone thinks we're doing so well. It's an illusion, leftovers from a prior launch's success. Last quarter's earnings fell short of our projections by nearly half. Confirmation that more challenges lie ahead. Competing with fast fashion in today's economy feels like pushing against a brick wall. Instant gratification is destroying us.

A sharp knock taps against the door.

Hannah enters, her presence brisk and businesslike. "Your seven o'clock meeting has arrived."

"Send them in," I say. It sounds harsher than I intended.

"I need to tell you something." Harper clears her throat.

The grin on my lips vanishes when I see *him* standing in the doorway, wearing a three-piece suit, looking like the Devil himself.

Asher Banks.

His light-brown eyes meet mine and nothing exists other than our hate for one another.

"Are you fucking kidding me?" I hiss under my breath, the words barely escaping my lips. "No. No way. Hell will have to freeze over."

The fact that my best friend didn't tell me that our important meeting was with Asher fucking Banks nearly sets me off. It's too early for my heart to be pumping this fast.

"Harper," Asher says. The light filters through the window, illuminating him like the angel of death. "*Billie.*"

A low growl escapes from my throat, and I nearly choke on the irritation that wells up inside me. Fuck *him,* and that infuriatingly attractive smirk plastered on his face.

"Harper, can I speak to you outside?" He glances at her, his chiseled jaw clenched tight.

The scent of his cologne—a blend of something that's so distinctly him and cedar—drifts through the room. I hate that he smells good.

The tension wraps around my throat like a fist, and it squeezes.

He's the only man on this planet that I purposely avoid because I can't be in the same room with him without getting into an argument. He's a pompous, know-it-all asshole. And I don't care that he's best friends with Weston. We've hated each other since undergrad. Nothing has changed in over a decade. Nothing at all.

Harper offers me a sweet smile, and her eyes display a hint of nervousness as she stands. "Give me one minute."

"Harp"—the frustration is evident in my tone—"this is low."

She knows we're enemies—that we have been. *Everyone knows.*

I'll file for bankruptcy before I allow him to save my ass. The mere thought of him having that power over me is unbearable. He'd never let me live that down.

She meets him outside my office door, but they speak loud enough where I can hear.

"You said she'd be aware," he mutters, his tone laced with annoyance, the chip on his shoulder barely hidden.

"I had no other choice. I apologize," Harper states, her voice urgent and tinged with desperation.

My heart drops at her tone. Are things worse than I thought? Are we so desperate we need *him?*

"I should go," he states in that deep growl that makes the hair on my arms stand up.

"Please, Asher."

Their voices lower, and I can no longer hear them.

A minute later, Harper returns with Asher following behind

her. They take their seats in front of my desk. The room is heavy with uncertainty.

"Why are you still here?" I ask, meeting his eyes. My irritation might bubble over.

"Because you need *me*," he says, his tone dripping with cockiness, a challenge written all over his face.

"I need you?" I scoff.

"Badly," he says, checking his watch. "And I won't help until you ask me."

"You can leave." I point toward the door.

"Perfect. You'll have to beg for my help next time."

"We can find someone else," I say, casting a worried glance at Harper, who's already calculating our next move.

"You'll beg on your knees." He leans back in his chair, licking his lips, his gaze intense.

I burst into sarcastic laughter. "Goodbye, Banks."

He stands and adjusts his tie before he moves across the room. "I'll have the last laugh, Calloway."

"Asher," Harper whispers urgently, before the door snaps shut. She glares at me, frustration radiating from her. "Billie, we *need* him."

"No, we don't." My response is immediate. "There are tons of marketing agencies who can help us pivot. Anyone other than him."

"Lustre offered Asher a contract," she blurts out.

"What?" I barely choke out the word.

My heart drops, a cold dread pooling in my stomach.

Lustre is our number one competitor. They play dirty and undercut us every chance they get. Somehow, they've stolen our designs and produced them faster and cheaper. It's why our share of the market dropped so significantly last quarter.

"They approached him and offered a contract. So, either he helps us grow and takes Bellamore to the next level, or he becomes our worst fucking nightmare."

"He's already mine," I snap back.

"Yeah, well, you need to decide if you hate him more than you love our company," she replies, her tone sharp. "This decision is yours. I got him here, and you pushed him away. You'll need to figure it out now."

"Anyone but him," I insist.

"He's the best. We both know that." She leans in, her voice dropping. "I just hope you're prepared to dip into your inheritance to save Bellamore. In less than six months, we'll both have to come up with millions so we don't go under thanks to your piece of shit ex."

The weight of her words press down on me. "Harp, I don't have access to my inheritance until I'm married. *This* is it. You know that."

"Then I guess your options are to find a husband or drop to your knees and beg Asher Banks. Which will it be?"

I suck in a deep breath, and I say the only thing that comes to mind. "*Fuck.*"

Continue Asher & Billie's story in
THE BOSS SITUATION
https://books2read.com/thebosssituation

Want more of Weston & Carlee?
Download an exclusive bonus scene featuring them here:
https://bit.ly/thefriendsituationbonus

WANT MORE OF MERRYVILLE?

A Very Merry Mistake

(Jake & Claire)

https://www.books2read.com/averymerrymistake

A Very Merry Nanny

(Hudson & Emma)

https://www.books2read.com/averymerrynanny

A Very Merry Enemy

(Lucas & Holiday)

https://www.books2read.com/averymerryenemy

KEEP IN TOUCH

Want to stay up to date with all things Lyra Parish? Join her newsletter! You'll get special access to cover reveals, teasers, and giveaways.

lyraparish.com/newsletter

Let's be friends on social media:
TikTok 🖤 Instagram 🖤 Facebook
@lyraparish everywhere

Searching for the Lyra Parish hangout?
Join Lyra Parish's Reader Lounge on Facebook:
https://bit.ly/lyrareadergroup

ACKNOWLEDGMENTS

An author friend told me that some readers just want a good love story. Nothing else. I will never forget those words for the rest of my life. It was a reminder that not everyone wants angst or third-act breakups. Writing about *falling in love* is my favorite part of this job. I'm a hopeless romantic and am proud to be a *palate-cleanser* author. It's a title I welcome.

I'm living in my soft girl era, but I'm happy and loving what I'm creating. When I'm old, *that's* what will matter the most. Thank you for giving my words the light of day.

I'm so grateful so many of you continue supporting me on this journey because ***MAGIC IS HAPPENING***!

Big thank you to my beta bishes (Brittany, Mindy, Lakshmi, and Thorunn), my lovely assistant Erica Rogers, Kate Kelly (for the pretty images), Bookinit! Designs (Talina & Anthony), my editor Jovana Shirley, and my proofer Kathy Coopmans. Thank you to JS Cooper for encouraging me to go *all in* on this series and for believing in it and me. It takes a team to help me publish on this crazy schedule, and I'm forever grateful for your help!

Thank you so much to my ARC readers and all the bookfluencers who always help me with cover reveals and will drop everything to read my books. I'm so effing honored to be doing this with all of you. To my readers, thank you for always showing up for me and for being excited. Thank you for going on this adventure with me. I'm having the time of my life.

As always, a big thank you to my hubby, Will (Deepskydude).

You're the love of my life. I wouldn't want to snuggle like fat little TSP piggies with anyone else. I love you so much! Thank you for being my number one fan.

ABOUT LYRA PARISH

Lyra Parish is a hopeless romantic obsessed with writing spicy Hallmark-like romances. When she isn't immersed in fictional worlds, you can find her pretending to be a Vanlifer with her hubby and taking selfies with pumpkins. Lyra loves iced coffee, memes, authentic people, and living her best life.

Made in the USA
Monee, IL
07 March 2025

13231669R10291